CHAYSING DREAMS

****

Jalpa Williby

outskirtspress
DENVER, COLORADO

Chaysing Dreams

v3.0

Outskirts Press, Inc.
http://www.outskirtspress.com

ISBN: 978-1-4787-0309-9

PRINTED IN THE UNITED STATES OF AMERICA

My Humble Gratitude…

To my beloved family, who patiently supported me as I buried myself in my computer for hours, every single day, for the last year and a half! Chaysing Dreams is dedicated to my husband, Roland, and my three children, Taj, Nikiel, and Jaelan; you guys have always given me the gift of vision.

To my parents, who always taught me to put my best foot forward. To my sister, Julie, who put in countless hours to help me, simply because she believed in me. I couldn't have done this without your endless support!

To my friends who read my original manuscript and pushed me to pursue this further, who did not let me give up, and who believed in this story and the characters.

To all who helped me become a better writer. Thank you, to all my editors, my publishing agency, and all of the supporting authors! I have a whole new respect for the literature world!

To all my patients in my physical therapy world, who made me who I am today. I'm a bit wiser each day because of you.

Finally, to all my readers, thank you, thank you, thank you. I hope you enjoy reading Chaysing Dreams as much as I enjoyed writing it.

One

"R*un!" Her inner voice yells at her. And she runs. She runs without looking back. She is scared. Something is chasing her. The sound of blood roars through her ears as her heartbeat is racing. What's happening? But she doesn't turn around. She runs because she knows her life depends on it. The wind howls and moans as she keeps running. She doesn't know where she is running. It's dark. She can't see anything and she trips. She tries to stop her fall. Her hands get scraped on the ground. She feels branches and twigs on the ground as she pushes herself back up. She runs faster. The bramble and vine that saturate the forest floor lacerate her feet. She doesn't know what she's running from, but she can tell it is closing in on her. She can hear something cutting through the fallen branches behind her. She is breathing so fast! She feels the cuts from the branches sting her face. She ducks and dodges as she tries to escape. She is gasping for air, but she doesn't care. She has to keep running. But she knows this "something" is getting closer. She's suffocating. She feels like she is trapped. No, no! Please! Not like this! She keeps running, but she's losing. She's desperately flailing her arms to fight off whatever that's chasing her. She screams, "No, no!" It has closed in on her. She feels it catch her. Oh my god! This thing has caught her! It's shaking her. NO, NO!*

"God, Tess! Wake up! Wake up! It's a nightmare! Wake up!" I hear a familiar voice yelling at me and shaking me.

I open my eyes. I look around, trying to focus. I am in my room--my safe room-- and my mom is holding me. She is looking at me, frantic and scared. I'm sure I look the same to her.

"Are you ok? Please say something, Tess."

"I think so, Mom," I mumble. "I'm just glad it wasn't real." I shiver in fright just thinking about the dream.

"Was it the same nightmare?" Mom asks, knowing the answer. I don't say anything. "What can I do to make you feel better?"

"I'm ok, Mom, really. I'm used to these by now. They just feel so real, though." I'm shaken up, but I don't want my mom to worry, so I act brave in front of her. What's the use anyway? I've been having these same nightmares for as long as I can remember. They haven't gone away yet, so I guess I just have to get used to them. I hate them, though.

Mom goes downstairs to the kitchen to fetch me a glass of water. When she returns to my room, she hands me the cup, and says, "Here, drink this, and maybe it'll settle you."

"Ok, thanks, Mom," I say sincerely. I take the glass, but avoid her concerned gaze. "I'm fine though, *really* I am. You have to go to work tomorrow, so go back to bed. I'm going to try and go back to sleep."

"Ok," Mom says, unconvinced. "Try to get some sleep. Don't forget, you have your basketball tryouts tomorrow." I know my mom is trying to distract me and focus on something else.

"Right, the tryouts," I respond, faking a smile. "Goodnight, Mom."

"Goodnight, sweets. Love you." She stands up, kisses my cheek, and walks out, closing the door behind her.

I get up from my bed and walk to the bathroom. As I open

the door, I notice my hands are shaking and my heartbeat is still erratic. I hate those nightmares!

I've racked my brain trying to figure out what they could possibly mean. Who is the girl in my dreams? My mom even put me in therapy for them and the psychologist told me they were just anxiety dreams. I never believed that.

I turn on the faucet and bend down to wash my face, hoping that would help settle me. What do these dreams mean? Why are they always the same with the girl running? They are terrifying!

When I grab a towel to dry my face, I see my reflection. My long, black hair is a curly mess. While my hair has always been difficult to manage, this takes the cake. My dark brown eyes stare back at me in shock and my olive skin is drained of color. God, I look crazy! I turn off the bathroom light and crawl back into bed.

Is it normal for fifteen-year-olds to have these same recurrent dreams? Shouldn't I be dreaming of boys or something? I can't analyze this again. I have to try to get some sleep. I say prayers in my mind, hoping it will help. I count sheep. I think about my history exam that I have the next day, and review the information in my mind. Somehow, I eventually fall asleep, but I toss and turn all night.

The alarm set for six in the morning rings way too soon. I wake up feeling groggy, and grumble as I rub my eyes. It's the day of my history test and the basketball tryouts. I have to find some energy to wake my tired butt up.

I shuffle downstairs and pour myself a cup of coffee from the kitchen. I can't help but smile when I see my dad's usual pile of science journals scattered around the kitchen table.

Mom is *not* going to like his mess.

The caffeine eventually kicks in and I take a shower. I quickly wash my wild hair and towel-dry it, letting it fall into spiral curls before pulling it back into a high ponytail. It will have to do. I'm blessed with long dark eyelashes, so I just touch them up with mascara and put natural colored lip-gloss on. I grab my skinny jeans from the closet and climb into them. I couple it with a fitted t-shirt and a leather jacket I bought from a thrift store on Fisherman's Wharf. Lastly, my short leather boots with my jeans complete the look. I glance at my reflection in the mirror. Not bad, considering it only took me twenty minutes to get ready.

I have an athletic build since I've played sports my whole life. I don't like to spend too much time on my hair or make-up--why bother? It would be a total waste of my time since I sweat playing sports anyway! I head downstairs and grab a protein bar.

My dad is sitting at the kitchen table, drinking his coffee. "Is that all you're eating for breakfast, Tess?" he asks, as he looks up from his iPad. I know he disapproves whenever I skip breakfast.

"I'll pick something up at school, Dad. I have to go! Bus will be here! Mom left for work already?" I change the subject quickly.

"Yep, I'm leaving soon, too. Remember, today is my late day at work. But have a good day and good luck on your try-outs." My dad is my biggest fan when it comes to my sports.

"Thanks Dad and you too!" I reply, as I grab my backpack, give him a quick kiss on the cheek, and run out to the bus stop.

As I'm walking down the hallway at school, I hear my friend, Kylie, yell, "Oh my god, Tess! Wait up! I have *so* much to tell you!" Kylie and I are best friends, inseparable since kindergarten.

"Hey, Kylie! What's up?" I reply, as she reaches my locker. Kylie always has some type of story for me. She is absolutely beautiful, so full of life, and always happy. If I ever want a good laugh, I find Kylie. She's hilarious but can also be dramatic, which translates well for her once she started landing all of the lead roles in the school plays. Unfortunately, this doesn't work so well in her personal life.

"You know who called me last night?" she says, leaning against one of the lockers.

I work on the combination of my locker and shake my head. "I don't know, Kylie," I say. "Who?"

She takes a deep breath and looks at me solemnly before responding, "Kyle."

"*What?*" I say incredulously. "He *called?* Wow, what did he say?" Kyle is Kylie's ex-boyfriend. It's weird that their names are so similar. I believe that is one of the main reasons Kylie first agreed to date him.

"Oh *yeah,* and get this. He acted like *nothing* had happened. Can you believe that? Where do these guys come from?" As Kylie says this, I smirk.

"Maybe it was his way of apologizing?" I try to be positive. Maybe guys just don't know how to fess up to their mistakes.

"You're kidding, right? I mean, he cheated on me," she says, frustrated.

"Well… I mean… you guys broke up last Tuesday, so, he didn't really *do* anything…" I say, trying to reason with her, but Kylie shakes her head and interrupts me.

"Don't even try it, Tess! Don't defend him! What he did was wrong, hooking up with that girl. So what if we were broken up? We were still talking. Oh, no way. Nobody plays me!"

I laugh because she's right. Nobody plays Kylie Roundry, the beautiful cheerleader. She is the perfect package: she's petite with long blond hair and almond shaped blue eyes, the color of the ocean. She can have any guy she wants, but she continues to find her way back to Kyle Keegan. Personally, I think she's too good for him.

It's funny. We're so different. Not only do we look totally different, but our personalities are like night and day as well. I'm more reserved and don't talk about all my issues, and Kylie has no problem sharing her deepest secrets. I am more of a jeans type of a girl, whereas Kylie wears the miniskirts, dresses, and the latest fashion trends. I can never see myself as a cheerleader. Not only am I awkward and ungraceful, but also, why would I cheer for others while they play sports? I'd rather be the one playing on the field or the court.

Kylie puts a stick of gum in her mouth and chews on it while pressing the sole of her kitten heel against the metal locker. "Anyway," she says, somewhat calmer than she was five minutes ago, "are you ready for the tryouts? And why do you have bags under your eyes?" Leave it to Kylie to be blunt.

"Oh…rough night," I reply reluctantly, slamming my locker door.

"Oh no! You had those weird dreams again? Why don't you see my therapist? She's like, *really* good with that sort of thing, Tess." I shudder at the thought of more therapy sessions. I had tried them, sitting in the room with a shrink asking me a bunch of questions, but I never once got any answers.

"No way! I just can't do it anymore," I say quickly. I want to change the subject. "Well, back to the tryouts...yeah, I'm kind of nervous."

I *am* worried about the basketball tryouts, because I'm probably one of the shortest girls out there. I'm only 5'3" so I have to make up for it in speed. I'm hoping I'm not done growing yet. My mom thinks I should still grow a couple of inches. She is a medical geneticist, so hopefully her prediction holds true.

"You'll do fine!" Kylie encourages. "When have you done badly in anything?" Kylie rolls her eyes.

It's true. My whole life, everything has been so easy for me. I chalk it up to my hard work mentality and being lucky.

"I have to go, Kylie. I don't want to be late for class. It's Mrs. Brunel's history final today!" I say, making a scared face.

"Oh, like you'll fail..." she says sarcastically, and then laughs.

"What's that supposed to mean?" I say, laughing.

"Seriously?" she replies. "You're *such* a nerd, Tess!"

"Oh, whatever," I say, smiling at her. Kylie smiles back, flips her hair, and is off down the hall. How does she do that? She's such a natural. Kylie is beautiful, inside and out.

I have a lot of people tell me all the time how pretty I am. But I don't notice that about me. I have big brown almond shaped eyes, surrounded by long thick eyelashes, full, puckered lips, and crazy curly black hair.

I think people are just intrigued by me because I have a

unique and an exotic look about me. I have such an unusual look because of all of my disparate ethnicities. I'm Italian, British, African American, Irish, Indian, Brazilian, and even Native American. Don't ask! I guess my family was just drawn to different cultures. Anyway, my mom is Indian, British, and Italian, while my dad is Irish, African American, Brazilian, and Native American. They both were born in America and met in college. I'm their only child. And yes, I have to admit, I have not met too many people who look like me. In winter, I'm much lighter, and in the summer, I tan easily.

Due to my distinct looks, many photographers and agents have approached me and said I should model. Even strangers say it! But I don't pay them any mind. Yes, I *am* flattered, but it's not something I really can see myself doing. I don't even like to look in the mirror too long. Can you imagine a photographer taking my pictures? No way! A model? Nope. A nerd? Yeah, probably. I've always been a straight A student. School has never been a challenge for me. It's strange. Whenever I take an exam and I don't know an answer, I just follow my instincts and pick one, and over ninety percent of the time, it would be the correct answer. I'm lucky that way I guess.

I make it through Monday and the tryouts. The coach tells us the tryouts are all week long since we have so many girls trying out. I'm up for the challenge!

When I arrive at school on Friday, I run straight to the athletic hall where the list is hanging. Even though I believe I did great at tryouts, I can't help but feel nervous. With my heart pounding, I gather my courage to look at the sophomore team list, under the S's for my last name. I don't see it listed. My heart sinks. Why is my name not on the list?

"Tess, congratulations!" I turn around and see my other best friend, Jack, standing behind me, his green eyes smiling with excitement.

"Jack, I didn't make the team. My name isn't there," I say, disappointed. I'm angry and confused.

"Tess," Jack says, "that's because you're on the varsity team! Look, here's the list!"

"What? Let me see!" Sure enough, there's my name: *Sanoby, Tessnia*.

I'm the point guard for the varsity team! It's unbelievable! In my excitement, I jump into Jack's arms and he twirls me around. He's just as excited as I am. He finally puts me down, but doesn't release me. He's still holding me in an embrace, and I continue grinning from ear to ear like a fool. All of a sudden, he leans forward to kiss me. Just as he brings his lips down, I turn my head, and his kiss lands on my cheek. I slip out of his embrace. I mean Jack is my buddy, why is he trying to kiss me? Jack starts blushing. I know he's embarrassed. I look up at him questioningly.

"Sorry, Tess, I just got caught up in the moment. I didn't mean to make it all weird," Jack mumbles under his breath.

"Don't sweat it, Jack. I know I have that effect on people," I tease, hoping to lighten the mood.

"Ha-ha, cocky much?" Jack jokes.

"Yeah, maybe a bit. Let's get out of here," I say as I laugh. Jack says goodbye and goes to his class, while I head to my locker where Kylie is waiting for me.

"Well hello, *Miss Varsity*! I'm so excited for you!" Kylie can barely keep herself from jumping on me.

"Who told you?" I ask.

"Ah, word got around…" she says.

"Oh my god, Kylie, I can't believe it! I'm *so* excited!"

"Well, I'm not surprised. You're good at everything you do! We *have* to celebrate tonight. I'm coming over!" Kylie is already making plans.

I interrupt her, needing to share what just happened. "Kylie, if I tell you something, do you promise not to tell anybody?"

"Of course, what's wrong?" Kylie is curious, but wary.

"Oh nothing's wrong, but I think Jack just tried to kiss me," I whisper to her.

"What?" Her eyes become wide. "What happened?"

"Well, he leaned down to kiss me, but I turned away so he got my cheek. It was all really awkward." I'm still flustered about the whole thing.

"Wait a minute, you almost got kissed by *the* Jack Thompson and you turned away? What's your problem? He's *so* hot! And he's the varsity quarterback. Any girl would have jumped at that chance!" she says, scolding me.

"Kylie, he's my friend. We've known him since kindergarten! I don't think of him like that! And he was embarrassed, too," I say. Truth be told, Jack is very good looking. He has light brown hair and deep green eyes. He's already six feet tall, and he has a great body because of his athleticism.

"Tess, he was embarrassed because *you* turned away. I've seen the way he's been looking at you lately. I think he has the hots for you. You need to open your eyes and recognize that he could be the perfect guy for you!"

"Perfect guy? Kylie, I'm only fifteen!" I have no interest in finding the perfect guy. If it doesn't feel right, I'm not going to force it. "Look, I just don't want you to blow this out of proportion. He tried and I wasn't interested. That's it. I doubt he will try again," I say.

"Whatever! I'll see you tonight?" Kylie says, before running down the hall.

"See you tonight!" I yell back. As I watch her walking away, I think about what she said about Jack. I shrug my shoulders, thinking there are more important things in life than kissing and boyfriends. So what if I haven't been kissed yet?

When I get home after my basketball practice, I share the big news of making it on the varsity team with my parents. They start grinning from ear-to-ear with pride.

"I knew you had it in you!" Dad exclaims. "But, I can still beat you one-on-one."

"I'll have to take you up on that, *old* man," I tease.

"*Old man*! Who are you calling old? Hey, I may be nearing forty-five, but I can still take you on the court, little girl!" My dad and I tease like this all the time. We both are very competitive and we love to mess with each other. In all fairness though, he is very athletic, and sometimes when we play, he beats me. Dad is fit, he gives no breaks, and he usually goes full force against me whenever we compete. That's probably why I'm good in sports.

"Ok, guys, we have to eat dinner. Nobody is playing against anybody," Mom interjects. My mom is also very fit. She has a fair complexion, long dark hair like me, and a feisty personality. She does not back down from any challenge, and pushes me to be the same way.

As we're eating dinner, Mom says, "Tess, you're going to be sixteen next month. I feel like you were just born yesterday. It's unbelievable how fast time flies." I hear Dad grunt under his breath. I smile knowing how much he hates being reminded that he's getting older. Mom turns to Dad, squeezes his hand and says, "You're even more handsome now, honey, than twenty years ago."

"You're just saying that to make me feel better," Dad responds, squeezing her hand back.

"Nope, I still get butterflies when I look at you." Mom smiles back to him.

"Ok, you two," I interrupt. "I'm already gagging." All three of us start laughing. My heart always fills with joy to see how much my parents still love each other after all these years.

Mom turns her attention back on me, and asks, "What do you want to do for your birthday, sweetie?"

"Well, I don't have any definite plans. It's on a Saturday so I was thinking about celebrating with my favorite guys," I reply, smiling.

"Oh, you're going to *The Angels* that day?" Mom asks.

"I think so. You know it's my happy place. Maybe I'll go for a few hours and play basketball with them or something." I become excited just thinking about it.

The Angels is a facility where autistic kids and adults reside. I volunteer there whenever I have spare time, because it's a nice escape for me, and they are some of my favorite people. I have been volunteering there since I was thirteen, and I've become good friends with some of them.

I eat my dinner and help my mom clean the kitchen. As we're doing the dishes, I say, "Mom, I'm so excited about basketball! It's going to be an amazing season!" I can't stop thinking about it.

"I'm really proud of you, Tess. You've always been able to accomplish whatever you set your mind to, though. I remember your dad and I were shocked that you started walking when you were barely eight months old. And you were so determined to learn to ride that bike. Dad hardly had to help teach you. You practically taught yourself! Tess, you were only three years old when you started riding it down the street!" Mom starts laughing as she shares the story.

"Well, you know I'm stubborn. If I want something, I don't stop until I get it," I say, lifting my chin up. I guess I've been that way my entire life.

"I'll give you that, Tess. You were never a quitter. You're a lot like your dad that way. I'm so excited for your birthday next month! Now tell me, what do you want? I mean it *is* your sweet sixteen, so it's pretty special."

"Um, I'm not sure, Mom. Have you and Dad thought about getting a puppy for the family?" I can't resist bringing that up again. My parents have never gotten me a dog or a cat, even though they know how much I love animals.

I hear my mom sigh before replying, "Tess, I know you want a pet, but it's just not the right time."

"Why do you guys always say that? What kind of *time* are you guys waiting for?" It's always the same excuse and it makes no sense to me at all.

"Let's change the subject, Tess. Just know that when we

decide it's time to get you a cat or a dog, you will be the first to know."

"Ok, Mom," I sigh, dropping the discussion. I don't want to argue with my mom. After finishing the dishes, I say, "I'm going to get my homework done. Kylie is coming soon."

"Ok," Mom says, "but don't stay up too late."

When Kylie arrives later that evening, she fills me in with the latest gossip on who is hooking up with whom. I have no idea how Kylie is able to find this information, but it's always entertaining to hear.

"I'm telling you, Tess, Kyle broke up with me because I wouldn't have sex with him. That's why he turned to Diane. She probably gave him what he wanted," Kylie says. She's still upset about this whole mess with Kyle. As far as I'm concerned, she deserves somebody much better than that loser.

"Kylie, forget about him. He's so cocky and stuck-up. I never liked the way he flaunted you around like you were some prize or something," I say. "Besides, you can get any guy!"

"I'm staying away from guys from now on!" Kylie responds. I start to laugh because we both know that's not going to happen. Kylie starts to laugh with me. "Ok, I'll at least take a break from guys for a week. I'm done talking about this. Let's talk about how Jack almost kissed you today!"

"No! There's nothing to talk about, Kylie!" I exclaim. I can't believe she's bringing that up again.

"Tess, how romantic it would be that your first kiss is from your best friend since kindergarten! You have to admit that he's really good looking!" Kylie says, giggling to herself. "Let's

FaceTime him!" Kylie grabs my iPhone.

"He probably has plans with his football friends, Kylie. It's Friday night!" I try to snatch my phone back.

"We'll see!" She starts to FaceTime him. I sigh in defeat, knowing I lost this battle.

"Kylie? What are you doing with Tess's phone?" I hear Jack's voice.

"I'm sleeping over at Tess's and we're bored," Kylie says. "But here, Tess wants to talk to you." I'm going to kill her! She hands me the phone. I see Jack's handsome face, smiling at me.

"Hey, Jack. Are you out and about or already calling it a night?" I say.

"I have a private training session for football tomorrow morning. I'm about to crash. What are you guys going to do?" Jack asks.

"Nothing. We're just hanging out here. Sorry to bother you," I say.

"Tess, you're never a bother! You know I love to hear from you," Jack responds.

"Thanks, Jack. I'll text you tomorrow. Good night."

"Good night, Tess," Jack replies.

After the conversation ends, I turn to Kylie, who's giggling in a corner. *"You know I love to hear from you,"* she mimics.

I can't help but laugh with her. She is so silly. "Kylie, you're making a big deal about nothing, as usual!"

"No, Tess! Jack is totally into you! He's had feelings for you for a while, and will continue to have them for a long time. Remember I said this. You're just too blind to see it for yourself!"

Kylie is impossible. There's no use arguing with her because she will always get the last word. So I take the pillow and throw it at her. It hits her right in the face. She picks it up and throws it back at me. I catch it and throw it again. The next thing I know, we have a full-blown pillow fight, just like we used to when we were five years old. We both fall back on the bed, laughing hysterically.

Two

It's Saturday, November 21st, and I turn sixteen. I open my eyes to the sunshine that pours through the blinds. I throw my duvet off of me and swing my feet around to the carpet. After a few moments of stretching, I pad across the carpet to the bathroom and wash my face. As I blot my wet forehead with a towel, the excitement finally wells up inside of me. I race through my bedroom, through the hallway, and down the staircase to the kitchen. The house, to my surprise, is silent and still dark in certain corners.

"Mom?" I yell. "Dad?" No one responds. As I pass through the dining room and into the kitchen, I expect to find the table stacked with my dad's science journals. But to my surprise, there's a large teddy bear holding a bouquet of small, pink roses and a tiny box, wrapped in gold paper on the table.

"I'm opening my present, you guys..." I call out to the house. "You better stop me!" I yell, as I unwrap the black velvet jewelry box. I gasp as I open it. I see a beautiful, antique silver necklace, with a rectangular locket. In front, it is simply engraved: *Tessnia.* I turn it around, and it says:

Strength
Peace
Happiness
Always

I open the locket, but find no picture. Beside the teddy bear, is a white envelope lined with gold paper with my name scrawled on it. Carefully, I unseal the envelope and read the card:

To our one and only child,

Words can't describe how lucky we are to have you in our life. Happy 16th!

And no matter what life brings you, we will always be here for you.

Love always,
Mom and Dad

PS: We didn't put anything in the locket because we wanted you to pick your own photograph.

My eyes fill with tears. I wipe them away, put my flowers in a glass vase, and run upstairs to put my new Teddy in my room. I then grab my cell phone and call my mom.

"Hey, Mom!" I say. I hear the sound of the Pacific Coast Highway on the other end. The cars rushing past sound like ocean waves.

"Hey, sweetie! Did you open your gift?" she asks me, knowing full well that I did.

I smirk. "Maybe..." I say, grinning to myself.

"Tessnia! I thought you were going to wait until your dad and I got home before you did that!" Mom scolds. After a brief pause, she says, "Well, did you like it?"

"I did! It's beautiful, Mom!" I exclaim.

"Really? I didn't know what to get you..."

"No, mom, it's *perfect!* I love it so much."

"I'm glad, sweetie," she says.

"Hey, where are you?" I ask.

"Running errands."

"Well, come home soon. I can't wait to go to *The Angels* today!"

"Ok! Well, stop buggin' me!" Mom replies, laughing.

"Love you, Mom," I say tenderly.

"Love you too, Tess," she says back, as we end our conversation.

I cross over to my window and open it. The sky is the color of a robin's egg with tufts of small, white clouds on the horizon. It's a beautiful, balmy California day and the winds from the Pacific Ocean are blowing. The Yarrow and Sea Rocket are especially fragrant today and I breathe them in. This is what I love about living in Pacifica. We have the breathtaking view of the endless ocean and the coastal mountains.

Placing my iPod on my stereo, I scroll until I find Joan Jett & The Blackhearts. I jump around in my room and sing loudly, "I Love Rock And Roll." I know it's an old song, but it's one of my favorites!

After my shower, I pull open my dresser drawers, and decide on a pair of Capri pants and a short-sleeved, fitted shirt that's opal pink. I rarely wear pink, but I know it is flattering against my skin tone. The neckline is a little low, so it shows the curves of my petite breasts nicely. My breasts are still growing, so I sometimes wear push-up bras to enhance my curves. Today is a good day to wear one of those miracle bras! I put on a light pink lip-gloss, and some eyeliner to make my eyes look even more exotic. I finish the look with black mascara on my lashes. I decide to wear my hair down. My wild spiral curls fall a few inches past my shoulders. I slip on my shoes with the one-inch heel and look at myself in the mirror. I can't help but smile at my reflection, knowing that Kylie would be proud of me. I'm learning to embrace my feminine side!

I find a picture of my parents and me, and size it to fit into the locket. It's when we were at an amusement park, and I'm only four years old. I'm laughing into the camera and both my parents are laughing with me and hugging me. I place it in my locket, and put the necklace on. It's perfect! It's a short necklace so it sits at my collarbone. I suddenly get teary-eyed. I guess I must be getting emotional in my old age.

My mom finally arrives and drives me to *The Angels*. On our way to the facility, she says, "You look beautiful, honey. I can't believe how much you've grown."

"Thanks, Mom. Oh, do you want to see the picture I put in my locket?" I ask, as I open the locket to show her.

She looks at the picture. "It's perfect! I clearly remember that day. You wanted to go on the big roller coasters! You had no fear, Tess!" Mom smiles. "Now remember, we're having your birthday dinner tonight after Dad gets home from work, ok?"

"Yes!" I reply. "You know I love your cooking more than any restaurant."

"Well..." she replies, tipping her head to the side, "Not as much as Chipotle..."

"Ha-ha!" I giggle. "Yeah, well... but that's different!"

"Hey, I make a damned good burrito!" Mom says, pointing

her index finger in the air.

"Ha-ha, if you say so..." I tease. "I love you, Mommy," I say, as the car pulls up to the parking lot of *The Angels*.

"I love you too, sweetie," she says.

I give her a kiss on the cheek. "Thanks again, Mom. And I'll see you around five," I say, as I jump out of the car and walk into the facility.

I sign into the volunteer sign-in book at the front desk. "Good to see you again, Tess. Welcome back," says Tina, who works at the front desk.

"Thanks, Tina! I'm looking forward to hanging out with my buddies," I say, smiling back at her. I begin heading back toward the residential sites.

"Tess!" I hear Tony yelling as I enter one of the sites. Tony comes running to me with a big smile. He's eighteen, and has autism. He doesn't make eye contact, clasps his hands together, and starts rocking.

"Hi Tony, I miss you so much!" I gently pat his back, and he gives me a shy smile.

"What are we going to do today? Did you drive? Where's your car? What kind of car do you drive? You look really pretty today. I like your hair." Tony shoots off rapid-fire questions.

"Whoa, slow down, Tony!" I say, laughing. "No, I didn't drive, but I'll be getting my license soon! I'm sixteen today!" I'm excited to share my special day.

"Tess, it's your birthday today?" Jennifer, the nurse, asks me. I nod, smiling at her.

Amy comes running to me. "It's Tess's birthday, it's Tess's

birthday. I want cake!" Amy starts yelling and spinning. Amy is fourteen, and she is adorable. She gets over stimulated easily though, so I have to be careful not to stress her out.

I look around and notice that there are six more of the residents surrounding me. They are all very excited. I decide to distract them. "Ok, guys, how about some games first? Who wants to play some basketball?"

It works like magic! All of the residents are now focused on the game. We set up the indoor basketball net, and play HORSE. It's so fun to laugh and run around with them.

After playing with them for half an hour, I decide to visit the residents in the other rooms. So, I take Amy with me for a walk. I figure she probably needs to escape for a bit, and she can visit her friends in the other rooms as well. After notifying Jennifer, Amy and I head out.

The facility is fairly large, so it is a pretty good walk to visit all of the ten rooms. As we're walking down the hall, suddenly, Amy starts running away from me.

"Amy, wait for me! Don't go anywhere!" I yell. I'm fearful that I won't know where she might end up if she keeps running. She leaves me no choice but to run after her. I remember her history of hitting other residents when fueled by too much excitement, and I cringe. "Amy, stop!" I yell.

She disappears into the multipurpose room. I run in after her, determined to use my stern voice on her. I don't even get the opportunity. As I stumble in, I hear music. I see Amy standing there, mesmerized, and slowly swaying in the corner to the sound of the music. I also notice there are at least thirty other kids in there, some sitting, and some standing. All of the kids are quiet and looking very peaceful. I can't believe it.

Usually, when too many of the kids get together in a room, they become excited or agitated, and it's harder to control them due to their disability. To my surprise, nobody is making a sound. All I hear is the music.

As I scan the room, I find the source. He's sitting on a folding chair in the middle of the multipurpose room. He's playing his acoustic guitar and I hear him singing.

I recognize the song, "Beautiful" by Christina Aguilera. I freeze. I'm literally unable to move. He has drawn me in. I'm captured by his music, his voice, his singing. He never looks up while he is singing. He keeps his head down, and keeps stroking his guitar to the notes. His voice has so much emotion in it; it feels like he's living the song. I vaguely remember noticing he has dark wild hair and he looks tanned.

The more he keeps singing, the more mesmerized I become. I have never experienced such a strong emotion. My eyes become misty with tears. I sense that he's singing the words of "Beautiful" from his heart. As I feel the goose bumps forming, I completely forget where I am. All I know is that I can't move and I can't look away. He keeps stroking his guitar, and finishes the song by humming the last couple of lines. After he finishes, the silence continues. It's as if nobody wants to break the spell.

Finally, he looks up, and one of the kids yells, "Again!" Then, some laugh, while some start yelling and rocking. The staff starts to clap, and soon after, some of the kids clap too. The guy looks up and smiles at the kids. His smile is warm and tender. I'm surprised that he looks so comfortable in this setting.

I walk over to Amy. She's grinning ear-to-ear. She runs

toward him and I walk behind her slowly. The kids and staff surround him; they're intrigued by him.

As I get closer, I notice he is tanner than I realized. He's fit, and he looks as though he's in his late teens or early twenties. He has dark brown hair, almost black, and it falls into a tousled mess. The look is carefree, and it seems to suit him. As Amy and I get closer, he looks up at us. I stop breathing. His eyes burn into mine. I can't look away. He holds my gaze with his intense gray eyes. They are deep and incredibly captivating. What is wrong with me? I attempt to break the eye contact, but I can't. He makes no effort to do so either. I don't notice anything around me, but him.

"Joe, sing again!" I hear Amy yelling excitedly, and with that, the spell is broken. I quickly look away, embarrassed.

"Hi, Amy. Did you enjoy that song?" This beautiful guy, named Joe, turns to Amy. As he stands up from his chair, I sneak a peek again. I'm surprised at how tall he is--easily over six feet. I notice he has a well-defined jawline, a narrow nose, and gorgeous high cheekbones. He looks like he could be a model. I'm taken aback by his gentle and sweet smile toward Amy. He then shifts his gaze toward me. I catch my breath, feeling like a fool.

"Hello," he says softly, as he slowly smiles at me.

"Hi," I say awkwardly. I smile shyly and lift my head to look up at him. I can't believe his eyes. Not only are they a unique shade of gray, but also a palisade of dark eyelashes surrounds them. Is it fair for one guy to possess such beautiful features? I notice that he has his arm extended to shake my hand, so I slowly place my hand in his. As soon as we touch,

I want to pull it away. I feel a wave of shock going through me. My eyes get wide and I quickly look up at him. I notice his forehead has a slight frown, and his eyes hold a glimpse of surprise, which he quickly conceals by lowering his lids. I swiftly withdraw my hand out of his hold, not prepared for the unexplained sensations from this brief touch.

He's the first to recover. "Hi, I'm Joe, you must be Tessnia?"

I'm surprised. How does he know that? I look at him puzzled. He points to my necklace and I look at my locket, stupefied. Right, my name is on my necklace.

"Oh yeah, I'm Tess. Well, Tessnia is my real name. But Tess or Tessnia is fine. Well, most people just call me Tess, though," I ramble. Why am I rambling? I sound foolish. I have to get a grip, very fast. "Oh, and that was amazing, you know, your singing. You were really great."

"Oh, thanks. I really enjoy it." Joe mumbles, as a sheepish grin begins forming on his beautiful face. I'm now having difficulty looking away from his boyish grin.

"Come on, Tess, we walk again," Amy interrupts. She's already bored of this exchange.

"Ok," I reply, disappointed that I have to leave this gorgeous guy named Joe.

"Joe come with?" Amy suggests. "Joe come for walk?"

I glance up at Joe, and I notice that he is grinning. He knows I'm nervous around him. His look is questioning, waiting for a confirmation. He wants reassurance from me that it's ok if he joins us.

"Um, sure. You can walk with us if you'd like, Joe.

Sometimes we go just to the park and back. It's perfect today because the weather is so nice," I say nervously. I'm glad that I remembered to grab Amy's jacket.

"Yeah, sure, I'd love to join you guys," Joe replies. *Yes!* My heart flutters at the thought of spending more time with him.

Joe leaves his guitar in a corner of the wall. As he bends down, I notice he has Levi's slim fit, faded blue jeans on that hang low on his hips. He is lean and muscular. His fitted black t-shirt hugs his muscular torso. From the back of the chair, he grabs his brown leather jacket. I can't help but notice how his muscles bulge out as he extends his arm to pull it into the sleeve of his jacket.

"So, do you volunteer here?" Joe says, interrupting my thoughts.

"Yeah, I've volunteered since I was thirteen. I've known all these guys for a while. But I haven't seen you around here?" I ask curiously.

"Oh, I pop in every once in a while. I can't volunteer too often because of my schedule. It's a nice escape for me," Joe responds.

"I feel the same way--about the escape, I mean. Puts life into perspective, you know?"

Joe turns toward me, and looks at me for a second, as if deep in thought. "Yes, I do," he says softly. His voice is quiet, as if he's analyzing what I just said.

When we reach the park, Amy jumps on the swing. She squeals in delight, and I start laughing. I turn to look at Joe, and I catch him staring at me with a strange look. It's a look of confusion, curiosity, and wonder. He conceals it quickly.

"So how long have you been singing?" I ask.

"Oh, I just do that on the side. It's another escape for me. It's no big deal, really," he mutters. As I watch his reaction, I realize he really doesn't think it's a big deal.

"What are you talking about? It *is* a big deal. Do you know the effect you have on people with your music? The entire room was hypnotized. It was pretty amazing to witness. You should really pursue your talent," I encourage.

"Nah, it's just a hobby. No big deal," he says uncomfortably. "What about you?"

I throw him a sidelong glance. "Hmm? Me?" I say, playing with my locket.

"Yeah," Joe says, smirking at me. "What do you like to do?"

"Um, there's really nothing interesting about me. My best friend says I'm a nerd," I answer, shrugging my shoulders.

"A nerd?" he asks.

"Yeah…I guess because I've always been really driven with schoolwork and I read a lot," I answer. "I also play sports on the side."

"Sports, huh? What do you play?" His smirk becomes a huge grin. His eyes are smiling at me, teasing me.

"I play basketball and run track," I reply, lifting my chin up. I don't understand why it's important to me that he approves.

"I bet you're fast," he teases, smiling at me.

"I'm decent," I say, watching Amy on the swing.

"Now look who's being modest. I know you can run. I can tell. I can tell by your build, and the way you carry yourself," Joe says. His voice softens. "I can tell when you run, you don't think about anything but just running. You don't look back. You know that you have to run as fast as you can, no matter what." He's looking straight into my eyes as he says this. It feels like he's looking into my soul, unveiling all of my secrets.

"What? How would you know that?" I question, frowning. I'm confused. What is he saying, and how does he know this about me? I become uncomfortable and begin rubbing my collarbone and my neck. I want to go back inside with Amy.

Joe notices my uneasiness. All of a sudden, he grabs the hook of my left arm with urgency. His eyes draw me in again. They are intense, and almost look troubled and confused. "Tess, you have to embrace your gifts--your talents. Don't fight them."

I pull out of his hold and take a step back. "What are you talking about? Look," I say, gathering my composure, "maybe we should head back." I nervously shift my weight from one foot to another. I want to run, but I know I can't because I'm responsible for Amy, who is still swinging.

Joe notices how uncomfortable he's making me. He smiles a warm, friendly smile. "Forget it, Tess. Let's go back." Just like that, the tension evaporates, and I begin to feel at ease again. I decide to ignore the strange exchange.

We head back to Amy's home. Joe walks with us. When we enter it, a bunch of the kids run to me and give me a big card that says, "Happy Birthday." They're laughing and some are jumping with excitement.

"Oh my gosh! Thank you, guys! Wow, you just made my birthday!" I'm so happy and touched by their gesture. From my peripheral vision, I notice Joe staring at me intently. I take the card and give them hugs, being careful to only hug the kids who can tolerate it. They all start to sing "Happy Birthday" to me. I'm really uncomfortable now because I hate being the center of attention.

"You're so beautiful, Tess!" Tony yells, after the song is over. My face burns from embarrassment because I feel Joe's eyes on me the entire time, piercing into me.

"Thanks, Tony," I smile at him.

I feel a hand on my waist, and again, the odd sensation travels through my body. I turn around to find Joe staring at me. He leans over and whispers in my ear, "I have to leave now. Walk me out?"

"Sure," I reply. My heart stops. Why does this guy have such a strange effect on me? I have no idea what's going on, but I don't care. I just want to be near him. He keeps his hand on my waist as we walk out and I don't pull away. I like how his palm burns into the small of my back and the electric sensation that travels up and down my spine. He walks taller as he holds me possessively, and the nurses and administrators glance up at us as we make our way through the building, past the lobby, and into the multipurpose room. As he goes to the wall where his guitar sits in its busted leather case, I feel the cold air of the room replace where his hand was. I miss his touch. After he hangs the guitar case over his shoulder, Joe puts his hand back on the small of my back. My heart does a happy dance.

"Shall we?" Joe says, cocking his eyebrow. I smile up at him, girlishly. We walk out to his car--a beat-up black Mazda sedan. "You didn't tell me it was your birthday," he says, as he pops the trunk. "How old are you?"

"I'm sixteen!" I reply proudly. He smirks. I love the way

his lips curl when he smirks.

"You're growing up!" he teases. After a brief pause, he says, "You know, Tony is right. You are beautiful."

"Thanks," I mumble, looking down. I feel nervous and I swallow hard. How can he call me beautiful? I slowly look up. He's waiting for me to make eye contact with him. I stop breathing. He has that same piercing gaze, as if he's looking into my soul. I can't look away. It feels as if he's reading my deepest thoughts and secrets. My heart quickens. I notice his eyes darkening.

"Why am I drawn to you, Tess?" he whispers. Oh my god, he's going to kiss me. I can't believe it! My first kiss is going to be from this gorgeous guy. And it's on my sixteenth birthday! What a great birthday present! Can this be any more perfect? I hold my breath as his head lowers. My lips automatically part and I close my eyes. I can feel the heat of his body coming closer to me. Then, his hand is in my hair. I feel his breath on my face. My legs feel like jelly. I vaguely remember praying that my legs would hold me up. I wait, and wait, and wait. Why am I not feeling his lips? I slowly open my eyes. Joe is standing in front of me, staring down at me, with his signature-teasing smirk. His eyes are smiling and he's holding his hand up. My gaze shifts to his hand, and I notice he's holding a leaf in his hand. "This was in your hair, Tessnia. I had to lean into you to get it out." I look at him, horrified and humiliated. His smirk gets even wider as if knowing the effect he has on me. Did he do that on purpose?

"Ok, you can wipe that silly grin off your face now. I'm totally embarrassed," I say candidly. What's the use pretending anyway? He knew what he was doing, and I fell for it.

All of a sudden, his mood shifts from teasing to sadness. He grabs my right hand with his left hand. With his other hand, he caresses my cheek, very gently, and almost too quickly. He brings my hand to his lips and opens my palm, kissing it softly while closing his eyes.

Joe looks into my eyes once more. He leans forward and whispers in my ear, "Happy birthday, Tessnia. Good luck to you, and remember what I said to you earlier." He releases my hand, jumps into his car, and drives away. I stare after the car with my mouth open, stunned at our exchange. He doesn't turn back once. I stand motionless for at least ten minutes, perplexed at what happened.

I slowly start walking back to the building. The whole encounter with Joe was so unreal. I feel confused and I'm almost in a state of shock. Am I ever going to see him again? Why did it feel so final when he left? My heart feels heavy. I don't even know this guy. Why am I feeling so sad? Did I feel a connection with him, or was that just my imagination?

I find out a little more information about him from talking to the Volunteer Coordinator. I find out his name is Joe Smith. Apparently, he occasionally pops in, usually when he's on his summer breaks or holiday breaks from his college. To my disappointment, no additional information is offered to me.

When my mom comes to pick me up, I'm still thinking about the events of the day in my mind on our ride home. I guess I'm still in a stupor because of Joe.

"Why are you so quiet, Tess? Did you have a good day?" Mom asks.

"Oh yeah, Mom," I say, rousing from my daydream. "Look at the card they made me." I show her the card from the kids.

"How sweet!" she replies, smiling at me.

My mind starts wandering again. I start to play back every exchange with Joe. I think about the way he was playing his guitar, and how he had sung from his heart and his soul. I remember how breathtakingly beautiful he was, and how comfortable he was with the kids. I linger on the color and depth of his gray eyes, and how they seemed to prod my soul. I remember how his eyes would dance when he was teasing me. I smile to myself as I remember loving the sensation going through my body when his hands were on me, and how they had burned into me. My smile widens as I think about his dark, wild and messy hair, falling all over his forehead. Then, I start thinking about some of the things he had said to me. He was talking about my running. I shudder when I remember he had told me to embrace my gifts. What did he mean by that? I sigh. Suddenly, all of the events of the day seem exhausting.

When we get home, Mom tells me to get the drinks from the basement. Even though most California homes don't have basements, my parents had insisted on building one.

I wander down the stairs, my mind reeling, when all of a sudden I hear a chorus of people yell, "SURPRISE!" Startled, I turn on the light and look around me. All of my friends are gathered in the basement. They laugh, while I stand there with a goofy smile on my face.

"Are you surprised?" Kylie asks, her eyes dancing with excitement. I'm sure she's behind the planning of this party!

"Yes! Oh my god, I had no idea!" I'm still looking around, trying to soak it all in. Everybody runs up to me and gives me hugs.

"Well, honey, we wanted to throw this surprise party for you with all your friends. Hope you're surprised," Mom says from behind me. I turn around and my dad is with her too, also wearing a goofy smile like me.

"Oh thanks, Mom and Dad! I had no idea. This is crazy." I laugh, still shaking my head. Then, I see a familiar face. My Aunt Jenna is here! She runs to me and hugs me.

"Happy birthday, my beautiful Tess!" she says, giving me a kiss on my cheek. "Where did the time go?"

"I can't believe you're here!" I say excitedly. Aunt Jenna is my mom's younger sister. She's in her late twenties and she's beautiful. There is a big age difference between my mom and her sister. After my grandparents died when they were young, my mom had practically raised her. I'm really close to my aunt, so I'm especially excited to see her.

"Let everybody eat and dance, Tess. We're running to your room to get you ready!" Kylie says, pulling me up the stairs.

"Wait, what?" I say. "I'm already ready." I don't want to leave the rest of my friends.

"Tess, you will *not* be wearing that to your sixteenth birthday party!" she says, rolling her eyes at me. "We'll be back down in no time. Now hurry, let's go." She takes me to my room. "I got you a cool outfit for your birthday present, and you're going to be wearing it!" She gives me a gift box. I hesitantly open it, because now I'm nervous of what she's going to put on me. I pull the clothes out. It's a sequin black mini skirt with a light gold sequin blouse. It's gorgeous, but it looks really skimpy.

"Kylie, it's really cute, but I can't wear it. Do you see how short this skirt is? First of all, my dad would kill me," I say, with disbelief.

"Don't worry, Tess. I got it all taken care of. I already warned Mr. Sanoby that he's not allowed to say anything. I told him that this was your night, and to let you enjoy it." Kylie is proud of herself, and smiles smugly.

"What did he say?" I ask curiously.

"He said nothing. He just threw his hands up in the air, started shaking his head, rolled his eyes, and walked away. So I took that as a yes. Now hurry." Kylie giggles, and she goes to work on me. I don't tell her anything about Joe, because I honestly don't even know what to say about that incident. The whole encounter seems surreal to me. I decide to fill her in with the details when we have more time.

As Kylie is getting me ready, I look in the mirror. My legs look long and toned because of the black stilettos I'm wearing. The outfit is skin tight, emphasizing every curve. She puts some more eyeliner and eye shadow on me, making my eyes stand out. Thankfully, she keeps the rest of the makeup light. She pins some portions of my hair up, and loose tendrils fall around my face.

"Kylie, are you sure? I never wear clothes like this." I'm nervous and feel out of my comfort zone.

"Exactly my point, Tess. All of the girls downstairs are wearing mini-dresses. Once in a while, it's ok to really dress up, you know? It's your birthday, and you should stand out. Let's go now."

I take a deep breath, smile, and hug her. We both run downstairs excitedly. As I descend down the stairs, people look at me in awe. Even though I hate being the center of attention, it feels good. About fifty of my friends are here, and excitement fills each of them. Instantly, I am caught up in it, too. As I look around the room, I notice my parents and Kylie have gone above and beyond for the party; there are countless appetizers, a full dinner to follow, a soda station complete with a root beer float area, a variety of homemade punch bowls, and even a dessert table topped with cupcakes that say "Tess" on them. The basement is decorated with Sweet 16 balloons, streamers, and disco balls. There is a DJ playing his music, and his strobe lights sparkle throughout the basement.

"You look breathtaking, Tess," Jack says behind me. "I'm not used to you looking like this."

"Me neither, Jack," I agree, as I turn to look at him. "But, thank you."

"Let's dance." Jack takes my hand and leads me to the middle of the dance floor. It's a fast number so we all dance in a group, basically jumping around, and singing the words out loud. Everybody looks like they're having a blast. After a few fast beat songs, it changes to a slow jam. I start to walk off, but Jack grabs my hand. "No you don't, Tess. We're dancing to this." He's wearing his boyish grin.

"Ok, you sure you can hang?" I tease.

"You're hard to keep up, but I'm up for the challenge." He responds right back. Jack puts his hands on my waist and pulls me to him. I'm glad to see there are a bunch of friends dancing with one another, so I don't feel too awkward. It feels nice to just lean into him. Jack is strong and muscular, so his arms wrapped around me make me feel secure. I decide to relax and enjoy myself. Jack smells really nice. He's wearing a fitted short sleeve green shirt and relaxed black jeans. Yeah, any girl would be lucky to be with Jack. He's not only good looking, but he really is a nice guy. I'm so caught up in the moment that I don't even notice when the song ends.

"Are you falling asleep on me?" Jack asks, as he nudges me. "Come on, let's get you a Coke or something." I start laughing as he teases me. That's one thing I love about Jack. I can be myself around him, without worrying about being judged.

After the party, I clean up, and climb into my bed. I can't believe all that my parents did for me for my birthday. I'm a lucky girl. I touch the locket around my neck, and before long, I fall asleep.

She is running. She can't tell where she's running. It feels like branches from trees are hitting her body and her face as she keeps running."Don't turn around. Keep running! Run!"Her inner voice is yelling at her. She's running as fast as she can."Please don't hurt me," she begs. She is scared. She's not going to give up. She's going to keep running. Her only escape is to run. Her heart is beating so fast, she can barely catch her breath! Something is reaching out for her, about to grab her!

"No!" I scream. I sit up in my bed, gasping for air. I try to slow down my breathing as I bury my face into my hands. I'm shaken up by the dream, as cold sweat covers my body. I take some deep breaths as I force myself to calm down. There was one thing different this time, compared to the previous dreams. This time, there were piercing gray eyes urging the girl in my dream to continue. The eyes were screaming at her to run and not give up. They were the same eyes that had pierced into my soul earlier.

Three

I continue to volunteer at *The Angels* whenever I get the opportunity. I find myself hoping I would run into Joe, especially during school breaks. Once, I decide to casually bring him up in a conversation while talking to Jennifer, one of the nurses. I just can't resist asking about him, hoping to find some information.

"Do you remember that guy who sang to the residents a while ago? I believe he sang *Beautiful* in the multi-purpose room, while playing his guitar," I say nonchalantly, as I continue organizing the activity closet.

"Oh, you mean Joe? We love him. But we haven't seen him since your birthday. I'm not sure why, because that's not like him. He normally would stop by every couple of months, and entertain these guys. I mean, clearly he is one of their favorite volunteers." Jennifer begins smiling to herself just thinking about Joe. I guess he has the same effect on thirty-year-olds, as sixteen-year-olds. It's been over six months already. Why hasn't he returned?

"Come on, Tess, now karaoke!" Amy demands, interrupting my thoughts.

"Ok, I did promise you, Amy," I reply. "Who wants to sing karaoke?" I look around the room for the response. All of the residents come running, full of excitement. Some are jumping up and down while clapping, and some are squealing in delight. I start laughing. How do these guys always cheer me up?

"Let's sing 'That's What Friends Are For'!" yells Tony. He loves that song. I set up the karaoke machine.

"Ok, guys, we all have to sing together. Come closer to the mic," I encourage. I'm a terrible singer, so there's no way I'm singing by myself. The residents circle around me. As we start to sing, I hold the mic in front of each resident as they take turns. It's so funny to watch them get excited when they hear their own voice. Some of the residents begin dancing while screaming. Nurse Jennifer has removed the residents who normally get over stimulated with loud noise. I see a few of the residents holding hands and swaying with the music as the song is coming to an end.

As I smile, I feel somebody reach for my hand. I look up to see Amy smiling at me. I give her hand a squeeze and we all sing and dance together. God, how I love these guys! I cherish my time with the residents at *The Angels.* They are unique in their own way. They'll always hold a special place in my heart.

Whenever I'm here, I find myself looking toward the front entrance frequently. A part of me always hopes to see Joe walk through those front doors with his guitar one day. But he never does.

As time passes, the details of meeting Joe start to become blurry. I'm not sure if I remember correctly what he looked like. I mean I remember his intense gray eyes and his beautiful singing. I'm sure he had really dark hair, but then I start questioning whether it was black or brown. The rest of the features are a haze to me. I may have started to make up what he looked like in my mind. I can't even remember if he had a round face or long face. I question if his eyes were big or narrow. Perhaps he wasn't even that tall. I mean, I was only 5'3" at the time, so maybe he just looked really tall to me. Or I was so caught up in the moment, that I might have conjured him up to be even better looking than he actually might have been. I'm annoyed at myself for not remembering clearly. I finally accept that it was one of those once in a lifetime experiences, and that I would never see him again. I honestly don't think about that encounter too much as time passes.

During the summer of my sophomore year, my family decides to go to Jamaica for a vacation. Although it is a long flight, I'm excited to get away for a week. Aunt Jenna decides to come with us as well, so we all fly out together. Our all-inclusive resort has a spectacular view of the Caribbean Sea!

My parents share a room, and Aunt Jenna and I share another room. Every day, we go to the beach and bake under the sun. Even though I'm not too far from the Pacific Ocean back home, somehow this feels different. It's more exotic out here. Maybe I feel that way because it's an island, or maybe I'm just caught up in the Jamaican culture.

Every evening, they have a stunning show for us. I'm mesmerized by the entertainment. One night during the dance show, one of the dancers grabs me and pulls me up on stage. I'm so embarrassed! He starts dancing around me, wanting me to dance with him. I can never dance like these dancers! They're moving their hips in directions that I don't think my hips are even capable of moving!

"Come on, Tess! Let's see what you got!" I hear Mom yell from her seat. Is she kidding me? There is no way I can dance like them! I try to walk off of the stage, laughing and shaking my head. The dancer pulls me back to him again, encouraging me to dance. Oh, what the hell. I'm on vacation, so I might as well just have some fun.

I start moving my hips to the rhythm. The crowd goes wild. The more the crowd cheers, the more I relax and let myself go with the music. It's so much fun to just let go! By the time the dance is over, I'm laughing and having a great time. I even forget that I'm on stage, with everybody watching me.

When I get back to my seat, I still can't stop laughing. My parents and Aunt Jenna are standing and cheering for me.

"You were absolutely amazing, Tess!" Aunt Jenna says. "You have some moves, girl!"

"Yeah, where did you learn to dance like that?" Dad accuses, narrowing his eyes at me. I know he's teasing me.

"Did I look totally foolish up there?" Now that the spell is broken, I feel self-conscious again.

"Honey, you looked beautiful up there. You could move better than the natives!" Mom says.

"Mom, you're just saying that because you're my mother!" I reply, rolling my eyes.

"She's not kidding, Tess! You looked hot up there. You need to teach me some of those moves!" Aunt Jenna beams.

"I would never be able to dance like that again. I can't believe I actually did it!" I laugh. I normally don't like showing off like that, but I must have gotten caught up in the moment.

Later that night, when we get back into the hotel room, Aunt Jenna and I have one of our talks again. During our vacation, before falling asleep, Aunt Jenna and I talk for hours. Our talks range from boys, to life, to sports, to good books, to our goals. My aunt may be almost thirty, but she is young at heart. I can always count on her for some great advice.

"Tess, you really looked good tonight dancing on that stage. I'm proud of you because I know that took a lot of guts," Aunt Jenna says.

"I was scared at first, Aunt Jenna. Then I started having fun, so I stopped worrying about it," I reply.

"That's what life is about, Tess. It's about enjoying yourself, and not to worry about what people think. I know that's sometimes hard, but trust me, you're not going to be able to please everybody all the time. Do you understand?"

"Yeah, Aunt Jenna," I say, nodding my head.

"No matter what life may bring, always remember to follow your heart. That's what ultimately is going to keep you happy," she says. I nod again. I love our talks.

The next day, we decide to go horseback riding on the beach. I'm very excited because I love animals, and I've never been horseback riding. My horse is a beautiful stallion named Thunder. He is all black with a shiny coat, has big brown eyes, black mane and tail, and a white diamond shape on his forehead.

Once the owner helps me mount him, my apprehension leaves me. I'm looking forward to our adventure together. Thunder remains graceful and gentle during our ride. As he trots along, I'm able to pick up the rhythm of his movement so we start moving in unison. I relax and enjoy this moment with Thunder. As he trots faster, the wind really begins to blow against my face and body. My heart beats faster with excitement, and it feels like I'm flying! I can feel the ocean breeze blowing through my hair and can almost taste the salt in the wind from the sea. I feel the strength of Thunder under me, as his beautiful mane flies with the wind, just the same as my wild hair. I'm surprised that even though I don't know Thunder at all, I feel so connected with him. The entire experience is exhilarating.

After the ride, I walk to Thunder, pet his coat, and thank him for the memory of our ride together. He brings his head to me, sniffs me, and then holds his head and tail up high, as if showing off. I start to laugh. Suddenly, Thunder bows his head down to me, bending one of his front legs so that he's lowered to the ground.

"I never saw him do that before," says the owner, frowning.

I continue petting Thunder, and ask, "Oh, what does it mean?"

"He's showing his respect for you," the owner says, looking puzzled. Surprised, I turn to look at Thunder again, and he stares straight into my eyes, keeping his head bowed. Instinctively, I bow my head to him as well, showing him the same respect. At that moment, I feel a powerful connection with him. I don't really understand it completely, but for some reason, Thunder makes me feel like he understands me more than I understand myself. I'm not prepared for the unexpected sadness when I have to say goodbye to him, as he finally leaves with the owner.

My dad and I jog on the beach every morning in Jamaica. We both love to run, and because of our busy lifestyles back home, we don't get too many opportunities like this. One morning, after we're done with our jog, we continue walking down the shore. Dad turns to me and says, "You know, Tess, you'll be leaving for college in a couple of years. What am I going to do without you?"

"Dad, I won't go too far, I promise. You can always visit me, and you know I'll always be coming back home. You can't get rid of me that easily!" I tease.

"Tess, you're all that your mother and I have. You're everything to us. You know that, right?" I realize Dad is not in a teasing mood and is having a serious heart-to-heart with me.

"You'll always be stuck with me, Dad," I reply.

"I can't believe how fast time flew. I mean, I feel like you were just born. I still remember when you first learned to walk and talk. And now look at you. You've grown up to be such a beautiful young lady. I can't even begin to tell you how proud I am of you, Tess."

Ok, now I'm starting to feel all choked up. My dad is rarely sappy. So when he does get to this point, that means he has a lot to get off of his chest. "Thanks, Dad," I slowly reply.

"Honestly, Tess, before I know it, you'll be walking down the aisle, and I'll be giving you away to some man. I'll probably want to kill this man for taking my baby away from me by the way!" Dad starts laughing.

I start giggling too. Dad is so silly. "Dad, why are you talking like this? Marriage is nowhere in sight, trust me! I want to accomplish so much before I even think about settling down!"

We continue walking for a while, just staring at the ocean, and enjoying the tranquility. Dad breaks the silence and says, "Tess, you know you can accomplish anything your heart desires, right? I have so much faith in you. You are strong; remember that. I don't say this often enough, but I am so proud of you. No matter what happens, you will always be my baby girl." We both stop and I give him a hug. I admire my father so much. He has achieved a lot in his life. He had no family, and he was raised in the slums. Somehow, he persevered when he could have easily chosen the life of gang violence. Against all odds, he got himself out of that environment, and put himself through college. Because of his intelligence, he also attended a top medical school, and is now considered one of the most respected neurologists.

"Don't worry, Daddy. I will always be your baby girl. I don't know what I would do without you and Mom. I'm so lucky to have you as my parents." I mean every word. If my tough father is pouring his heart out to me, I'm not going to hold back either. We aren't really the type of family who analyze our feelings, or have long family discussions. That's just not us. That's why moments like these are even more precious.

For the rest of the vacation, we go zip lining, hiking, and climb the Dunn's River Falls. It ends up being one of my most memorable vacations. I love creating memories like these with my parents and Aunt Jenna. I can always count on Aunt Jenna to make sure we're doing something adventurous. She loves living on the edge, and is the first to try anything new.

The week is over way too fast, and before we know it, we're already flying back. I'm happy to get the window seat because I love looking at the sky from such a high viewpoint.

I start to think about Thunder, the beautiful black stallion. I say a silent goodbye to him as the plane takes off, and I see the island of Jamaica become smaller and smaller the further we fly. I have no idea why we had bonded, but I know I will never forget him.

The plane ascends up and through the clouds. As I look out of the window, I see the wing of the plane and the clear blue sky straight ahead. I glance down and notice the sky is layered with a blanket of white fluffy clouds. I sigh, feeling content and peaceful as I soak in the beauty.

Just then, for a brief second, a dark cloud passes before my eyes. I automatically jerk my head away from the window to avert my gaze from the blackness that has just passed by the window. My heart skips a beat, as fear passes through my body. I begin to breathe rapidly. Why am I having a panic attack? And where did that dark cloud come from? When some of my courage returns, I hesitantly peek out of the window again. There is nothing there! The sky is completely clear. I quickly turn my head toward the tail end of the plane, thinking we must have passed that cloud very quickly. But all I witness is a clear sky. The only clouds I see are the white clouds that are below the plane, but they are the harmless cotton-like, scattered clouds.

I glance at the other passengers to see if they had noticed that black cloud. I don't notice anything unusual in their facial expressions. When I look toward my parents, both are oblivious and reading their medical journals. I force myself to slow my breathing down. In time, my heart rate settles down as well. I wonder if I had just imagined that cloud. My body had instantly reacted. I decide to put it behind me, deliberately not thinking about it anymore.

As high school years pass, Jack and I continue to stay close. He comes by the house often, and many times Dad, Jack, and I play basketball in my driveway, while Mom prepares snacks. She always makes her ice cold, homemade lemonade that hits the spot.

Jack and Dad are both very competitive. Neither gives any breaks while playing sports. Once, when Jack shoves me down with his shoulder, following up with a dunk into the basket, I yell, "Hey, no fair! This is not football!"

"Stop complaining," Jack says, while laughing. "You're just mad that I dunked on you."

"Let's see what you got, Tess. Get back up and play your game!" Dad encourages.

Ok, I can just keep complaining, or do something about it. I'm so angry! I'm going show them that this is my sport! I snatch the ball back and get myself in the zone. I take the shot, and "swoosh".

"Ha! Nothing but net!" I yell. I get the ball back and quickly drive in, toward the basket. Dad tries to cut me off by jumping into my path. I do a spin move and get around him. I see Jack is running toward me to block my shot. But I sidestep and go up for a reverse layup. Yes! I'm on fire!

"Nice!" Dad says. "But this is where it stops." Dad is so funny when he starts his trash talking.

"Ok, come on, old man. You're playing like you're forty-six or something!" I tease. Dad hates it when I throw his age in his face. As I get the ball back, before they even realize what I'm about to do, I take a quick fade away shot, which goes straight into the hoop. "Oh, what were you saying, Dad? You have nothing to say now?" I can't resist rubbing it in.

"Come at me, little girl!" Dad teases back, bracing himself to stop my next move.

"Ok, I'm going to have to stop holding back," says Jack, taking his shirt off. I start laughing, but then I notice Jack's ripped body. I'm surprised how his body has changed. How did the boy I grow up with, become a man overnight? To my horror, I must have been staring at him because I hear Jack say, "What? You've never seen a guy without a shirt before?"

That makes me laugh even more because I know he's teasing me. "Not Jack Thompson, I guess. You've grown up," I reply.

"I've been growing. You've just been too busy to notice," Jack says, his green eyes dancing as he smirks.

"Come on, you two. Are we going to play some ball or you guys going to stand there and flirt all day?" Dad yells. Leave it to Dad to be so blunt! Jack and I laugh and we start playing again.

Jack is ready to stop any moves I have up my sleeve. But I'm on fire, and all my shots are falling in. Before long, I have beaten both of them, and I run around the driveway, doing my victory lap. Both Jack and Dad can't resist but laugh at my silly victory lap. They both walk up to me and shake my hand.

"Impressive, Tess," Jack compliments, smiling at me. I plant a smug smile on my face.

"Who wants lemonade?" Mom steps outside with three glasses of lemonade.

"Perfect timing!" Dad says, as we each grab one and chug it down.

"Thanks, Mrs. Sanoby," Jack says, after he finishes the

drink. "It's just what I needed after your daughter just beat me in basketball!"

"You let her beat you, Jack?" Mom asks. "You have to play her as if you're playing against one of the boys."

"I tried! But she was still unstoppable!" Jack begins laughing.

"He's right honey," Dad interjects. "I couldn't stop her, either. And she's never going to let me forget about this loss."

"Yep! You got that right!" I say. I'm pleased with myself. Not often can a short seventeen-year-old girl say that she beat two strong, competitive guys.

Kylie and I spend a lot of time at the beach in high school. One day, we decide to drive up to San Francisco. We love shopping at the small shops at Fisherman's Wharf.

After shopping, we sit on the ledge by the beach, staring at the ocean, sipping root beer floats. As I stare into the ocean, listening to Kylie tell me a story about some guy who's trying to ask her out, I see something dark pass before my eyes. My root beer float slips out of my hands and I gasp. Immediately, my heart starts beating fast, and I start having difficulty with my breathing.

"Oh my god, Tess. What's wrong?" I close my eyes and shake my head. When I slowly open my eyes again, the darkness is gone. I look behind me and in every other direction, but I see nothing out of the ordinary.

"Did you see a dark cloud pass just now?" I ask Kylie, as I force myself to calm down.

"What? No! Tess, there are no dark clouds. Look, the sky is completely clear. What are you talking about?"

I take some deep breaths. "Nothing, don't worry about it, Kylie."

"No, really, what happened?" Kylie insists.

"I don't want to talk about it, Kylie. Please, let's just change the subject." With my hands still convulsing and my skin a frightful shade of pale, I kneel down to pick up the cup of root beer float that had fallen, and throw it away. Kylie, shaken and confused, continues talking about the guy while I try to settle my heartbeat.

When I'm alone in my room later that day, I think about that black cloud again. Something similar had happened almost a year ago when we were flying back from Jamaica. What in the world is going on? Should I tell my parents? Could something be happening to my brain? But no, I'm not having any episodes of dizziness, headaches, or any other symptoms. I decide against telling my parents, not wanting to cause them unnecessary worry.

Four

Throughout my high school career, I receive straight A's. Also, my mom's prediction of growing a few more inches comes true. By the time I'm eighteen, I'm 5'5".

For basketball, we make it to state playoffs. During my junior year, we take third place, and during the senior year we come in second. I average twenty-five points, fifteen assists, and twelve steals per game.

Track is another high school experience I will always remember. I break some high school records, make it to state, and win some gold and silver medals there. I mostly run the 400 and the 800-meter runs. My high school sports give me the memories that I will always cherish.

I attend all of my high school dances. My mom tells me that it's important to create memories. She says that one day, I would appreciate these experiences. For most of my dances, I end up going with a group of my friends.

One of the guys from my Anatomy class, Danny Kites, asks me to my junior homecoming dance. Danny has that guy-next-door look. He wears glasses. He's bashful, which makes him incredibly charming, and he is a perfect gentleman through the entire dance.

"You look really pretty tonight, Tess." Danny barely is able to look at me as he compliments me.

"Thanks, Danny. You look really handsome too," I respond, smiling back.

Before I realize what's happening, he simply leans forward and kisses me. I'm completely caught off guard. I think to myself that maybe I should pull away, but then I don't. I decide to just relax and enjoy the kiss. Danny is really cute, and a good guy for a first kiss.

I wait for the fireworks. They always mention the fireworks and the butterflies in your stomach in the books and the movies. But none of that happens. I can't believe those books make up lies like that! Overall, it's not an unpleasant kiss, but still a bit awkward. I decide to just ease back from the kiss without hurting his feelings. Danny doesn't take offense. He just smiles and says, "Thanks, Tess." And that's that.

The evening ends and he brings me home. *My first kiss was with Danny Kites,* I think to myself. *At least the first kiss bit is over with!*

After Danny, I sort of date a couple of other guys. There's Tyler Kanes. He's in my AP Calculus class, but dating him doesn't go anywhere. Then there's Rick Motiski, who's also very nice, but again, it ends as soon as it starts. I never let it get further than a few kisses with them. It just didn't feel right, and I never do something if it doesn't feel right. Besides, all that just isn't important to me. Sometimes, I think that it's more of a distraction. I mean, I have a lot of goals that I want to accomplish. I want to make something of myself. And sometimes, trying to deal with boy problems just isn't worth it.

While my dad doesn't have any desires to know about the boys in my life, my mom is very curious. I have a great relationship with Mom, so I like asking her for advice.

One day, as I'm lying on my stomach in my bed, studying

my Physiology notes, I hear Mom yell, "Tess, look what I bought for you!" She sounds excited, so I run down the stairs, curiosity getting the best of me. I see Mom standing in the kitchen with at least a dozen shopping bags surrounding her.

"What's going on, Mom?" I ask, wondering what she's up to now.

"Come and see, Tess!" Mom replies. She starts to pull the items out of the shopping bags. I notice many different outfits. They're not the usual jeans and t-shirts that I wear. They're cute fitted dresses, mini-skirts, flattering shirts, and shoes--lots of different shoes!

"Mom, what is this for?" I ask, now curious.

"They're clothes for you, honey," Mom answers.

"Oh, thanks. Why did you get so many clothes? I mean there are enough clothes and shoes for a whole new wardrobe here." I'm confused as to why she bought clothes that I normally don't wear.

"Well, Tess, you're growing up. I thought you might want to wear more flattering clothes. I know you've been noticing boys lately. This is all part of growing up, you know?" Mom begins to hold different outfits up to show me.

"Mom! I do not notice boys!" I exclaim. How embarrassing!

"What's the big deal? You've dated a few boys here and there. One day, you'll fall so hard for a guy, that you'll think a hundred times about what you want to wear to impress him."

"I can't even imagine that, Mom," I say, still baffled. "But tell me how you fell for Dad." Maybe shifting the attention away from me might work getting off of this topic.

"Well, as you know, I met him at college. I fell for him right away, but of course, I wasn't going to let him know that,"

Mom says, laughing as she's reminiscing. "You see, Tess, you have to keep it interesting. You have to keep them guessing, you know, to keep them coming back for more." Mom starts giggling.

"Mom!"

"I'm being serious, Tess. This is some great advice I'm giving you." Then Mom's tone of voice changes from teasing to serious. "One day, you'll fall for somebody. At first, you'll fight it, because you won't understand. But when you do, Tess, you'll know that he's the one--the one you would die for."

I remain quiet for a few minutes thinking about what she said. I then walk up to her and say, "I'm so glad you and Dad found each other. And thanks for the clothes, really." I kiss her cheek and grab the shopping bags.

I take the clothes up to my room and hang them into my closet. The clothes are really cute, but not what I wear normally. They are more Kylie's style. Oh well, maybe Mom is right. Maybe one day, I will want to wear these flattering clothes to impress somebody. I wonder if everybody finds the type of love my parents have for one another. Without a shadow of a doubt, I know my parents would die for each other in a heartbeat.

My accomplishments and grades get me noticed by prestigious universities. My dream is to attend Stanford, not only because of its reputation, but also because it's only forty-five minutes from home. I'm not ready to go too far from my parents yet.

One day, as I'm anxiously waiting for my admission letters,

I finally get an envelope from Stanford. Too afraid to open it myself, I run to my mom and hand her the envelope.

"I can't do it, Mom. I'm too nervous. You open it for me," I say, as I start to pace the floor.

"Are you serious, Tess? You need to open this. This is something you've worked toward your whole high school career. I'm sure it's good news," Mom encourages, handing the envelope back to me.

"Ah!" I scream, taking the envelope back. "Ok, I can do this. Wait! Hold my hand, Mom! I've never been this nervous about anything!" My mom comes by me, and hugs me around my shoulders.

"Of course you can do this. Remember, everything happens for a reason. So just lift your chin up, and face your destiny, Tess."

I sigh. She's right. I close my eyes, and tear the envelope open. I slowly open my eyes, taking the letter out. All I see are the words, "Congratulations, Miss Tessnia Sanoby." I start jumping up and down, screaming and running around in the kitchen. My mom starts laughing and reads the rest of the letter.

"Oh my god, Tess. They are giving you a full scholarship because of your academic achievements. And they want you to run track for them! I guess the scout who came to watch you liked what he saw."

"What? You're kidding! This is one of the happiest days of my life, Mom!" I run to Mom and hug her tight. She's still laughing. "We have to call Dad!" I dial his number while we're both still screaming. For the first few minutes, he can't even understand what we're saying. We're laughing and screaming too hard. Finally, we're able to clearly explain the acceptance, the scholarship, and my chance to run track for them.

Dad is silent for good thirty seconds. Then I hear him say softly, "I can't even express to you how proud I am of you, baby girl! The best news is that you're only forty-five minutes away from us!" I start laughing. Leave it to my dad to focus on the distance over everything else!

As my senior year comes to an end, I start having mixed emotions. The thought of it all ending is sad, but starting a new phase in my life is exciting.

One night, as I'm sleeping, I hear loud music outside of my bedroom window. Who's blasting their music this loud in the middle of the night? As I try to sleep through it, the music gets even louder. Wait a minute! It's "In Your Eyes" by Peter Gabriel.

I jump out of my bed and look outside. Jack is standing there on my driveway, holding a giant boom box over his head, and looking up at my window! What in the world! I start laughing because it's from one of my favorite old movies, "Say Anything", when John Cusack was serenading his girlfriend, Ione Skye, by playing the song. I run downstairs and out the front door.

When I approach him, I see that he's laughing just as hard as me. "What are you doing, Jack?" I ask.

Jack turns his boom box off, walks back to his car, and pulls a huge sign out that says, *"Would you do me the honor of going to prom with me?"*

Wow! Jack is asking me to prom! I run into his arms and say, "Of course! I can't imagine a better date than my best friend!"

Jack sighs, and then smiles. "Thank God! I would have been really embarrassed if you had said no after all that," Jack says, and he starts laughing again.

"I'd love to go with you! Let's go tell my parents! And by the way, I love that song! It's one of my favorite movies!" I can't stop babbling. I'm so excited!

"I know it's one of your favorite movies, Tess. That's why I played it for you!" Jack says, rolling his eyes. We both laugh and go back in the house to wake up my parents. I know they would want to share this moment with me.

The senior prom ends up being a big deal. Kylie is going with Kyle, her ex-boyfriend. At first, I was surprised she said yes to him. But I guess she let go of the whole "cheating" thing, because her response to me was, "Oh well, shit happens."

I end up wearing a beautiful, lightly sequined silver, strapless dress that is snug until the waistline and loosely flows down to my ankles. The material is soft, and hugs my body at the right places. I wear silver heels with tiny Swarovski crystals to match. I get my hair done at the salon, and choose to straighten it for a sleek, silky look. As I'm looking at my reflection in the mirror, I can't believe how long my hair is when it's not curly.

When my mom sees me, her eyes fill with tears. "Oh Tess, look at you! You look absolutely gorgeous!" Mom walks over to me and gives me a tight hug. Dad is watching TV in the family room. As Mom and I walk to him, she says, "Honey, look at your daughter!"

Dad glances toward our direction. He narrows his eyes and says, "You're wearing that?"

"Oh my god, Dad! What's wrong with this dress, now?" I reply. I'm not surprised that he has something to say about the dress. "It's covering everything!" I hear my mom giggling behind me.

"It's too tight!" Dad complains. He gets up from the sofa and walks toward me. "But you look beautiful, Tess. I'm glad you're going with Jack. I like him and trust him. I know he'll be a gentleman with my baby girl." I sigh, shaking my head at my overprotective father. He walks up to me and kisses my cheek. "Have fun but be careful, ok?"

"Yes, Daddy." I smile up at him.

Kylie, Kyle, Jack, and I are all meeting at my house before prom and all four of us are going to take a limo. Their parents come to our house as well to take pictures of all of us.

When Jack sees me, he says, "Damn, Tess, I'm one lucky guy to be going to prom with you."

That makes me smile. I tell him, "I feel pretty lucky to be going with you too, Jack." He looks amazing! He has a black tux with a black shirt and a silver tie. His broad shoulders fill the jacket nicely, as the dress pants hug his muscular thighs. Yes, any girl would love to have Jack as her prom date.

Everybody takes a ton of pictures, especially my mom. She loves "capturing the moments." Our prom theme is *Red Carpet,* and the theme song is *Good Night* by Black Eyed Peas. I can't wait to see everybody dressed up, especially my basketball and track teammates.

The prom is at the Marriott, and has a beautiful view of the ocean. The entry way is lined with a red carpet, leading into a ballroom with shooting stars falling from the ceiling. It's breathtaking. We see our closest friends from school and dance the night away. Hugs, laughs, and even some tears fill the room, as we realize this is our last high school dance together. Kyle and Kylie stay with us throughout the night, and I feel like the luckiest girl in the world being able to share this night with my two best friends. Just as Dad predicted, Jack is a perfect gentleman.

When the night is over, we ride back in the limo to my house since everybody's cars are there. Kylie jumps into Kyle's car and they drive off. Jack walks me to my front door.

I turn to him and say, "Thanks, Jack. Because of you, I will always remember my prom."

"No, thank *you,* Tess. Do you have any idea how many guys envied me tonight?" Jack is towering over me as my back is leaning against my front door, smiling and teasing me with his eyes.

"Shut up, Jack!" I laugh.

"I'm serious! You looked beautiful tonight, Tess. I had a wonderful time." He then leans forward and kisses my cheek. I hug him and turn to go into my house. As I start unlocking the front door, something makes me turn to Jack again. I reach up and give him a gentle kiss on the lips. It's a sweet kiss, a kiss filled with friendship, respect, and mutual love for each other.

To top off my senior year, I receive the title of the valedictorian for my class! I'm really proud of myself because I was able to maintain straight A's throughout all four years of high school. When I share the good news with my parents, they are ecstatic! Everything is just falling into place for me. I can't believe how lucky I am! My life is going just as I planned it!

I prepare the valedictorian speech on my own. I really want to say something that my class will remember. As I'm standing on stage with the microphone, looking at my graduating class, and both my parents staring at me with so much pride, the speech flows. I end my speech with, "There will always be ups and downs, twists and turns in our lives. But we have to find the strength to keep moving forward. The past is done, it's over, and you can't change it. You can hold on to your memories and learn from them. Look at what's in front of you, focus on your vision, and run toward it! Because when it's all said and done, only you are in charge of your strength, your peace, and your happiness." The crowd gives me a standing ovation, cheering and whistling.

I look at my parents, smiling down at them as they smile back. Before I have a chance to look away, I see a dark cloud passing before my eyes again, obscuring my parents from my view. My breathing automatically changes, as my heartbeat becomes erratic. No! No! I have to get myself in control! Why is this happening right now? I don't want everybody to witness my anxiety attack. I close my eyes for a few seconds, taking a deep breath and holding on to the podium with dear life. I take some slow, deep breaths again. Please God, let the black cloud be gone when I open my eyes. When I slowly open my eyes, thankfully everything is back to normal. The crowd is still standing on their feet, clapping for me. I look around to see if anybody noticed my strange behavior. But it looks like everybody is still smiling.

When my parents find me later, my mom is crying. She says, "What happened to the time, honey? I feel like you were in your diapers just yesterday. This is one of the happiest moments of my life!"

Even my dad looks like he has tears in his eyes. He's normally a tough guy so it shocks me. "Love you, baby girl," he says and gives me a tight hug.

"Thanks, Mom and Dad. I got the smart genes from you guys," I tease.

Although they both start laughing, we all know how true that is. Not only is my dad, Dr. Trent Sanoby, a neurologist, but also a big shot director at his hospital. My mom, Dr. Nina Sanoby, is involved with some big genetic research. I know both of these positions are an enormous responsibility, and my parents are very dedicated to their work.

My Aunt Jenna makes it to my graduation too. "You made it!" I exclaim when she sneaks up on me.

"Now, why wouldn't I make it to my favorite niece's high school graduation?" she says, as she hugs me.

"I'm your only niece, Aunt Jenna."

"So? You're still my favorite! And I'm so proud of you! That speech was amazing!"

"Thank you. I had a bit of help on that speech from the locket that my parents gave me for my sixteenth birthday though," I confess.

"Well, I still loved what you said. Those words are so true." My aunt gives me another hug. I say a silent prayer that I would live true to my words throughout my life. Ultimately, only I am in charge of my strength, my happiness, and my peace.

My dad pulls me to the side and asks, "Was everything ok on stage, Tess? You had turned really pale at the end of your speech."

"Oh, must be the nerves, I guess," I lie. My dad is just too observant for me to get away with anything!

"Ok, if you say so, Tess," Dad replies after a brief pause, knowing full well that I am lying.

I continue to have my strange dreams, and occasionally that darkness creeps up when I would least expect it. My dreams are similar with the mysterious girl running every time. Once in a while, the same gray eyes show up, looking just as intense and piercing as ever.

That senior summer, I work at Nordstrom in the mall. I work all the time to get some money saved up for college. Even though I received the full scholarship, I want some extra spending cash. Once in a while, Jack would show up at the mall and take me out to eat during my lunch break.

Kylie is going to attend San Jose State University. This is only thirty minutes away from Stanford. We convince our parents to let us get an apartment together. At first, my dad is hesitant. He finally agrees when we find an apartment complex that has a 24 hour doorman downstairs. Kylie wants to live by the Stanford campus, and plans to just drive to her school. That works perfect for me.

Jack is going to be attending UCLA, which is over six hours driving distance from Stanford. I'm happy he stayed in state and did not decide to attend a college across the country. I'm going to miss him once college starts, but I'm excited that

Kylie and I will finally be roommates.

When our parents bring us to our apartment to drop Kylie and I off, it's the strangest feeling. I mean, we're going to be totally on our own! Eighteen and independent! Nobody is going to be checking up on me. No curfew! No rules! I can do whatever I want! Wow, it feels amazing to have this freedom.

Both of our parents give us really tearful goodbyes. My dad can barely look at me. He just mumbles to be careful under his breath and walks out.

After they leave, Kylie and I just lie on our beds in our apartment, staring at the ceiling. We both have separate bedrooms, but because the two bedrooms are across from each other, we can see one another. Instead of feeling excited, it feels empty. Just that quick, the appeal of "freedom" is gone.

Finally, half an hour later, Kylie interrupts my thoughts and says, "Well, we can't just lie around here. I won't allow it. Let's go explore the campus." I have to agree with her. We can't keep feeling sorry for ourselves.

So we go exploring. As we check out the campus, we see the library and the other study areas. Our classes are going to start in a week, so we walk my schedule first, then drive to Kylie's campus and walk her schedule. We still need to get the books for our classes. Instead, we decide to first grab some lunch, and then some ice cream from Baskin Robbins. We're starting to have a really good time. We see all types of kids, basically our age, walking around. We start people watching as we sit on the bench, eating our ice cream. There are people roller blading, kids on their bikes, couples holding hands, and there are those students who are carrying their books, looking stressed and lost. I guess those students are probably freshmen like us.

As we're sitting there, my phone buzzes. I look down and notice a text from Jack.

"Hey, Tess. How are you adjusting there?"

Kylie says, "Who is that?"

"Jack," I reply.

"He's so sweet, Tess. Tell him I say hi and we miss him already."

I text back:

"Jack! It's cool. Kylie and I are sitting here eating ice cream. We've been here for couple of hours. How about you? Are you meeting new people? We miss you."

Couple of minutes later, I get a reply.

"Oh yeah, my roommate is pretty cool. He's from the east coast. Been here for about five or six hours. We're just hanging out. I wanted to check in on you guys. I'll text later. Oh and miss you guys too."

"Alright, Jack. I'll talk to you later."

We head to the local bookstore to buy some books for our classes. By the time we get some books, we're a few hundred dollars broke. We decide to head back to our apartment to put our books away.

Back in our apartment, I try to organize my closet in my room. To my disappointment, the closet is *very* small compared to the one in my bedroom back home. Even though we're lucky enough to get a two-bedroom apartment, our bedrooms are small, and so are our closets. Kylie is very frustrated.

"This is ridiculous, Tess. I miss my closet back home!" she complains.

"Me too, Kylie!" I agree.

Our first night in college is low-key. We go out and get some pizza from the fast food pizza restaurant on campus. Then we come back to our apartment and watch a movie together. We're both exhausted from walking all over the campus.

"This is really different then high school huh, Kylie?" I ask.

"Yeah, I miss everybody, Tess. This university is so huge. We used to know everybody in our high school," Kylie sighs.

"Yeah, it's depressing. I'm just glad you're here with me, Kylie," I say. I can't imagine what it would be like without Kylie here.

"Me too. I'd feel really lost without you," Kylie says.

We finish watching our movie, call our parents to say goodnight, and go to bed. As I'm falling asleep, I think about how much I miss my room, my home, and my parents. I guess this is another phase in my life.

During the rest of the weekend, we buy the remaining of our books, check out the gym, my track field, and other study areas. Saturday evening, Kylie convinces me to go to the local bar where other students hang out. Although we can't drink alcohol, most of the bars are eighteen and over on campus, so we're able to get in.

I wear some fitted jeans and a tank top. I also wear my Converse gym shoes. I don't feel like dressing up. I pull my hair up in a high ponytail, and keep my makeup light.

There's music playing at the bar. We order some pop and hang out. A few guys come by to talk to us. There is a "Josh" and a "Frank", who end up staying with us at the bar.

Apparently, they belong to one of the fraternities. We tell them we're freshmen, and don't know too many people.

"Oh, no worries. Give it some time, and you'll get to know a lot of people," Frank assures us.

"And once you adjust, you will have a blast," Josh says. We find out that they both are sophomores. "When we have our frat parties, we'll invite you." We all exchange our numbers. It's nice meeting new people, but I'm already thinking about next week. My fall training for track starts on Monday.

Five

I run to the track field bright and early on Monday. They're having us start the training at 8:00 am. I decide to get there by 7:30 because I want to impress my coaches. I start stretching and doing my usual warm-up. Fifteen minutes later, the other athletes begin to come. At exactly eight o'clock, the coaches arrive and stand around us in an intimidating half-circle.

The head coach, Coach Williams, says, "Welcome, all of you. According to the rules, we aren't supposed to start official practices as of yet. But, I always like to start with these informal training sessions to get you guys in shape for the practices. I'm going to tell you right now, you're here to run. I want no excuses. You will give me 200% at every practice and at every meet. If I find out you're only giving me your 100%, you'll be kicked out. Any questions?"

Nobody says a word. We're all ready to prove ourselves. Coach has us first stretch and go for comfortable runs around the track. He says something about becoming one with the track field. During our water break, I look around at the bleachers. I estimate there are less than ten people watching the practice session. They're far so I can't really see them clearly. But they're all sitting in groups of two's or three's.

Coach has us running against each other in groups of five. Every race I run, I take first. I feel comfortable in my prowess and coach is pleased with my accomplishment as well. The second time I take a break, I look around again. Basically, the same people are on the bleachers. But then I notice one guy is sitting by himself. He's on the top bleacher, in the far left corner. He has a baseball cap on, but I really can't see much more than that. It's interesting that he's watching alone. Then again, maybe he's a boyfriend of one of the athletes, and is here to support her.

After practice, I jog back to the apartment. When I finish taking a shower, I text my parents:

"Mom and Dad, the fall training for track was awesome today. I took first every time."

*"Proud of you baby."*Dad texts back.

*"Go Tess!"*Mom replies.

The "informal" training sessions are Monday through Friday, three hours every morning. I don't mind it though. It keeps me busy, and it keeps me in shape. We have some loyal fans that show up to watch us practice. And I always see that guy sitting in the same spot with his cap on. I can't tell whose boyfriend he is though. I don't remember him talking to anybody after practice. But maybe I don't even notice because I usually jog back to the apartment as soon as the training sessions are over.

That weekend I get everything ready for my classes because school begins on Monday. I'm ready to take over the world. I want to impress my teachers. Track practices change to every evening once classes start.

My first class on Monday morning is Biology. Right away, the teacher starts with, "I'm Mrs. Lackly. I know all of you were probably on top of your high school class. I'm here to tell you that at this university, you guys are going to be average, if that. All top students come here, so you will be competing against them. And just so there are no misunderstandings, I give no breaks. Frankly, I don't care what happens in your life. We all have our problems. When you are in my class, you are here to learn biology. That's it. Any questions?"

Everybody remains silent. I wonder why I was in such a hurry to grow up. I'm totally feeling the stress. That first Monday feels never-ending. I'm exhausted, but I still have to go to practice. I hope track practice will alleviate some of the stress I'm feeling.

I arrive at my practice right on time. Without even realizing it, my gaze wanders to the bleachers at the top far corner. The guy with the baseball cap isn't there. Guess he's not as dedicated to his girlfriend as I thought. Coach pulls us over just as I'm about to start warm-ups.

"Team, I'm going to be having some helpers pop in occasionally. They really have some impressive background, and I think they can give you guys some great hints and help you train. I've got Chris helping us out today. He's going to be assisting us quite a bit. Chris?" The coach looks behind him, searching for Chris. I follow his gaze, and I see the guy who normally sits in the bleachers with the baseball cap, walking toward us. As he's approaching us, he takes his cap off. I notice he has blond wavy hair. As he gets closer, I note that he's bigger than I originally thought. He looks easily over six feet tall and is muscular--I mean *really* fit. He looks strong, and his muscles are nicely defined, as his Under Armour shirt hugs his torso.

The coach continues, "I've had the opportunity to witness

Chris run in the past, and believe me this kid is talented. So, when he offered to help, I jumped on it. From now on, whenever Chris can make it, treat him like your assistant coach. Chris, you have anything you want to say?" Coach looks at Chris. We all also turn to look at Chris. I realize that he's not really a kid. He looks like he's maybe in his early twenties. Guess he's not anybody's boyfriend on the team. What a weirdo! Why was he just sitting on the bleachers by himself all week? Maybe he was trying to decide whether he'd like to even assist us. Maybe he was checking to see if there was talent on this team, and making sure he wasn't just wasting his time.

As I'm trying to study him, Chris looks up suddenly, and he holds my gaze. He has ocean blue eyes with long dark eyelashes. I catch my breath. He is gorgeous.

"Well, I'm glad I can be here, and hope to be of help," Chris responds.

I notice he has some type of accent. English? Unfortunately, I'm still having difficulty looking away. Ok, I have to focus, and not act like a fool! Everyone starts doing warm-ups, so I reluctantly stop staring at him.

Chris is standing on the side, timing everybody's runs, and recording it. He doesn't say anything more.

Brandy, the girl who is warming up next to me, says, "Wow! He's really hot! He can help me any day, any time!" I smile politely at her, but I really want to just roll my eyes at her. Great! Another girl falling for a guy just because of his pretty face and hot body! I hope I don't have to listen to these girls lust after him at every training session.

When I get home, I'm drained. Kylie is already there,

also exhausted. While we're eating dinner, Kylie says she's homesick, and wants to go home this weekend. I'm happy she suggests this because I'm feeling the same. We both finish our homework quickly, and pass out on our beds.

For the rest of the week, I get into my routine of my classes, fall training, studying, and sleeping.

Chris, from track, never says much to anybody. He stays to himself and just records our times and takes notes. It's annoying. Really? I mean he's supposed to be this amazing athlete, and he has not done anything for us. What is he here for anyway? He's starting to get on my nerves and I'm not sure why. It's not like he's doing anything specific to bother me. Maybe the fact that he just stays to himself and never talks to anybody is probably more annoying to me than anything. But truth be told, he really is an attractive guy. I can't believe how good-looking he is, and maybe that's another reason he's starting to bother me. He gives me no attention at all. Not even a "good job" after I win every single race during practice. It's like he doesn't even notice how fast I am, or for that matter, that I even exist.

The girls on the team keep talking about him and giggling behind his back. There are a couple of girls who have even gone up to him to try to flirt with him. I'm impressed with their courage because he always presents himself as unapproachable. I'm not sure if he notices that he is very popular among the girls, because he doesn't give any of them a second glance. He continues to keep the conversations short and terse, and remains aloof.

Finally, on Friday, I decide to engage him in a conversation. I march right up to him, and ask, "So, have my times been improving throughout the week?"

He looks up from his stupid paper that he has his head buried into, and says in his "English" accent, "Let's see, yeah, it looks like you're doing all right."

Is this guy crazy? I'm doing better than all right. How does he not see that I'm kicking everybody's butt on the team? I'm starting to get even more irritated.

"Well, can I see my times please? I mean, I need to see how I'm doing so that I can meet my goals. If I'm just doing 'all right', I guess I have a long way to go still," I reply, annoyed. I see his lips curl into a smile. It's almost as if he wants to laugh, but he holds back.

He looks up at me, his eyes almost teasing, and says, "Yes, Tessnia, you *do* have a long way to go still."

The fact he calls me by my full name throws me off. Then I realize that's probably how my name is listed on that paper he keeps writing on. Ok, I'm ready to give him a taste of his own medicine.

"Oh, really? Well, I guess you should step it up and start actively training instead of just sitting there in your little corner. For somebody who supposedly knows it all, what have you really taught this team so far?" I am so angry. If he's going to cut me down, without even justifying his comments, I'm not going to hold back either.

Then all of a sudden, he starts to laugh--a genuine, full-blown laugh! He's actually laughing at me!

"Are you laughing at me? I'm not sure what's so funny." I put my hands on my hips, lifting my chin up, ready to take him on. This guy is rubbing me the wrong way!

"No, Miss Tessnia, I wouldn't dare laugh at you," he says in that funny accent. "I'll tell you what. I can start your training this weekend. Tomorrow morning at seven sharp, I'll see you right here."

"Uh, no. I don't think so," I reply. "I'm going home this weekend." Does he think I'm going to just change my schedule like that? "And my name is Tess by the way. And just out of curiosity, where are you from anyway? I can't place your accent."

He gets another smirk on his face. As much as I hate admitting it, I can't help but notice again that he truly is beautiful. "I'm from Australia, actually, but I've been here in the States for some time now. I can't shake the accent though." He smiles again.

God, this guy is so good looking, especially when he's teasing and not grouchy. His wavy blond hair is blowing in the wind, and his blue eyes are teasing me. There's something familiar about him, but I can't place it. I have never met anybody from Australia. Besides, I'd remember him if I had met him in the past. Although he has the typical blond hair and blue eye coloring, he undeniably has a unique look about him. He's not pale at all. He has a dark and even tan everywhere. He also has a beautifully structured face. And his body seems to be hard as a rock, the way his muscles bulge out. Normally, I don't find blond haired guys attractive, but apparently he is the exception. I'm definitely drawn to him. Great! Just my luck to be attracted to a guy who gets on my nerves!

"Are you done checking me out now?" He suddenly interrupts my thoughts.

"Wha.... I'm not... wait, why would you think... look

I'm not checking you out." I start stumbling over my words. God, am I that obvious? I'm embarrassed, humiliated, and even more annoyed. "Look I have to go. I still have to pack before I leave."

I run off sprinting back to the apartment. As I'm running off the field, I think I hear Chris chuckle behind me! How humiliating! I don't dare to turn around. I'm pretty sure that even when I get back to my room, my face is still scarlet red. Unbelievable! Who does he think he is anyway? He sure is arrogant to think I was actually checking him out. I mean, I was just curious since I never really got to see him close-up. And why am I letting him get under my skin? He is a nobody!

On our drive home, I tell Kylie about him and how cocky he was during our exchange. She can tell that I'm still really worked up. "Wow, Tess. I can't believe there's actually somebody out there capable of shaking you up like this. You're always so in control. I kind of like this new you. You know, I never see you frazzled like this." Kylie begins laughing, apparently finding this situation funny.

"Well, I don't like it at all. And I promise you, he will not get me *frazzled* again." I'm determined to take control of this situation, and not let his stupid smirks get to me.

Being home for the weekend is amazing. It's so nice to spend some quality time with my parents. And since Jack is home for the weekend too, we catch a movie on Saturday night. He tells me college life suits him, and he's just living the dream.

When we return back to the campus on Sunday, I decide

to apply at some places for a part-time job. I want some extra cash, and I figure I could work on weekends.

When I arrive to track training on Monday, I'm curious to see how Chris is going to be involved with helping us train. But once again, he doesn't acknowledge us, keeps taking our times, and gives us absolutely no advice. He just keeps recording our times on that stupid paper of his. I can't believe it. It's like our talk never happened last week. What a waste of time! As the week progresses and he makes no move to change his style, I can tell my irritation is increasing.

"Calm down, Tess. Don't let him get to you," I whisper under my breath. Great! Now, I'm even starting to talk to myself. I decide to play his game, and proceed to completely ignore him as well. I treat him as if I don't even notice he's there.

Friday after practice, as I'm grabbing my backpack, I hear, "Tessnia, wait up." Yes, it's that familiar, annoying accent. I don't know why even his accent is bothering me. He catches up to me. "I'm going to be out here tomorrow at seven in the morning if you want to train with me," he says.

"Tomorrow is Saturday," I reply, not making eye contact, still pretending to fix something in my bag.

"I'm aware what day of the week it is. I know you were concerned about my lack of involvement with this team last time we talked. I was offering this time slot to you for training if you're interested," Chris explains. He looks directly into my eyes, almost challenging me to turn him down.

"Um, I'm not sure about Saturday mornings. I try to catch up on everything over the weekend, including my sleep," I reply back to him.

"Ok, suit yourself. If you change your mind, I'll see you bright and early." I guess he's not going to try to convince me any more. Chris turns, puts his cap on, and walks off. Does he really think I'm going to drop what I'm doing, disturb my sleep, just to come train with him?

At 6:30 the next morning, I find myself jogging to the track field. I have a hoodie on, and loose sweatpants. I have my t-shirt and track shorts on under the sweatpants. I'm not sure exactly what Chris had in mind for this training session.

When I woke up literally five minutes ago, I barely got ready. I brushed my teeth, and pulled my hair up in a high ponytail. I put no makeup on, but washed my face to help me wake up. When I glanced in the mirror before I left, I couldn't believe how young I looked with the baggy clothes and no makeup.

I arrive around 6:50 and notice Chris is already there. He's wearing baggy shorts and a sweatshirt. His blond hair looks crazy and messy in the wind. He probably just rolled out of the bed too. The difference is that he looks just as beautiful as he always does.

As I jog up to him, he turns to me and says, "Changed your mind?"

"Yeah, I was curious to see what you had to offer for my training I guess," I reply, shrugging my shoulders. It's the truth. I really am curious.

"Fair enough," he says. Then I catch him looking at me, lost in his thoughts. It makes me feel uneasy.

"What's up? What are you looking at?" I demand.

Chris looks startled that I had caught him staring. But he recovers just as quickly and replies, "Oh, I'm just not used to you looking like this," he mumbles. "You look beautiful. You know, young and innocent."

"What? I just woke up." I'm surprised he actually gave me a compliment. Usually, Chris has seen me wear some light makeup, such as mascara, eyeliner, and lip-gloss. Today, I am all-natural.

He flashes a lopsided grin, tilts his head to one side, and replies, "I guess I must like that look. Well, let's get started. Let's just go for a comfortable jog couple of times first to warm up." I'm surprised at how quickly he changes the subject. He's a hard one to figure out.

As we both start to jog next to each other, I notice that he is light on his feet. Considering how tall he is, he does not come down hard on his feet as he jogs. Chris looks comfortable with a perfect stride and form, and makes it look effortless.

After we warm up, he turns to me and says, "Ok, here's the deal, Tessnia. You are good; I'm not going to lie. But I meant it when I said you have a long way to go." I open my mouth to argue, but he interrupts, raising his hand. "Now, before you start huffing and puffing at me for saying that, let me explain. You're thinking too much about running while you're running. You're concentrating too hard on your form, your strides, and your arm swings. You're almost too stiff when you run. You have to learn to shut everything out, and just run. You need to become one with this track field; nobody else exists, but you and this field. You should run like you're flying. And all this should be effortless, you know, automatic. If you do this right, you'll be always winning the gold medals, not just some of the times."

"Ok, show me," I say to him, raising my chin.

"What?" he asks, looking surprised.

"Show me what you mean. Let's race. I may even beat you." I'm so ready to shut his mouth up.

"I doubt it, Tessnia," Chris replies confidently.

"Well, then why don't you race me? Ok, let's just say you do beat me. I'll guarantee you, it won't be by much. I'll be right behind you." I'm determined to prove myself to him. "And by the way, I told you, most people just call me Tess."

"I like the way Tessnia sounds," Chris answers back, shrugging his shoulders. He sighs, shakes his head, and then says, "Ok, let's do this. Let's line up at the starting line. We'll run the 400. I'll even give you a head start if you'd like." His eyes are smiling again. Ok, he is back to the teasing.

"I don't need a head start!" I snap back at him. I decide to take my hoodie and sweat pants off, not wanting any extra clothing weighing me down while I run. Of course he makes no move to take his sweatshirt off. I take my position at the starting blocks.

He looks at me for a second, shrugs his shoulders again, and says, "Suit yourself. On your mark, get set, go." And we take off. I run like I had never run before. I want to so badly show this over-confident guy what I'm capable of. Does he have any idea how many races I've won already?

As I'm running, I realize he is way ahead of me. I can't believe it. I've never seen anybody run so fast. And he's a natural. It doesn't even look like he's trying. Chris is completely relaxed, light on his feet for the entire distance. I finally understand what he means when he says, "Run like you're flying."

Chris looks like he's flying on the track field--just gliding along, like it's no big deal. By the time I get to the finish line, he's already waiting for me, smiling.

I'm breathing heavily, trying to catch my breath. I look up at him, and while gasping for air, say, "You can wipe that smug look off your face now. You've proved your point."

"Actually, that may have been your fastest run yet, Tessnia," he says proudly. "I see that motivation and challenges work wonders for you."

"Great!" I say sarcastically. "Now tell me Chris, what are you doing here? I mean, with talent like yours, why are you wasting your time with this track team and at this university? Shouldn't you be training for the Olympics or something?" I'm still irritated that he basically just blew me away in that race.

"Actually, I'm not attending this university right now. I'm part of that military program that's based out of here," he casually answers me.

"Wait, that intense military program that I hear is really tough to get in?" I ask, surprised.

"I guess they felt they could use me. No biggie, it helps pay the bills," he answers. I don't know much about the details of this military program. As a matter of fact, I don't think many people know too much about it. I do know it's supposed to be really intense, and it's near impossible to be accepted. I know you have to be exceptional not only physically, but also intellectually.

I can tell Chris is done with this conversation, because he's already heading back to his bag. He grabs it, and says, "Ok, Tessnia, good job today. I'll be seeing you."

Next thing I know, I'm left standing there, staring at his back as he walks off.

Six

That evening, Kylie says she's starting to feel restless. She wants to go out and meet new people. Josh had invited us to his fraternity party that night so she suggests that we go. I haven't gone to a fraternity party yet, but I've heard that they get wild.

We've been so stressed in college, always working, that tonight we just want to have some fun. I wear my black fitted jeans and my black fitted tank top. I put on my short black boots that has about two-inch heel, which brings me to 5'7". I leave my hair down, and put some extra mascara with eyeliner to make my eyes appear mysterious. The dark maroon lip-gloss emphasizes my full, pouty lips. When I examine myself in the mirror, I'm pleased with my appearance. The fitted clothes accentuate my curves at the right places. My long, curly, dark hair falling down my back, gives me the appearance of being wild and carefree. The silver bracelet and silver earrings are just enough accessories to help bring the outfit together.

"Tess, you look hot," Kylie says when she walks into the bathroom. Kylie looks really good, too. She has a cute little mini-skirt on, some leggings under, and an off-the-shoulder shirt. She has a bright red headband on, with red lipstick to match. She always knows how to put things together, and only she can carry it off. Kylie is only 5'2", so cute clothes like this suit her.

"You look damn good yourself, Kylie. Let's show these

college kids how to party!" We both laugh and leave our apartment.

When we arrive at the party, I'm shocked at what I witness. There are a couple of hundred college kids there. And they're all wild. They're partying in the house, in the yard, in the bathroom--wherever they can find room.

"Kylie, I think most of the people here are drunk. Aren't they underage?" I ask, in disbelief. They're all drinking either the spiked punch that's in the corner or beer. They aren't even trying to be discreet!

"Tess, what do you think college kids do? Don't be such a prude. Besides, don't you even notice all these hot guys here?" Kylie thinks this is no big deal. I look around, and notice that there are a few guys who are turning to check us out. Maybe they're curious because we're new.

"Hey guys, I'm so glad you guys made it!" We hear Josh yelling to us as he crosses the room. "Welcome to the other world of college. This is what it's all about."

I'm starting to wish that I was back in my apartment. I'm feeling out of place and uneasy here. There are people making out everywhere, and one is throwing up in the front yard, with everybody cheering!

"Thanks for inviting us, Josh," I answer back politely.

I notice Kylie is already mingling with some guy in the corner. Thanks for leaving me and making me feel even more awkward, Kylie!

"Come on, let's get you started with something to drink," Josh says, his mouth reeking of cheap beer. He leads me to the punch bowl and starts pouring me a cup.

"Oh, no thanks, Josh. I'm going to take it easy tonight. I

have an early start tomorrow." I look around nervously, wondering how to get out of this situation discreetly.

"What? Here's the rule. When you're out, you don't think about the next day. You think about here and now, and having fun. Here, drink up." He hands me the cup.

I decide to try to play it off, pretending like I'm going to drink it. When he turns or walks off, I plan on throwing it away. But to my dismay, he's still standing there, waiting for me to drink it. I lift my chin up and say, "I'm not going to drink this, Josh. Not interested."

"Wow, here, let me show you how it's done." He takes the drink and chugs it. He empties the content in one gulp. "See how easy that was?" he says, crushing the red solo cup. When he proceeds to fill another, I decide to walk away. He grabs my arm and says, "Come on, Tess, just one cup, that's it."

I nervously scan the room for Kylie, hoping she would catch my eye. When I don't see her anywhere, my heart plunges into my stomach. "Josh, can you let go of my arm? I told you I'm not drinking tonight." I'm starting to get irritated. Didn't anybody teach him that "no" means no?

"You won't regret it, Tess. Trust me on this. It'll help you loosen up and not be so stressed. You know, just let loose. You're too uptight. Here, drink!" Josh still hasn't let me go. I try to pull my arm out of his hold. His grip becomes even tighter. It's obvious he's either drunk or high. Either way, he's totally out of line.

"Let me go, Josh!" I say sternly, trying to get myself free from his hold.

"I said *drink!*" Now his grip is painfully tight. He has the cup to my face as if he's about to force it into my mouth. Is this guy crazy? I turn my head from him and try to pull my arm out of his hold. But his grip tightens and becomes even more painful.

"Let her go, Josh! Right this minute!" I hear a familiar voice, with the familiar accent.

I spin around, and there he is. Chris is standing there, furious, his jaw clenched tight, and his eyes flashing with fury. He's staring Josh down, daring him to challenge him. Josh releases me immediately.

"Oh hey, Chris. No big deal, man. It's all good," Josh mumbles.

Chris pulls me behind him. "If I find out that you went within even fifty feet of her, ever again, your ass is mine. Do I make myself clear?" His tone is slow and deliberate, and so low, that I know he's doing everything in his power to maintain his control.

"I gottchu man. Damn." Josh turns around and leaves us without another word.

"What are you doing here?" Chris asks me angrily. It's intimidating the way he's glaring at me.

"What? What are *you* doing here? Are you following me?" I accuse him.

"I'm partying here," Chris snarls. "I'm very familiar with this university and all the frat parties. I did attend here, remember?" Chris is still furious.

"Aren't you a little old to be partying with the college kids?" I challenge him, putting my hand on my hip.

"Like I said, I'm partying here. And no, I'm not too *old*." Chris narrows his eyes at me. "There are many graduate students here my age. Besides, I'm legal age. You're not. What do you think happens at places like this?" Chris takes a step closer, towering over me.

"Hey, Tess, is everything ok?" Kylie comes over to check what's going on. She must have noticed the commotion.

"Uh, fine, Kylie," I reply. Kylie is looking at Chris, waiting for me to introduce him to her. "Oh, and this is Chris--you know, from track. Chris, this is Kylie, my best friend." Chris barely glances at Kylie. I can tell he's still angry, as he continues scowling at me. I stubbornly avoid his gaze. Why is he mad at me? It's not like I drank the alcohol or anything.

"Nice to meet you, Chris. Tess, do you want to leave soon? I'm ready to call it a night," Kylie suggests. She's trying to get me out of this awkward situation.

I can sense Chris glaring at me, daring me to glance his way, but I completely ignore him. "Yeah, I am too, Kylie. Let's go home."

"Chris! Babe, here you are. I've been looking all over for you." A redheaded girl strolls toward us. Kylie and I both turn to look at her. She's looking with adoring eyes at Chris, pouting her lips at him. She hooks her arm around his arm and leans her head into his shoulder.

Chris finally tears his eyes away from me, looks down at the redheaded bimbo, and smiles at her. The girl's breasts are hanging out of her low-cut, skintight dress, and she has voluptuous curves in all the right places. No doubt, any guy would love to be in her arms. And here she is, hanging all over Chris.

"Yeah, sorry, Roxy. Just got tied up a bit. You ready to leave?" Chris says to her. Roxy? Really?

"Yes, I'm anxiously waiting for my alone time with you," Roxy sulks in a husky voice, flirting with him. She, apparently, wants us to know that he is taken. Kylie and I stare at the exchange with our mouths open, looking like fools.

I finally snap out of it. I can tell my blood pressure is rising. "Oh, perfect timing. We were just leaving ourselves. And you can have all your alone time with him as you please. We were done with him anyway." I want to send the message loud and clear that we definitely are *not* interested. I grab Kylie's arm and storm out of that claustrophobic room, leaving the most annoying, overbearing guy standing there with that redheaded disgusting slut hanging all over him.

"Damn, Tess, you never told me how good looking this guy was. I see he still has the power to get under your skin." Kylie giggles, as we're walking away.

"Do not want to talk about him or this night anymore. I just want to crawl into my bed." Kylie knows me well enough to drop the subject.

That night, I have my dream again. It's the same dream, but this time, there are different colors in it. I see red, blue, and even the familiar gray. I wake up in panic and splash cold water over my face.

The next day, I find out that I got a weekend job at the Starbucks by the campus. I'm grateful because I need the extra cash.

I decide to ignore Chris at practice on Monday. There's not much to say. I don't understand him, and honestly, I don't want to understand him.

I keep busy with my studies. I'm able to pull off all A's on my first set of exams! I'm off to a good start.

I continue attending the Saturday morning "extra" training sessions because I have to admit, Chris is helping me. He's working on "visualizations" with me. Instead of being so technical while I run, he says I should be visualizing the run and to just go for it. He says only then, I will become more of a natural runner.

I don't bring up the incident from the frat party, even though I'm still bothered by the events from that night. I don't even know how Josh knows him. Whatever! There's a lot about Chris I don't know. Actually, whom am I fooling? I don't know him at all. I don't even know his last name for heaven's sake!

And why should I be surprised that he had a hot girl throwing herself all over him? Chris can get any girl with his looks. I guess I assumed he was a loner because of how he portrays himself during track practices.

Every Saturday after our warm-ups and our exercises, Chris and I end our session with a race. And every time, he beats me. I never even come close. To make the loss even worse, I can tell that he's not even giving his all. But each time, I try harder.

One day after our race, as he watches me cross the finish line, Chris turns to me and says, "You know, that's what I love about you. You never quit. You keep going, and give all you've got, no matter what."

"Just wait, I'll beat you one of these days," I say, trying to catch my breath.

"Maybe you will. I know that you are improving," he encourages.

Once my breathing becomes more regular, I turn to him

and say, "I have a question." Chris lifts his eyebrow, waiting for me to continue. "Why are you spending these extra sessions on me? I mean, why me? What about the other runners?" I ask curiously.

"You're the only one with any potential, Tessnia," Chris answers nonchalantly, shrugging his shoulders. He picks up his bag, turns around and asks, "Do you want to grab breakfast or something?"

"What? You actually have time to grab breakfast? I thought you might have to get back to your girlfriend for some alone time. You know, the red headed bombshell, flaunting her breasts for the whole world to see!" Too late! I have no idea how the words slipped out of my mouth. That incident was over a month ago. Why am I bringing that up now? Even Chris looks at me with a puzzled look. Then, he finally understands.

He smirks and says, "Oh, a bombshell, huh? I'm not sure about that. But no, I don't have to get back to her *for some alone time,"* Chris mocks me. "And for the record she is not my girlfriend. I don't have time for *girlfriends.* Roxy and I have a more mature relationship."

"Mature relationship?" I ask, as the unfamiliar emotion of jealousy creeps over me. Why am I feeling jealous? I shouldn't have brought this topic up.

"Yep, we both are able to meet each other's needs without expectations. Just the way I like it," he answers back, looking smug.

"And what kind of name is Roxy?" I mumble under my breath as I start walking away from him.

"What's wrong with her name?" Damn it! He was not

supposed to hear that. "Be careful, if I didn't know better, I would think you're sounding jealous." Chris teases, lifting his eyebrow.

"Good thing you know better," I reply, turning back to look at him, putting my hand on my hip. "Forget I even brought anything up. I don't want to know any more about *Roxy.* And to answer your original question, no, I can't have breakfast. I have to go to work soon." I'm ready to leave now, wanting some space from Chris.

"Work? You're working now, Tessnia?" Chris asks me as he catches up to me, his eyes full of curiosity.

"I started at Starbucks a few weeks ago," I answer. "I've got to go now."

I don't want to spend any more time with Chris than I have to. Normally, I'm always in control, but not around him. I especially lose all control of my emotions around him. The only way I can think clearly again, is when he's not near me.

When I arrive at work a few hours later, the place looks like it's getting busy. I'm half way done with my shift, and my mouth drops open when I see Chris walking in.

He walks right up to me, and says, "Hello, I'd like a cup of coffee, black."

"Are you kidding me? What are you doing here, Chris?" I ask.

"I'm here for my coffee, Tessnia. Is there a problem of some sort?" he asks, flashing his famous lopsided grin. He's really enjoying himself!

I curl my lips and attempt to act civil. I ask sweetly, "What size, sir?"

He answers back, just as sweetly, "Grande, please."

When I serve him the coffee, he gives me his killer smile, lifts his one eyebrow, nods at me, and sits down at a booth nearby. He makes himself comfortable as he pulls out his laptop. God, he's annoying! He works for two hours, then closes his laptop, puts it in his backpack, waits to catch my eye, smirks, and walks out. My body relaxes instantly as soon as Chris leaves.

When I return to my apartment, I tell Kylie about Chris showing up at my work. "Tess, I think he likes you." I roll my eyes, knowing it's far from the truth.

"No, Kylie, trust me! It's not that at all. It's weird. I can't really explain it. Sometimes I feel like it's not accidental that he shows up wherever I am."

"Of course it's not, Tess. He's trying to bump into you because he likes you. Hello?" I can see that Kylie is exasperated with me.

"Kylie, I'm telling you, it's difficult for me to explain it. There's something about him, and I'm not able to pinpoint it. He's so secretive," I say, shaking my head. "Oh forget it, I'm overanalyzing as usual."

"Yes, you are overanalyzing, Tess. He likes you, period. Don't read into it more than that," Kylie explains. She really wants me to believe that he likes me. In reality, I know it's far from the truth. The guy can get any girl at this campus.

"I know for a fact that he does not like me like that, Kylie." My frustration starts to intensify. I just want to forget about Chris.

As time passes, the routine becomes more consistent. Chris's presence is more and more regular in my life. Not only do I see him every day for practice, but I see him every weekend at work as well. He never says much--just smirks at me, and does his work at the same booth. Sometimes he brings books with him, and he frantically takes notes. And before he leaves, he always waits to make eye contact with me, smirks, raises his one eyebrow, and walks out.

I continue to ignore him. I know he's waiting for a reaction from me, which I refuse to give him.

Seven

I'm looking forward to the Thanksgiving break because I'm ready to spend some quality time with my parents. The Saturday before the Thanksgiving break, Chris and I practice as usual.

At the end of the practice, he says, "Wait a minute, Tessnia, I have something for you." Chris motions me to walk to his bag.

"What?" I ask, confused. He pulls a folder out of his bag and hands me an 8 x 11 white sheet of paper. At first glance, it looks like a blank paper.

"Turn it around, Tessnia," Chris says, smirking at me.

I gasp as I turn the paper, my eyes wide with bewilderment. It's a pencil sketch of me. I'm sitting at a table, with books in front of me, lost in thought. The back of my pen is in my mouth and I'm holding it with my right hand. My hair is falling forward in a curly mess and my brown eyes are large and contemplative. This is exactly how I look whenever I'm doing my homework or studying. I have a bad habit of chewing on my pencils and pens. On the bottom right hand corner, I see the words, ***"Happy Birthday, Tessnia."***

"What?" I ask, confused and having difficulty finding the right words.

"I know your birthday is this week. I'm not going to see you, so I wanted to give you a little something," Chris explains.

"That's me studying," I say incredulously.

"Yes," he says simply.

"How...wait...you drew this?" I ask, still trying to process it.

"Yeah, I do a little drawing here and there," Chris answers, shrugging his shoulders.

"I don't understand. How did you know about my birthday and how did you know how I look when I study? I mean this is so me." Then I notice that the background is the university's library. I often go there in-between classes to study. "This is at the library."

"Yes. I walked in one time and there you were studying at the library. I didn't want to disturb you because you were concentrating so hard. So I drew you a little sketch of how I remembered you from that day. The rest, I used my imagination. And I know your birthday because it's written next to your name on the list for your track team."

"Oh," I whisper. I look at the sketch again, and start to giggle. "You even got me chewing on my pen."

"Yeah, you were chewing extra hard that day. You must have been studying for an extremely difficult exam," Chris teases, as a slow grin begins to form.

"I don't even know what to say. I mean, thank you. You're really talented. This looks exactly like me." I shake my head in disbelief as I examine the drawing.

"It's no big deal. I'm glad you like the drawing," Chris says nonchalantly. "Well, happy birthday, and have a good trip." Chris turns, grabs his bag, walks to his truck, and drives off.

I'm left standing there completely dumbfounded. The thought of Chris even getting me anything is shocking enough! He actually noticed my birthday? I look down at the drawing.

Unbelievable! The girl in the drawing is breathtakingly beautiful. But it's me. It's me from Chris's eyes.

Spending time with my parents for Thanksgiving and my birthday is exactly what I needed. It's a much-needed break to help me relax. When I return to school, time flies quickly.

As my first indoor meet starts, I'm especially nervous. My parents take time off of their busy schedule to come and watch me. I'm running the 400-meter dash. I line myself at the starting blocks, and when the gun goes off, I take off. The only person on my mind as I'm running is Chris, and all of the training he did with me. I want to show him that I was listening.

When I take first place, all of my teammates run to me, hugging me. They're yelling and screaming, practically knocking me over. And through all of the laughter, my eyes search for that familiar face. When I find it, he's looking straight at me and gives me a nod. This time, his eyes are full of pride. My heart skips a beat. Why is it so important to get praised by him?

This ritual becomes a routine. After every meet--and I always take first--I try to find him. He waits for my eye contact, and smirks at me or gives me a nod. He never verbally tells me how proud he is of me. And he never approaches me. But I know. He shows me his pride through his eyes.

That Christmas, the gift I receive from my parents changes my life. Even though I'm nineteen years old, I've never outgrown the joy of waking up on Christmas morning. I race down the stairs that morning, and find my parents sitting around the tree, smiling ear to ear.

"Santa got something really special for you this year, Tess," my dad says.

He slides a medium sized box toward me. I squeal in excitement.

"Hurry! Open it, Tess!" My mom is just as excited as me.

I lift the lid off of the box and peek inside. Inside the box, is a tan and white puppy staring back at me. He has big blue eyes, and he's wagging his tail.

"Oh my god! He is *so* cute! He's mine?" I can't contain my excitement.

"He is a *she,* Tess. And yes, she is yours to keep. You can take her back with you to the apartment if you'd like," my mom replies.

"She's special, Tess, just like you. You'll see that she is really smart. And I would like her to go with you. She can watch over you and protect you. It would help your mom and I sleep easier," Dad says. Dad is always so protective of me, thinking about my safety first.

The puppy jumps into my lap, and starts licking my hand. I start laughing. She's so cute! I fail to see how this little helpless pup can look out for me. But if that's what my dad wants to believe to feel better, then that's just fine by me.

"Finally, I got my own dog! And of course, I'm going to take her back with me. I absolutely love her already! What should we call you girl?" I start tickling her behind her ears. "What type of dog is she?"

"She has multiple different breeds in her, Tess," Mom answers.

"She's rare, Tess. She's one of a kind," Dad explains.

"Of course she's one of a kind! Look at her! She's perfect. I'm going to call her *Gem*. She's a rare Gem to me." Gem barks as if she likes that name as well, and starts to jump up and down with excitement. Then, she climbs up my shirt and starts licking my face. I love her so much already!

Suddenly, she looks right into my eyes. She stops moving, and her big blue eyes stare straight into me. I stop laughing, as I'm unable to look away. Gem gives me the same look that Thunder, the horse from Jamaica had given me. Gem is looking deep into me, into my soul. I tear my eyes away and glance toward my parents to see if they noticed the odd exchange. I catch my parents look at each other. But just as quickly, they compose themselves and they both smile at me. Gem is jumping up and down again, doing her happy dance. Everything is back to normal. Maybe I imagined that entire incident. I jump up and give both of my parents a hug.

"You guys are perfect, do you know that?" I really mean it. I'm so lucky to have them in my life.

"No, honey, you are perfect. And don't ever forget that," Mom says, as she gives me a kiss on my forehead.

Gem and I get familiar with each other during the rest of the Christmas break. I'm impressed at how smart she is. I show her to use the bathroom outside only once, and she just stands by the door whenever she needs to go. Even when she's outside, she never tries to run away. She just stays by the door, runs around, and plays. If she starts to wander off, I just call her and she runs back to me. I notice that for a new puppy, she's incredibly fast.

For New Year's Eve, we have a small get-together at Jack's house. There are only about twenty of us there, and we're all friends from high school. Most of us haven't seen each other for a long time since we had gone our separate ways. It feels good to catch up with them.

Kyle and Kylie wander off to a corner. Jack takes my hand and leads me under the mistletoe. He lifts my chin up to look at him and says, "Ok, Tess, don't freak like you did last time I tried to kiss you."

"What? I didn't freak. I didn't know..." Before I can finish my sentence, he leans forward and plants his lips on me. It's a brief kiss, but full of tenderness.

"See, not too bad, right?" Jack asks.

"Shut up, Jack," I say, laughing with him. Jack takes my hand, leads me to the rest of the guests, and we begin mingling.

Right when midnight is about to strike, we start the count down.

All of us yell, "10, 9, 8....4, 3, 2, 1!" We all jump around, hugging one another, and screaming, "Happy New Year!"

As I'm hugging everybody, suddenly, my phone buzzes. I look down at my phone and notice a text that says,

"Thinking about you as this new year starts. Happy NewYear!"

I don't recognize the number. So I reply:

"Thank you.Who is this?"

"Come on, Tessnia, you know who this is."

Oh my god, it's Chris! My heart skips a beat.

"How'd you get my number?"

"You gave it to me, a while back."

"I don't remember giving it to you?"

I know I hadn't given it to him.

"I guess when there's a will, there's a way. Have a good night, Tessnia."

"Happy New Year to you too, Chris."

And that's that. I get no reply back. He has ended the conversation. I quickly save his number on my phone. Feeling almost giddy that Chris texted me, I can't help but smile. I refuse to analyze this feeling!

I return to the university with Gem, and she immediately adjusts to the apartment. When I explain to her that she can't bark because it would disturb the neighbors, it's as if she understands. I'm also glad to see that Kylie instantly falls in love with her, as she plays with her non-stop.

I add Gem to my routine of my crazy college schedule. I don't like her to be alone in the apartment all day so I decide to take her to my track practice. I tie her up by the nearby tree and tell her she has to wait while I practice. Gem sits there obediently until I finish.

When I bring her with me to Saturday practice, Chris comes up to us as I'm tying her up. "She's beautiful," he says.

"Thanks, her name is Gem. My parents got her for me for Christmas," I tell him. I can't help but show her off.

"Huh, maybe she can go running with us on track when we start," Chris suggests.

"Really?" I ask, liking the idea.

"Yeah, let's try it. But let's warm up first."

After we stretch, and warm up, we bring Gem to the

starting line. Chris leans down to her level to take a closer look at her. They both stare at each other for at least a minute straight. It's as if they see something that nobody else can. I tell her he's a friend, while rubbing my hand through her fur. He brings his hand to her. She sniffs his hand, tilts her head as if intrigued by something, and then kisses his hand.

"It looks like you made a friend, Chris." I'm surprised at how quickly she bonds with him.

"I guess so," he replies, and pets the top of her head.

"It's strange how she stared at you for so long. She did the same to me when I first got her. It kind of reminds me of the horse I bonded with when I went to Jamaica," I mumble, deep in thought.

"What?" Chris turns to me, narrowing his eyes curiously.

"Yeah, it's strange. Thunder, the horse I rode in Jamaica, looked at me the same way as Gem just looked at you," I say, shaking my head in confusion.

"Hmm, interesting. Maybe animals have some sort of sixth sense, and Thunder knew you were special," he replies with a smirk. I look up at him, and his eyes are teasing me.

"Ha! There's nothing special about me. I'm just an ordinary girl, trying to make it in life," I say dramatically.

Chris's smile broadens. "Come on, let's run," Chris says, walking toward the field.

I explain to Gem we will be running, and she has to stay by me. She barks up at me once, wagging her tail. After I release her leash, Gem and I follow Chris to the starting line.

When Chris says to go, we all take off. The entire time she stays right by my side. She doesn't wander off, and she doesn't try to pass me up.

When we reach the finish line where Chris is waiting for us, he says, "You know, she's really smart. And fast. How old is she?"

"She's only twelve weeks. And yeah, she is smart and fast. She's one of a kind, right girl?" I look at Gem, smiling at her with pride.

She barks once at me as if answering me while wagging her tail. I laugh and rub behind her ears. Chris laughs with me. His laugh catches me by surprise. It's a rare sound. He sounds so happy, and I can't help but wonder why he doesn't laugh more. I look up at him, with a puzzled look.

"Now what?" Chris asks.

"You're just a confusing guy, that's all," I say, shaking my head. "Do you know that I don't even know your last name?"

"Jones," Chris replies.

"Your name is Chris Jones? You don't look like a Chris Jones to me," I say, narrowing my eyes.

"Really? Strange. Hmm, well, let's do some more laps," Chris suggests, shrugging his shoulders.

Gem, Chris, and I work out for at least another hour. It feels good to get such a great workout in. I know Chris is helping me. And as much as I hate to admit it, I enjoy our time together. I'm starting to get used to him being around. Maybe that's not good.

On the last lap, right when I'm sprinting my hardest, my ankle twists. Damn! That hurt! I keep trying to run because I don't want to quit. When Chris notices how I limp through the finish line, he says, "What happened?"

"Nothing!" I say quickly. I don't want him to know that I hurt my ankle. I just want to get home and ice it.

"Come here, let me see. You're limping. You hurt your left leg. Is it your ankle or your hamstrings?" Chris asks.

"Oh my god! I said it was nothing. I just rolled my ankle. I'll ice it when I get home, ok? It will be fine." I don't like this type of attention. And I'm certainly not used to it from Chris.

Suddenly, I see the black cloud pass before my eyes. Oh no! Not now! My breaths become shallow, and my heart rate becomes erratic. I try to calm myself down because I don't want Chris to see me this way. My eyes close instantly, as the intimidating black cloud surrounds me. I put my hand to my temple hoping to get a grip very quickly. I take some slow deep breaths, knowing that the cloud is not really there. I don't want to look like a fool in front of Chris, but I don't think my legs can support me anymore. Suddenly, I feel strong arms grab hold of me, and lower me to the floor. I slowly open my eyes, and to my relief, the black cloud is gone.

"What happened?" I hear Chris whisper in my ears. He is sitting on the grass behind me, and his strong arms are still wrapped around me. I've never been this close to Chris. I know I should move away, but his proximity gives me the strength I need to calm myself down.

Gem comes by us and starts to lick my face. She looks just as worried as Chris. "Tell me what happened," Chris repeats.

"Nothing," I say. I'm not about to share my crazy visions with Chris. He lifts my chin up to look into my eyes. His gaze is penetrating into me, as if he's trying to read whether or not I'm telling the truth. "Honestly, it's nothing, Chris. I just had a sharp shooting pain in my ankle, that's all. I needed to sit down," I lie.

"What? You're lying. Something happened just now. You

looked like you saw a ghost, and looked scared out of your mind." Chris is not ready to let this go.

"Yes, I was scared. I didn't realize it was going to hurt that bad, Chris. That's it. But it feels better already. I think I can get back up on it." I try to divert his attention back to my ankle.

He releases me and moves himself closer to my legs. He takes my left leg, and pulls my shoe and sock off. I'm sure my feet smell since I just ran, and they must be full of sweat! How embarrassing!

"I'm checking it myself!" Chris says, as he assesses my ankle.

"Look, you're making a big deal about nothing. I'm going to be fine," I insist.

Chris does not reply. He moves my ankle around. I wince when he rolls it outward. "It looks like you have a sprained ankle. You need to rest that so you don't hurt it even more."

"Yes, sir!" I want to lighten up the mood. Chris touching me like this is doing strange things to me. I'm very uncomfortable with the way it's making me feel. I try to pull my leg out of his grasp, but he holds on and starts to massage my foot and ankle. As much as I hate admitting it, it feels really good. I guess my poor feet take a lot of beating from the running. God, he's good. The pads of his fingertips move into my swollen tendons and muscles. I sigh with relief.

Chris's hands start to move up my leg as he massages my calf muscles. I can't look away as I watch his strong hands stroking against my bare skin. His touch brings my nerves on high alert. Even though he's just touching my leg, and it is a therapeutic touch only, my body starts to react. I just want to close my eyes and savor this moment. It feels too good. No, this cannot happen. I'm entering the danger zone.

I look up at him, and he's looking right at me as he's working on my leg. His gaze is open and unguarded. To my disbelief, Chris looks vulnerable. Is he reacting to his touch the same as me? It takes me by surprise. He *never* lets his guards down. As though he read my mind, he shields his eyes from me by lowering his eyelids and focusing on my leg again.

Chris clears his throat and abruptly releases his grip from my leg. "Yeah, I don't think you should try to jog home now. I have my truck here. I'll take you and Gem back."

"Honestly, it's not necessary, Chris," I say, regaining my composure. I need to get some space from him.

"As your trainer, I think it *is* necessary. Here, drink this water first," he instructs, as he hands me the water bottle. I know it's no use arguing with him. He's too strong-willed to change his mind.

Sighing in defeat, I drink the water. Chris helps me up to my feet and then leads me to his truck. He has a black Toyota Four Runner. It suits him. He gives me a boost up into the truck, and Gem jumps into the back.

As he's driving, I turn to him and ask, "What type of work do you do in the military anyway?"

"Ha! Aren't you a curious one? That contains lots of top secret stuff that I am forbidden to talk about," he teases, smirking at me. Why does he have to look so sexy when all he's doing is smiling? His wind-blown hair and his teasing eyes are making it difficult for me to concentrate. I quickly look away, pretending to be interested in watching out of my window. Once I get more control of my emotions, I turn back to answer him.

"Well, forget you. Who said I'm interested anyway? I was just making small talk with you," I say, folding my arms in front of my chest, stubbornly.

Chris laughs. "Ok, whatever, Tessnia." I don't respond. Within minutes, he has pulled the car to the apartment parking lot.

He helps me out of the car and into my apartment. He even brings me to the sofa in my living room. "Now remember to rest, ice, and elevate. You may even want to wrap that up. Ok?"

"Got it!" I reply. And then he's gone. I'm finally able to breathe again.

As I'm sitting there thinking about how he had taken care of me, I realize I never told him how to get to my apartment. How does he know where I live? I shake my head. I don't think I'll ever be able to figure him out.

To make matters worse, I had the episode of the black cloud right in front of him! Just my luck! Thank goodness he bought the story about the ankle, and didn't continue to pursue for more information.

For some reason, Chris's touch has tremendous power over my emotions. My nerves are on such high alert whenever he's around me. I'm not ready to understand why I feel that way. I just know that after some time, I have to put some distance between us so that I can think clearly again.

Later that day, Kylie tells me that Kyle is going to come

and visit her the following weekend. She says he's going to stay at our apartment if that's ok with me. It doesn't bother me. I probably should let them be alone for the weekend. Maybe that would be the perfect weekend to visit Jack! He has asked me several times, and I never had the opportunity.

First, I need to ask my work if I can have that weekend off. They like me, so I'm sure it wouldn't be a problem. When I ask Jack about it, he's really excited. He tells me that he can't wait until I get there. As I'm planning my trip, I notice a text from Chris.

"How's your ankle?"

"Fine!"

"Are you still limping?"

"No!"

"Are you icing regularly?"

"Yes, I told you! It's fine!"

"Are you going to work tomorrow?"

"Of course! Why wouldn't I?"

"Well, you staying on that ankle for eight hours is going to aggravate it more! That's why! And what's up with all your exclamation points at every reply??"

"OMG, I told you the ankle is fine! And I will be going to work! Gotta go now!!!!!!!"

In truth, the ankle is still sore. I elevate it and ice it the rest of the day, hoping it would be ready for work the next day.

I wrap it up with ace wrap before going to work on Sunday. I figure the compression should help. Chris comes to my work earlier than usual. I know his order, so I get it and hand it to him.

"You're still limping," he accuses.

"Nope, I'm not. It's your imagination," I lie.

"Guaranteed you won't be able to practice tomorrow," Chris says.

"Guaranteed I will," I challenge. Chris rolls his eyes, shaking his head. He takes his coffee and sits at his booth with his laptop. I want him to leave early today because I don't want him to notice that my ankle is getting worse. To my dismay, he stays there longer than usual.

As the day progresses, the pain is becoming excruciating. Maybe it's not a good idea to stay on it for the whole eight-hour shift. But pride keeps me going. I try to minimize the limping to the best of my ability, praying that Chris wouldn't notice.

Finally, when my shift ends, I want to get out of there. I glance around the room for Chris, but he's already gone. That's strange since I just saw him still sitting there five minutes ago. I guess it's just as well. My pain is unbearable. Now that he's gone, I don't have to try to hide my limp.

"Hey, Tess, are you ok?" My boss becomes worried when he sees me limping.

"Yeah, I'll be fine. I just hurt my ankle at practice," I answer as I walk out the door.

I limp outside. God, I have a long walk to the apartment. Why didn't I drive my car to work? I should have brought some pain medicine with me. What was I thinking? I take a deep breath to brace myself for the painful walk.

Suddenly, I feel somebody grab me from the hook of my arm.

"Come on, I'm driving you home," Chris says.

"I'm fine. I can walk home," I say stubbornly. I hate giving him the satisfaction that he was right.

"Whatever, let's go. My truck is parked in the lot. And I picked up Chipotle for your dinner. Hope you like burritos." Chris guides me to the truck and helps me get into the passenger side.

"You don't have to do all that, but thank you." During the drive to the apartment, neither of us says anything. I'm in too much pain to try to make small talk. He's too annoyed with me to say a word.

Chris helps me into my apartment. Kylie is not in. She's probably at the library. This time, Chris doesn't leave immediately. He helps me to the sofa, and then he takes my shoes off.

"Really, no need for this. I am totally fine," I say, completely embarrassed. Chris ignores me and unwraps the ace wrap. My ankle is really swollen. "Ouch!" I wince.

Chris sighs in frustration. He goes to the freezer and grabs an ice pack. He wraps it around the ankle. Mm, it already feels better.

"Where's your medicine cabinet? Do you have any ibuprofen?"

"In my bathroom. Yeah, I have Advil," I answer. What's the use arguing with him? He's going to do what he wants anyway. When he returns, Chris hands me two tablets of Advil with a glass of water.

"So, I noticed you hung up the sketch I drew of you in your bedroom," Chris says, as I'm swallowing my pills. I almost choke on my water.

Damn! I forgot I have it hung up on the wall next to my

bed. I hung it up as soon as I got home that same day he gave it to me. I couldn't help it. I love seeing it every morning when I wake up and right before falling asleep at night. For some strange reason, it makes me feel closer to him.

"Um, yeah. Guess I really like that present from you," I confess. I sneak a peek at him. I catch his smile, and then just as quickly, it disappears. Chris looks down at my ankle again.

"I'm sorry to say this, but you can't practice for the next few days. I'm sure the athletic trainer will agree with me." Chris is still irritated with the choice I made today about going to work, but I think seeing that sketch hanging in my bedroom had pleased him. He's not as abrupt with me and his voice is much more sympathetic.

"Ok," I reply. I don't want to argue with him, and he's probably right.

"Are you going to stay off the ankle as much as possible?" he asks.

"Yes, sir! I will just sit and watch at practice tomorrow, ok?" I can't help rolling my eyes at him.

"You are one stubborn girl. But just remember, I'm more stubborn." Chris grabs his jacket and leaves out the door, leaving me wondering what just happened.

Eight

The athletic trainer has me sit out for the next three days. She sends me for an X-ray, and thankfully nothing is broken. By the third day, my pain is almost gone. That Thursday, I'm running almost to my full potential. I can tell Chris is happy with my progress.

After Friday's practice, I race home. I've been driving to practice all week to avoid jogging back to the apartment. I still need to pack for my visit to Jack's university.

Finally, when I'm done packing, I grab my bag, my books, and Gem, and we head to UCLA. It's over a six-hour drive, so by the time we arrive there, it's almost midnight. Jack comes running out, kisses my cheek, and grabs my bag from my car.

"I'm so glad you were able to visit me! And this must be Gem!" he exclaims. Gem jumps up and starts to wag her tail.

"Yes! Gem, this is Jack." Gem barks again.

"Hello, Gem! I heard a lot about you! I finally get to meet you," Jack says as he pets her. Gem kisses his face, as if showing him she's happy to meet him as well.

"So this is your place, huh, Jack?" I ask, looking up to the apartment building.

"Yep! This is it. Come on. You had a long drive. You must be exhausted," Jack says, as he leads us up the stairs and into his apartment.

When I walk in, I can tell that Jack must have cleaned up. There's a sofa and a TV, a small kitchen table, and two bedrooms, with two bathrooms. It's clean and tidy for college guys.

"This is nice, Jack," I say, as I walk around. He lives with his roommate, Doug. I begin wondering where I'm going to be sleeping.

Jack must have read my mind because he says, "Thanks. Oh, and it's the perfect weekend for you to visit, because my roommate went out of town. He told me you could use his bedroom."

"Oh, ok. That's nice of him. Tell him thanks for me," I say, grateful that I didn't have to sleep on the sofa. "I thought I might have to crash on the sofa."

Jack was putting my bag in Doug's bedroom. He comes out of the room and walks up to me. "I would take the sofa, Tess. I wouldn't let you sleep out here. You'd use my bedroom," Jack says, shaking his head. "I can't believe that you actually think that I would let you sleep on the sofa."

"I'd feel bad taking your bed, Jack," I mumble, feeling bad that I insulted him.

Jack lifts my chin up to look at him. "Hey, I know we've known each other since kindergarten, but believe it or not, I've grown up to be a gentleman." And then he smiles. I love Jack's smiles because it takes me back in time when he was just a little boy.

"You were always a gentleman, Jack," I say as I hug him. The strong stable arms embracing me feel good. Jack has always made me feel safe and secure.

"Let's get you something to eat first of all," Jack says, as he plays with my hair. "I made some fried chicken. What do you think?" I step out of his embrace and smile. Jack is always in tune with your needs. I'm famished.

"Perfect! Thanks, Jack," I say gratefully.

I set Gem up with her food and water. Jack and I eat the chicken with biscuits and gravy. We start catching up on things. I confess that all I do is study, work, and track practices.

To that he replies, "Not healthy, Tess. You have to get a life outside of that."

"But I'm content, Jack. I don't feel like I should be doing anything else. And you're going to kill me, but would you mind if I crash after we eat? I'm exhausted!"

"Tess, you know in the college world, the night is just beginning," Jack says, smiling at me.

"I know, Jack. I'm an old woman, what can I say? Hey, but you can go out if you want. It would be ok with me. Besides, we have all day tomorrow, right?" I feel bad, but I can't help it. I truly am exhausted. And honestly, lying down with a good book until I fall asleep sounds heavenly right about now.

"I didn't make any plans tonight, Tess. I'm not going anywhere. Let's go walk Gem, and then we'll call it a night, ok?" Jack suggests.

"Alright, let's go." We walk Gem for half an hour. He shows me the campus since his apartment is not too far from it.

When we return to the apartment, I say goodnight to Jack. He kisses me on my forehead, and I go into Doug's room. After changing into my pajamas, I wash my face, brush my teeth, and crawl into bed. It feels strange to sleep in somebody else's bed besides my own. Gem finds a spot on the floor next to the bed. I don't even grab a book to read. I fall asleep instantly.

She is running. "Visualize!" It's Chris's voice. She runs faster. "Run!" Again, it is Chris yelling. She keeps running. She has to keep running if she wants to live. She is exhausted! "Don't stop! Run!" Chris yells. She wants to give up. It's so hard to breathe. But his urging won't let her stop. She has to take a breath and get some air! She is gasping for air. She needs air! She can't breathe!

I sit up in bed, gasping. Beads of sweat are rolling down my forehead. Gem jumps on the bed, into my lap, and begins licking my face. She wants me to know that she's here for me. I slow my breathing down, and recognize where I am.

I roll my fingers through her fur, and say, "I'm ok, girl. It's just these crazy dreams!" I'm shocked that I'm hearing Chris's voice in my dreams now! That had never happened before. God, my dreams are getting more and more messed up.

I look at the time. It's just past seven in the morning. I would have started my practice with him at this time. I didn't even tell him that I wasn't going to be there. He'll figure it out when I don't show up. Saturday practices are extra, and he said that he practices on his own on Saturdays anyway.

I can't fall back asleep though, so I put some sweatpants and a sweatshirt on, and Gem and I go for a run. I don't want to wake up Jack, so I leave the front door unlocked. After an hour, we get back, and I jump into the shower. I quickly put on my robe when I hear my phone ringing in the bedroom. I run to the phone, thinking my parents are probably checking in with me.

"Hello?" I answer.

"Where are you?" It's Chris. And he's angry. He's very angry. I can tell because his voice is low, and he is talking very slowly, like that day at the frat party.

"Oh, sorry. I forgot to tell you, Chris. I'm out of town," I say hesitantly. Suddenly, I'm annoyed. I don't owe him any explanations!

"You're out of town? Where?" he demands.

"That's not your business, Chris." Now I'm really irritated. If he's going to make demands on me, I'm definitely not going to answer him. Who is he anyway? It's not like I can just call him and demand *his* whereabouts. There is silence for a few seconds.

Then I hear him say, "You are really trying my patience. Don't push me. Just answer my question."

"Are you crazy? I don't owe you any explanation!" I say courageously. Actually, I yell it. I am furious!

The bedroom door opens. Jack is standing there with a questioning look on his face.

"Hey, Tess, you ok?" he asks, concerned. I give him a hesitant nod.

"Oh, ok, I get it. You're visiting some guy," Chris says angrily. There is a brief pause, and he continues, "So much for Miss Innocent Act. The joke is on me, I guess." And then there's a click.

I'm left staring at my phone. What in the world is going on here? God, this guy just infuriates me! Can't he leave me alone for one day? And why is he so mad?

I still have a frown on my face when Jack walks up to me, and says, "Hey, you ok? You have a crazy look on your face."

"Thanks, Jack. And yeah, I feel kind of crazy. Let's just go get some breakfast."

"Breakfast it is!" Jack smiles. I smile back. He has such a calming effect on me.

I do not want to talk about Chris, so I don't bring it up to Jack. He takes me around his campus. I meet some of his college buddies, and they're all very nice. I'm happy to see that Jack is hanging out with people with goals, and are driven like him.

Later that night, we go out to dinner at a pizza joint on campus. It feels nice to unwind with the Rock and Roll music in the background and the casual atmosphere of the restaurant. Suddenly, Jack says, "You know, Tess, I'm kind of dating somebody."

"What? Really?" I ask, surprised.

"Yeah, her name is Sara," he continues, focusing his attention on his plate of food, as he avoids looking at me.

"Well, where is she? I'd love to meet her." I seriously want to meet her because I'm very protective of Jack.

"No, you won't be meeting her, Tess. We're not *that* serious yet. We're just kind of hanging out, and she's cool. I just wanted to be the one to tell you," Jack explains.

"Ok, Jack. I get it. But honestly, I am happy for you. You deserve the best. You know that, right? She's a lucky girl." I want him to know how special he is.

I hear Jack sigh. He stares at me for a few seconds, shakes his head, and says, "Tess, you have no idea how amazing you are." He reaches across the table, and squeezes my hand. "And you know what? *You* deserve the best. Don't ever forget that. I envy the guy who's going to win your heart one day." I squeeze his hand back. I realize at that moment, that Jack will always be in my life, in some shape or form. He is just too important.

Chris does not call me the rest of the time while I'm with Jack. I'm relieved because I don't want any type of confrontation. I wonder how it's going to be when I see him on Monday at practice. I go over several scenarios in my head of what I should say to him but decide against every single one of them. Why should I explain myself to him?

I drive back Sunday morning, giving Jack a tight hug before I leave. God, I love this guy. He kisses my cheek, and says, "Tess, remember to be spontaneous and have some fun in your life, ok? Promise me."

"Ok, Jack, I'll try." Gem gives him a kiss on his face and we begin our drive back to Stanford.

As I drive home, I wonder how everything went with Kyle and Kylie. I hope she had a good time. I get back in the afternoon, and decide to go to the library to get some studying done. I return to the apartment around seven o'clock and decide to text Kylie to check on her.

"Kylie where are you? I'm home now."

"I'm eating dinner with Kyle.We've been out and about. He's leaving in a couple of hours so I'll be home around 9. How was your visit with Jack?"

"Great! We'll talk when you get back."

I decide to make spaghetti for dinner. Just as the water for my noodles is beginning to boil, I hear a knock on my door. I wonder who that can be since the doorman didn't call up. Normally, I don't open the door if I'm not expecting anybody.

My parents always taught that to me since I was a child. But I see Gem is standing by the door, wagging her tail. So I figure it has to be somebody we know.

I yell, "Coming!" I open the door, and in walks Chris.

"Oh, come on in, Chris, why don't you?" I say sarcastically. "And by the way, how do you know where I live? I never asked you when you brought me here for my ankle. I mean, are you stalking me?" All of my annoyance toward him comes flooding back as I see him. He has all black on, and damn does he look good. I know he's still angry. I can feel it radiating through him.

"Reality check, Tessnia. I know all your business. I'm practically your assistant coach, so that would give me access to your phone numbers, your address, your emergency contact information, your birthday, and whatever else I fucking want!" Chris says, his tone low. He turns to me, folding his arms in front of him, as if challenging me to question that.

"Oh." I mumble, unable to think of any smart response. He's still standing there with his arms folded in front of him as if waiting for further explanation from me. So finally I ask, "Ok, so what are you doing here?"

"I think you owe me an explanation, Tessnia," he responds slowly and deliberately.

"About what?" I ask innocently. Even though I know what he's talking about, I don't think I owe him any explanations.

"I'm going to say this once, and only once. If you make an appointment with me, I expect you to be there. If you can't make it for some reason, you damn well better contact me and let me know. Not only is it the courteous thing to do, but do you have any idea how worried I was? I nearly went crazy." He sighs, and runs his fingers through his hair as if that gesture helps calm him.

"Why in the world would you be worried?" I ask, still confused.

"Why? Well, for months now we've been practicing every Saturday together, and all of a sudden you don't show up one Saturday without a word. I get no phone call, no message, nothing. Why wouldn't I be worried?" Chris is irate.

I walk past him and head to the kitchen. With my back still turned to him, I say, "Well, as you can see, I'm fine--actually, more than fine. I had a great weekend." I have no idea what makes me say that. I sneak a glance at him, and notice that his jaw is clenched and his hands are balled up in a fist.

"Don't push me, Tessnia," Chris says, so quietly, that I have to strain my ears to hear him.

"And how am I pushing you, Chris?" I can't stop myself. God, it's like I have no control of the words that are coming out of my mouth. His anger is making me angry. Before I can say anything else, Chris strides toward me, grabs me at my waist, and pulls me against him.

"Do you really want me to show you how you're pushing me, Tessnia? What you do to me?" he whispers in my ear.

I freeze, unable to move a muscle. I have never been this close to Chris. God, why does he have this effect on me? My whole body is on fire. My breathing becomes uneven and heavy. He lifts my face, looks into my eyes, and then he claims me. His lips are on mine. He comes down hard. There is no tenderness in his kiss. It's a possessive kiss, a passionate kiss.

My body instantly responds. I melt. My lips automatically open, and to my horror, I start to kiss him back just as passionately. My arms wrap around his neck and I hold him tight as I kiss him hard. I have never experienced such a loss of control. His body has pinned me against the wall. He pulls my hips against his, and moans. I feel a deep pressure in my gut, a sensation unfamiliar to me. There is no point of return. I love how his body feels against me. I'm so turned on. What the hell is wrong with me? I don't even care. This feels too good. I just let myself go, as I surrender myself to him.

"Tell me, tell me nothing happened with that guy, Tessnia," Chris says against my mouth as he's kissing me.

"Nothing, he's a friend, that's it. A childhood friend," I say breathlessly. I can't even think clearly, let alone articulate anything. All I know is that this feels too good. Not only have I never been kissed like this, but also my body has never responded like this. Chris kisses me hard once again, and then he pulls himself off of me. No, I don't want him to stop. I open my eyes in protest. He's breathing heavily, just as I am. He runs his hand through his hair.

When he looks at me, he says, "Never again. That can never happen again. Do you understand?"

I stare at him, speechless. I'm still too shocked of everything that just happened to respond. I desperately try to catch my breath, wondering how he's able to recover so quickly.

"Mistake. I messed up. Look, we have to stay apart. Saturday practices--not a good idea. From now on, just the regular practices." He sighs, and as if talking to himself, he continues, "Damn, this is crazy. What did I do?" Chris starts heading to the door. I'm still standing there, leaning against the wall, unable to move. He opens the door, but instead of bolting out, he lingers as if contemplating what to say. He doesn't turn around to look at me. Instead, he slowly says, "I'm sorry, Tessnia. I screwed up." And then he walks out without a second glance, closing the door behind him.

I close my eyes, attempting to get my bearings. My legs are unable to support me anymore. I slowly slide down the wall and sit on the floor. I hug my knees, trying to make sense of what just happened. I'm so confused. God, I lost all control. And when he kissed me, I never wanted anything more. I wanted him, shamelessly. Not only did I forget where I was, but also who I was. I had never felt like that, ever. Kissing him felt so right. But then he said it was a mistake. Why did he say it was a mistake? Did he mean that? I know he wanted me just as badly as I wanted him. I felt it. We both lost control.

Why am I always confused when it comes to Chris? It feels like I'm always riding an emotional roller coaster with him. Gem comes up to me, whimpers, and puts her head on my leg, looking up at me with her big blue eyes. She looks as sad as I feel.

"It's ok, girl. I'll be ok," I whisper to her. I just feel so lost sometimes in my life, and this is one of those times.

By the time Kylie and Kyle get back, at least I've gotten off of the floor. Kyle walks in, gives me a hug and says, "It's nice to see you, Tess. You look good."

"Thanks, Kyle. How are you?"

"Good, now that I saw my girl." He moves to Kylie, and wraps his arms around her. Kylie is beaming, looking up at him. "But I have to head back now."

Kylie and Kyle say their goodbyes, and he finally leaves.

When Kylie and I are alone, she says, "Oh Tess, that was a perfect weekend! I had missed him so much."

"I'm glad you guys are working things out, Kylie," I say. I like to see my best friend happy.

"Tell me about your weekend. You don't look good. You ok?" Kylie gets straight to the point.

"Oh, I'm fine, Kylie. I had fun with Jack. You know he's so great," I tell her. "Oh and he's seeing somebody. Some girl named Sara. He said she was pretty cool."

"What?" Kylie asks, surprised. "Really? Are you ok with that?"

"Why wouldn't I be? I just want Jack to be happy. You know I never thought of him like that," I clarify. "I mean, I *am* protective of him, so of course if this Sara girl hurts him, I'll rip her heart out." And then we both giggle. It feels good to giggle after what happened earlier with Chris.

"That's what I love about you, Tess. Nobody messes with those you love. But you do look crazy. Did anything else happen?" Should I tell her? What the hell. If I can't tell her, whom can I tell?

"Well, Chris came here earlier. And, um he kissed me, like crazy kissed me. You know, one of those kisses that just melts you and you can't think clearly anymore? That type of kiss."

"You're kidding! *Oh my god!* I want the details." Kylie's eyes are full of excitement.

"There are no details. He pulled himself off of me, said it was a mistake, and left," I explain. It all happened so fast. And now, I'm even more confused than ever.

"Well, he's probably just trying to sort out his feelings for you. I told you he's into you!"

"No, Kylie, you don't understand. He was so final and

matter of fact about it. I just don't understand it. No, actually I just don't understand *him*," I say, exasperated.

Kylie walks over to me. "Hey, hey look at me. I've known you since kindergarten, and I've never seen you like this. You were always the strong one, knowing exactly what you wanted, and never lost control. Do I need to worry here?" Kylie puts her arm around my shoulders, trying to look at me for some type of reassurance.

I take a deep breath and sigh. "No, you don't need to worry, Kylie. I'm going to figure this out. I just need some time, I guess." I answer her with the confidence that I really don't feel.

Nine

Chris is true to his word and he completely ignores me the following week. He stays out of my way at practice and avoids all eye contact.

Finally, on Wednesday, I decide to confront him. After practice, I march right up to him and say, "We need to talk."

His shoulders instantly stiffen up. Not taking his eyes off of the clipboard he's using, he replies, "There's nothing to talk about."

"How can you say that? You owe me an explanation. This is crazy." I start getting angry because he continues to ignore me.

"Look, I already apologized. It was a stupid mistake. I'm your trainer. I crossed the line. It's not going to happen again." Bending down, he picks up his backpack, saddles it over his shoulder, and begins to walk away.

Really? How can he just ignore what had happened? And as much as he likes to pretend that it meant nothing to him, I know it's a lie. We had connected that night, and it was a connection I had never felt with anybody else.

I catch up to him. "I'm not done yet, Chris. You call yourself 'my trainer'? I'm pretty sure you haven't *trained* me all week! And you said no more Saturdays. You said you're going to help me get better. How can you help me if you're avoiding me? And why are you acting like nothing happened between us. I felt something, and you did too!" My breathing is heavy now from frustration. I lower my tone, hoping to calm myself down. "Besides, I have a lot of questions. I'm confused. And I think you're the only one who can help with these questions."

Chris stops. He turns around and looks directly into my eyes, clenching his jaw tight. His cerulean blue eyes are fierce and determined. "No, Tess. You have to help yourself. I can't help you. You're your own worst enemy. You constantly restrict yourself from what you're capable of doing. It's not me who can help you. And as for that damned kiss? Trust me, I'll probably end up hurting you. Stay away from me. You have to get that through your head," Chris says, pressing his index finger against his tousled blond hair. He's angry and his words sting. I stare at his back as he walks away, warm tears forming behind my eyes.

Stay away from me. That's what he said and he meant it. He was mean and cruel. It felt like he stabbed me through my bleeding heart. I was so stupid! How did I read more into all this then it really was? There was no connection! It was just a 'damned' kiss, that's it. Sure, he was turned on, but which guy wouldn't be from a passionate kiss? And all those times he showed up at Starbucks? Who knows? Maybe it really was a place where he could get his work done. I probably read more into my track meets as well. He was coming because he was the trainer and that's it!

I blame myself for the predicament I'm in. I let my guard down and set myself up for this pain. I imagined something that really wasn't there. I let myself get too attached to him. Damn him!

I have to stay busy. I can't allow myself to fall apart. When Saturday morning comes, I go to track as usual, knowing he's not going to be there. Gem and I practice together. I don't need him to train me! I can do this myself!

The following week, I'm a mess. I really miss him! I miss seeing him on a regular basis. Not only does he not come to my work anymore, Chris is showing up even less frequently at the track practices. And this week he hasn't come at all yet. I keep looking up to see him walk down the field, my heart in my throat. But, no Chris.

We have a meet this week. He has to come to my meet! He just has to! All the way until my race comes, my eyes search for him. I never see him. I line up at the starting blocks. I feel nauseated. How can he not come to watch me race? He never misses any of my meets! When the gun goes off, I run! This time, I run with a heavy heart. That's the first race I lose this year.

By Thursday, depression hits me hard. I don't even want to get out of bed. I haven't seen Chris in a week.

After practice that evening, I come home and go straight to my room. And then the tears come flooding out. I can't stop myself. I don't even care. I glance up at the drawing he made for me. It makes me cry even harder.

I used to think that people who feel sorry for themselves are weak. But damn, sometimes you just need a good cry. I can tell Gem is worried about me. She keeps coming by me and licking my tears. How did I get so attached to Chris? When had all this happened? I want him back in my life. But how do you force somebody to be in your life when they walk away without a backward glance?

Friday evening, Kylie says, "You look like death, and I'm sick of seeing you moping around. I will not have my best friend feel sorry for herself over some guy. We are going out tonight. You will go out, and you will have fun. You are going to flirt with guys, and forget about that one guy whose name will not be mentioned anymore. You're going to wear a hot outfit and go out there with a new attitude. Do I make myself clear?"

I don't want to go out. I want to lie in my bed, bury myself under the blankets, and feel sorry for myself some more. I sigh. I know Kylie is right. Maybe redirecting my attention on other people might help me stop moping over Chris.

Taking a deep breath, I get my butt off of the sofa, and say, "Ok, Kylie, you're right."

That night we go to the local dance club. I have my fitted colorful mini-dress on, with my three-inch heels. The dress is very flattering, and is splashed with deep rich colors, which perfectly suit my skin tone. It's one of the dresses that my mom had bought me and I never wore until now. I feel beautiful and confident in it. I'm glad Kylie talked me into going out.

My hair is down, and loose, with big curls. It looks wild, and I'm glad, because I want to feel wild tonight. I put on a little more makeup than usual. I make my eyes look more almond shaped and I thicken my already long eyelashes. I even have some eye shadow on, which makes my eyes appear mysterious. I use a darker shade of lip-gloss to emphasize my full lips. I put on some long earrings, and a matching bracelet.

Tonight is going to be a new beginning for me. The over-cautious, over-analyzing, always doing the right thing Tess, is gone. I'm going to let loose and enjoy myself. Tonight, I'm not going to think about anything else but having fun.

Even Kylie is in awe at my appearance. Before we walk out, she says to me, "You have no idea how beautiful you are, Tess. You look beyond stunning."

Kylie and I hit the dance floor immediately. Within five minutes of dancing, we have a group of guys swarming around us, dancing with us. After a few dances, we take a break and get some drinks. Some of the guys offer to buy us drinks, but we decline. It's tempting to drink some alcohol tonight to help me forget. But I can't get myself to do it. It doesn't feel right. Besides, I don't need to drink alcohol to let loose! Instead, Kylie and I both have Sprite.

After a quick break, we hit the dance floor again. Numerous guys come up to dance with me, and I dance with every single one of them. I just move my body with the music and the atmosphere of the club relaxes me. *Be more spontaneous,* Jack said. Hey, being spontaneous and carefree is fun.

Finally, around eleven o'clock, Kylie says she's starting to get tired and we should head back.

"Oh, Kylie, I'm not ready to go back yet. You can go if you want. I'll head back later. I only have to walk about four blocks." I'm having too much fun to leave now.

"I don't know, Tess. I think I should stay with you," Kylie says warily.

"Trust me, Kylie, I'll be fine. It's not like I've been drinking. I'm totally in control. I can take care of myself," I insist.

"Are you sure, Tess? I don't know about this." Kylie is reluctant to leave me.

"Kylie, I don't want to leave yet. How about this? As soon as you reach our apartment, text me to let me know you're there safe, so I don't worry. And I will text you before I head back, so you have an idea of when to expect me."

"Alright, Tess, sounds good. And if you decide to crash somewhere else tonight, shoot me that text too," Kylie teases.

"Shut up, Kylie," I laugh.

Fifteen minutes later, I receive a text from Kylie, saying she is home safe.

I continue to dance at the club. Josh is at the club as well and to my relief, he is being courteous. He doesn't try to force alcohol down my throat like last time.

"Look, Tess, I'm really embarrassed about my behavior from last time. I'm sorry. I was completely out of line," Josh mumbles, looking apologetic.

"Thanks, Josh. All is forgiven," I smile. I'm glad he takes accountability for his actions. The rest of the night, Josh and I dance together.

"You're gorgeous, Tess. You especially look stunning tonight. I've never met anybody with such a rare beauty like you," he says in my ear as we dance.

"Wow, thank you, Josh!" I respond with a grin. I don't care if they're lines; it still makes me feel good. And Josh is a good-looking guy, so why not? He has brown hair and brown eyes. He has a nice body, and a nice smile with dimples. Yeah, I can get used to attention from a good-looking guy like Josh.

Finally, when the club ends, he says, "Come on, I'll walk you back to your apartment so you don't have to walk alone."

"Ok," I say, relieved that I don't have to walk back by myself. "Thanks, Josh."

During our walk, Josh asks, "Did you have fun? I like to see you let loose and enjoying yourself."

"Yeah, it was a lot of fun, Josh. Thank you," I reply politely.

"You look really hot tonight, Tess," Josh continues.

"Um, thanks, Josh," I answer, looking around me. I notice the street is deserted. I can't believe that nobody is around. Josh reaches for my hand to hold it. I really don't want to hold his hand, so I slip out of it. When we walk further, he tries to put his arm around my shoulder. I'm beginning to feel uncomfortable. I sort of wiggle out of that as well. What is he doing? It's making me uneasy.

Suddenly, he stops me by grabbing my arm and says, "What's wrong with you? Why are you brushing me off?"

"What?" I ask. "What are you talking about, Josh?"

"You were totally leading me on at that club," Josh accuses.

"What? We were dancing, Josh. I was not leading you on," I explain, wanting to clarify this to him.

"You were all up on me. Don't think I don't know how to read your signals," he says angrily.

"No, Josh, you misunderstood." Now I wish that I walked back alone to the apartment. Better yet, maybe I should have left with Kylie.

All of a sudden, he grabs me tighter and yells, "Nobody leads me on!"

Before I can react, he puts his mouth on me. It's disgusting. He smells like beer, his lips are hard and brutal. His grip on me is tight. I try to push him off of me, but he's too strong. He pushes me into the alley next to the building we walked past. He keeps trying to force his nasty tongue into my mouth.

I start to push harder and shake my head to get out of his hold. Somehow, I get my mouth away from him to say, "Stop, what are you doing? Let me go!" I'm mad, but I'm also starting to get scared.

"Shut up, bitch! You fucking deserve this. You asked for it. This is what you wanted all along." Josh sounds crazy.

Next thing I know, I'm on the ground, and he's on top of me. This cannot be happening. God, I have to get out of this situation. I try to scratch him and bite him. He then hits me, hard, on the left side of my face. That hurt! Nobody has ever hit me. Even my parents never spanked me. I'm shocked. I know I'm losing control of this situation. I can't get his nasty mouth off of me, so I can't even scream. I muster up my strength to try to push him off of me. He's too heavy. I try to kick him, but his legs are wrapped over mine, restricting any movements from my legs.

Oh my god, how did I get myself into this? I have to do something to get out of this mess! Is he really going to try to rape me? I get my answer. I hear him pulling the zipper of his jeans down. Then, I feel his filthy hands all over my breasts. I feel nauseated with disgust and fear. He tries to pull my dress off of my shoulder, but because it's so tight, he has difficulty getting it off. I struggle even harder. I start shaking, terrified as the situation continues to get worse. I don't want to get raped. Please God, not like this. The more I struggle, the more pressure he puts on my body. I feel the burning on my back as my body scrapes against the concrete floor. I panic even more when I feel him pull my dress up.

"You're going to like this, bitch!" he says against my mouth. I try to squeeze my legs tighter as he tries to spread them. "You want a fight? Hell yeah, it just turns me on more."

His disgusting words against my mouth are making me

feel like I'm going to vomit. As I struggle and moan in pain, I start to cry. Is he going to kill me after this horrible ordeal is over? When I feel him trying to get my panties out of the way, I know it's over. I know that I'm just a helpless victim and he's going to have his way with me. I remember thinking about all of the advice my dad had given me about safety. *I'm sorry, Daddy, I made bad choices tonight.*

"I'm about to rock your world, baby! Hell yeah, you are so hot. And I'm so fucking turned on!" Josh continues his filthy words against my mouth as he brutally keeps trying to kiss me. By now, I feel defeated. There is nothing I can do to get out of this nightmare. There is nothing left in me. I'm crying and I start shaking like a helpless prey cornered by the evil predator. My body goes limp as I prepare for the inevitable.

Suddenly, his weight is pulled off of me. I open my eyes, and there's Josh, and he's being held up by his shirt... It's Chris! Chris is here, holding Josh off of me! Chris is standing over me, so furious that smoke is practically coming out of his ears; he looks like the devil himself. I exhale a deep sigh of relief, because devil or not, I have never felt safer.

"You disgusting bastard! I'm going to kill you!" Chris says venomously. His voice is even scary to me. Josh tries to swing at him. Chris blocks him. Then Chris throws Josh to the ground.

"What the fuck! Ok, bring it. I'm a black belt in karate, Chris. You don't know what you're getting yourself into. This is not your business!" Josh yells.

Chris doesn't say one word. Instead, he kneels down to check on me. He's taking deep breaths, and I know he's doing everything in his power to control himself. Josh tries to jump on him from the back but Chris throws him off easily, as if he's swatting a fly.

At that moment, I see a side of Chris I've never seen before. Every time Josh tries to swing or kick Chris, he easily deflects the strikes. I'm in awe at his quick reflexes. I notice that even Josh is shocked. Then, just as quickly, Chris switches to offense mode. He swings and kicks. Before Josh can register what's happening, he's knocked out cold. Chris's movements are lightning fast! I don't even know what happened. All I know is that Josh is lying on the floor, not moving.

Chris is still furious as he walks over to Josh to finish the job, as if to finish him off for good. I pull myself into sitting position. I have to stop him.

"Chris, please no. Don't," I whimper hoarsely. Somehow he hears me and it snaps him back to reality. He turns to look at me, and then at Josh who's out cold. Chris stands still for a few seconds as if to calm himself down, and I watch him as he kneels down to check Josh's pulse. He gets back up and comes by me. He tries to pull my dress down, attempting to help cover me better. My dress is ripped so it's useless. He takes his jacket off and puts it on me. I'm still shaking. Chris picks me up in his arms like a baby, and holds me against him. He doesn't say one word. He just carries me all the way to my apartment. He uses the entrance from my parking lot to avoid any unnecessary questions from the doorman.

When we get into my apartment, Kylie is wide-awake. She comes running to us, screaming, "What in the world? What happened? Why didn't you text me? I've been worried sick."

"She's ok," Chris replies. "Call Josh's frat brothers and tell them to get him from the alley by First Street. Tell them he is passed out cold."

"What? Did Josh do this to you, Tess? I'm calling the police!" Kylie cries. She is very upset. I have no energy to reply back to her.

"No need. Trust me, he won't be bothering Tess again," Chris answers her.

Chris takes me into my bedroom and lies me down on my bed. Gem comes running to me to check on me. She starts whimpering and then growling, knowing somebody has done this to me. I give her a brave smile. "I'll be ok, girl," I say in a shaky voice.

Gem runs to Chris and starts to whimper to him. He kneels down in front of her and looks at her dead in the eyes, and says, "Don't worry, I handled it. And I'll make sure she's ok." I see Gem lick his hand, as if thanking him. I just want to cry.

Instead, I lie there in shock. My whole body shudders as my mind keeps replaying the events of the night, and how bad it would have been if Chris hadn't been there.

"You need a bath, Tessnia. Come on, I'll help you," Chris says softly.

I vaguely remember him taking his jacket off of me first, and then the dress. He had already run the water in the bathtub. He brings my towel to my bed. He gently takes my bra and panties off. I don't even move. I let him do it all because I know he's going to make sure I'm ok. Chris is going to take care of me. I completely trust him. He saved me tonight. He may have looked like the devil ready to kill, but he was my guardian angel, my protector.

He wraps the towel around me and carries me to the bathtub. Chris gently lowers me down into it. He takes the soap and the washcloth and softly rubs the lather into me. He washes off all of the dirt and the mud, while he gently rubs over the scratches. As he looks down at the bruises, his lips close into a thin line, and his jaw clenches tight.

"I should have killed him," he whispers. I'm too numb to say anything. He gently washes my face and I wince when he touches my left cheek. "Sorry, Tessnia. You are swollen here. It looks like that son of a bitch hit you in the face. I'm just trying to clean you up." Chris takes the shampoo and washes my hair and then rinses it out. He gently massages my scalp, and I slowly give myself to him as I begin to relax a bit.

Chris carries me out of the tub and has me stand on the bathroom rug. He takes the towel and wraps it around me, and with the other towel, he dries my hair.

He picks me back up and brings me into my bed. I hear him opening my drawers, searching for something. He must have found what he was looking for, because he comes back to my bed and helps put my panties, tank top, and my pajama bottoms on me. Afterwards, he helps me lie back down, and covers me with my blanket. I'm still shaking.

He holds my chin and turns my face toward him as he stands over my bed. He examines me with his deep, penetrating gaze. "You haven't said a word. Tell me you're going to be ok. Look at me and say it."

I look up at him. Before I can respond, Kylie knocks on the door. "Can I please check on Tess? I'm really worried."

Chris looks at me for permission. I nod my head, and he walks to the door. As Chris opens the door, Kylie rushes to me and sits on my bed. She winces when she sees the bruise on my face.

"Tess is strong. She's going to be fine," Chris says to her.

Ignoring Chris, Kylie says, "Tess, are you ok?"

I nod.

"What happened? This is crazy!" Kylie is frantic.

I turn to Chris and notice he is putting his jacket on. "Are you leaving?" I ask softly.

"I think so. I'll call you first thing in the morning. But first, I need to know you're going to be ok," Chris insists.

"No, stay. Please stay. I need you to stay, Chris," I beg.

Chris looks at Kylie and me hesitantly, not knowing how to respond.

Kylie gets up from the bed and says, "Chris, you need to stay. You're the one who can help her." She leans over and kisses my forehead. "Let me know if you need anything, Tess," she whispers to me and walks out of my room, closing the door behind her.

I turn my attention on Chris and notice he still has his jacket on. I don't want him to leave. Just his presence makes me feel safe and protected. I start to panic. "Please," I beg. My voice is shaky again and I feel the tears gather in my eyes.

"Hey, hey, it's ok. Look, I'm right here," he says. He gets into my bed and gathers me into his arms. He holds me for a few minutes. Then, he shifts his weight and stands up again.

"No," I whimper.

"I'm just taking my jacket off, see?" Chris says gently. His eyes are soft. After he takes his jacket and shoes off, he crawls back into my bed. He gets under the cover and pulls me into his arms. I bury my face into his chest. As I relax, the tension starts to ease off of me. He brushes his fingers through my hair. After a few minutes, he buries his face into my hair and kisses my head. "I'm going to make sure you're ok, Tess. Please just close your eyes and go to sleep. I won't leave, I promise," he whispers softly against my ears. I finally let go, feeling safe in Chris's strong arms. In time, the exhaustion from the night catches up to me, and I sleep.

Ten

It's dark. And she's running. RUN FASTER! She's running even faster. It's getting darker. God, who is chasing her? She can't catch her breath, but she keeps running. She knows something evil is after her. Suddenly, Josh is there. And he's laughing. A horrible, evil laugh, as if he knows she's about to get caught. She runs even harder. She falls. "Get up! Don't stop!" It is Chris's voice, urging her to get back up. She pulls herself up and starts running. Chris's face flashes. He looks desperate, urgent, and forceful. "Keep running!" She runs, and he's still yelling to run faster. But something is different. It is Chris's face, but something about his face is not the same. It's his eyes. They are strong and powerful. And they are gray.

I wake up with a start and sit up. I'm gasping, and I begin shaking. The room is spinning. I attempt to breathe deep in order to calm down. It doesn't help, and I shake more. I get startled when I feel somebody's arm on me. When I look, I see that it's Chris sitting up next to me.

"Hey, what's wrong? It's ok. It's going to be ok," he says in a comforting voice. At that instant, the awful events from the night flash before my eyes. I shiver. Chris pulls me closer to him and wraps his arms around me, but I resist and tense up. "What's wrong, Tess? Talk to me." Chris says, sounding worried.

I sigh and explain, "I have these dreams--nightmares, actually. I've had them for as long as I can remember. But they're always the same. A girl is running in these dreams and something or someone is chasing her. For her to escape, she has to run as fast as she can. I wake up right before she is caught. They scare the hell out of me because I can feel everything that the girl is feeling." I shudder, hating to talk about my dreams.

"Have you ever seen the girl? Any traits of her?" Chris asks, deep in thought.

"No, I never see the girl," I say slowly, shaking my head.

"Do you see anybody else in these dreams?" Chris questions, with a slight frown on his forehead.

I hesitate at first. Then, avoiding his gaze, I slowly mumble, "Yeah, I do. Sometimes you're in it, yelling to run faster. Tonight, Josh was in it, laughing because the girl was almost caught. But then you were also in it, encouraging to not give-up. It was you, but you kind of looked different. And that woke me up."

"Hmm, I see. What do you think these dreams mean?" Chris asks, his frown deepening.

"I don't know. To be honest, I don't even want to know," I reply and I put my fingers on my temple. My head is spinning even more.

"I think dreams mean something. I think it's usually your subconscious talking to you. Do you think this girl is you? Are you trying to get away from something?" Chris asks.

"No! At least, I don't think so. But I feel everything that she's feeling. I can even feel her fear," I slowly reply.

"Ok, maybe they're premonitions. You know something about the future?" Chris suggests.

"What? I hope not. God, that would be really scary if that's the case," I say, frightened at the thought of my dreams becoming a reality. "Don't say that."

"Ok, come here. Look, I'm just thinking of what they could possibly mean, that's all. Let's drop it, ok?" Chris pulls me tighter into his arms, and we lie back down. Instantly, I feel myself relax. I have no idea how he does that. Just his touch makes me want to melt into his arms.

"When I saw that good-for-nothing bastard on you like that, I wanted to kill him. I almost did. It was your voice that stopped me. God help me, Tess, I would have killed him," Chris whispers, as his muscles start to tense up.

"Chris, how did you know? How did you find me in that alley?" Now that I'm able to think more clearly, I wonder how he showed up when I needed him.

Chris caresses my back as he holds me. "I was at that club, Tessnia. I go there occasionally to unwind. So by coincidence, I already was there. Then, I saw you walk in. And you had that skimpy dress on, clinging to your body. You looked so wild and carefree. I almost walked out. I've been trying to keep my distance, as you know." Chris pauses, thinking about the night. "But then you jumped right on the dance floor with your friend. And I saw how all those guys were swarming around you like some hungry wolves. I didn't like it. I couldn't leave. When I saw that pig hanging on to you again, I knew I should just keep an eye on him. I didn't trust him from the previous incident at the frat party. So when you left with him, I was furious. Why would you trust a loser like him?" Chris sighs in frustration.

"I don't know why, Chris. I was being stupid," I reply, shaking my head. I'm still angry with myself for that decision.

Chris hugs me tighter and says, "Well, needless to say, I

followed. But I didn't want to look too suspicious, so I waited a few minutes before following you. I think I must have waited too long because I couldn't find you when I came out of the club. I started to panic. I didn't trust him, Tess, and I didn't want you to be alone with him too long. I started scouring the area and finally started running toward your apartment," Chris says, taking a deep breath. He pulls me closer into his arms and says, "And then I saw you guys when I passed that alley. Seeing you buried under him like that, it nearly killed me, Tess! I was beyond furious!" Chris shudders in anger. He reaches out and gently caresses my bruised cheek.

"Chris, how did you learn to fight like that?" I remember his quick reflexes and his incredible moves he had used against Josh. Chris doesn't respond. I lift my head to look at him. I sigh and shake my head. "I don't understand why you're always so secretive."

He remains silent for a few minutes, but he doesn't look away. Finally, he sighs too, and says, "There's a lot you don't know about me and it's best that way. Look, it's late. And you need your rest. Please, get some sleep, Tessnia." Chris brings me back into his embrace. He isn't going to share any of his secrets with me. I know nothing about him, but I know lying here in his arms, feels right.

"Ok, no more questions. Thank you. Thank you for everything you did for me tonight. I don't even know how I could ever repay you for all you did." I'm so grateful to have Chris in my life.

"Don't say that. I'm just mad I didn't get there faster," Chris replies.

"It was horrible. He was filthy and mean. God Chris, his

hands and his disgusting mouth..." I shiver thinking about it.

"Stop, please. If I could take your pain away, Tessnia, I would. I can't bear to hear this," Chris says, as he shudders. I look up at him. He whispers, "You have no idea the effect you have on me, Tessnia. The thought of anybody hurting you, ever... I swear, Tess." And then he gives me a very gentle, soft kiss on my lips. My lips automatically melt under his, and I instantly respond. It makes me feel safe and secure. To my disappointment, it doesn't last. He pulls away, and then kisses my forehead.

"Sleep. You need to sleep." I *am* exhausted. I sigh and snuggle closer to him. Eventually, I fall asleep.

The next morning, when I wake up, Chris is sitting on the chair in my room. He's watching me. Suddenly, I feel shy. It's strange. I felt so close to him last night. But now with the distance between us, it feels different.

I slowly whisper, "Hey."

"Good morning," Chris replies, his tone distant.

"I'm going to run to the bathroom real quick," I say and make my escape. What is going on? Why am I acting like this? I guess reality of everything from last night is finally sinking in.

I brush my teeth, and look in the mirror. I gasp. My left cheek is swollen and covered with a red and purple bruise. Splashing my face with cold water, I go over in my head the events from last night with Chris. I remember how he had seen me naked and a wave of shock and pleasure cascades over me. I curl my lips in and remember how he'd kissed me softly and tenderly. Finally, as I dry my face with a towel, I think about how distant he seemed this morning and how upset I was that he hadn't let me wake up in his arms. Leaving the towel on the sink, I turn the doorknob and open the door. When I enter my room, I see he's still sitting in the chair as if in contemplation.

Taking a deep breath, I say to him, "Chris, I really want to thank you again for last night." I figure this is a good place to start. Besides, how can I possibly thank him enough for what he did for me? Chris doesn't say anything. He just lifts his one eyebrow, and keeps staring back at me, with that same intent look. I start fidgeting with my hands as I'm starting to feel nervous. I look down at my hands, unable to look at him. Why is this so awkward? Finally, I mumble, "Why are you so quiet?"

"I'm just thinking, Tessnia, that's all," he replies, his tone impersonal.

"What are you thinking about?" I ask, almost afraid of the answer.

"I was wondering why you didn't fight that bastard off of you last night," Chris answers.

"I tried, Chris. You don't think I tried? He was too strong," I respond, bewildered.

"You're stronger and quicker! You didn't try hard enough!" Chris insists.

"Did you not notice how he had me pinned down? I tried to struggle but I couldn't move! I'm definitely not stronger than him. Do you think I liked him on top of me like that? Do you know his nasty hands were all over me?" I ask incredulously. What is Chris insinuating?

"No! I don't think you liked it!" Chris yells. "That's not what I'm saying. What I'm saying is that you froze up. When I walked up, you looked like a helpless, trapped rabbit, about to get devoured by the big bad wolf. You gave up, Tess." I glare at him, shocked that he truly believes that I just gave up.

"Unbelievable! Why are you saying all this? I did not ask for what happened to me!" I yell.

Chris jumps up off his chair and starts to walk toward me. I can tell he's angry. Instinctively, I step back to keep some distance between us. I can't think clearly whenever he gets too close to me.

"Why am I saying this? Because, Tess, what are you going to do if something like this happens again? You're just going to give up? You could have screamed. You could have run. I know you can outrun that son of a bitch. You could have fought him. I know you don't think you can fight, but trust me, you are stronger than you think. You just have to learn to use it. You can *not* give up like that, ever! Do you hear me?" Suddenly, Chris is right in front of me and I have nowhere to go. I try to walk around him but he grabs my arm. "Tell me that you understand. Promise me that you won't give up like that."

"Stop it, Chris. You are starting to scare me!" What does he expect from me? I tried to do everything in my power to fight that bastard off.

"Scare you? Are you kidding me? Are you even listening to a word I'm saying to you? You drive me up the wall! Why don't you ever listen?"

And then, his lips possess mine. But this time, it's not like last night. This kiss is not gentle and sweet. It's full of frustration and anger. To my dismay, my body betrays me. My lips open up automatically, and my body starts to respond. He somehow leads me back into my bed, and he's on top of me. And the kiss changes from anger, to passion. I can feel his hard body against me. He is aroused, and I respond. My back arches so that my hips can be closer to his hardness. A moan escapes me. I want him right now.

Chris moves his lips to my neck. As he kisses my neck, my fingers tangle into his hair. I feel his tongue on my neck, and I arch my back, rubbing my hips into him. His breathing changes, and I feel his hand on my belly. Slowly and seductively his hand begins exploring under my shirt. The anticipation is driving me wild. As his hand finds my breast, I can't hold back another moan. Since I don't have a bra on, he has full access to my breasts. God, I'm so turned on, as he begins playing with my nipples.

Chris attacks my lips as he continues to explore my breasts. As our tongues dance together, I tug on his shirt. I want to feel his hard chest against me. He pulls his t-shirt off and all I can do is stare at his magnificent body in awe. My hands reach to touch his tight six-pack stomach and then his chiseled chest. He is perfect. In the next instant, my tank top is pulled off of me. I open my eyes to look at him when he stops kissing me. Chris is staring down at me, his eyes full of passion.

"God, you're beautiful," he says, and he buries his face into my breasts. I hold my breath, as he sucks. I've never experienced such a sensation! I feel like I'm going to burst. I press his head down into my chest even harder. He's playing with one of my breast with his mouth, and the other with his hand. The sensation is too much!

"Chris, please. I'm going crazy." Somehow, I get the words out. My voice sounds so husky, that I don't even recognize it.

"Mm, you are delicious," he whispers, as he sucks even harder, his tongue playing on my nipple. Another moan escapes me, this one louder. I'm going insane!

I feel him pull my pajama pants off of me and his hand ends up between my legs. I want to scream! What is going on? Oh my god, I'm going to burst.

"Ah, Chris," I say breathlessly.

"You have no idea what that does for me. Hearing you scream for me is a total turn-on," Chris whispers.

"I'm going crazy, Chris, please," I whisper. Sensations are traveling through my body that I've never experienced before.

"Please? You need a release, Tessnia. And I'm going to give it to you." I have no idea what he's talking about. But I don't care. Chris is in control, and I have no problem with that. He knows what he's doing, and it feels too good. "Do you know how long I have dreamed about this? I've wanted you in my arms squirming for me for so long. Do you want this, Tessnia?"

"Yes, Chris, I do. I want you--right now," I beg. I want him to continue with whatever he's doing to me. It's driving me wild.

Suddenly, I feel his hand in my panties. First, he puts his entire palm against my naked flesh. "So soft and warm...and wet, Tessnia," he whispers. "Just the way I imagined it."

And then his finger is right *there,* where I'm the most sensitive. I gasp for air and then hold my breath. Chris moves his finger up and down, slowly and deliberately. His finger plays with me as his mouth is still working on my breasts.

My breathing becomes even more erratic, as I completely lose control of myself.

"Ah," I sigh. God, all these sensations are too much. I'm on edge. "Chris!" This is all I can muster out. I'm practically wiggling under him, feeling as if I'm going to explode.

"Shh, baby, just wait. This is only going to get better." Better? How can that even be possible? It already feels like I'm in heaven. As Chris moves down, his lips reach my belly. He plays with my navel with his tongue, and instinctively, my pelvis arches. I feel him pull my panties off of me. "Mm, so beautiful. I'm going to taste you now, Tessnia. I have fantasized this over and over." Taste me? Before I can process what he said, his mouth is buried into me.

"Ah, Chris!" I scream. What is he doing to me? I bite my lower lip as I feel his tongue inside me. I can't take it anymore. I start to move against his tongue as he devours me. He is relentless, and I can't hold back anymore. I let it all go. I scream, "Chris!"

I lose it. I reach my peak and let myself go. I fall, and what a wonderful experience it is! Chris guides my fall all the way down. It's the most unforgettable intimacy I've ever imagined. Chris does not stop until I finally come back down to Earth.

Chris pulls himself up and kisses me passionately. He looks down at me, and raises his one eyebrow, slowly flashing his lopsided smile. "You take my breath away, my beautiful Tessnia."

I start to get embarrassed. God, I'm a vixen. Who knew? I smile back and bury my face into his neck. "I'm embarrassed," I say shyly.

"Why are you embarrassed? You are perfect. Do you have

any idea how gorgeous you are? The other weekend when you had gone to visit that guy, I went mad! The thought of you with another guy! God, Tess, I thought I was going to kill somebody. You have no idea of the power you have over me." I sneak a peek up at Chris and he's smiling down at me.

"You don't have to worry about any of that, Chris. I've never done any of this," I whisper shyly into his neck. "Tell me what to do. Tell me what feels good to you." I bury my face deeper into his neck, hiding from embarrassment.

Chris freezes. If I didn't know better, I would think that he stopped breathing. I feel him tense up. "What do you mean? You've never..."

"Never! I mean a few kisses here and there, and that's all. This is all so...Never!" I say, shaking my head.

Chris doesn't move. I glance up at him. He frowns and stares off in space. I feel him shifting. He's moving away from me. I try to hold him tighter but he releases my hands from around him and rolls off of the bed.

"What's wrong?" I ask. I'm confused. What did I do wrong? Chris shakes his head and sighs. He runs his fingers through his hair, as if frustrated. He then leans forward, and covers me with my blanket. I blush as I realize that I'm stark naked. Chris is already putting his t-shirt on. Clearly, he's done. "What's wrong?" I try once more.

"I'm sorry, Tessnia. You don't deserve this. When I'm around you, I don't think clearly. I lose all control and make stupid choices," Chris responds, sounding somber.

"I don't understand. Did I do something wrong?" I'm baffled. One minute he's telling me he can't get enough of me. The next minute, he's moving away, saying it's all a mistake.

"No! Please, *I'm* the screw up. You're a good person. You are so innocent, so naïve. God, I'm so sorry. I didn't realize. It's my fault." Chris is rambling to himself as he begins pacing back and forth. Clearly, he's trying to find the right words to explain why he's walking away, once again.

"So, because I haven't been with another guy, you're leaving? I mean, that's not me. I don't just hook up with whomever. If it didn't feel right, I didn't pursue it. This, you and me, felt right. I was waiting for the right guy, Chris," I explain. Why doesn't he understand that?

"Tess, I am not the *right* guy, trust me. As a matter of fact, I'm the wrong guy for you. You don't even know me. God, what have I done? Look, I can't really explain it, but you have to trust me. I am not that guy who you think I am," Chris sighs, running his fingers through his hair again. "You need to keep your distance from me." Chris sounds desperate for me to understand.

"You know what, Chris? You're right; I don't know you. All I know is that when I'm with you, it *feels* right. I know it doesn't make sense. It doesn't make sense to me either. When I didn't see you the last couple of weeks, I literally went through depression. I missed you. And that's not me. I don't get attached to people. But I'm not going to be afraid of my feelings anymore. I don't know what's going on with us, and I certainly don't know who you are, especially when you say crazy things like this. But I do know that I love being with you. And I'm not scared to admit that to you--not anymore." There! I finally come to terms with my feelings. I want to just lay it all out there. At least, I know that I didn't hold back.

Chris sighs in frustration. "Look, this is getting out of

hand. I never wanted to let it get to this point. And God only knows that I fought for so long to avoid this. And here I was, in your bed, selfishly taking everything you wanted to give me. I can't do that to you."

"Are you kidding me? You're going to give me the line, '*It's not you, it's me?'* Please don't treat me like a complete idiot, Chris!" I'm humiliated!

Chris shakes his head. He then rubs his forehead as if he's having difficulty finding the right words. "Look, you're not going to understand, ok? Just promise me one thing. I don't know what the future is going to bring, but promise me you'll always look out for yourself. You're too nice, too gullible. I want you to learn to trust your instincts. I don't want you to trust anybody. You always need to be smart about your choices. Here you are, trusting me with everything, and you don't know me at all. Tessnia, please, I need you to hear me on this. Promise me," Chris says, exasperated.

"Wow, that sounds like a goodbye," I whisper.

"I told you I don't know what the future is going to bring. And I have to do the right thing here. You need to live your life, without me in it. You have a good life, Tessnia. Actually you have a great life. And I would never take that away from you. You are too important. I know nothing makes sense right now, and maybe it never will. I don't know. But I need you to promise me that you will take care of yourself." Chris sounds desperate.

"I always take care of myself," I reply, confused at where this is going. "Look, if this is your way of breaking things off with me, just have the guts to say it. Spare me all this crap of you not being good enough for me. Damn you, Chris. I just poured my heart out to you. Like I said, have enough respect for me to just be honest. Once you walk out of this door, is it over? You're not going to call me or contact me, are you?" I'm getting upset, knowing the answer.

"Tess, I..."

"Just say it, damn it!" I yell at him.

Chris brushes his hand through his hair. Then, he takes a deep breath, and says, "No, I won't be calling you, Tessnia. You won't be hearing from me again." He then turns, grabs his jacket, and walks out of my bedroom.

I stare at the ceiling for a long time after he walks out. Eventually, I sob into my pillow until there are no more tears left. I'm emotionally drained. I know Chris enough to know that he meant what he said to me about not trying to contact me again. At that moment, it feels like I lost my best friend.

Eleven

When I finally come out of my room, it's the afternoon already. Thankfully, Kylie already took Gem out in the morning. I feel terrible. What a night! I want to erase everything from last night except for my precious moments with Chris. I don't want that erased. Even though he doesn't want anything to do with me, I'm not ready to let it go. I want to remember the tender way he bathed me, and how he made me feel safe in his arms. I cherish the way he held me all night, reassuring me that everything will be ok. I remember our passion, how he wanted me as much as I wanted him, and finally his bittersweet goodbye.

"I'm glad you're finally out of your room, Tess. Now can you *please* tell me what the hell is going on?" Kylie demands.

"A lot happened last night, Kylie. I can't even talk about it right now," I mumble, shaking my head. "I have a huge headache."

"Ok, fair enough. Just tell me you're ok. Did Josh hit you on your face and give you that bruise?" Kylie walks closer to me to get a better look at the bruise.

"Yes, I will be ok. And yes, it was Josh," I answer.

"Bastard! He called me couple of hours ago. He said to tell you and your boyfriend to stay away from him. He said he can file charges against Chris, but he's willing to forget everything about last night, if you do the same," Kylie says.

"Wow, the nerve of this guy. Unbelievable! Well, I don't

know if he would have anything against Chris, but Chris did beat him down pretty good. I don't want any more problems. I just want the whole nightmare behind me. And I don't want unnecessary attention on Chris when he was just trying to help me. Whatever, as long as that scum stays away from me, I'm willing to let it go," I say. I shudder at the thought of what almost could have happened last night.

"Tess, I'm so sorry. Please know that I'm always here for you. Please talk to me when you're ready. Chris stormed out of here earlier. Is everything ok with you guys?" Kylie asks, full of concern.

"No, we're done. It's over. Again, I can't talk about this right now," I mumble. I don't want to start crying all over again.

"Hey, I get it, Tess. Look, I made you some lunch. Why don't you eat something, jump in the shower, and you might feel better. Also, the Talent Bar down the street is having local talent perform on stage impromptu. I thought that might help get your mind off of things. It will be low-key. Maybe we can walk over there for a couple of hours? It starts like at seven or so. Do you want to get out of here for a bit?" Kylie suggests.

"I'm done going out for a while, Kylie. I think I'm just going to study here in the apartment." I don't have any desire to see anybody.

"Ok, I'll stay with you then," Kylie says without a second thought. She's so sweet, and always trying to take care of me. I can't expect her to stop having her fun just because I'm in a miserable place.

"No, I think it'll be nice to be alone, Kylie. Sorry, I'm just a mess right now," I reply. "I'm going to take Gem for a run soon. It will do me some good to run as well. Maybe it will help to clear my mind."

Gem and I run together for a long time. It feels good to have the wind rushing past my face and to push my body to the point of exhaustion. I want to run away from everything, from my problems, from Chris… if only for a little while. I hear the sound of the redwood trees rustling in the refreshing breeze. It's nice to become one with it all, and I lose track of time. It's all very exhilarating, and I do feel a little bit better. Gem is always great at cheering me up. As the sun begins to set, we reluctantly head back to the apartment.

When I return, Kylie is getting ready to go to the Talent Bar. She looks cute with her miniskirt and her leather jacket on. Before she walks out, she asks me once more, "Are you sure you won't change your mind, Tess?"

"No, I'm good. Just text and let me know when you get there, and when you're planning on returning. And have fun," I say to her. I get up and give her a hug because I want her to stop worrying about me. She hugs me back.

"You're my best friend, Tess. Whatever you need, I'm here," she says slowly.

"I know, Kylie. And thanks," I reply. "Now go have some fun, will you?"

Kylie laughs and heads out.

After Kylie texts me that she's there, I jump in the shower. Then I sit at the kitchen table, and preoccupy myself with my homework. I need to keep my mind busy and not think about anything else. I know waiting for a call that's not going to come is useless.

A little past 7:30, my phone gets another text. I notice that it's from Kylie.

"OMG get your butt over here, Tess. Chris is here."

"What?" I text. What the hell is Chris doing there?

"He's here!"

"What????" I'm so confused. Maybe Kylie is wrong. Why would he be two blocks away from my apartment? He left, giving me the impression that he's going to stay away from everything and everybody for a while.

"Stop saying what! Just get your ass over here!!!!!"

"I'm on my way!"

My heart is racing as I jump up and quickly change out of my sweats. I climb into a pair of faded, skinny blue jeans with a brown leather belt and put a tan colored blouse on. There's no time to get ready. I look in the mirror. Wow! That bruise on my cheek looks *really* bad. I try to put some powder cover-up to help hide it. The makeup does help a little. I quickly put some mascara and lip-gloss on. I keep my hair down and curly, hoping to cover that side of my face. I look at my reflection, and shrug my shoulders. This is the best I can do. I grab my brown short jacket, and put on my short brown boots.

The whole time while I'm running to the bar, my heart is racing and I can't stop thinking about what Chris is doing there. I tell myself that I'll stay in the back corner once I get there so he doesn't notice me. The last thing I want, is for him to think that I ran over there just to see him. Even though I am doing just that, my pride won't allow it. I want to see him. I don't care if that sounds pathetic.

When I walk in, the place is really crowded. I text Kylie to let her know that I'm in the back. Within minutes, she comes and finds me.

"When I saw him sitting at the bar, Tess, I knew you'd want to see him again," Kylie says excitedly.

I search to find Chris but I can't see him. My stomach is in knots. I'm so nervous. And although I really don't want him to know I'm here, I try to scoot up closer to the front. I know I can't leave until I see him! Where is he?

I'm still trying to locate Chris by the bar, when the announcer says, "We now have a new singer with us tonight, ladies and gentlemen. Let's give Mr. Chris Jones a warm welcome, everybody."

My head flings to the stage, shocked, and I see Chris walking up. He sits down on the chair in center stage, slings a guitar around his chest, and begins tuning the chords. As he adjusts the microphone and licks his lips, I take in everything about him--from his tousled, honey blonde waves, to his faded denim jeans, and to his fitted gray t-shirt. He does not look up once.

Chris clears his throat and speaks into the microphone. "I had to make one of the toughest decisions of my life today. This song, *Leave Out All The Rest*, says it all." His voice is full of sorrow, so resolved. Just hearing his voice makes me tremble. I hold my breath as he starts to sing.

Chris is singing *Leave Out All The Rest* by Linkin Park. He has really slowed down the rhythm, singing his own version of the song. It's just his voice and his guitar. It's breathtakingly beautiful. My heart is beating so fast, as I'm drawn to his voice, to the stroke of his guitar.

As his singing continues, the entire room has become quiet. Chris has captivated the whole crowd to him and his singing. I realize the words of the song are meant for me.

My whole world starts spinning. Could this be possible? I go back in time. Oh my god! I start visibly shaking as he keeps singing. He never looks up. He just keeps singing, and I am unable to move, to even breathe.

With each line he sings, my head spins more. I become nauseated, and I'm gasping for air. I vaguely remember Kylie asking if I'm ok. Chris then slows down his singing, lowers his voice, and is barely playing his guitar. He sings the last verse into the mic, his heart and soul open to the world.

I can barely keep standing there. My legs are shaking uncontrollably. I have to get out of here. As I'm trying to process what is happening, suddenly Chris looks up, right at me. With both my hands clasped over my mouth in utter shock, I'm incapable of looking away. He stares right into me. He stares with gray piercing eyes, deep into my soul, willing me to see what is right in front of me. I gasp. No, it can't be possible. Tears pour from my eyes, and my skin drains of color.

I have to leave, *right now*! I turn and run to the exit. I have to get out of there. I can't breathe. I need air. Somehow, I push my way through the crowd, and out of the front door. I run out and I keep running. Oh my god, oh my god, oh my god. Please, somebody explain what is going on. I don't even know if I'm screaming this out loud or if it's all in my mind. I feel completely lost.

"Tess, Tess, are you ok? What's wrong? Talk to me." Kylie has caught up to me. She grabs me and starts shaking me. "Why are you crying?"

I'm hysterical, unable to catch my breath to answer her. I keep shaking my head, sobbing.

"Oh, Tess. Please tell me," Kylie begs, confused. Without releasing me, she continues shaking me as if to snap me back to reality.

"It's Chris," I mumble, in between my sobs. "It's not Chris. Chris is Joe. Oh Kylie, Chris is Joe!"

"Tess, calm down, ok? You're hysterical. I have no idea what you're talking about," Kylie says, looking worried. She glances toward a crowd of people who has stopped to watch us. "Look, let me get you to the apartment. You can explain everything to me there."

"You don't understand! Chris is Joe! Damn, how did I not know? He's been lying all this time!" I say frantically.

"Take a deep breath, Tess, ok? Please, let's just go back to the apartment. You're not even thinking clearly right now." Kylie puts her arm around me to encourage me to start walking, instead of standing there sobbing uncontrollably.

I pull myself out of her hold. "No, No! I have to find him. I have to go back to the bar and confront him." I turn and start running frantically back to the bar. I have to find out why. Why did he lie all this time? Kylie runs with me. When we get back to the bar, he is no longer on the stage. We look all over the bar, but we don't see Chris. I'm desperate. I have to find him. I need answers!

I run to the bartender. "Excuse me. Where is the guy who sang on stage? Chris Jones? He sang *Leave Out All The Rest?*" Maybe he's in the back.

"Oh yeah, Chris! He was fantastic, wasn't he? He was clearly the crowd's favorite! The whole place exploded with applause when he finished." The bartender chuckles. I'm getting more frustrated because he is not answering my questions!

"Ok, but where is he now?" I interject impatiently.

"Sorry, honey, he left as soon as he was done. He didn't say a word to anybody and just left. There were a lot of good looking ladies sad to see him go, I'll tell you that." The bartender starts laughing even harder. I just want to throw something at him.

"Tess, please. I'm really worried about you. Can we go back to the apartment? Maybe he came there. I know he looked straight at you, so he knew you were here." Kylie is trying to help me think reasonably. I take a deep breath. I tell myself to calm down and try to think clearly. Maybe he did go to my apartment. Maybe he wants to explain everything. Should I call him? No, I have to see him in person. I'm going to force him to look at me in my face and explain what the hell is going on. It can't be a coincidence that I bumped into "Joe" again. He must have known it was me! And why did he lie? Why did he keep lying? No, I have to see him in person.

I start to run toward the apartment. Please, please let him be there. The doorman would have let him come up because he knows Chris by now. I race up the stairs to my apartment. Half expecting to see him standing by my door, a wave of disappointment envelops me when I don't see him.

Kylie unlocks our door, and there's no sign of Chris. Of course not! He probably has no idea what to say to me! What kind of lies can he possibly finagle now?

Gem comes up to me. She starts barking and pushes something from the floor toward me. I look down and notice a folded piece of paper. I pick it up and see the letter. I slowly unfold it with my shaky hands, knowing who it's from, but afraid to read what he has to say.

> ***Dear Tessnia,***
>
> ***I never meant to hurt you. Ever. I can't even express how sorry I am for dragging you into my mess. I have to leave. I don't have a choice. But before I leave, I want you to remember when we first met on your 16th birthday. I want you to know at least that much about me, with the hope that it helps you hold on to some good memories between us. I know you are probably wondering why I never told you the truth. Again, there's probably another time and place for that.***
>
> ***Please remember what I said. Don't trust anybody. But always trust your instincts. Embrace your gifts!***
>
> ***Tessnia, please know that if there is any way that I could spend even one more minute with you, I would in a heartbeat. I never got the chance to even begin to explain what you mean to me. I guess some things are better left unsaid.***
>
> ***Please don't look for me. You won't find me.***
>
> ***Yours always...***

I feel the tears fall from my eyes and they dampen the paper. My lip quivers and my head feels like it's going to burst. He must have slid the letter under the door. I can't even see the words any more. They're blurry. The letter slips from my hand. I stand, motionless for quite some time.

Kylie picks up the letter and I hear her say, "Oh, Tess, what is he talking about?" I start to feel dizzy as the room begins spinning. I vaguely remember Kylie bringing me to the sofa. I sob for at least half an hour while Kylie holds me. Everything was a lie. He had lied about everything. Gem stays by my feet with her head down, with her sad eyes staring at me. Finally, I wipe my tears.

"I hate him," I whisper.

"Oh, honey, you don't mean that," Kylie says, trying to be helpful.

"Yes, I do. I hate him! He lied to me from the beginning. I don't know what he was doing in my life. I don't know what he wanted from me. But whatever we had was a lie. He pretended to be somebody he wasn't. I don't even know if his name is Joe or Chris. He knew what he was doing from the beginning. The jerk even faked an accent! And he didn't even have the guts to tell me all this in my face! He left me a letter! What kind of a man does that?" I'm furious! "And I now have more questions, then answers!" I take the letter, crumple it, and throw it across the room.

Gem slowly walks to the folded paper, picks it up in her mouth, and places it on my lap. She whimpers.

"I don't want the stupid letter!" I yell at her.

Before I can throw it again, Kylie takes it from my lap. She opens it back up, straightens it, folds it up neatly, and puts it in her purse. "I'm going to hold on to it until you're ready for it, Tess," she states calmly.

"I don't want the stupid letter! Ever! I hate him, do you

hear me? How could he do this to me? What did he want from me? He couldn't even meet me face to face? He owed me some type of an explanation! After everything we had been through, he just left me a letter and said his goodbye!" I yell.

Kylie takes my phone and scrolls down my address book. She finds Chris's phone number and dials the number. "I'm calling him," she mumbles under her breath.

"What are you doing? Do NOT call him. Did you not hear me say I hate him?" I try to grab my phone, but she dodges into the kitchen. I run in there to snatch the phone from her, but she has already hung up.

"It's disconnected, Tess," she slowly says to me.

"Well, are you surprised? He left! And he said not to look for him. He said I wouldn't be able to find him! He's gone Kylie. Damn him! He came into my life, screwed it all up, and left! And you know what? Good riddance! Thank God things didn't get even more serious!" I can't stop yelling. This guy made me an emotional mess from the first day I met him. No more! I need to take control of my life.

Kylie squeezes my hand and says, "Let me just get something straight. Chris is Joe? Joe, the guy you told me about from *The Angels*? The guy you met as a teenager? I don't understand. Are you sure, Tess? I mean it makes no sense. What kind of a coincidence is that to run into him all these years later?"

"It's not a coincidence! Don't you see? It was all planned! He planned the whole damn thing! Nothing about us was real. Nothing! And yes, I'm positive Chris is Joe! Only one guy could sing like that, trust me! And when he looked at me, he had Joe's eyes. They were gray! And didn't you read the letter?

He mentioned our meeting on my sixteenth birthday! Damn him!"

"I just don't understand, Tess. Why? What did he want from you? And why did he have to leave so suddenly?" Kylie is confused, trying to make sense out of everything.

"He used me for something, obviously! I don't want his name mentioned again. Not ever again!" I want him out of my mind and out of my heart. I storm into my bedroom. I see the sketch of myself he had drawn for me for my birthday still on my wall. Seeing the drawing makes me even angrier! It just reminds me of the deceit! I snatch it off and throw it across the room. I have never hated anybody in my life. But at that moment, I hate Chris, or Joe, or whatever the hell his name is! He has made a complete fool out of me. I promise myself that I will never let my guard down again!

Twelve

After Chris is gone, I bury myself in my school work and my running. I finish the year with high A's. I win most of my races. Gem and I run together for training every Saturday just as we had done previously. She's getting really fast and can easily fly past me, but she always stays right next to me.

Initially, after Chris left, I kept thinking about the why's and the how's. It got me no answers and more headaches.

Finally, as days become months, I come to terms that Chris is not coming back. I can't keep feeling sorry for myself anymore. I'm stronger than that. No, I don't have any answers about my life, but my life is fine. I'm back in control. I'm not an emotional wreck like I used to be around Chris. I have no idea what he meant when he said in the letter that he had no choice but to leave. But, it sounds like a lame excuse to me. On the bright side, Josh completely stays away from me.

It feels good to be home during my summer break. I always feel safe and secure to be back with my parents. Jack and I hang out together during the summer. I don't mention anything about Chris to him. It just doesn't feel right to talk to him about it. He's the loyal guy in my life, the one who never walks away, and the steady force that gives me a peace of mind.

Gem and I keep running together during the summer months. Gem is my faithful companion, who's always there for me. Her intelligence never ceases to amaze me.

One day during the summer break, my mom and I go on a lunch date. While we're eating on an outdoor patio of the restaurant, my mom says, "You know, Tess, you're different somehow since you've been back."

"How do you mean, Mom?" I ask.

"Well, you're more withdrawn. You're not your usual joking self. It's almost like the light in your eyes has disappeared," Mom explains. Apparently, my mother has no problems getting straight to the point. I take a sip of my Coke, wondering where this is going. "Did something happen at college that I should know about?"

"No, Mom. I'm fine, really," I say. I've been keeping myself busy, thinking that I was doing just fine. What is she talking about?

"Tess, I'm your mother. I know you better than you probably know yourself. Tell me what's going on with you," she says.

I sigh and decide to open up to her. "Ok, remember how I went to *The Angels* on my sixteenth birthday?" Mom nods, leaning forward, listening intently. "Well, I met a guy there. His name was Joe, and for some reason, I felt a strong connection with him. Nothing happened. He said his goodbye and that was that."

"Ok, go on," Mom encourages, nodding again.

"In college, I met a guy named Chris. There was an intense connection between us. Later, I found out that Chris was actually Joe," I try to explain, rubbing my temple. All this is probably sounding very confusing to my mom.

"I'm not following, Tess," Mom says, shaking her head.

"Ok, let me start over. You see, I didn't recognize that

Chris was Joe because they looked different. Joe had dark hair, and Chris had blond hair. Joe had gray eyes, and Chris had blue eyes. To top it all off, Chris had an Australian accent. He faked it all. The whole thing doesn't make sense. But Chris admitted he was Joe and left. He simply wrote a letter saying not to look for him." Just talking about it, gets my heart racing again. I'm not sure if it's still from my anger about the situation, or simply because he still has that effect on me.

"Honey, this guy Chris, was the same guy you met when you were sixteen? Has he been following you?" Mom starts looking over her shoulder nervously.

"No, I mean I don't know. Look, I don't think he was following me. But I also don't think that it was all a coincidence." I pause, gathering my thoughts. "Look, Mom, I don't want you to worry. He wasn't dangerous or anything. Actually he protected me when this fraternity guy was out of line one night." I decide not to go into details about that night. My mom would absolutely lose her mind if she found out what Josh almost did to me.

"What? What happened?" Mom is looking even more frantic. Why did I even bring this up?

"Nothing, Mom. Look, please don't tell Dad. He's so overprotective. Just know that Chris was not a mean person, ok? We connected. I was drawn to him. And to be honest, I cared about him. I think he felt the same way. Well, at least I thought so, but then I found out that everything was a lie." I take a deep breath. Mom looks at me with concerned eyes, waiting for me to finish. "But now he's gone. He just disappeared, and I'm moving on with my life. That's it."

"Oh honey. This is all too much. Why didn't you tell us

what was going on with you?" My mom is upset, but I don't want her to worry about me.

"It's no big deal, Mom. Life goes on, you know?" I try to sound strong.

"Oh, sweetie, I'm so sorry. Is there anything I can do to help you?" She is still distraught.

"Mom, please don't worry. It's over. Nothing lasts forever. It's life. I told you, I'm over it," I insist. I'm not sure if I'm trying to convince her or myself.

"Ok, Tess. But I do have a question for you, and be honest with me. Did you ever feel like you were in danger around Chris or Joe? I mean, did you ever feel that he was trying to hurt you?" Mom whispers, looking over her shoulder again anxiously.

"Well, no. Actually, I always felt protected and safe. I mean, I barely knew Joe, but I really felt like I knew Chris very well," I reply slowly. "But don't you see? That's why I feel like a fool. I trusted him, and he was lying the entire time."

"Ok, I get it. But can I share something with you? I believe that everything happens for a reason. It may not make sense right now, but maybe one day it will. And you know what else I believe? I believe in destiny. I believe that if it's meant to be, you guys will see each other again. Somehow, the universe will find a way for you two to run into one another again. If he is part of your destiny, Tess, he will find you," Mom says softly, but with conviction.

"Oh Mom, you're such a romantic! But thank you. You did make me feel better." I reach across the table to squeeze her hand. As my mom smiles at me, I sigh deeply. I love her so much. She is so wise, and always knows the right things to say to make me feel better. Although, in this case, I'm doubtful that Chris will find me.

My sophomore year goes well. I continue to work hard at school. I don't go out much. Once in a while, I hit the local bar with Kylie. Kylie and Kyle broke up again. She says she's not the one to brood, and is ready to meet new guys. I, on the other hand, want nothing to do with guys. Sports and studies are my "safe zone." I focus my attention on things I'm good at, and I'm back in control of my life.

Gem goes everywhere with me. I love to talk to her because she always acts like she understands what I'm saying to her. She's a great listener. She's her full adult size, weighing solid eighty pounds. She's lean and beautiful, resembling a tan and white Siberian Husky with big blue eyes. She's loyal like a Labrador Retriever, smart like a German Shepherd, and fast like a Greyhound. I'm amazed at her perfection.

Jack visits us several times throughout the year. It's always fun when Kylie, Jack, and I hang out. It reminds me of the olden days, when we were just kids. Jack and his girlfriend Sara broke up. When I ask him if he has anybody else lined up, he says that he's going to "play the field" for a while. And why shouldn't he? He's really good looking, and I'm sure every girl at UCLA is interested in him. As long as he's happy, I'm happy.

As far as Chris is concerned, although I hate him most of the time, I really miss him. Since he's been gone, he's always in the back of my mind. I find myself hoping that somehow he will show up again in my life. I miss his lopsided smiles, and the way he raised his eyebrow whenever he smirked at me. I miss him showing up at Starbucks just to annoy me. I miss our running sessions, and how he would yell at me the entire time to run faster in that stupid accent. Hell, I even miss his overprotectiveness. And even though I have no idea what he meant when he had said to not trust anybody, I find myself always watching my back. I constantly feel like I'm being watched. It's an eerie feeling, but then again, he probably made me paranoid.

And yes, I did try to look for Chris. He told me not to bother, that I wouldn't be able to find him. He was right.

One day, as I was trying to finish my Anatomy homework, on impulse, I jumped in my car and drove up to the military site. They didn't let me through the gates, even though I tried to explain to them that I was looking for a "Chris Jones." They told me there was nobody there by that name and only authorized personnel were allowed through the gates.

The next day, I called there. But everybody I questioned, informed me that they didn't know anybody by that name.

I asked my track coach if he knew where he had gone, and the coach told me he had no idea. He said that he remembered Chris saying his job was relocating. I even tried to Google search him. He actually popped up as Chris Jones for his track accomplishments at Stanford. His name also popped up for graduating with High Honors in all subjects. Apparently, Chris was not only very athletic, but also extremely intelligent. Nothing popped up for Joe Smith during any online searches. This little information did not help me at all. I finally gave up looking for him, but a small part of me never gave up hope that he would find me one day.

I get the letter back that Chris had written to me. Kylie had kept it safe for me because she knew one day I was going to ask for it. That letter and the sketch he had drawn for me are really the only solid memories I have of Chris. I'm going to always hold on to them. I keep the letter and the sketch in my jewelry box with my locket from my parents. Periodically, I pull the letter out and read it over and over, hoping there's some type of clue of his location. It's useless though. It's a goodbye letter. I have to face the fact that Chris is gone. He has made no attempt to contact me.

I never open the sketch of me. That is too painful. It reminds me too much of the tender and loving side of Chris; Chris who had called me beautiful, and had portrayed me as such through his drawing.

I continue to have my strange dreams. Sometimes when the girl in my dreams is running, I would see a guy in the background. Sometimes, he has blond hair, and sometimes he has dark hair. But his eyes are always gray. Sometimes his eyes look really sad. Sometimes he yells at the girl to run even faster and to never give up.

When I wake up from these dreams, I visibly shake for at least half an hour. I have Gem jump on the bed so that I can hold her close to me. She's the only one I can draw strength from after these dreams. In her quiet way, she is my steady rock.

During my breaks from school, I continue to volunteer at *The Angels*. They're always happy to see me. They know that during Thanksgiving, Christmas, spring, and summer breaks, I will be there. I have my special friends there at *The Angels* whom I've known since childhood, and they really are my peace and serenity. Truth be told, I probably need them more than they need me.

When I turn twenty-one, it's a big deal to my friends and family. My parents drive down to spend the day with Kylie and me. We go out to eat breakfast at a fancy restaurant. At the restaurant, my parents give me two tickets to Hawaii to use whenever I want for a birthday present! I'm so excited! Maybe Kylie and I will just jump on the plane for Spring Break!

When we get back to the apartment, there are roses waiting for me with the doorman. He says a delivery man had brought them. It's a bouquet of twenty-one roses. I'm thrilled because I never had roses delivered to me. I grab the card, and all it says is,

Happy Birthday, Tessnia

Although there is no name or signature, time stands still and the room starts spinning.

Kylie becomes impatient and snatches the card from me saying, "Who is it from? Wait, nobody signed it. Tess, you have a secret admirer!"

I stay quiet, as my mind races. Can it be from him? Am I being unrealistic for thinking that? After all this time, would it really be him? And why would he remember my birthday? It has been almost two years! But he's the only one who calls me Tessnia. Am I just thinking it's him because of wishful thinking? Suddenly, I don't feel much like celebrating.

With my heart in my throat, I remain quiet the entire

elevator ride up to the apartment. When we get to the apartment, I excuse myself and go to my bathroom. I sit on the closed toilet seat and start to tremble, overwhelmed with emotions. Unbelievable! I'm not even positive if the roses are from him, and this is the kind of effect he has on me! I have to get a grip. I take some deep breaths to try to calm my racing heart. I wash my face with cold water to help me snap out of whatever I'm going through. This is crazy! I had my life back in control, and after all this time, he still holds the power over me to fall apart.

I can't resist. I call the flower company to inquire about the order. Just as I predicted, they tell me it's an online order. I ask if it's from a Chris Jones or Joe Smith. They say no it's not. They tell me it's just pre-paid by a temporary credit card, with no name and no further information. Of course not! Why would I think that Chris would actually walk to a flower shop and leave all of his information? He already told me that I wouldn't be able to find him.

I have to get myself to calm down. My parents are still here. I don't want them to witness me falling apart like this.

When I come back out of my room, Kylie had already put the roses in a vase. I avoid looking in that direction.

"Well, we still have a lot of plans for your birthday," Kylie says, skipping back to the living room where we're standing. "I'm going to pack for you because we're out of here!" She gives me a quick hug and disappears in my bedroom.

"And that's our cue, honey. We're driving back and we'll dog-sit Gem until you come back," Mom says.

"Wait, what's going on? Where are we going?" I'm confused, looking at Mom and then Dad for some answers.

"Too many questions, Tess," Dad laughs. "And happy birthday again, honey. Have fun with Kylie, but always be safe, ok?"

"Of course, Dad. Don't worry," I assure him. They both give me a hug and tell me how proud they are of me. My dad kisses my forehead and Gem kisses my hand.

Before my mom leaves, she whispers to me, "Remember what I said about destiny." Then, they both leave with Gem. Why did my mom say that? Does she think that the roses are from Chris, too?

Before long, Kylie is already out of my room with my bag packed, smiling from ear-to-ear. She also grabs her already packed luggage. "Let's go," she says excitedly.

"And I'm not allowed to ask where we're going?" I ask.

"You'll know soon enough," she says, with a mischievous grin and her eyes dancing.

She drives us to the airport. Now, I'm starting to get curious and even excited. I'm looking forward to getting out of here. When we check in, I find out we're going to Vegas.

"Vegas? Wow, Kylie!" I exclaim. I'm really touched by everything she's doing for me.

"Hell, yeah! We're about to party!"

I smile. Kylie always knows just how to make me happy. The plane ride is only a couple of hours long. When we land, we catch a cab. As I hear Kylie tell the cab driver where we're going, I find out that we're staying at Bellagio! I look at Kylie because I know how expensive that place is.

She smiles and simply says, "Nothing but the best for my best friend!"

I embrace her, saying, "Thank you."

Bellagio is incredibly beautiful. There's Italian art on the walls and beautifully carved pillars. Kylie has booked us a one bedroom suite. After checking in, we run to our room. When she opens the door, Kylie says, "After you, birthday girl!"

I walk in, curious to see our suite. In the middle of the room, I see Jack! He's smiling with his arms open for an embrace.

"Oh my god, Jack!" I scream. I run to him, wrapping my arms around him, and he swings me around. "What are you doing here?"

"Are you kidding me? Do you honestly think I would miss my best friend's twenty-first birthday?" He still hasn't stopped smiling.

"I can't even tell you guys how happy I am right now! I have my two best friends here with me at Vegas! I'm a lucky girl!" I exclaim.

"Look guys, we have a view of the entire city!" Kylie says, as she opens the curtains. All three of us are in awe of the lights and the fancy buildings. So here we are, in the city that never sleeps.

We go to the restaurant downstairs to grab a bite to eat and then walk around to explore the city. There is so much life here! None of us really gamble, so we're apprehensive to try it. Jack tries his luck in the slot machines, but he ends up losing thirty dollars. Afterwards, we eat dinner at the steak house.

When we get back to our hotel, Kylie tells me to take a shower. "The night is just beginning. We're about to hit the town."

Uh-oh. Here we go. I jump into the shower. When I come out, there is a black dress laid out on the bed. "Is this what I'm supposed to wear tonight? It looks tiny," I yell.

Kylie walks in as I'm staring at the dress. "Yep! You're wearing that dress, Tess," she confirms.

"I don't think I will fit into it, Kylie," I say, shaking my head.

"Um, yes you will, and you will look fantastic in it," she assures me.

To be a good sport, I put the dress on. And wow! Is it tight and short! It leaves nothing to the imagination. I groan.

"Absolutely gorgeous!" Kylie exclaims, apparently pleased with her selection. As she hands me black heels, she instructs, "Go do your hair and makeup and then you're wearing these heels."

"Yes ma'am," I reply. Why bother arguing with Kylie? It's a no-win battle.

I wear my hair down, and finish putting on my makeup. I keep it light, but put on crimson lipstick. It compliments nicely with the little black dress.

I step out of the bedroom, and Jack and Kylie are waiting for me. Jack is already drinking beer, and almost chokes when he sees me. "Wow! You look fantastic, Tess!" He kisses my cheek and pulls me into his arms. Leaning against his strong chest feels really good. He holds me against him a moment longer, and then releases me. Jack is no longer that shy boy I knew at one time. He is now a confident, experienced man, whose presence alone makes heads turn.

As I step back, I smile up to him and say, "Thanks, Jack. You both look gorgeous yourselves!" Jack has on an indigo shirt, with faded blue jeans. Kylie has a beautiful crème colored mini dress on, which looks very flattering against her pale skin.

"Let's do this!" Kylie says, shaking her little hips.

We hit the strip, wandering through the different hotels and casinos. Jack and Kylie insist that I have to drink now that I'm twenty-one. I don't want to initially, but their persistence convinces me. Hey, why not! It's my twenty-first birthday after all!

I first try the beer that Jack's been drinking. Gross! I almost spit it out. Jack laughs and says, "You need the girly drinks, Tess."

"What are the girly drinks?" I ask.

"Hold on, I'll be right back," Jack says and he disappears by the bar. A few minutes later, he brings a cocktail back with him. He asks me to try it.

I hesitantly take a sip. Hm, not bad. It tastes fruity and sweet. "What is it?" I ask.

"Don't worry about it. I know your taste, so I'll get your drinks for you," Jack says, his eyes mischievous. Kylie starts to giggle. I take another sip. If the drinks taste this good, I could drink all night! As the evening progresses, I start feeling really good.

I decide to try my luck at the casinos. We pass through the sea of tables and wander through the valley of slot machines. I walk over to the Roulette table. Maybe I can handle this. All I have to do is pick the numbers that I think the ball might land on. I have to bet at least twenty dollars to sit at this table. Well, I'm not going to put any more of my money than that, win or lose. Jack, Kylie, and I watch the other players first.

Kylie whispers in my ears, "Are you going to try this, Tess?"

"I think so, Kylie. It looks easy enough," I reply, shrugging my shoulders. I step up to the table at the next round. I close my eyes and think of a number. The first number that pops into my mind is 17. I put all of my chips on that number.

"Tess, you're supposed to spread out the chips. That increases your odds of winning," Jack says.

"Well, for some reason, that number came to my mind. I'm just going for it!" I laugh. Kylie starts giggling with me. Jack shakes his head, but starts laughing as well. They know I'm not a serious gambler, and I'm just playing to have a good time. When the dealer starts spinning the wheel, Kylie grabs my hand, squeezing it in anticipation. The wheel spins, and eventually starts to slow down. The white ball is going round and round. We're all holding our breath. As it really starts slowing down, I notice that 17 was still six slots away from the white ball. Finally, the ball lands! Yes! It lands on 17! I can't believe it. Kylie claps her hands and starts jumping up and down, screaming in delight. Jack starts to laugh and gives me a hug from behind.

"Tess, how did you do that?" Kylie says, still jumping up and down.

"Beginner's luck?" I respond. "I'm doing it again!" I close my eyes and number 11 pops into my mind. This time, I put my twenty dollars of chips, plus the chips I had just won, on number 11.

"Are you sure, Tess?" Jack whispers, getting nervous.

"I'm going for it!" I exclaim, grinning ear-to-ear.

We all watch the wheel turn again, and the white ball goes

round and round. Kylie has a death grip on my wrist. The ball lands on 11! I throw my head back in joy and laugh. This is great! No wonder people get addicted to gambling. I must be having great stroke of luck!

"Maybe you should stop while you're ahead," Jack suggests.

"Relax, Jack!" Kylie replies, waving her hand toward him. "Let her have some fun! She deserves it!"

"I don't want her to lose all her winnings, though," Jack says warily.

"I'm going to try one more time. Then I'll stop, I promise." I smile sweetly at Jack.

I take all of my chips. I close my eyes, and I envision number 29 in my mind. I place all of the chips, plus another hundred dollars' worth on number 29. I hear Jack sigh behind me in defeat, which makes me giggle. As the wheel starts turning, Kylie yells, "Come on, number 29!" The ball lands on number 29! I start laughing. This is absolutely crazy! I have no idea why I'm having this luck. The other players at the table laugh in disbelief as well. The dealer looks baffled, and he has a frown on his forehead.

When I get my winning chips, I contemplate whether to play again. Jack grabs me from the hook of my arm and says, "You promised, remember? And look around you. You hate being the center of attention."

I turn around and notice that people are gathering around the table, curious. Jack is right, I better stop. I smile up at him and say, "Fine, party pooper! Let's cash in!"

With the money I won, we spend it at the club. Jack has a couple of beers, Kylie doesn't drink at all, but I'm getting wild drunk! I'm on the dance floor, with no inhibitions. My shoes are killing my feet but I don't care. I'm feeling carefree and having a time of my life.

Jack and Kylie remain with me on the dance floor, and many times poor Jack has to hold me up. By the time we stumble back to the hotel, it's three in the morning. I am so tired and drunk. I'm staggering all over the place and Jack and Kylie have to help me to the bed.

"I love you guys," I slur.

"We love you, Tess, you know that," Jack replies, tenderly moving my hair out of my face. He's always so thoughtful and sweet. Why is he always so nice?

I grab his hand and say, "You know nice guys finish last, don't you?"

"I guess I'll finish last," Jack softly answers. "You need to go to sleep."

Ignoring Jack's suggestion, I say, "I don't know what I would do without you guys. I'm so lucky to have you two in my life." I start to get teary-eyed.

"Ok, Jack, I'm going to help her change if you could please step out," Kylie says. She knows I probably need some one-on-one.

Jack exits the bedroom and I hear him turn on the television. "I'm going to sleep on the bed with you," Kylie says. "And Jack will take the sofa out there."

"Kylie, you know how much I love you, right?" I want her to understand how important she is to me.

"Yes, I do sweets, but you need to sleep now," she insists. She already has my pajamas for me.

"Kylie, can I ask you something? Do you think those roses

were from Chris?" I want her opinion. I guess even in my drunkard state, I'm still thinking about Chris.

"Do you want an honest answer?" she asks.

"Yes!" I reply, without hesitation.

"Ok, then yes, I do think they're from him. But I don't like it. You haven't been able to move on since he left. It's not healthy. God only knows who he really is. From the sound of it, he's not coming back. Please, can you find a way to at least try to date somebody? It may help you. Damn it, Tess, it's been almost two years since he left! It's been over Tess, please accept it and move on. I can't stand seeing you like this. No guy is worth your tears!"

Just as I hear those words from her mouth, tears start flowing down my face. "I know you're right, Kylie. I've been doing pretty good though, right? It's just that when I saw the flowers with that note, all of the memories came flooding back! And honestly, I've had no desire to date anybody."

"Oh, Tess, I'm sorry. I don't mean to upset you." Kylie wipes the tears off of my face.

"No, Kylie. You're right. And I know it." I sit up and give her a tight hug. I pull my dress off and put my pajamas on. "Thanks for an amazing birthday, really." My head is still spinning. "Ugh, don't feel good," I complain as I lie back down.

"Ok, time to sleep!" Kylie demands and puts the covers around me. In a matter of seconds, I fall asleep.

"Wake up, sleepy head. We have to check out!" It's Kylie. Why is she yelling? And she is tearing my blankets off of me.

"No, my head, Kylie. I can't move," I moan. I can't believe

she's making me get up.

"Go jump in the shower. You have ten minutes," Kylie demands.

Unbelievable! I slip off the bed, and stumble into the bathroom. Somehow, I take a shower, get dressed, brush my teeth, and manage to put my hair up in a bun. Kylie, the true friend that she is, already has my bag packed.

I feel like complete shit and vow to never drink again. We all check out and catch a cab to the airport. All three of us are too tired to talk. I'm thankful that I have my sunglasses because the sun is way too bright, and my head is killing me.

Jack has the same flight as us, so we're able to fly back together. Once we land, we say our goodbyes to Jack. "I meant what I said last night, guys. I am really lucky to have you two in my life. Thank you so much for everything." Then, all three of us share a group hug in the parking lot. As we hug, I remember how we used to do the same "friendship" hug when we were young, promising that we'd always remain friends. I become misty-eyed when I think about how after all this time, we managed to stay friends, despite all the trials and tribulations between us. Somehow, I know they will always be there for me. I smile.

Thirteen

I excel the rest of my junior year. When I take my MCAT's, I receive an extremely high score. All of my professors are excited for me. With my MCAT score and my GPA, I can get into top medical programs!

My parents are ecstatic when I tell them about the score, but tell me they expected nothing less from me. My dad says, "We knew since the day you were born that you were destined for greatness."

I laugh and reply, "Don't all parents think that of their kids?"

Everything, as usual, comes easy for me. I get faster and faster. As I run, I remember everything Chris taught me. All of the coaches are very impressed with me, as are my professors. I guess it's just as well that I continue to bury myself in my studies and sports, because I don't hear anything more from Chris.

During my senior year, I find out that I've been accepted to some of the most prestigious medical schools, such as Johns Hopkins, Harvard, University of Chicago, and Stanford. Everything is falling into place!

For spring break of our senior year, I decide to use the two tickets to Hawaii that my parents gave me for Kylie and myself. I really want to do something special for Kylie since she has always been there for me. We go to Maui and the island feels like paradise. The magnificent view of the endless ocean and the mountains brings a sense of serenity.

We go hiking, helicopter riding, kayaking, swimming with the dolphins, whale watching, and simply lie on the beach, baking in the sun. It's another one of my most memorable vacations. Although Kylie and I are always together in college, it's nice to hang out in a totally different setting. We really open up to each other.

One night after we return to our hotel, she shares with me that she fantasizes of being a television reporter.

"Kylie, you would be perfect for that job!" I encourage. "I can totally see you in front of that camera." I smile at Kylie. She would be a natural!

Kylie smiles back. "I hope so, Tess." She pauses, and then says, "Tess, do you ever wonder who we'll end up marrying? I think about it all the time."

"Nope. I have never thought about marriage, Kylie. I feel like we're still so young!" Marriage? Wow, I can't even imagine that.

"Tess, you're older than me! You never think about that?" Kylie gets up to go to the bathroom to wash her face.

"No, I don't. Honestly, I just want to focus on my career for now," I say. That's the truth.

"Well, do you believe in soul mates?" Kylie yells from the bathroom. I climb out of the bed and walk to the bathroom. I stand with my arms folded in front of me, leaning against the doorway as Kylie washes her face.

"Like, finding your perfect mate and being with them forever?" I think about that for a minute. Then, shaking my head, I say, "No, I don't think so, Kylie. I think when two people are compatible, they just work at making it work." I guess I've always been practical when it comes to romance.

Kylie dries her face and then turns to me. "Well, I believe in soul mates. I think two people are destined to be together. Maybe sometimes some people never find their soul mate. But I hope we do." Kylie is obviously the more romantic one.

"I don't know about all that," I say. This conversation is too deep for me.

She replies, "Everybody has soul mates, Tess. You'll see. When you find yours, I will remind you of this conversation." I don't know why at that moment, Chris's face flashes before my eyes. I ignore the vision.

By the time I'm ready to take my senior finals, I'm already getting solid A's in all of my classes. I can't wait to go back home for the summer and spend some time in my own bedroom and eat some of my mom's cooking on a regular basis! I can't believe my undergraduate studies are coming to an end.

I feel good about my first few finals. I only have one more final on Friday. I just want to get it done and get out of here. That Friday morning, I wake up feeling a lot of anxiety. Did I have a strange dream again? As my breathing and heart rate become irregular, I lie back down, hoping to calm down. When I look at the time, I notice it's six in the morning. Can I be that stressed out about this last final? I mean, it's the Physics final, but I know my material! Why am I feeling so anxious? I close my eyes and try to relax.

Suddenly, a vision of my parents flashes before me. I hear my dad's voice saying, "It's going to be ok, Tess." As he's talking, the dark cloud passes in front of them.

My eyes pop open! What the hell! My breathing becomes even more erratic. Why am I seeing my parents? I don't like it. I take some deep breaths to calm my nerves. After a few moments, when my shaking somewhat subsides, I grab my phone and send them both a text:

Hey, Mom and Dad! Last final today at 3 o'clock! So ready to come home!

A few minutes later, Mom replies:

We miss you so much, Tess! Good luck on your exam and can't wait to see you! Love you!

Dad replies as well:

Hey, Tess! You'll do fine on this last final! Hurry home because I'm ready to kick your butt in basketball.

His text makes me smile. I feel a little better after hearing from them. I jump in the shower and decide to review some things for Physics. As I drink some tea and sit on the kitchen table to start studying, I see the dark cloud again! I nearly drop my cup of tea. I close my eyes to shut out the vision. I've never had that dark cloud vision show up so frequently! As a matter of fact, the dark cloud presents itself maybe twice a year! My heart starts racing and I begin sweating profusely. Keeping my eyes closed, I rest my head on the table, hoping to calm myself.

When my body relaxes slightly, I muster up the courage to open my eyes. The darkness is gone. I get up and wash my face to cool myself down. I just want three o'clock to hurry and come so I can get this exam over with already! When I sit back down to study, I force myself to focus on the material in front of me.

A few hours later, I decide to head toward the class. As I

lean forward to place my books into my backpack, I notice the black cloud floating by me again! Oh my god! What is happening? I know it's not real, and it's all just in my head. But my body reacts and I start feeling nauseated. I can't breathe, and I begin to gasp for air. I grab the chair and quickly sit back down in case I pass out. I put my head on the table again, resting it on my arms, keeping my eyes closed. I don't understand why this darkness keeps creeping up on me. I feel helpless to the point of wanting to cry. As my body relaxes, I slowly open my eyes, and the darkness once again is gone. I decide at that moment that as soon as I get back home, I'm going to discuss these episodes with my parents. There has to be some type of explanation for it.

I slowly walk to the sofa and lie down for a while. I need to try to calm myself down, and focus on this final I have to take soon. Forcing myself to get up eventually, I head to my last final. I pray silently the entire walk through the campus. I'm in such a daze that I can't even remember how I arrive to class.

When I start the test, my anxiety gets worse. I try to focus on the exam just so that I can quickly finish. If I just get it done, maybe my anxiety would disappear. Miraculously, I'm able to complete the exam. I have no recollection of the questions or the answers. I'm the first one to finish, and I quickly dash to the front desk and turn it in.

I feel nauseous again, and fear that I may vomit right here in the middle of the classroom. I have to get out of here. I run toward the door, seeking some fresh air. As I bolt out of the classroom, I nearly run into a woman, who's just about to enter our classroom. She's wearing business casual attire. I mumble my apology and attempt to dodge around her.

"Wait, Miss Tessnia Sanoby?" The woman stops me.

I turn around and suspiciously reply, "Yes?"

"Your dean would like to see you in his office. He wants you there right now."

"Why?" I ask. I don't understand what's going on, but I know something isn't right.

"I think it's best if you go there immediately, Miss Sanoby," she slowly replies.

I turn around and start sprinting toward the dean's building. Confused and scared, I run faster, wanting to find out what's happening. When I reach the building, the secretary tells me to go directly into his office. She says in a kind voice, "He's expecting you, honey."

I open the door, not knowing what to expect. I see him sitting in his chair, and sitting across from him is my Aunt Jenna. As she slowly turns to me, I notice that her eyes are swollen and bloodshot red as if she has been crying. She looks like she's in a state of shock. As soon as she sees me, her eyes start tearing up, and her face turns red. Why is Aunt Jenna here? It would have taken her at least three hours to travel here. My heart sinks. Something terrible has happened.

"What's wrong? Where are my parents?" I ask immediately.

"Tess, honey, sit down," Aunt Jenna mumbles, her voice husky.

"NO! I'm not sitting down. Just tell me! What's going on? Where are my parents?" I demand.

Aunt Jenna walks toward me. The dean stands up and starts to come toward me also. They're both looking at me with pity in their eyes.

"Please, Tess, sit down," Aunt Jenna begs, holding her

hand out to me. Her hand is visibly shaking.

"Damn you both! Just say it! What are you guys doing? Just say it!" I start to cry. The room is spinning. "Tell me! Say it!" I'm yelling and crying.

"Tess, ok, please… Oh my god, Tess. There was a terrible accident this morning. They were driving to work together. And there was a bad car accident, Tess. And neither of them made it. I'm so sorry, Tess." Aunt Jenna's voice is quivering and she starts crying. She is unable to say any more, as she continues to sob. She tries to reach out to me. I back away. I don't want anybody to touch me. What is she saying? I don't really understand her. I need to replay everything again. Maybe none of this is real. Is this one of my bad nightmares again? I'm getting confused. I start to feel dizzy. Why is the room still spinning? I try to walk out the door. I need to get away, get some space, and try to think clearly. Right now, Aunt Jenna is not making any sense. I take a few more staggering steps toward the door, and then everything goes black.

The rest of the day is very difficult to remember. I know Kylie is with us. Somehow, we end up at my parents' house. I think Aunt Jenna got me there. Aunt Jenna is there the entire time. I vaguely remember seeing Jack at the house also.

I don't talk to anybody. I don't comprehend what's happening around me. A lot of people keep coming in and out of the house, and there are a lot of phone calls. But I don't answer any calls, and I stay in my room. I just want to go to sleep and not wake up. I'm completely numb and still very confused. A part of me still thinks this is one of my horrible dreams and when I wake up from it, everything is going to be back to normal.

Kylie comes to my room at one point and says, "Tess, honey, I unpacked everything for you. I will get the rest of your things from the apartment later. But right now, you have to eat. Can I get you soup or something? You haven't even eaten anything all day. Please eat." I don't respond. She sighs and reluctantly leaves my room. When she comes back fifteen minutes later, she has a bowl of some type of soup and tells me to eat it. I have no desire to eat anything. I have this terrible lump in my throat and I just want to vomit. I ignore her and lie down on my bed.

"Tess, please tell me what you need. Do you want to talk? What can I do?"

I look up at her and think, "What is there to talk about?" I close my eyes. She sighs again, and leaves the room. At some point, I must have fallen asleep.

She is running again. This time it's different. There are a lot of visions going in and out. She sees a guy standing in the deep woods. He has blond hair, and he's staring at her. She sees another guy on the other side of the woods, staring at her. He has black hair. Both guys have gray eyes. Neither says anything to the girl. They just look at her with sad gray eyes. Then there are two more figures in the distant--a man and a woman. Who are they? The girl starts running toward them. The man and the woman look sad. The girl runs faster. Maybe if she runs even faster, she can reach the man and the woman. But they are beyond her reach. The woman buries her head into the man's chest as if in distraught. The girl wants to reach them to comfort them. She tries even harder. The man shakes his head in sorrow. The image of the man and the woman starts to fade away. "NO!" the girl yells. "DON'T LEAVE ME!" But the man and the woman keep fading. "NO!" the girl yells again. "DAMN IT, I'M ALMOST THERE! JUST WAIT! DON'T LEAVE ME!" The girl is desperately trying to reach for them, but they completely disappear.

I feel something shaking me, and I hear the familiar bark. There's wetness on my face. When I open my eyes, Gem is on my bed, desperately trying to wake me up. And then it happens. I start to cry and can't stop. I'm sobbing so hard, it's difficult to catch my breath.

The dream really shook me up. Were my parents in my dream? It must have been them. But then they both faded away.

My parents are gone. They both left me. Gem is whimpering, and puts her head on my lap. I start to rub her head, and say in between my sobs, "What am I going to do, Gem?" The pain is too much to bear.

I hear my door open. It's Jack. He must have been sleeping somewhere in my house, and probably heard me. He comes into my bed and pulls me to him. He doesn't say anything while I cry into his chest. I cry for hours. I can't stop. He keeps his strong arms around me the entire time. I eventually calm down enough to fall asleep in his arms.

The next few days pass in a haze. I vaguely remember my aunt running around, trying to make arrangements. I can't process my surroundings, so I withdraw away into my safe place. I don't want to talk to anybody, and I don't want anybody to talk to me. Kylie tries to force food down my throat.

It's no use. I can barely eat.

Kylie and Jack move into the house during that week. I don't even care. My aunt, Jack, Kylie, Gem and I live together in my parents' home. Jack takes Gem for her runs every day, and helps maintain the house. Aunt Jenna is on the phone a lot, making plans for the funeral and the wake. She is cordial to the neighbors and friends who drop in to give their condolences. I stay in my room. I have no desire to flash a fake smile and hug anybody.

Once, when I'm coming down the stairs, I hear Aunt Jenna say on the phone, "I don't know, it was just a horrible accident. It was all instantaneous. Neither suffered… They found my information on my sister's phone and contacted me. They told me to come to the hospital immediately… I was just glad they got a hold of me before Tess. It's all been too much for her. No, she's not even talking to anybody… I think she's in a shock… I might need to get her help when all this is over… I'm trying to stay strong for her… Everything has been too much, horrible…" I hear her crying on the phone. As I come into the kitchen, my aunt stops talking, and quickly wipes her tears. "Hey, let me call you later, ok?" she says quietly into the phone. After she hangs up, she turns to me and says, "Hey, sweetie. Can I get you anything?" I ignore her, grab a water bottle, and head back upstairs to my room.

The wake and the funeral are unbearable. All these people keep coming and hugging me. My high school and college friends are there. The entire track team comes, including my coach. There are family members there, who I barely know, neighbors, and my parents' work colleagues. The only family I'm close to is my Aunt Jenna. My parents were not close to the rest of the family. Both sets of my grandparents had died when my parents were young. My parents were loners and preferred to stay to themselves.

Everybody at the funeral means well, but I hate it. I'm wearing some clothes that Kylie had handed to me earlier, instructing me that I had to put those on. I'm here somehow, but functioning as a robot. I just do whatever they tell me to do. I'm having difficulty even processing the ordeal. Gem doesn't leave my side, standing next to me during the wake and the funeral. She remains protective of me through the entire affair.

At one point during the wake, a gentleman, probably in his forties, comes to me and says, "I'm really sorry for everything. My name is Tom Sterns. I was a close friend of your parents and worked with them as well. I was closely involved with your mom's research. They were extraordinary people, and will truly be missed." And then he gives me a hug. It's a strong hug, full of compassion and empathy. I wonder for such a close friend, why I had never met him.

By the time everything is over, I'm exhausted. I don't even remember the speeches, or when the caskets are lowered. I tune out and I'm just going through the motions. All I want, is to go home, and crawl under my blankets in my bed. I want nothing more than to go back to sleep, and shut the world out. Sleep appears to be the only thing that seems to help with the pain, even if it *is* temporary.

After the torturous event ends, we all come home. Aunt Jenna says, "Tess, remember there's a nine o'clock appointment tomorrow morning with the lawyer for the will. He will be coming here to meet with you." I can tell that she really doesn't want to bring the topic up to me, but it's not something that can be avoided. Why do I have to meet with the lawyer? Why can't somebody just tell me what comes out of it? This is so stupid. I'm not ready for this. Please God, make this horrible pain go away. I can't bear it.

"I'm going to take Gem for a run," Jack says. I know it's Jack's way of trying to change the subject. Plus, he's probably looking for an escape. "Come on, girl," Jack calls for her. Gem looks up at me as if asking for permission. I nod to her and then head to my room.

Kylie follows me into my room. "Tess, can I get you anything?"

I shake my head and fall into my bed. She pulls my shorts and t-shirt out of the drawers and puts them on my bed.

"I'm right here if you need anything. I'm here for you, Tess, ok?" I nod, avoiding the eye contact.

After Kylie leaves, I strip out of my clothes, and put my t-shirt and shorts on. Without even taking a shower, I bury myself under my blanket. I want today to be over.

I wake up in the morning, with a severe headache. As I step into the bathroom and look at my reflection in the mirror, I notice the horrible bags under my eyes. I have to meet with the lawyer today, so I force myself to take a shower. I put some jeans and a white blouse on, and pull my hair up in a bun.

My head is killing me now, so I reluctantly go downstairs to find some Ibuprofen. As I step into the kitchen, there's coffee and toast waiting for me on the table. I haven't been able to eat too much more than toast once in a while. I can barely even force that down my throat.

Jack, Kylie, and Aunt Jenna are sitting at the table, eating breakfast. Everybody stays quiet. I grab a couple pills of Advil, and sit down at the table, nibbling at my toast. I swallow my pills with my coffee.

Precisely at nine o'clock, the doorbell rings. Aunt Jenna lets Mr. Klein, the lawyer, in and brings him into the kitchen. Since I'm the only child, the attorney asks to meet with me alone. I lead him into the study and I take my seat on the chair by the desk, and gesture him to sit on the chair across from me.

As he sits down, he says, "Listen, Miss Sanoby, I am truly sorry about everything. I've been your parents' lawyer for some time now." Mr. Klein pauses as if waiting for me to say something. When I remain silent, he continues. "They were very precise of their wishes in their will. All of their bank accounts and this house belong to you. I will be meeting with your mother's sister as well. Your mom left all of her jewelry to her sister, with the exception of their wedding rings. They left those for you." The lawyer pauses again before continuing. "I don't know if you realized, but your parents were very wealthy. Here are all of the statements to their bank accounts." Mr. Klein hands me some papers. I don't even open them. "I'd like to advise you to please look those over. That way, if you have any questions, I can answer them," he explains.

Reluctantly, I start to skim the papers. As I force myself to focus, the numbers on the statements begin to register. Am I reading this right? There's an account with over five million dollars! There's another with eight million! As my eyes get wide with disbelief, I start flipping through the papers faster. What the heck!

I put the papers back down on the desk and say, "There must be some type of mistake. My parents were not this wealthy." Great, now I have to deal with this lawyer's mistakes?

"No mistake. Your parents' bank accounts equal to almost thirty five million dollars. They were very successful and hard workers," Mr. Klein explains. I start to become more confused. What is going on? There is no way my parents could have money like this. I mean our house is a decent size home, but I wouldn't consider it a mansion. And we never drove fancy cars or anything. It's not like we went on too many extravagant vacations. There must be some type of misunderstanding. This makes no sense. How could they have made this much money? They weren't even old for goodness sake. "Oh, and one more thing. They wanted me to give you this in case something happened to them," Mr. Klein says, as he hands me a sealed envelope.

"In case something happened to them? What does that mean? Did they think something was going to happen to them?" My head is spinning. Are there things I didn't know about my parents?

"It's perfectly normal, Miss Sanoby, for people to prepare like this. It's nothing unusual. Most of my clients actually plan ahead like this." Mr. Klein is very matter of fact about it. "And their wish was that you read that in private."

Mr. Klein has me sign a bunch of papers, to ensure everything transfers to my name. He also gives me his card, and says, "Please don't hesitate to contact me if you have any further questions or concerns. I will meet with your aunt on my way out to discuss what was left for her." After shaking my hand, he takes his leave.

I stay in the study and open the envelope. It's a letter from my parents. I immediately recognize my mom's writing.

Our Dearest Tess,

If you got this letter, that means we are no longer in this world. I'm so sorry, baby.

We want you to know that we did everything in our power to give you the most normal childhood and life. We felt this was very important. You see, Tess, you are anything but normal. You may not quite understand, but you have many gifts. You are more intelligent than the norm. You are more athletic than the norm. That's because you have what we call "excelled genes." This is extremely rare. You were, by chance, born with these excelled genetics. And to be honest, we aren't even sure of all your talents from possessing such genes. But what we do know, is that you need to realize that you are extremely special. It's just as important that nobody knows this about you, Tess. This would not be to your benefit. You have to live as normal of a life and try to blend in as best as you can. The wrong people can NOT find out about this. You must do everything in your power to protect yourself. We love you, Tess, and you must persevere. Live Tess, follow your destiny, and be happy.

With all my love- always,

Mom

Then the writing changes to my dad's writing.

My precious baby girl,

Oh baby, I'm going to miss you so much. But I will be watching you. Watching you conquer this world- because that's how amazing you are. Tess, I knew you were born to do some greatness, and you haven't disappointed me as of yet. I know that right about now, you feel alone in this world. But Tess, you have no idea how strong you are. You have no idea of your capabilities. You have to believe in yourself, baby. And be happy. You must be happy in life.

I know there are a lot of things we haven't told you. I'm sorry sweetheart. We were waiting for you to graduate from college and talk to you. But since you are reading this letter, I guess we didn't get that opportunity. Tess, remember what Mom said. You must blend in. Nobody can find out about your elite genetics. Nobody can find out that you're different.

I will always be by your side, baby girl- in life or death. I will be there.

Love you with all of my heart and soul,

Dad

PS. Destroy this letter as soon as you read this. It can NOT get into the wrong hands.

I can't hold back the tears from rolling down my face. My parents are truly gone. And they had prepared for it. My dad said he's going to be with me in life or death. Is he with me now? Is he watching me fall apart?

I must have stared at the letter for at least thirty minutes, reading it, and re-reading it. I have no idea what they're talking about. I'm a mess. My life is falling apart around me and I have no idea how to stop it. Not only do I not know many things about my parents, but apparently I don't know shit about myself either.

"I can't do this, Daddy," I whisper with tears still rolling down my face. "I need you. Why did you leave?" I wait for some type of sign, but there's nothing. Eventually, I muster up some energy and force myself to get up from the chair as I slowly walk to the fireplace in the study. I turn it on and throw the letter into the fire to destroy it. I stare at it until it burns down to ashes. I wipe the tears off of my face and step out of the study, knowing that my eyes are bloodshot red and swollen.

Aunt Jenna, Jack, Kylie, and Gem are all anxiously staring at me, wondering if I'm ok. They can see from my swollen red eyes that I've been crying.

"I'm alright," I whisper, and slowly climb the stairs and lock myself in my room.

Fourteen

Aunt Jenna stays with me for another week. When I go downstairs to get some water, she says, "Tess, I want to talk to you about something." Jack and Kylie are sitting in the kitchen with her.

"Yes?" I ask, not wanting to have a conversation.

"Jack, Kylie, and I were talking just now. You know, to plan things out. I have to go back to work, Tess. I have to go back to my condo," she says reluctantly.

"That's fine, Aunt Jenna," I answer.

"Do you want to move in with me? I only live couple of hours from here, Tess. Maybe we can sell this house?"

"No thanks, Aunt Jenna," I interrupt. "This is my parents' home, and there's no way I can sell it." My parents had this home custom built. They loved their home. I wouldn't even dream of selling it. "I'll be ok," I lie.

"Ok, I understand. Kylie, Jack, and I discussed a few things, Tess. They will be staying with you for now. We're not comfortable leaving you alone yet. And if you need anything, you know I'm not far. I'll be calling every day, and I'm coming here every weekend. You know that right?" She walks up to me and takes my hand. I nod because I already know that Aunt Jenna will be here every weekend. "And Tess, did you decide about counseling?"

"I don't think I want the counseling, Aunt Jenna," I answer her, shaking my head. "But if it's that important to you, I will think about it some more, ok?" I assure her so she doesn't worry so much about me. She has her own life to live. Losing her one and only sister must have been heartbreaking for her. My Aunt Jenna needs to get back to her life.

"I'm going to hold on to one of the spare keys to the house," she says. I can tell that she is hesitant about leaving me.

"Sure, no problem. Remember, Kylie and Jack are still here with me. I'll be fine," I say, trying to sound optimistic.

Aunt Jenna gives me a big hug. When she releases me, her eyes are filled with tears. "I love you so much, Tess. Just know that. And I'm always here for you," Aunt Jenna says, her voice quivering. "No matter what, ok?" She kisses my cheeks. Jack stands up and comes to stand by me. He takes my hand and squeezes it.

"Don't worry. We'll watch over her," he assures Aunt Jenna.

Later that day, when Aunt Jenna leaves, Kylie and Jack take Gem for a run. It feels good to finally be alone. I look around the house. Everything looks the same, as if my parents are still around. I close my eyes, hoping I can feel their presence somehow. I concentrate, thinking if I try hard enough, somehow we would make a connection. I feel nothing.

The other night, when I dreamt about the girl, I saw the man and the woman who faded away. Were they my parents? Maybe that's how they'll try to connect with me. I shake my head thinking that I'm really starting to lose it now. God, so many thoughts are racing through my mind. Their note said I have some special genes. What does that mean? Yes, things have always come easy for me. But I've heard a lot of people say that. My parents said in their letter that even they weren't sure of all of my talents. Did Chris once say that to me? Maybe it was "Joe" who first mentioned that to me. I think he had said to embrace my talents. Maybe he knew something that my parents knew. Did they know each other somehow? But no, when I had told my mom about Chris, she was genuinely surprised.

God, my head feels like it's going to explode! I have so many questions and I have no idea who can answer these questions. But then again, maybe I don't even want to know. I'm driving myself crazy. I can't think about this anymore.

I just want to go back to sleep again. It's an escape from reality. How ironic, since all of my life I hated to sleep because I dreaded the nightmares. Now, my real life is worse than those dreams. I would rather deal with the nightmares if I can just escape from this horrible pain. This constant dead weight in my gut, the lump in my throat, my head always spinning, and feeling like I want to vomit--it's all too much. I have nothing left in me. The only way I can cope is to try to sleep and to shut the world out.

When Jack and Kylie return, Gem runs to me and kisses my face. She has truly been my rock through this entire ordeal.

"Are you ok with your aunt leaving, Tess?" Kylie asks. "Tell me the truth."

"Yeah, why wouldn't I be? I mean she has a life. She has a job, obligations," I answer. "And that reminds me. You guys don't need to stay here and stop your lives. I mean, you can stay if you want, but please, I can't stand all this. I know you guys would already be working if it wasn't for me. I feel pathetic with all of you stopping your lives."

"Tess, we're here because we want to be here. What you

went through, we can't even imagine. It's horrible, and that's what friends do. Friends help each other," Jack explains. Kylie nods in agreement.

"Suit yourselves. I'm going to my room," I mumble. I'm done with this discussion. I slowly climb the stairs leading to my bedroom, wanting to be left alone. I'm starting to get annoyed but I'm not sure why. Jack and Kylie mean well, but I don't want their pity anymore.

That evening, Kylie brings me dinner to my room. I don't say anything to her. She leaves it on my table and tells me to call her if I need her. I don't even touch the food.

My life goes on like this with Jack and Kylie doing things for me for another two weeks. My aunt calls me every day, and she comes to stay with me every weekend. I start to take Gem for her walks. I can't run. I have no energy for that. Even during the walks, I feel miserable.

I start to drive a bit, especially for grocery shopping. I do nothing regarding the money my parents left me, except I try to remember to pay the bills on time. I barely eat, but occasionally, I try to eat a sandwich or a microwave dinner. After every meal, I want to vomit. Nothing tastes good to me.

At the end of the two weeks, Jack comes up to me in the kitchen and says, "Tess, what can we do to make this any easier? We really don't even know what to do anymore."

"I just want to be left alone, Jack." There, I said it. If that's selfish of me to say, then so be it. I'm sick of all this attention. I hate looking at them, and their eyes are so full of sorrow and pity. It kills me. Stop feeling sorry for me, damn it! "There's not much you guys can do. I'm able to feed myself, and I'm taking Gem for her walks now. It's kind of good to have some alone time. I'm not sure why you guys think you need to stay here."

Jack stays quiet for a minute. He tries to make eye contact, but I have no desire to look at him. I keep my gaze down. Jack sighs, and then says, "Ok, Tess, that's fine. I will tell Kylie that you'd like your space. But we will still be stopping by here frequently whether you like it or not."

I start to feel guilty. I'm pushing them away, and I don't know how to stop myself. I look up at him and say, "Fair enough. Take the two spare keys and you guys are welcome here whenever you want. Just help yourselves in." After a brief pause, I soften my voice and say, "Jack, I do appreciate everything you guys have done."

"You don't have to say that, Tess." Jack walks over to me and kisses me on my forehead.

That evening, after Jack takes Gem for a run, they pack up their clothes. They eat dinner with me because Kylie made lasagna for all of us. After they finish washing the dishes, they both give me hugs goodbye.

Kylie says, "Tess, I went grocery shopping so you have enough food in the fridge to last you a month! But you know I'm right down the street right? You can call me for anything, anything at all. And I will check on you every day." I hug her back and nod.

When Jack gives me a hug, he whispers in my ear, "You can try to push us away all you want, but it won't work. We love you too much." And then he leans down, pets Gem and says to her, "Take good care of her, Gem." Gem barks in response.

After they leave, I lock the door behind them. I turn to Gem and say, "It's just you and me, Gem." She wags her tail and barks. Since it's late, we both settle in for the night. Gem stays in my bedroom the entire night. I wake up in the middle of the night and tell her to come on the bed. It feels strange for the two of us to be completely alone in this house. It would probably do me some good to cuddle with her. She hops on, and I hug her. Feeling her next to me helps me to relax and I fall asleep again.

The next month goes from bad to worse. My aunt calls every evening. I answer her calls because I know she needs to hear my voice. Kylie and Jack call daily as well, but I usually just text them saying all is well. I have no desire to interact with anybody.

During the weekends, they all visit. Jack takes Gem for runs every time he visits. I mostly lock myself in my room.

My typical day consists of brushing my teeth, trying to eat, trying to watch TV, taking naps, taking Gem for walks, and going to bed for the night. Even though I attempt to eat, I can barely get the food down. All my actions are performed robotically. I go through the motions because I know it has to be done. I don't even get ready. I barely even brush my hair. I just exist. I know I'm hitting rock bottom, but I don't care.

Jack comes over one morning and sits down to watch TV with me. I have no interest in talking, or for having company. I fall asleep watching TV. I don't know how long I sleep, but I feel him wake me up and say, "Come on, we're going for a drive."

"I don't want to, Jack," I reply. I want to go back to sleep.

"Tess, you have no choice. We're going for a drive. Let's go." Jack grabs me from the hook of my arm and forces me off of the couch. After being practically dragged outside to his car, I hear him call for Gem. Jack is not going to take no for an answer so I don't fuss in the car. He drives to the neighborhood park. It's the same park we used to play at when we were children--the same park he used to push me down the slide.

"Come on. You're getting some fresh air," Jack says as he opens the passenger door. He takes my hand and leads me to one of the swings, and I sit down. He sits on the swing next to me while Gem walks around the park.

As we begin swaying on the swings, he says, "Tess, I can't watch you do this to yourself anymore. I feel helpless. I mean medical school is about to start in a month, and you're just sleeping your life away." I remain quiet. What does he want me to say? Jack tries again. "Tess, I know you've gone through a lot. I can't even begin to pretend that I understand your pain. But Tess, I can't let you do this to yourself. You have to get help. It's ok to get help. People do it all the time."

"What kind of help, Jack?" I ask. "I'm fine."

"Look, you're not fine. You're a mess, ok? You need help. You know, like therapy or anti-depressants. Something for God's sake! Please, Tess, it will help you. It can just be temporary. It'll help you get through this." Jack stops swinging and turns to me for a response. Jack is desperately trying to make me understand him.

I feel myself becoming more upset. I stop swinging, stand up, and walk a few steps away. Then I turn back to him, and shout, "Get through what Jack? I lost my parents! They're dead! Do you think I want to forget that? I lost them forever. They're gone! Do you get it? No, I don't want to get through this. They were all I had. They were my everything. Now, I have to just accept that they're gone? And move on with my life? Are you kidding me?" I am so frustrated and angry! How can I possibly live my life when my parents' lives were just taken from them? "Look, Jack, I'm probably not going back to school anyway. I don't want to. I have no desire to go to medical school anymore. I'm done."

"What?" Jack gets off of the swing and walks over to me. He grabs my chin and lifts it up, forcing me to look at him. "Tess, for as long as I remember, you've wanted to be a physician. What about your dreams to go to poor countries and making a difference? You know, helping the less fortunate? You've been talking about that since you were a little girl," Jack insists.

I move away, turning my back to him. I fold my arms in front of my chest and say, "Well, dreams change Jack. I have no desire to do that anymore. I've changed. I'm not the same."

"I know you've changed. And that's why I'm worried, Tess. You're not yourself. And that's totally understandable. But Tess, you shouldn't make such life-changing decisions right now. You may regret it later. You're too fragile to make such permanent decisions. When you're feeling better, you can think more clearly."

I turn to face Jack and say, "No, Jack. I've already thought this through. I'm going to take a break. Maybe after a break, I may change my mind. Who knows, I may re-apply to medical school next year if I feel like it. But right now, I have no desire to go back to school." I start walking to the car. I want to go back home and bury myself under my blankets again. Reluctantly, Jack follows me. He calls for Gem and she jumps in the car.

Jack is silent all the way back to the house. When he stops in my driveway, he turns to me and says, "Listen, Tess, I just want you to be able to smile again. Will you at least think about what I said?"

I reply, "Sure, Jack." Both he and I know full well that it's a lie.

When Gem and I get into the house, I look around. I haven't touched any of my parents' belongings. Their shoes and coats are still in the closet. I haven't even gone into their bedroom. The door to their bedroom has stayed closed. Aunt Jenna offered to pack their possessions, but I had refused. Why would I put any of their things away? That seems so final!

I force myself to open their bedroom door. The bed is neatly made. I shake my head. Mom was such a neat freak! I see my dad's jacket hanging on the rocking chair in the corner. I smile. My mom used to get so mad because he always left his things everywhere. I can still hear her say, "It would take you only two minutes to hang that coat! Why is it on the rocking chair? It does not belong there!"

And I can hear my dad's response, "That's two minutes of my life I would have wasted on hanging that coat." He would purposefully have silly responses just to get her even more frustrated! My smile widens as I shake my head.

I walk into their bathroom. I can still smell my mom's perfume lingering in air. I stand there, close my eyes, and take a deep breath, filling my nostrils with Mom's scent. I soak it in for a few minutes, just remembering her. I finally open my eyes, sigh, and walk into their walk-in closet. Both of their clothes are hanging neatly on either side of the closet. I sit down in the middle of the closet and pull out the box of the photo albums. Mom always wanted hard copies of all of the photos. I smile as I remember how much she loved organizing them in the photo albums or making scrap books out of them.

All of the albums are in chronological order. Even though I've seen all of the pictures before, I want to see them again today. I just want to remember the happier times. I first look through their wedding album. Mom looks so beautiful, and in every picture, Dad is staring at her with so much devotion. I sigh as I see her wedding dress hanging in the closet.

The next album is about me. This album is when I was born. There are a ton of baby pictures of me. In every picture, my parents are just in awe by me. I laugh as I come across the picture when I had come in first place as a baby in a beauty pageant. There's another photo where I'm sitting on my dad's shoulder as he's carrying me through Walt Disney World. I remember I kept complaining that my legs hurt too much to walk. Finally my dad had just picked me up and tossed me on his shoulders and carried me the rest of the day. Besides pictures of me from every single birthday, there's a separate album of me playing sports! There are pictures of me playing soccer in Kindergarten, and many more playing basketball, softball, and running track. My parents attended every single game. Even when I was in multiple sports, my parents made sure that they were there, cheering for me! I smile as I remember my mom being the loudest in the stands.

I go through the pictures from all of our vacations: Jamaica trip, Chicago, Florida, Hawaii, Canada, and even India! I was only twelve years old when we had decided to go to India. My parents had really wanted to visit the Taj Mahal because it's considered one of the Seven Wonders of the World. I find the picture of my parents in front of the Taj Mahal. Their eyes are full of happiness and love.

Before going there, my mom was teasing my dad saying, "Now remember, they say if two people go together to visit the Taj Mahal, that means they will always be together. Are you ready for that?"

Dad had laughed and said, "Guess I'm stuck with you then." As I reminsce, I can't stop the stream of tears going down my face. The lump in my throat comes back again, and I feel as though I'm suffocating. I have to get out of here. I run out of their bedroom, slamming the door behind me.

I wipe my tears and hurry downstairs to get a glass of water. Maybe drinking the cold water will help. As I pour the water into my glass, my hands start shaking. I can barely hold the glass. Why did this happen in my life? It's not fair! I throw the glass across the room and it shatters everywhere. Gem comes running, looking around the room. I take the coffee maker off of the counter, and throw it.

"Why?" I scream. "Why did you leave me?" I'm screaming so loud that my voice is screeching. Gem starts to whimper. I lose all control. I take everything off the counter and slide it off. I start throwing the utensils, while screaming like a mad woman. "Why? You guys were all I had! What am I going to do?" As I scream and yell, more things are thrown across the floor, shattering, just as my life around me has shattered. Gem starts running around, probably scared to death. It must have been half an hour later, when I finally sink down on the floor, exhausted.

I have hit rock bottom, and there's nothing I can do to stop it. I slowly lower my head onto the floor and lie there on the cold tiles. I start sobbing uncontrollably and hysterically. Gem comes by me, trying to cuddle with me. I don't even recognize the horrible noises coming out of me as I sob.

Eventually, when all my tears dry up, I force myself to gather up enough energy to clean up the kitchen. Since I have broken everything that I can get my hands on, it takes me at least an hour to get it all cleaned up.

I gather up the strength to climb the stairs and go up to my room. I pull out my parents' wedding rings and hold them close to my heart. The rings are always in my jewelry box with the locket they had given me. I remember getting that locket on my sixteenth birthday as if it was just yesterday. I open it and look at the picture. All three of us are so happy in this picture. God, how I miss that! I want to go back in time. I read what they had inscribed on the locket.

Strength
Peace
Happiness
Always

My life has turned upside down in a matter of seconds. How can that have happened? God only knows how many times I wished that I was in that car with them. I close my eyes. I have to snap out of this. God, give me the strength. I sigh, and close the locket. I can't look at it any more. I put it back in my jewelry box. I see the folded sketch of me that Chris had drawn for me and after all these years, I still can't get myself to open it. I'm just too depressed, and seeing that drawing would make me even more depressed. I then notice the folded letter that Chris had left me. I pull that out and read it again.

Dear Tessnia,

I never meant to hurt you. Ever. I can't even express how sorry I am for dragging you into my mess. I have to leave. I don't have a choice. But before I leave, I want you to remember when we first met on your 16th birthday. I want you to know at least that much about me, with the hope that it helps you hold on to some good memories between us. I know you are probably wondering why I never told you the truth. Again, there's probably another time and place for that.

Please remember what I said. Don't trust anybody. But always trust your instincts. Embrace your gifts!

Tessnia, please know that if there is any way that I could spend even one more minute with you, I would in a heartbeat. I never got the chance to even begin to explain what you mean to me. I guess some things are better left unsaid.

Please don't look for me. You won't find me.

Yours always…

I sigh deeply. I must have read this letter over and over a million times already. But I have to let Chris go. He's gone, just like my parents are gone. I fold the letter back and put it in my jewelry box again.

It's starting to get late. I turn to Gem and say, "I still have to take you for a walk. Come on, Gem."

As we're walking, I feel guilty that I don't run with her anymore. I just don't have it in me to find the energy. It's a miracle that I'm even walking her.

When we return home, I try to feed Gem. To my disappointment, the dog food bag is empty. "Gem, there's no food. Let me run to the grocery store and get you some. I'll be right back, ok?"

The grocery store is only a ten minute drive. I grab the dog food, and decide to pick up some treats for her. She has been just as miserable as me lately. The only time she's even semi-happy is when we have company. Otherwise, she mopes around with me all day. Seeing me lose total control of myself probably didn't help matters. Maybe the treats will cheer her up.

I return home half an hour later. When I open the door, Gem comes running to me, wagging her tail. I give her the food and also the treats. "Sorry, Gem. I know I've been neglecting you lately," I whisper, while scratching behind her ears. She stops eating and kisses my hand. "You're a good girl, Gem. I love you so much. I don't know what I would do without you." I kneel down and give her a big hug.

I go back to my room. I need to jump into the shower before I go to bed. I haven't eaten dinner, but I'm not even hungry. I take a long hot shower. Sometimes the hot steam really helps to wind me down and sleep. I decide to wash my hair since I can't even remember when I washed it last. It must have been easily a week.

After the shower, I wrap myself in my towel. I haven't looked at myself since this nightmare started. I sneak a peek at the mirror as I wipe the condensation off. I'm shocked at the reflection that stares back at me! Besides losing so much weight, my eyes are surrounded by deep, dark circles. My cheeks are hollow and my collar bone and ribs are disgustingly protruding out. There's barely any meat left on me! Where did my muscles go? I can't look at myself anymore. It's a horrific site which makes me even more depressed.

I wrap the towel back around me and step into my room. I notice that Gem is already in my room, wagging her tail at me. I walk to my drawers to get some clothes. As I open the drawer, the hair in the back of my neck stands up. Something isn't right. I quickly turn to see if anything is out of place. But everything appears normal. I glance toward Gem, but she isn't acting strange at all. I must be losing my mind. I quickly grab my panties, my sweat shorts, and my tank top, throwing them on. I'm still feeling uneasy. What is wrong with me?

I creep toward my window. Is something going on outside? I slowly peek out but I don't notice anything unusual. I decide to get a better look. I deliberately pad across the carpet to get closer to the window, squinting to see if I notice anything suspicious.

That's when he grabs me! I feel a strong arm grab me from behind and the other hand is on my mouth before I can scream. He's holding a handkerchief against my mouth. I squirm and push at his arm to shove him off of me. But he's too strong.

I start to shake my head back and forth to try to free myself. I'm having difficulty focusing! I can't think straight. Oh my god! He's drugging me with the handkerchief covering my mouth and nose. I try to hold my breath as I struggle to push his hand away from me and get out of his hold. But it's useless. He's too strong. Somebody please help me! But nobody comes. Then, in a very low tone, I hear him say in my ear, "Sorry, sweetheart."

I fade into darkness.

Fifteen

God, my head is hurting! And I feel so groggy. I guess I should get my ass up and start the day. Maybe coffee will help. I reluctantly start opening my eyes, still having difficulty focusing. I stare up at the ceiling, looking at the white ceiling fan, as it goes round and round. As I focus on the fan slowly spinning, my eyes fly open. I don't have a ceiling fan! This is not my room! Where the hell am I?

"Well it's about time you decided to wake up." I hear a male voice say from the corner of the room. I spring into sitting position and the memories come flooding back. Somebody had grabbed me! My gaze flies to that corner of the room. I try to focus, but I'm having difficulty seeing the man. It's dark where he's sitting, and I can see only his shadow. Maybe the drugs are still in my system.

"Who are you and what do you want?" I ask bravely. In reality, I'm scared out of my mind!

The man is sitting in a chair in the shadows. He has all black on and he looks big, strong, and intimidating. He stands up from the corner chair and starts to stroll toward me. Instinctively, I sink back into the bed, shaking like a leaf. "You forgot me already, Tessnia?"

My head jerks up to meet his eyes. It's Chris, but wait--he looks like Joe! He has dark hair again, with those same gray eyes that have haunted me for so many years. "Chris? What... what is going on?"

Is this a dream? He has come into my dreams so many times, but the dreams are never like this. Maybe Jack is right. Maybe I really do need some serious help. Maybe if I close my eyes for a few minutes, and open them again, I'll snap back to reality.

"Chayse," he replies, with that same smirk I remember so well.

"What?" I ask. I'm still having difficulty staying focused. I have no idea what is happening.

"Chayse, that's actually my real name," he answers back.

"So, you're not Chris or Joe? Now you're Chayse?" This guy in my dream is starting to frustrate me. If this is a dream, it's time to wake up.

"Truly, my name is Chayse," he explains. Somewhere in the back of my mind, I note that he now has an American accent.

"Look, is this a dream? I haven't been myself lately and I think I may be losing it," I explain. This is all too confusing. Wake up, Tess! This is getting out of control!

Chris, urr, I mean Chayse sits next to me on the bed. He looks straight into my eyes with his deep, gray, penetrating gaze. He leans forward and gives me the gentlest kiss on my lips. It's sweet and full of tenderness. I close my eyes to savor the moment. If this is a dream, there's nothing wrong with enjoying it.

When he pulls away, he caresses my cheek and says softly, "Did that feel real enough to you?"

My eyes fly open as reality begins to sink in. He's looking straight into my soul with the same intense gaze that I remember so vividly. Oh my god. This is real! I jump off of the bed.

"What the hell! Stay away from me. Do *not* touch me, ever! What am I doing here? Why are you here? And where am I anyway? You kidnapped me?" I am so angry! The nerve of this guy to just show up back in my life, bringing me here against my will, and then kiss me like nothing ever happened!

"Relax, Tessnia, let me explain," he says.

"Stop calling me Tessnia!" I yell. "My name is Tess! Damn it!"

"You're hysterical. Just take a deep breath. One question at a time, ok? And I'll try my best to answer," he says calmly.

"Wait, where's Gem? What did you do to Gem? I swear, if you hurt her at all!" He wouldn't hurt her, would he?

"Gem is fine. She's here with us," he answers back, smiling proudly.

"What? You kidnapped her, too?" I ask incredulously.

"Kidnapped, or is it dognapped? Well, I didn't do either of those things. I didn't have to. Gem came here willingly. I have to say she was just as happy to see me as I was to see her," he answers arrogantly.

"Let me see her. I want to make sure she's ok," I say, lifting my chin up, challenging him. I don't trust him at all.

Chayse--if that's really his name--throws his hands up in air, sighs, and walks to the closed bedroom door. He opens it and yells, "Gem, come here. She's finally awake!"

I hear Gem running down the hall. She trots in, runs to me, and barks happily. She even jumps around, wagging her tail and doing her happy dance. She then kisses my hand. She has lost her mind! I stare at her in disbelief, thinking, what is she so happy about? What a traitor! Thanks, Gem.

"Told you she was fine," Chayse says smugly, rubbing it in even more.

"Ok. Well, I don't really know what we're doing here. But we need to leave now. It was nice seeing you. Just tell me where we are, and we'll be on our way." I have no interest in finding out what kind of game he's playing. This is not a safe zone. I have to get out of here. Being near him is very dangerous for me. I've already learned that lesson!

"Well, that's impossible. You're too far from your home. You see, I drove all night to get you here. This is my temporary residence. And you will be staying here for a bit," he answers confidently.

"You're going to now hold me against my will? I'm calling the police. This is ridiculous!" I am utterly shocked that he's acting as if this is not a big deal.

"You can't call the police because there are no land lines here. And unfortunately for you, I am in possession of your cell phone." Chayse smiles as if he's proud of himself.

"I have people checking on me every day. Somebody will miss me soon and they will be searching for me," I challenge him.

As if rising to the challenge, Chayse takes a few steps toward me. He shrugs his shoulders and says, "No worries. I already texted Kylie, your aunt, and that male friend of yours, what's his name? Jack is it? In any case, they got the text from your phone, basically saying that you're fine but you needed to get away for a bit. You're taking Gem with you, and not to worry."

"Wow, unbelievable! You have some nerve! What do you want from me? Why am I here?" I'm furious. He has no right to take my phone and pretend to be me answering to my loved ones!

Chayse runs his hand through his hair, just the way I remember. "Why are you here? Because I missed you, Tessnia," he says slowly and deliberately. His voice is low and husky. My heart skips a beat. Oh no! I have to get out of here.

I take a deep breath and say, "You missed me? It's been three years! And aren't you a bit dramatic? Couldn't you have just called me or even simply rung my door bell if you missed me? You clearly knew where I lived. Why drug me, snatch me out of my own home, and then drag me here against my will?"

"Good point. But a bit hard to explain right now. Let's just say that I had no other choice," he answers, shrugging his shoulders again.

"Wow, that sounds like the same lame ass excuse you gave me when you left. Whatever! Look, this is insane. What do you want from me? I don't even know who you are!" I start wondering if I should be worried or frightened. But strangely, I don't feel either. I'm just really angry. I can't believe that he would just come into my life like this. To top it off, he's acting as if he still has rights in my life! And the worst part is that my dog is absolutely fine with it. As a matter of fact, she had watched him as he attacked me in my own bedroom, and hadn't done anything about it.

"That's strange. I would say you know me better than anybody else in this world," Chayse replies, sounding somber.

"I don't know you! I don't even know your real name!" I exclaim, with disbelief. I don't know anything about him. He is a complete stranger to me.

"I told you my real name is Chayse. And that is the truth. I dyed my hair blond when I was Chris, wore blue colored contacts, and had a fake Australian accent. That wasn't me. I am an American, and I have dark hair. But I wasn't talking about superficial, Tessnia. I'm simply saying that nobody knows the real me more than you." Chayse's voice lowers and he slowly starts to stroll toward me, minimizing the distance between us.

I instinctively start to back up. I have to keep my space from him. As much as I hate to admit it, I notice instantly how beautiful he looks. It's Joe, but now he's a grown man. His body is that of a man. Solid as a rock! His hair holds that same messy look--dark and wild. And his eyes are piercing as ever! They haven't changed at all, but may have actually become even more intense gray than how I remember them. He has a beautiful tan on him, as he always did, making me think he's probably an outdoor type of guy. He has a black t-shirt that hugs his torso and relaxed black jeans which are falling right below his hips. He looks sexy. I force my gaze away, fearing that I may give away the effect he still has on me.

"Please, please don't come any closer," I beg. I have no strength to fight this gorgeous man off. My emotions are all over the place. I just need some space to try to gather my thoughts and figure out why he has brought me here.

He sighs, running his fingers through his hair as if he's frustrated. "Ok, Tessnia. Let's just go downstairs and eat some breakfast. I cooked for you." He appears to have abandoned the idea of coming closer to me. For now.

"I'm not hungry," I quickly reply back.

"I don't care. You'll be eating full meals here. You look sickly. You're skin and bones. Nothing like the Tessnia I remember." Chayse is adamant.

"You can't order me around!" I raise my chin up in defiance. The jerk just called me "sickly"!

"Here's how it's going to work. Either you come down willingly, or I carry you down and make you eat anyway," Chayse threatens, lowering his voice.

"First of all, you can't force me to do anything. But right now, I'm going to use the bathroom!" I notice a connecting door and hope that's the bathroom.

As I dash to the door, yanking it open, I breathe out a sigh of relief that I'm right! I quickly close the door and lock it, desperately craving some space. Once I'm alone, my body starts to tremble. I can't believe how much he can still affect me. I haven't seen him in over three years! Why is he back in my life? I have no idea why he forced me here. Where the hell am I anyway? I look for windows in the bathroom but to my disappointment, I find none.

I reluctantly sneak a peek at the mirror and I cringe! My hair is a tangled, curly mess all over the place! I try to put some water to wet my hair down, praying it will help to control it somehow. I help myself to the mouthwash that's on the counter. I splash cold water on my face, hoping it will clear my mind. After taking a deep breath, I force myself to go back out, bracing myself for whatever awaits me.

Chris--I mean Chayse--is standing in the middle of the room with his arms crossed across his chest, waiting patiently for me. "Ready to eat now?"

I turn my back to him. I am so angry! Who does he think he is? Just as I'm about to reply a smart comment back, I feel him pick me up and throw me over his shoulder.

I gasp in shock and scream, "Put me down! Now!" How infuriating!

To make matters worse, I hear him chuckling as he carries me out of the room. He really thinks this is a big joke! Then, I see Gem following us, jumping around, wagging her tail, and barking excitedly as if she thinks this is fun and games too! So much for loyalty from your dog! He carries me through a long hallway, then down the stairs, and eventually into the kitchen. He lowers me down on the chair by the table.

"Here we are! You will be impressed with the breakfast," Chayse announces. I am too shocked to reply back. Chayse brings two plates full of scrambled eggs, pancakes, and wheat toast to the table. He also pours two glasses of orange juice.

"I can't eat all that," I complain, knowing that I'm purposefully being difficult.

"You will eat all that. I'm putting my foot down. You'll clean your plate up. You need to get healthy and try to gain some of your weight back." I'm tempted to throw the plate of food in his face. That would show him! But I hold back. The aroma of the food is making my stomach growl so I decide to take a few bites. When I taste the breakfast, I'm impressed with his cooking skills. This is the first time I'm enjoying the taste of food in a very long time. Without saying a word, I keep eating. And to my surprise, I clean up my plate. I must have been hungrier than I realized. I haven't eaten this much since my parents' accident. After I finish the food, Chayse takes the plates and puts them in the sink. He comes back and sits in his chair, focusing his attention back on me again.

"Thank you," I say to him. "It was good."

"You'll be surprised with my cooking talent. Wait until

you try my lunch and dinner dishes," Chayse brags. He's apparently not humble about his cooking.

I slowly shift my gaze up at him. I sigh and softly mumble, "I'm really having a hard time calling you Chayse. Even though your hair and eyes are different, I still see you as Chris."

"You can call me Chris if you'd like. It doesn't matter," he replies, shrugging his shoulders.

"Why would I call you Chris? You're not Chris. You are Chayse," I say, shaking my head in disbelief. Does he think it's perfectly ok for people to call him by false names? I sigh, and then ask, "What do you want from me? Why am I here?"

"I already told you, you're here because I missed you. That's the truth," he answers, as if it's the most obvious answer.

"You missed me? Hmm, well, if I remember correctly, you left. Remember?" I say incredulously. "You left over three years ago. You just took off, with no explanations. You broke my heart, *Chayse*! But to top it off, our whole relationship, or friendship, or whatever we had, was a total lie. You lied to me about everything. You had met me years ago, as Joe! Then I see you years later, and you had changed not only your appearance, but your name too! You knew who I was, and not once did you respect our friendship enough to be truthful. You kept lying. And then, you just took off!" I'm yelling at him now, as my blood pressure rises. But I can't stop. "And now, here you are again in my life. You have no idea what I've gone through since you've been gone. You have no idea about my life, and you just show up saying you missed me? You're three years too late, *Chayse!* And you haven't really answered any of my questions. I still don't know what I'm doing here." I am breathing heavily by now, my anger getting the best of me. Damn it!

This man still has the power to frustrate the hell out of me.

Chayse watches me for a few more minutes as I wait for a reply. He gets up from his chair, saying, "You will get your answers soon enough. But right now, we're going to take Gem for a walk." Gem starts walking toward him when she hears her name. "Come on, girl. Let's get you some fresh air."

I sigh, because I know that he tactfully just avoided answering everything that I asked him. Knowing that the answers won't be given until he's good and ready, I follow Chayse and Gem outside. Maybe I might get an idea of our location from the surroundings. I might see something I recognize.

Unfortunately, as I step out, I just see open land and meadows. There are no houses around. I don't even see a main road, except there's a long dirt road leading to the house. I turn to look at the outside of the house. It's a two-story red brick house. It has a white door and white shutters on the windows. It's not a large house or anything, but it has a lot of charm to it. I wonder how far the main road is from this dirt road. From the looks of it, there is no end in sight.

As if reading my mind, Chayse says, "We are in the middle of nowhere, Tessnia. Don't even think you can make a run for it. You'll probably get lost in this open land and the woods." I glare at him, and he's looking down at me with his lopsided grin flashing, waiting for me to challenge him.

"This is your house?" I ask, not wanting to give him that satisfaction.

"Well, I never said that. I said it was my temporary residence," he replies.

"Where's your car?" I ask, as I notice there's no car by the house.

"I put it in the back. I didn't want to leave the car in plain view."

"Why so many secrets? You've never been straight-forward with me. I don't understand. Why the disguises?" I ask, wishing for once he would be truthful with me.

"I had no choice, Tessnia," Chayse answers, gazing off into distance. He does not elaborate more than that.

We continue our walk with Gem as she explores the land, enjoying herself. As I watch her, I come to terms that she really likes Chayse. I'm not sure why she likes him so much. She had recognized him, and hadn't even questioned when he'd taken us out of our home. I reluctantly admit that she trusts him. The fact that Gem trusts him, helps me to relax and I find myself enjoying the fresh air and the soft breeze.

As the rays of light glimmer and shine across the landscape, I can hear the birds singing their love songs. The fresh breeze blowing softly through my wild curly hair feels refreshing as it fills my senses. I am invaded by the scent of the pine trees and wild flowers. I can't remember the last time I had noticed the simple beauty of Mother Nature. I take in a deep breath to savor the outdoor scent of my surroundings.

We must have walked quietly for an hour before Chayse says, "The outdoors is working its magic on you, Tessnia. I already see some color on your cheeks." As I turn to look at him, I see that he's grinning with approval. I don't say anything. I don't want the spell to break just yet. For the first time in a long while, I actually feel at peace.

How ironic.

I am, God only knows where, with this man who I don't know much about, and I have no way of leaving. But somehow, right at this moment, I feel peace. I cherish the feeling.

To my disappointment, we eventually start to head back. Perhaps he's tired from being up all night. For all I know, he may have also driven all day to get to my house.

When we arrive back, Chayse says, "How are you feeling? Are you tired?" I shake my head no. "Maybe you should jump in the shower and get cleaned up." I guess that's a hint that I probably look a mess and in desperate need of a shower.

"I don't have any of my clothes here, remember? What am I supposed to wear?" I challenge him, rubbing it in that I'm here against my will.

"Actually I packed for you, Tessnia. I grabbed some clothes for you and some of your personal items. I even remembered your phone charger," he says proudly. "Look in the bedroom drawers and closet for your clothes. And your toiletry is already in the bathroom."

I'm debating whether to argue with him, but the thought of a hot shower *does* sound appealing. I could use a good clean up. Without saying a word, I climb upstairs to the bedroom. A lot of my clothes are already hanging in the closet. I note that many of his clothes are also hanging on the other side of the closet. There are more clothes in the drawers. I grab clean underwear, bra, a pair of jean cut off shorts and a white tank top. My cheeks scorch with embarrassment at the thought of Chayse unpacking my personal undergarments.

As I step into the bathroom, I notice more details. It's a nice, clean bathroom, big enough to fit a shower and a Jacuzzi. The bathroom is decorated with antique wall tiles and floor tiles.

When I glance toward the mirror, I wince. The only thing

I have going for me is that I do have some color on my cheeks from the sun and the wind. How embarrassing that I went like this all morning with Chayse!

I strip and jump into the shower. I shave my legs, desperately needing it. I take a deep breath as the hot stream collides onto my skin, releasing tension. As I close my eyes, the steam envelops my body. After washing my hair, I finally step out of the shower.

After drying myself, I put my clothes on and brush my teeth. Towel drying my hair helps my spiral curls fall softly down my back. My hair finally appears slightly more manageable and I'm surprised at how long it's getting from not having a haircut in the last few months. I haven't used any makeup in a long while either, but today I decide to put light mascara and lip gloss on. I check at my reflection in the mirror once more and my big brown eyes stare back at me. I sigh. I still look "sickly" but at least I feel a little cleaner.

When I step out of the bedroom and head downstairs, I can smell something delicious cooking. Italian maybe? My stomach responds as I'm already feeling hungry. Strange, since I ate more breakfast than what I usually eat the entire day. It must be the country air.

When Chayse sees me, he smiles with his perfect white teeth and his eyes full of approval. My heart skips a beat. Damn! This is one beautiful man. His hair is damp, and he has different clothes on than this morning. I guess there must be another shower in this house because it appears that he has also taken a shower. He's wearing faded, loose fitted jeans, and a white t-shirt. The jeans are his typical style, hanging right below his hips, making him look sexy as hell. The way his damp hair falls over his forehead, and the way he is standing, leaning against the kitchen sink with his legs slightly spread, makes me swallow hard from nervousness. Chayse folds his arms across his chest, and smirks at me, raising one of his eyebrows. Having difficulty concentrating, I force myself to look away.

"You look gorgeous, Tessnia," he simply says. What is he looking at? Has he looked at himself lately?

"I thought you said I looked *sickly*," I reply, as I reach the kitchen table. I can't resist letting him know that I noticed what he had said to me earlier.

He laughs--a genuine, full blown laugh--throwing his head back and apparently getting a kick out of my comment. I narrow my eyes at him, crossing my arms in front of my chest, as he finally stops laughing.

"Sickly, yes, but still gorgeous," he clarifies. "Come on, time for lunch. You won't be sickly for long because I'm going to make sure you get some meat on you. I made some spaghetti with meatballs for lunch." Chayse walks toward me, takes me by my hand, and pulls my chair out. When I sit down, he presents me with a plate of spaghetti, Italian salad, and garlic bread. It smells delicious. He then asks, "What would you like to drink, Tessnia?"

"Water is fine, thanks," I answer.

He goes back to the fridge and brings two bottles of water. He returns with his plate of food as well and sits down to eat with me. As I take some bites, I'm again impressed with how delicious the food tastes. I look at him and wonder what he wants from me.

I decide to try my luck and ask, "What do you want from

me, Chayse?" My voice softens as I say, "At least answer that much. Please."

Chayse takes a few more bites before answering. He concentrates really hard on the food from his plate, with a slight frown on his forehead. It's as if he's thinking about how he wants to answer that question. He finally looks up at me, and slowly says, "Whatever you can give me, Tessnia."

What does he mean by that? Maybe he knows about my parents' accident and the money they left me. He seems to know an awful lot about me.

So, I stare right at him and ask directly, "Is this about money? You want me to pay you to let me go?" As soon as the question slips out, I regret it. I already know the answer. Even if I know nothing about this man, I know he's a man of integrity. He would never stoop to that level.

Chayse's eyes become wide with disbelief. "You think you're here because I want your money? Why would I want your money? I have plenty of my own." He looks shocked and I start feeling embarrassed that I even asked that question.

Knowing that I've insulted him, I whisper, "I'm sorry." I look down again. "I just don't understand." Too many things are happening too fast.

Chayse reaches for my hand across the table. I don't pull away and instantly, I feel the same sensation that I remember so clearly go through my body whenever we touched. He holds my hand and says, "Come on, let's take a quick nap. I'm exhausted from being up for at least twenty four hours straight."

I snatch my hand out of his hold as I panic. "Nap? Um, no thanks. I'm good," I quickly reply. I hope he's not thinking that I'm going to sleep in the same bed as him. There must be another bedroom upstairs. Maybe he can just use that other bedroom.

"Well, you don't have to take an actual nap if you don't want to. But I want you with me, so you don't try anything stupid and end up getting hurt," Chayse insists.

"Are you kidding me? What am I going to do anyway? I'm not going to the bedroom with you," I say sternly. I *will* find the strength to fight this battle.

"You don't have a choice. Now, stop being so dramatic." He takes my hand and starts leading me upstairs. I am fuming as I try to resist. There is no way!

"Where the hell am I going to go? We are in the middle of nowhere!" I try to plead my case.

"I know. But I want to have a peaceful nap," Chayse explains, as he continues to take me toward the bedroom. "At least I won't be worried about anything if you're right next to me. Besides, it might do you some good to rest as well."

By now, we're almost by the bedroom. My resistance is useless. He has already made up his mind. My mind races, trying to think of a way to get out of this situation. Ok, maybe I can just lie next to him, and as soon as he's asleep, I can slip out of the bed.

When we enter the bedroom, he throws his shoes off, moves one side of the blanket aside and climbs under it. As he lies there perfectly content, I stand there awkwardly, twirling my hair with my fingers nervously. "Come here, Tessnia," Chayse says, lowering his voice. I sneak a glance at him, and he starts flashing his famous crooked grin. "You're acting like we've never shared a bed together," he teases, raising one of his eyebrows.

"Don't go there with me," I reply tartly, crossing my arms in front of me.

His grin gets wider. He opens the blanket on the side he's not sleeping to make room for me. I sigh and hesitantly climb on that side. I remain on the edge, stiff as a board and hold my breath. This is so awkward. How did I get myself in this situation? Maybe if I just count to myself and keep my mind preoccupied, I won't focus on the fact that he's lying right next to me. My heart is beating so fast, that I'm sure he can hear it. Please God, have him fall asleep soon so I can get out of this bed, and out of this room.

As if Chayse can hear my mind, his arm comes across me, holding me. "What are you doing?" I ask incredulously, as my body becomes even more rigid.

"I'm just making sure you don't attempt to sneak out. Besides, I like holding you. Now hush, close your eyes, and go to sleep." Wow, I can't believe how demanding he still is!

I'm just about to say something smart back, when I notice that he's already falling asleep. His breathing is slowing down, and I feel his whole body relaxing. I sneak a peek and notice that his eyes are closed. I quickly look away, for fear that he may open his eyes and catch me staring at him. I lie still, afraid to move a muscle for at least fifteen minutes. He doesn't move either. I glance at him again. He is sound asleep.

I am incapable of looking away as I continue to stare at him. I'm in awe by his flawless beauty. His wild hair is even more unruly as it's falling all over his forehead. He has a sharp, strong jaw line, with a narrow nose. Despite the relaxed expression on his face, his five o'clock shadow makes him look rugged and dangerous. His full, soft lips are partly open, making them appear even more luscious. I love his skin color. His natural tanned skin is clear and flawless. As his gray eyes remain closed, they're surrounded by long and thick black eyelashes.

I wonder if he even realizes how gorgeous he is or if he even cares. Probably not. He doesn't seem like the kind of guy who would worry about the exterior appearance. That seems too shallow for his personality. Chayse is much more deep and intense. I sigh. I have to admit, I love just lying here and staring at him while he sleeps so peacefully. When he's awake, I can barely look at him. His presence is so overwhelming and almost intimidating.

Chayse--he said that's his real name. I don't even know his last name. *Chayse*, hmm, I have to get used to that. As I continue to stare at him shamelessly, rehearsing his name in my mind, I have to admit that he does look like a "Chayse" to me. The name's not a common name like a "Joe" or a "Chris". Chayse, yeah it suits him--masculine and unique, just like him.

I find myself edging a little closer to him. I can smell him, that same familiar, rugged scent I had missed. I smile to myself because he has not changed his cologne from three years ago. I have no idea what cologne he uses, but it's a huge turn on. And it's so him. I take in a deep breath, savoring this moment, knowing he will leave my life again.

Maybe one day he'll explain everything to me. Or maybe he'll always keep his secrets from me. But I know, that at this moment, I don't want to be anywhere else but right here. This is my cherished moment, and I'm going to remember every detail of his image as he sleeps. Eventually, I start to relax with the rhythm of his breathing. Maybe it will be ok if I close my eyes just for a minute.

Sixteen

When I open my eyes, I feel Chayse staring at me. I glance up at his face and he's looking down at me, with a far-away look, full of emotion. Before I can pinpoint the emotion, Chayse shields his eyes.

"Sorry, I didn't realize I was going to fall asleep," I mumble, breaking the spell.

"Why are you sorry? Come on, we should take Gem for a walk." Chayse is impersonal again, and the strange look is gone. He jumps out of the bed and pulls me up with him.

"I need to use the bathroom real quick," I reply, trying to escape. Just because he wakes up beautiful, doesn't mean everybody has the same luxury!

"Ok, I'll meet you outside by the front door," he says. As he leaves the bedroom, I hear him whistling for Gem.

After stepping into the bathroom, I brush my teeth, and put my hair back into a loose braid. I put my light lip gloss back on, and head downstairs. When I step out of the front door, Chayse is sitting on the porch steps.

"Where's Gem?" I ask.

"Oh, she's running around. Don't worry. I told her to be back in fifteen minutes." He looks up at me and smiles mischievously.

It's hard not to smile back. "Fifteen minutes, huh? You sure she got that? Are you going to ground her if she's late?" I can't help but joke with him. It feels good to not be so uptight and stressed out constantly. But suddenly, I can't help but worry at the thought of her being out there by herself. "Wait, you don't think she'll get lost or hurt, do you?" I ask, scanning over the landscape, hoping to see her.

"Nah, she'll be fine. And I bet she'll be back in fifteen minutes. Don't you think she's really smart?" he asks.

"Well yeah, I think she's smarter than most dogs, sure. But I doubt she understands the concept of time!" I laugh. Does he really believe that or is he still joking around with me?

"Ok, let's make a bet," Chayse challenges.

"Are you serious?" I ask, baffled. "Ok, I'll bite. What's the bet? But you know I'll win this bet right?"

"We'll see," he answers. He gestures me to sit down on the porch step next to him, holding out his hand. I take his hand and lower myself down. His touch brings my sensations on high alert. Once I take my position next to him, I slip my hand out of his hold, not wanting to let my guard down. Chayse smiles, as if he knows exactly why I pulled my hand out. I don't dare respond, deciding to ignore the whole exchange. He continues, "Ok, here's the bet. If I win, we sleep on the same bed every time we go to bed. If you win, I sleep in the spare bedroom."

"Well, you can always force me, like you did today. Why bet?" I ask, now curious.

"True. But I don't like to force any woman to share my bed with me. It doesn't sit right with me," Chayse teases, as he lifts his one eyebrow. I can't help but laugh.

"Ok, you got yourself a bet!" We shake hands to make it official.

We remain silent as we watch the sun setting. The beauty

and the tranquility bring me peace that I've been craving for a long time.

"Thank you," he says to me, switching his attention on me.

"For what?" I ask.

"For lying next to me. It was probably the most restful nap I've had in a long time," Chayse explains, as his eyes penetrate mine.

"To be honest, I rested pretty well, too," I confess. I start to get nervous, needing some space from him. Pulling myself up to stand back up, I walk down the porch steps. I take a deep breath. The country air feels amazing.

As I continue to enjoy this picturesque scenery, I wonder what I'm doing here. I'm letting my guard down with him and I'm setting myself up for getting hurt again. I have to keep staying strong. I can't let him in. Not into my heart. Not into my soul. I know that if I did, and he leaves again, I won't be strong enough to make it this time. I take a deep breath and quickly say a silent prayer to give me the strength. I hear him approach me and he stands next to me.

"Well, Gem's got five more minutes. Let's see what happens," he says, his eyes dancing. Chayse seems to be very excited to find out the outcome of our bet.

"I can't believe that you actually think that she'll be back in exactly fifteen minutes," I say, rolling my eyes.

"I truly do believe that," Chayse responds, smiling at me. "You got her for a Christmas gift right?"

"Yeah, my parents gave her to me," I respond automatically. *My parents*. I sigh. I haven't thought about their death in almost twenty-four hours. Suddenly, guilt starts to eat me up as my eyes fill with tears. I don't want to cry, not in front of Chayse. I turn my head away from him abruptly, staring into the horizon. My parents are gone. I'm all alone in this world. I don't want to fall apart again, not here.

I feel Chayse reach for my hand. He takes my hand and kisses the palm of my hand, just as he had done when I had first met him. I slowly shift my gaze up at him, and I know he can see the tears in my eyes. I don't want his pity. He doesn't give it to me. He just squeezes my hand, his eyes full of understanding. His hand on mine somehow grounds me, as if he's transferring his strength into me. It's a squeeze of re-assurance. I'm thankful that it's not that same look of "poor Tess, what's going to happen to her now."

Just then, we hear a familiar bark. I look up and Gem is running toward us from the fields. Chayse checks the time on his watch.

"Yep, fifteen minutes," he says, with pride. Gem races to us, doing her happy dance. "Good girl! Exactly fifteen minutes. Proud of you, Gem!" Chayse is laughing while petting her. Gem is jumping up and down, just as happy to get that attention from him. I guess he has that same effect on all females, no matter what species. "Guess I win the bet." Chayse's eyes tease me, as he rubs it in.

I smile back at him, shaking my head. "Guess you did win that bet."

"And I intend on collecting my prize!" Chayse threatens. I take a deep breath, and start to become nervous again. I don't think I can handle sharing his bed every day. I can't even think of a good comeback for him, so I mumble something unintelligible under my breath. As we start heading back to the house,

I hear Chayse chuckle. It's humiliating that he knows exactly the reason for my nervousness!

I decide to change the subject, and say, "I think it was a coincidence that she came back in exactly fifteen minutes."

"Why is it so hard for you to believe that she knew?" Chayse asks, his gray eyes wide.

"Because she's a dog, Chayse. And dogs aren't supposed to know the concept of time," I answer back.

"The world is not black and white, Tessnia. There aren't always just practical answers. You have to open your mind," Chayse insists.

"I can't even talk about this. I don't understand you at all." I think it was a strange coincidence that she came back in time. Chayse truly believes that she knew what she was doing. Shaking my head, I ask, "What's the plan for the rest of the evening anyway?"

"Let's do dinner first," he suggests.

Chayse doesn't allow me to help with dinner so I finish up the dishes from earlier. He makes us chicken and rice. I have no idea why I'm always hungry here, but my stomach begins to growl as the scent of the food fills the kitchen. I haven't eaten three full meals in so long, never feeling hungry. But right now, I'm famished, and I clean my plate spotless. After dinner, I tell him that I'm cleaning up the kitchen.

Once everything is cleaned, we watch TV in the family room. We're both sitting on the sofa, while Chayse is flipping channels. Nothing interesting is on, so Chayse says, "Let's play a game."

"What kind of game?" I ask, now curious.

He gets up and brings a deck of cards. He shuffles them

up and instructs me to pick a card. He tells me to hold on to the card, but to not show it to him. He then instructs me to look at the card and think about it in my mind. It's the queen of hearts, so I start to visualize it in my mind. He then makes three piles of the cards, has me put my card in the middle of one of the piles, and shuffles it all up.

"I know the card," he says confidently.

"Really! So what is it?" I tease.

"Queen of hearts," Chayse says, with a smug smile.

"Wow, not bad," I say, impressed with him. "What's the trick?"

"I'll do it again," Chayse says with his cocky grin.

He does the same trick five more times, and each time, he amazingly guesses the card correctly. I know a lot of people perform impressive tricks with cards, but unfortunately, I don't know any of these tricks.

"I'm going to make it harder," Chayse says. "Let's get rid of the cards. I want you to think of a number from one through ten. Just think of the number in your mind, and I bet I can figure it out."

"Hmm, that *is* hard. Ok, let's see what you got," I challenge him, enjoying playing these games with him. He is so funny when he's in a playful mood. I close my eyes, and I think of the number nine in my mind.

He starts humming and then puts his hands on my temple and closes his eyes. He does this for about twenty seconds, and then opens his eyes, and says, "Nine."

I'm taken aback by his answer, assuming he was going to guess wrong. "Wait, how did you know that?" I ask, bewildered.

"Magic," he replies, his eyes dancing.

He has me pick a number from one through twenty next. I pick sixteen in my mind. Chayse does the same ritual and gets it right! Then, Chayse goes all the way to fifty, and he's able to guess number twenty-eight correctly. How the hell is he doing this?

"I can't figure your trick out. How are you doing this?" I finally ask.

"No trick. You can do it too," Chayse replies.

"What? No, I can't. How can I possibly know what number is going through your mind?" I ask, shaking my head.

"You're limiting yourself, Tessnia. Open your mind. Just do what I tell you. Trust me." Chayse takes my hands into his hands.

"Chayse, I'm telling you.." I say, trying to refuse.

"Close your eyes, Tessnia, and make your mind go blank," Chayse interrupts, squeezing my hands. "I'm going to make it easy for you. I'm going to think of a number between one through five. And I want you to blurt out whatever number comes to your mind. Not yet though. I have to think of the number." Chayse pauses, and closes his eyes, still holding my hands. "Ok, I got one. Now you say whichever number comes to your mind. Remember, to say the first number that you think of, Tessnia. Don't analyze this too much," he explains.

"Ok, the number four popped into my mind," I answer. I want to giggle because this is so ridiculous.

"Yes! My number was four!" Chayse exclaims.

"Ha-ha, really funny. I know you're just saying that to make me think that I really guessed the number that you had in your mind." He's so silly to think I'm actually going to believe him.

"I'm not, really. How about this? I will now write a number from one through ten on a piece of paper." He grabs a note pad and a pen from the coffee table and writes a number, keeping it hidden from me. "Now I want you to say the first number that pops into your mind."

"Eight," I reply, still finding all this hilarious.

Chayse shows me the paper. It has the number "8" on it.

"What the hell!" I exclaim, snatching the paper out of his hand. "How did you do that?"

"I didn't do anything. *You* did it," Chayse says proudly.

"I don't understand," I whisper, closing my eyes. I put my hand on my temple because suddenly my brain feels fatigued.

"I see you're starting to get tired. Come on, it's getting late. Let's get you some sleep. I'll take Gem outside real quick." Chayse whistles for Gem and she trots behind him out the front door.

As I climb up the stairs, I'm still in awe at the game. How was I able to guess those numbers? It doesn't make any sense.

Then it hits me. Chayse is not here. I'm alone in this house. This is my chance to see what he's up to! I quickly walk down the hall to investigate the other rooms. There's one more bathroom down the hall. I see nothing of interest in there. The other closed room is the second bedroom. Maybe I'll find my phone in here. I quickly start to scan the room. I notice some of his clothes are thrown on the bed. I search the pockets for my phone. Nothing. I inspect all of the drawers but there are just few of his clothes in there. I glance through his closet, and to my disappointment, nothing out of ordinary is in there. I scan the shelves and I notice a safety case with a lock on the top shelf. Because the key is still attached to the case, I pull it down, and turn the key. As I'm about to open the case, I feel a twinge of guilt for invading his privacy. Just as quickly, I brush the thought away since he's the one who brought me here against my will!

When I open the lid, I gasp as I stare down into the case. I see at least eight different driver's licenses with a picture of Chayse. Each license has a different name and a different look. What the hell! I flip through the licenses in disbelief. Who is this guy? Why does he need so many different identifications? God, I'm so stupid. I've barely been here for twenty-four hours, and I've been playing housewife to this guy. I don't even know him! These fake ID's just prove that he has too many secrets. I absolutely can't stay here. I have to find a way out. I shuffle through his identifications again, my hand trembling and my heart racing.

"Find what you're looking for?" Chayse is standing in the bedroom doorway, leaning against the frame, with his arms crossed in front of his chest. He is irritated. "You know, it's not polite to snoop."

I instantly react, becoming irritated as well. "You're kidding right? You know all this information about my life. You even knew about my parents, and you're lecturing about politeness and snooping?" I ask incredulously.

Chayse stares at me for another minute and says, "As usual, point well-made, Tessnia." Chayse then smiles. "But let's put my personal belongings away for now."

"Why do you have so many fake ID's? What is it that you're not telling me? I have a right to know!" I demand.

Chayse walks toward me, closes the case, locks it up, and places it back on the shelf. He grabs the hook of my arm to lead me out of the room, saying, "Come."

I snatch my arm out of his grasp. "Just don't touch me, ok?" I quicken my pace and practically run into the bedroom I've been using. Before he can say one more thing to me, I race into the bathroom and lock the door. I take some deep breaths to calm myself down. I have to think things through without him being in the same room as me. Whenever Chayse is near me, I am incapable of thinking straight. I quickly wash my face, hoping it will clear my mind so I can think rationally.

I start pacing the bathroom, trying to gather my thoughts. I don't know anything about him. He's been secretive since the day I met him. Is he dangerous? Yes, I believe Chayse *can* be dangerous. But no, I don't think he would be dangerous toward me. I can't see him intentionally trying to hurt me. I'm not scared of him. If anything, I see him more as a protector.

I still have not received a clear explanation regarding what he wants from me and why I'm here. He keeps talking in riddles, never giving me direct answers. He frustrates the hell out of me!

Unfortunately, he still holds power over me. I'm still drawn to him, and there's a strong connection between us. I'm playing a dangerous game because I know in my heart, he's going to disappear again--just as he had in the past.

I sigh and jump in the shower. After the shower, I notice I don't have my pajamas with me. I have no choice but put my jean shorts and t-shirt back on. As I step out of the bathroom, Chayse is already in bed, flipping through the channels on TV. He must have taken a shower in the other bathroom because his hair is wet. He has changed his clothes to a gray tank and a pair of shorts. I force my gaze away from his bulging shoulder and chest muscles.

I ignore him as I grab my pajamas out of my drawer and run back into the bathroom. I have my cotton boxer shorts and a matching cotton tank top. I'm relieved that they cover everything. I take a deep breath, and bravely step back out.

"I have two questions, and you have to answer them," I say to Chayse, putting my hand on my hip. "And I don't mean some vague answers, but truthfully answer them." This time, I'm not going to budge until I get my answers.

Chayse looks at me, and raises his one eyebrow at me, waiting for my questions.

"First question, why do you have all of those ID's? And I want the truth." I start to tap my foot, lifting my chin up stubbornly.

Chayse stares at me for a full minute, and then sighs in defeat. "Ok, Tessnia. Remember a while ago I had told you that I was in the military? Well, they've given me specific training. And many times, I have to use different ID's for my assignments. Trust me, it's all part of the job."

"Like the CIA or something? Are you in special forces?" I ask, prying for more information.

"Something like that. Yes, I work for the government. I'm not even supposed to share that with you. Everything is classified information, so please do not repeat that to anybody. Plus, it's not safe for you to have any more knowledge. So I'm not elaborating on that question. What's your second question?" He is ready to move on.

I fold my arms in front of my chest and say, "Alright, that

answer will have to do for now. My second question is why are we both sleeping on the same bed if there are two bedrooms here?" I need to keep my distance from him, knowing I can't afford to get too close to him. The closer I allow myself to get to him, the harder I'm going to fall.

Chayse smiles, and responds, "Well, that's easy. I like lying next to you." Chayse turns to his side, facing me, and props himself up on his elbow. "And, you lost the bet, remember? Besides, I rest better when you're by me." Chayse's smile widens as he teases.

"Hmm, you seem to have done fine the last three years, Chayse," I snap back.

Chayse doesn't say anything at first. After thinking about his answer, he says, "Well, the couple of nights I've laid with you have apparently made an impact on me." Then his voice lowers as he says, "Especially that first time." My face burns from embarrassment as Chayse relentlessly continues his teasing.

Determined to prove to him that I'm not at all affected, I say, "The way I remember it, you just got up and left. Actually, that's pretty much all I remember about it."

"Well, I remember every detail, Tessnia. I have carried that memory of you with me for three long years." I can't tell if he's being serious or is still teasing me.

"Let me make it clear. There will be no repeat of that night. Absolutely not! Not ever, do you understand?" God, I can't believe that he's bringing that up! Where is he going with this?

Chayse laughs. "Who are you trying to convince, Tessnia? Me or you?" Chayse flashes his crooked grin, waiting for me to respond. I open my mouth to snap a smart comment back, but nothing comes out. So, like a fool, I stand there with my one hand on my hip and my mouth open. He chuckles, probably at how foolish I look. "Don't worry, Tessnia. As much as I'd love to pick up where we had left off, I've never had to force myself on any woman. And I don't intend to start now. Believe me, that is not something I get off on."

No, of course he doesn't. I vividly remember his reaction when that creep, Josh, had attacked me that night. He had nearly killed him. Besides, I can't ever imagine Chayse having to force himself on any woman. I'm sure he's used to women just throwing themselves at his feet.

I stomp to the bed, take my pillow, move it all the way to my edge, and lie down. I pull the covers over me and swiftly turn my back on him.

When I hear him laughing under his breath, it takes every ounce of my willpower to not hit him with my pillow. He turns off the light and lies back down.

I am so tense, that I'm having difficulty closing my eyes to fall asleep. But, as his body starts to relax, mine automatically responds. Before I know it, I'm asleep.

She is running again, desperate. But this time she is running toward something. She has to get there. She feels the urgency. She sees a man and a woman. They are in a car, driving and talking to each other. They are laughing and relaxed. NO! She has to reach them! Something is not right! "Please stop!" she yells. They are not stopping. They can't hear her. She runs faster. She has to reach them! RUN FASTER! KEEP RUNNING! She gives it her all. She has to get to them on time. She's almost there. Just a little more! And then it happens! A truck comes from nowhere and crashes into them! The car blows up instantly! NO, NO! PLEASE NO! GOD PLEASE!

"Get up, Tess! Please, it's me, Chayse! It's just a dream, please wake up." Chayse desperately tries to wake me, shaking me frantically.

I open my eyes and try to free myself from his hold. "Let me go! Let me go! They were almost saved." I begin to cry, unable to stop. I am hysterical. I keep trying to push him off, screaming. I lose all control as I start hitting him. As I sob hysterically, punching into his chest, Chayse does not let me go. He holds me tighter, and brings me closer into his chest. My wailing does not stop, but he keeps holding me and rocking me.

"I'm so sorry, baby. God, I'm sorry. If I could take your pain away..." he keeps whispering into my ears. Eventually my wailing turns into sobbing. Finally, exhaustion takes over and I have no more tears left. I am drained. Chayse never stops rocking me, holding me, and caressing my back and my hair.

"Another bad dream," I whisper.

"Tell me, Tessnia," Chayse encourages.

"I think it was about my parents. The girl in my dream was running to save them," I tell him. "But she doesn't reach them in time. They were driving, and then the truck came. It was too late. She was too late." I start shaking uncontrollably.

Chayse squeezes me tighter to him. "Was the girl in your dream you?"

I catch my breath. "I can never see the girl, but I feel her fears, her anxiety, and all of her emotions. I don't know Chayse, it's just too much. If only I could've saved them!"

"Tess, there was nothing you could do!" Chayse insists.

I pause, deep in thought. I take a deep breath and explain,

"It's just that I think I had a warning. I would get visions of a black cloud passing before me, and it would scare the hell out of me. These episodes were so rare, that I didn't worry about them too much. But on the day of the accident, I had multiple visions of the black cloud. That had never happened before. Chayse, I knew something was wrong! In my heart, I knew! But I just didn't figure it out. Maybe I could have saved them!" My voice quivers, as my eyes fill with tears.

"Stop it, Tess! How could you know? You're punishing yourself, and I can't bear it! Trust me! Even if those visions were related to your parents, there was nothing you could do. I wish there was something I can do to help you through this." His voice is husky and full of pain.

I glance up at him and notice that his eyes are misty. Chayse is hurting because he can't bear seeing me in pain like this. I hug him tight, not wanting to see him hurt because of me.

"I'm sorry, Chayse. I lost control. And thank you," I slowly whisper back.

"Don't apologize, Tess! You've been through hell and back. And I'm here for you, to help you through this. I promise you, I'll do whatever I can. But I'm not going to let you give up, Tessnia. You have to somehow overcome this horrible pain. You have to keep going, live again."

"You have no idea how many times I wished I was in that car with them," I mumble into his chest.

Chayse pulls me off of him. He puts his hand under my chin and lifts my face. He looks directly into my eyes, with that same familiar intensity in his gray eyes, desperate for me to understand. "Don't you ever say or think that again! Your parents would never want that. They would want you to live,

Tessnia. Tell me you know that." Chayse looks frantic.

"I know, Chayse, but honestly, before I came here, I felt my world had stopped. I had never felt that kind of pain. I didn't have the will to keep going, Chayse. But being here, with you, it's different," I confess. I look up at him. "But I know you're going to leave me too. Just like you did last time. And just like my parents left me. I just don't think I'm strong enough, Chayse." I can't stop the tears from flowing down my face.

Chayse sighs, and pulls me back against his chest. "Trust me, Tessnia, if I had it my way, I would never leave you. But I don't know what tomorrow is going to bring. And above all else, your safety is the priority for me. Unfortunately, being with me is not safe. I could never forgive myself if something happened to you because of me. That's why I brought you out here. It's isolated, hidden, and hopefully safe."

"You broke my heart last time you left, Chayse," I whisper. It's important he knows the truth.

"I'm so sorry. I kept telling myself that I have to stay away from you because I'll just end up hurting you. But I'm powerless. I can't seem to stay away. Eventually I find my way back to you, Tessnia. And I know that's not fair to you." Chayse pauses, and then softens his voice and says, "I know it's not fair, because I can't offer you any future with me." He lifts my face toward him and looks deep into me. "All I can offer you is here and now." As I stare back at him, I see that he is speaking the truth.

He has put it all out there. He wants me to know, so that I can make my choices accordingly. I have no idea what he means by my safety. I have no idea why he always has to leave.

But at that moment, I know that I would hold on to any time I can have with him. Then it hits me. I love this man. It has always been him. He's the reason why I couldn't be with any other man.

I'm going to lose him soon. I feel it in my gut. But there's nothing I can do about that. I just need to take advantage of whatever amount of time I'm given with him.

Losing my parents taught me that life is too short. If this is all I have with Chayse, then I will take it. I'll hold on to each and every memory, just like I did when he was Joe, and when he was Chris. I will keep my memories with me and cherish them.

I reach for his face with my hand and slowly lift my lips to his. He doesn't move as our lips touch. With all the love I feel for him, I gently kiss him. As I reach up to the back of his neck, wrapping my fingers into his hair--that thick wild hair I love so much--I deepen my kiss. I hear him moan, surrendering himself to me and he matches my kiss. I turn him onto his back and roll on top of him. I continue kissing him as my hands explore his face, his arms, and his chest.

His tank is still on, and I want it off. As I start to kiss his neck, I bring his tank up over his head and pull it off. I'm in awe at his beauty as his chiseled chest feels hard as a rock under my fingers. As I glance up to meet his eyes, he's staring back at me--cautious, curious, and questioning. I lean into him again, and start kissing his face. I want to savor every inch of him. The feel of his bristles against my cheek sends goosebumps down my spine.

My body is on fire as we continue to kiss. When I pry myself off of him eventually, my breathing is erratic. Then, my mouth finds his chest. I kiss his chest, and when I travel to his nipples, I suck. I hear him gasp, and then hold his breath. He feels so good. I roll my tongue around one nipple and then go to work on the other.

As he moans, I smile. I like this power I have over him.

Then, my mouth starts to travel lower. I kiss his belly and my tongue rolls in his navel. Chayse moans louder. I want to go lower. Do I dare? Yes, I do. As my mouth plays with his navel, my fingers start to pull at the string of his sweat shorts.

Just as I'm about to pull his shorts down, he grabs my hand. He pulls me back up to him, and before I know what's happening, he has rolled me over. I'm lying on my back and he's on top of me.

"You're playing with fire, Tessnia," he slowly says to me, narrowing those beautiful eyes at me.

"I want you, Chayse," I simply say. It's the truth.

He shakes his head slowly. "No, not like this. You had a horrible night. When we do this, I want to make sure that your head is clear. Tonight was a very emotional night for you. As much as I want to do this right now, Tess, I know the right thing to do is to comfort you."

"I want you, Chayse. I want this," I insist. I hold him tighter and whisper, "I need you."

"And you have me, baby. Always, you have me. But not like this. Not tonight. Not when you were crying your eyes out just an hour ago. You've got a lot going on, Tessnia. And I don't want you to jump into this because it's a nice diversion--you know, to help you escape. No, when you and I make love, it will be just about us, with only the two of us, and nobody else. Period."

"I don't use people for 'diversion' Chayse. I would never disrespect you or anybody else like that," I respond.

"I know. You're a good person, Tess. Tonight, you need to rest. You're exhausted, and it's been quite a night for you." Chayse rolls off of me to lie on his side again. Then, he pulls me back into his arms and says, "Come, sleep now."

He pulls my hair back, kisses my forehead, and pulls my head into his chest. Although I'm disappointed, this feels good. I feel my body relax into his body. How does he do that?

Somehow, my body always responds to him. It's as if we are in sync. I sigh and close my eyes. I take a deep breath to take in his scent again. Mm, I love his smell--so masculine, so him.

I accept my revelation of my love for him. I know now that I always loved him, but I was just too stubborn to recognize it. I also know that no matter what happens between us, I will never stop loving him. I close my eyes, and hold him tighter. I feel him bring me even closer to him as he sighs. I am content. I can lie in his arms like this forever.

Seventeen

When I open my eyes, I'm alone. It's early morning hours, and I notice sunlight faintly peeking in through the windows. Everything is quiet. I don't even hear Gem. Maybe Chayse took her for a walk already.

I jump out of the bed and walk to the window to check if I see them. As I glance down, I catch my breath. Chayse is outside, with only his sweat shorts on, and his chest is completely bare. He is performing an exercise routine. I can't help but be mesmerized watching him move with the sun rising over the horizon. I am spellbound by his grace and beauty as he performs a mixture of yoga and karate.

Chayse is holding positions that seem impossible, and they emphasize the strength and definitions of his muscles. Suddenly, he switches position and executes high kicks in the air and couples them with flips. Sometimes he moves very slowly and deliberately during the routine, and other times he moves so fast that my eyes can barely keep up. I'm in awe at the fluid movements of his sculpted body and shocked by his ability to control his muscles through such demanding positions and motion.

The complex routine challenges his strength, his balance, his coordination, his flexibility, and his discipline. Some of the moves he's performing make him appear as if he's flying in air. I'm stunned, yet fascinated, at how he's capable of jumping so high, and doing moves while he's still in air. I sigh. Not only is Chayse unique, but he is extraordinary. There is so much I don't know about this man.

I see Gem sitting on a rock, mouth open, tongue out, wagging her tail. Even she seems like she's in awe of what she's witnessing.

I'll be damned if I just stand here watching him. I put on my black yoga pants and my athletic tank. I quickly brush my teeth, pull my hair up in a high bun, and run downstairs. I put my gym shoes on, and dart outside to join him, heart beating fast with excitement.

Gem barks and runs to me, wagging her tail. I hug her, as she kisses my face.

Chayse stops his workout and watches me as he smiles. "So the sleeping beauty awakens," he teases.

I smile back, and say, "Teach me what you were doing." Even though I know I can't get remotely close to his performance, I'm so impressed, that I'm ready to rise to the challenge.

"Oh, somebody was busy spying this morning?" Chayse asks, lifting his eyebrow.

"Yep, I sure was. And I liked what I saw. Now, I want to learn that," I reply, raising my chin up stubbornly.

Chayse's grin widens as he says, "Yes ma'am. Let's do this."

I walk up to him, my anticipation rising. "Ok, what should I do?" I ask, ready to get started.

"We're going to start out with learning specific positions. I want you to just imitate what I do. Here, stand next to me, so you can see."

Chayse starts to stand on one leg and then lifts his arms up over his head. I'm able to follow his lead. Ok, this isn't *too* bad. I can do this! Then his arms extend out to the sides, and he shifts his weight, still standing on one leg. All of my muscles are working to help stabilize my stance. He continues to challenge our balance, our strength, and our focus. Then, he performs the same routine while standing on the opposite leg.

As we continue, Chayse starts moving with the routine. Although it's becoming more difficult to keep up with him, I'm determined to learn. He instructs me to shut the world out, and really become one with my body. He says it all has to do with my focus. I close my eyes, and push my body.

We must have been working out for at least half an hour before he adds the kicks into the routine. They are powerful kicks, and I swear I can almost hear the "swoosh" of his legs. I try to keep up knowing I don't look as graceful or as smooth as him. But I don't give up, trying my best. Suddenly he performs flips, along with the kicks, as if he's in a one-on-one combat. He's moving so fast, that it's impossible for me to keep up. I stop and watch him, fascinated.

"Why did you stop?" he asks me after he finished.

"I can't do that, showoff," I tease.

He laughs and says, "Yes, you can. If you keep saying you can't do something, you won't be able to do it. You have to believe in yourself. Remember to trust your body and your instincts." Chayse pauses, and then gestures me to stand next to him. "Come on, I'll break it down for you. But I don't want you to stop. I want you to at least try, and remember what I always said, even when you ran track. Visualize!"

I sigh and take my position next to him, deciding to give it my best shot. When he does it, he makes it look so easy. Chayse slows the movements down at first, while I watch. I see him soaring in air as he sidekicks, then he completes a backward flip, and lands back on his feet. He then swings his right leg behind him while he spins, and finally comes back to his original stance. After he completes his moves, he gestures me to do the same.

I close my eyes as I take a deep breath. I picture Chayse doing the routine in my mind. I relax my body as I focus and visualize. I don't think anymore, and I just let my instincts take over. I open my eyes, and go for it without analyzing anything. Just as quickly, I'm standing in the original stance again. I turn to Chayse and he's standing there, grinning from ear-to-ear and clapping his hands. Gem is barking even louder, wagging her tail in excitement.

Chayse walks up to me, grabs my hand, and kisses my palm. "You are amazing."

"I did it?" I ask, shocked.

"You probably did it better than me, Tessnia! I told you to just believe in yourself." He leans over and kisses my cheek. "I'm proud of you," he whispers in my ears.

"Wow! How did I do that?" I'm so surprised for completing such a difficult move. It looked impossible! I start to laugh. Now, I definitely want him to teach me everything. "Let's do some more!" I exclaim.

Chayse laughs with me. "I miss that. I miss your laugh. Do you know that I haven't really heard that full blown laugh of yours since the first time I met you? When you were only sixteen? It's nice to hear it again."

"That was a long time ago. Guess I need to laugh more often," I mumble, surprised that he remembered from so long ago.

"You just always held back whenever you were around me. You were never really relaxed," Chayse explains.

"Well, truthfully I *wasn't* relaxed around you. I felt uneasy around you. It's like you knew things about me, that I didn't know myself. I always felt intimidated. I still think you know more about me than I know myself. And by the way, we will be talking about that, whether you want to or not. But for now, I want to continue our workout."

Chayse raises his eyebrow, but then shakes his head in defeat as he says, "Ok, let's continue."

For another twenty minutes, he adds more and more complex moves. I'm surprisingly keeping up with him, although I'm nowhere close to perfection like him. His advice of not analyzing too much, visualizing, and following my instincts is working.

Finally, Chayse stops, folds his arms, and says, "Did I ever tell you how amazing you are?"

"Um, maybe," I reply shyly. "But I like hearing it." I slowly smile back.

Chayse stares at me, narrowing his eyes, as if deep in thought. Finally he says, "Let's go and get some breakfast, Tessnia. I still need to fatten you up." Chayse begins his teasing.

"Hmm, while you do the breakfast thing, I'm jumping in the shower," I say, as we start walking back.

"Come on, I'll race you back," Chayse challenges, and takes off.

"Hey, not fair!" I yell, and run after him. Gem races with us too, barking happily. I'm right at his heels by the time we reach the door. Chayse and I both are laughing the entire time.

By the front door, Chayse turns to me and flashes his

famous lopsided grin. "I guess I can still beat you."

"I was at a disadvantage. You caught me off guard," I complain, narrowing my eyes and pouting my lips.

Chayse steps closer to me, towering over me. Our bodies are almost touching. He lifts my face up with his hand, and lowers his head toward me. He then gives me a tender kiss on my lips.

"I love when you get that feisty look in your eyes," he says, as he pulls me into his arms and holds me. I close my eyes, enjoying the embrace. Chayse then whispers in my ears, "And don't ever let yourself be at a disadvantage. Never let anybody catch you off guard." He steps away and looks at me, his gray eyes burning, waiting for my confirmation. "Do you understand?"

I nod.

Once we step inside, I sprint up into the bedroom. I'm sweaty, so I'm desperate to clean myself up. I strip in the bathroom and jump in the shower. Satisfied after washing my hair and shaving my legs, I step out.

I'm irritated with myself when I notice that I forgot to bring my clean clothes in the bathroom. I contemplate whether to put the sweaty workout clothes back on me, and decide against it. That's gross! That means I need to sneak back into the bedroom to get my clothes. I lean my ear against the door. I don't hear anything in the bedroom. Chayse must be still downstairs cooking.

I wrap the bath towel around me and slowly open the bathroom door to peek out. Nobody's there! I run to my drawers and pull my panties and my bra out. I then sprint to the closet and grab my jeans and a casual top. Still nervous, I quickly throw my towel off and put on the hip hugger panties and my matching cream colored bra. Just as I lean down to grab my jeans from the ground, I feel his presence in the room. Damn it! I quickly spin around, and to my dismay, there's Chayse standing there, leaning against the open door, smiling his beautiful smile at me, as if he can't get enough of what he's witnessing.

"Do you mind?" I exclaim, eyes wide. "Can I get some privacy?"

"I'm actually enjoying the view, Tessnia. You know, it's quite a sight, with you leaning over like that reaching for your pants and all. You have a nice, um, back side." Chayse's grin broadens. My face turns scarlet red from humiliation. "And those panties of yours are sexy as hell on you. Besides, it's nothing I haven't seen before, Tessnia."

I shake off my embarrassment and reply tartly, "I'm sure this is no big deal to you, with all your women who are probably more than willing to show you whatever your heart desires. But that's not me. Can I have some privacy?" Then I notice that I'm so preoccupied arguing with him, that I completely forgot I'm still standing there with just my panties and bra on. I hastily snatch my shirt to slip it on.

But before I can do that, Chayse is already right next to me. He grabs my arm and takes the shirt out of my hand. "Not yet," he says softly. "And I wasn't talking about my other women. They were nothing but distraction."

"A distraction? What kind of an adjective is that to describe one of your women? Is that what I am to you? A distraction?"

Infuriated, I try to pull my arm out of his hold. His grasp tightens. Suddenly, he's so close to me that our bodies are almost touching.

"Not only are you my distraction, Tessnia, but you are my heart as well. And you see, that's not a good combination." Chayse's voice lowers to barely a whisper. "I was talking about you when I said it's nothing I haven't seen before. My dearest Tessnia, I remember everything about you, every single detail. You have no idea how many nights I have stayed up thinking about what we shared; the time I saw every inch of your body. Believe me, I have embedded that memory into my brain, into my soul. I will always remember how you were screaming for me."

I look down, nervously biting my lower lip, as my face scorches with embarrassment. As I keep my gaze down, I whisper, "Please."

I sense him step closer. "Please what, Tess?" he challenges.

"I...", No other words come out of my mouth. My heart is beating so fast and even my hands begin to perspire. As my legs become weaker, I fear that they won't be able to hold me up much longer. I'm helpless as I lose all control, and my body betrays me.

"Look at me, Tessnia," Chayse commands, his voice hypnotizing me. With no will of my own left, I look up at him. His gray eyes are full of desire. He leans down toward me, and his lips touch mine. This time, the kiss isn't so tender. This time, the kiss is full of desire and demanding a response. Automatically, my body responses.

As my mouth instantaneously opens, I inch closer to him so that our bodies are touching. My hands caress up to his chest and he puts his hands on my hips and pulls me even closer against him. I can feel that he's just as turned on as me and to my horror, I hear myself moan under him. Chayse moves his hips against me as he deepens our kiss. Losing all control of rational thoughts, I just want him to throw me on the bed and have his way with me.

"Damn, I want you," Chayse whispers. But suddenly, he's pulling away. I protest by holding him tighter. Chayse doesn't move away immediately and we hold each other for another minute until both our breathing slows down. Finally, he steps away from me, and I'm left standing there, still trying to get some control of myself.

Chayse reaches in his back pocket and hands something into my hand. I look down, and notice that it's my phone.

"My phone," I say, confused. "What…"

"Your friend, Kylie, keeps calling and leaving messages. She said the text messages are not good enough. She said if you don't call her soon, she's calling the police. She's worried about you," Chayse explains.

"Oh." I'm not surprised that Kylie is insisting on hearing my voice. "What do you want me to say?"

"You can say anything you'd like, Tessnia. I don't want to hold you here against your will. If you're ready to go back, then just tell her you're heading back." Chayse then turns his back on me and walks out the door.

I'm left standing there, wondering what just happened. He left me the phone and said I could leave if that's what I wanted. Does he want me to leave? He was kissing me passionately just a minute ago. I shake my head, as I sit on the bed, confused more than ever. What does he want from me?

I scroll down my messages and note that several of them are from Kylie, Jack, and my aunt. They've tried to contact me numerous times every single day. Chayse was replying back to every one of them, pretending to be me, assuring them that I was alright. I then listen to my voicemail and there are six messages from Kylie, a couple from Jack, and a few more from my aunt. I have to call Kylie and let her know that everything is ok. As soon as I call, I know Kylie is going to attack me with questions. I'm not quite sure yet how to answer her. Chayse is leaving it all up to me. He wants me to choose. I can either walk away right now, or stay as long as he will allow it. Either way, I'm going to get hurt badly.

I sigh, knowing what I'm going to choose. I haven't felt this alive in a long time. Truth be told, Chayse gave me a reason to go on. The funny thing is that I haven't even been here for two full days yet. I'm simply not ready to walk away from him. Not yet. He has made it clear that he's not able to promise anything for the future, but I'm just not ready to let go. Whatever Chayse is willing to give me, I know that I'm going to take it. I sigh, and dial Kylie's phone number.

"Oh my God, Tess, where are you?" Kylie answers immediately.

"I'm fine Kylie. Don't worry," I reply.

"Don't worry? What do you mean? You simply vanished into thin air, Tess. All of us here have been worried sick." Kylie sounds frantic.

"Didn't you get my texts? I told you not to worry. I'm fine. To be honest, I haven't felt this good in a while Kylie. Trust me," I assure her, not wanting her to worry.

"Well, you do sound stronger, Tess," Kylie replies hesitantly. *"Maybe this getaway is what you needed. But where are you and when are you coming back?"*

"I did need to get out of there for a bit. And yes, it's been good for me. I'll be back maybe in a few weeks? I'm not sure yet. Either way, you can text me and we'll keep in touch. It's just that getting my space from everything and everyone from back home is what I need right now, Kylie. Gem is with me. And we're doing some bonding time. I promise I'll keep in touch. Tell my aunt you talked with me, and I love her and miss her. And tell Jack I miss him, and not to worry. Ok?" I deliberately did not answer her question regarding my location. Besides, I have no idea where the hell I am!

I hear Kylie sigh. Then she says, *"Ok, sweetie. Don't worry about anything here. I'll check on the house. You take your time, but keep in touch with me or I'll worry. Love you. And honestly, Tess, you do sound better to me. And that's all I care about."*

"Thanks, Kylie, and I love you, too. I have to go now," I reply, and end our call.

I remain sitting on the bed for a while. Well, that's that. I've made my decision. I guess I probably would do anything to be with Chayse. It's scary how much power he has over me.

"You're going to regret this, Tess," I say to myself, as I slip my clothes on and head downstairs.

When I reach the kitchen, Chayse has omlet ready for us. I notice that he's also taken a shower. He has dark gray jeans on, hanging just below his hips. This is coupled with a light gray fitted t-shirt, hugging his beautiful torso. It amazes me that I'm still in awe at his beauty.

He turns to look at me but doesn't say anything. As he brings our breakfast to the table, there's an awkward silence between us. I can tell he's waiting for me to say something about the phone conversation but I don't know how to start.

As I'm about to sit down, I reach my hand out to give my phone back to him.

"Why are you giving that back to me?" he asks, not taking the phone out of my hand.

"I figured you'd want it back. I told Kylie I'm fine, and not to worry." I pause, look down to avoid his gaze, and shyly say, "I told her I'm not coming back just yet." I put the phone down on the table in front of him without looking at him.

Chayse remains silent at first, deep in thought, and then hands the phone back to me. He says, "I'm not going to keep your phone, Tessnia. I want you here on your own free will, and you can leave whenever you'd like."

I start to feel annoyed, wondering if maybe he doesn't want me here after all. He keeps bringing up about leaving whenever I want. I look up at him, narrowing my eyes at him. "Sounds like you're ready for me to leave, Chayse. If that's the case, just say it."

Chayse looks at me in disbelief. "You really think I want you to leave, Tessnia? These last two days have been some of the happiest days of my life. I'm just worried. I don't want you to get hurt." Chayse reaches for my hand across the table and holds it.

"Neither of us know what's going to happen tomorrow, do we, Chayse? But we're here now. And I don't want to worry about the future. I just can't do it. I have to live for here and now. If I keep worrying about tomorrow, I will never get past today." I'm ready to put it all out there.

Chayse runs his hand through his hair, like he always does when he's unsure. But finally he sighs, and replies, "You're right. Let's not worry about anything but what we have here and now." He then squeezes my hand and smiles. "I have a great idea. Let's go on a picnic for a late lunch."

I can't help but laugh as his eyes smile back at me mischievously. "Where do you want to go?" I ask.

"I have a spot in mind. We'll pack some sandwiches. It'll take us a couple of hours to walk there. But it's a beautiful walk, and I think you'll like the location," Chayse explains, getting excited about the trip.

"Ok! I'm game! I'll make some sandwiches, and you grab some snacks and drinks." We finish our breakfast, pack, and an hour later, we are on our way.

Eighteen

Gem is just as excited as me to go on our picnic. We hike for a couple of hours. It's a beautiful hike, through meadows, up and down hills, and we even pass by some caves.

During our hike, we stop frequently to admire rare plants, unique species of birds, and animal tracks. To share the wonders of nature with Chayse is a gratifying and fulfilling experience for me. Chayse never ceases to amaze me with his vast knowledge of different topics.

During our walk, he holds my hand as if we've known each other forever. Gem trots next to us the entire time. If we find any animal tracks, Gem starts sniffing around it to see if she can track the animal. I laugh, and tell her to stay away from the wild animals.

When we reach the top of one of the hills, Chayse says, "Here we are."

As I look around, I'm taken aback by the scenic view. We're on top of a hill, full of beautiful wildflowers. Just on the other side of the hill, there's a lake with a magnificent waterfall, cascading into the clear water. Serenity and peace flows through me as the surroundings invade my senses. I can feel the gentle breeze blowing through my hair. The wind carries the soft fragrant scent of the wildflowers and the clean fresh scent of the water from the waterfall. Ever so slightly, I can smell the wood from the pine trees. The birds are chirping their love songs, and even the sound of the bees buzzing is peaceful.

"Come on." Chayse takes my hand and brings me to an open area, under a beautiful willow tree. He opens his backpack and spreads a blanket on the grass. He gestures me to sit down on the blanket, as he hands me a water bottle. Chayse plants himself next to me, and we soak in the calm water from the lake, the clear blue sky, the sound of the waterfall, and the colorful wildflowers, as we drink our water.

"It's beautiful, Chayse. Thanks for bringing me here," I say sincerely. The sound of the waterfall is doing wonders for calming my body, mind, and spirit.

He leans over and kisses my cheek. "I'm glad you like it." Then, he turns and whistles for Gem. She comes running and barks excitedly. "Here's some water for you girl." Chayse holds his water bottle to her mouth and starts pouring one gulp at a time. After she finishes, he says to her, "Ok, go explore, but I don't want you to go too far. I want you to be able to hear us when we call you. Understand?" Gem barks as if she understands his instructions. She then runs and disappears into the meadow.

"Is she going to be ok, Chayse?" I ask, looking at the surroundings. I'm worried because this place looks like it's full of wild animals.

"Oh yeah, she'll be fine, trust me. She's smart," he assures me.

"Do you really believe she understood what you just said to her?" I ask curiously.

"Of course! I already told you that she's a special dog," Chayse replies, without any doubt.

"That's what my dad said when he gave her to me. He said,

'She's special, Tess, just like you,'" I say slowly.

"Your dad was right, Tessnia. He was a very intelligent man," Chayse says softly, squeezing my hand. "Come on, let's eat."

The hike must have made me hungry because I devour my sandwich along with the juice bottle. "This is perfect, Chayse," I say smiling.

"Oh, and I remembered the dessert!" Chayse suddenly exclaims. He pulls out two lollipops. I start to laugh, and take the red one from him, while he keeps the orange one. We both sit there, sucking on the lollipop like two little kids, staring at our breathtaking view.

Finally, I say, "Tell me everything."

Chayse hesitates at first and then says, "I don't know where to start."

"Start with you, Chayse. I want to know everything about you," I encourage gently. Knowing Chayse is very private and hates talking about himself, I reach for his face and turn him to look at me. "Please," I whisper softly.

Chayse gets a faraway look in those beautiful gray eyes of his. He focuses his attention toward the lake, as he contemplates on what to say. He sighs as he runs his hand through his hair, and says, "My oldest memory consists of growing up in different foster homes as a little kid. My parents died when I was a baby. I don't remember them at all."

"Oh, I'm sorry, Chayse," I reply, shaking my head. I can't imagine not having memories of my parents. How horrible.

"It was a long time ago," Chayse says, shrugging his shoulders nonchalantly. "I never knew any of my family. I was probably given up very quickly to foster care, because like I said, that's all I remember. My birth certificate said my name was 'Chayse Pierce', my mother was 'Shae Pierce' and my father was 'Jared Pierce'. And to be honest, I don't even know if all this is true information. But it's all I know." Chayse is talking as if he's telling a story about somebody else, speaking indifferently, with no emotion.

I reach for his hand, holding it tight. "Go on, Chayse," I encourage him to continue.

Chayse says, "As I got older, I began to realize that I was different than other kids my age. School came really easy for me. I was faster and stronger than most kids my age. Sometimes, I would have visions or dreams and they would come true. As time passed, I learned to trust my instincts. My instincts never failed me. And my instincts told me to not tell anybody of these special talents that I possessed. As a matter of fact, I would purposefully pick the wrong answers on exams to avoid perfect scores. In sports, I would purposefully attempt to not do as well, not giving all my effort. I really tried to avoid attention in every way. Somehow, I knew that if the wrong people found out about me, things would not go in my favor." Chayse stops and sips another gulp of his juice. He then lies down on the blanket. I lie down next to him. He pulls me into his arms, and we both stare at the sky, preoccupied in our thoughts. I can't help but picture poor Chayse as a young boy, lost, and not understanding his circumstances. I imagine him all alone, not trusting anybody, and my heart goes out to him.

"Chayse, did you have any friends as a child? You know, did you get close to anybody? Somebody you could talk to maybe?" I ask.

"No, not really. I kept my distance. I had a hard time

trusting people. And like I said, I learned to trust my instincts. I had no desire to get close to anybody. And I certainly was not going to tell them anything about me," he explains. "In my spare time, I continued to volunteer at places like *The Angels.* I volunteered there because it really helped me get away from all of the stress. Those guys really were therapeutic for me."

"Yeah, I know. I loved it. It was a nice escape for me too." I remember my friends that I made there. I haven't seen them since Christmas break and I miss them.

"Then one day, as I was playing my guitar for them, I looked up, and there you were. I swear I think my heart stopped for couple of beats. I had never felt such a strong emotion. I couldn't understand why I felt an intense pull toward you. I knew I was somehow connected to you, and for the life of me, I had no explanation for that. It was so strange and it confused the hell out of me. I wanted to investigate why I was so drawn to you. So I decided to talk to you a bit and spend some time with you. As I found out more about you, I started to have a hunch that maybe you were like me. So I took a chance, and hinted about your talents. When I saw the panic in your eyes, as if I found out your deepest secrets, I knew for sure. I also knew that you didn't understand any of it."

I nod, remembering that day. "I remember it all, Chayse. You were singing *Beautiful* to them. It was so hypnotizing. And I was drawn to you as well. I didn't understand why I felt so connected to you, either. I still don't understand. And when you mentioned about running, and embracing my talents, I got really freaked out," I explain. "And by the way, why were you 'Joe Smith' at the time?"

Chayse chuckles, and says, "I changed my name as

frequently as I was able to do so. Luckily, I knew a lot of people on the streets, so they always hooked me up with different fake ID's. Even for college, I had to become Chris Jones because I didn't want people to know the real Chayse Pierce. I knew I wanted to get my college degree, but staying for that many years under my real name was too risky. So I became Chris Jones. I had forged all of my transcripts, records--everything. Through the years, I had become really good at personifying different people. As for track, I just walked up to the college coach and asked if he would give me a shot. Of course, as soon as he saw me run, he knew he had hit a goldmine. And luckily, that helped pay for my college." Chayse is smiling as he's remembering.

I smile back at him. "I was so young when I met you. I thought you were so cute," I confess.

Chayse's smile widens. "I was actually attracted to you, Tessnia. And when I found out you were only sixteen, I felt so ashamed. I was the adult and was contemplating how to ask you out on a date," Chayse laughs, shaking his head in disbelief.

"What? You teased me. You pretended that you were going to kiss me, and then you just pulled some leaf or something out of my hair. I was so embarrassed. And I never saw you again. You never came back. Do you know that every time I went there, I would search for you?" I remember how I would always look for him each time I went back to the facility. I remember my disappointment when I wouldn't see him.

"No, I didn't go back. I realized that you were so innocent, still a child. I couldn't involve you into my mess. I was always on the run. I had people after me, Tess. And if you were anything like me, I didn't want them to know about you. I wanted you to have a normal life. You were so beautiful, carefree, innocent, and believing the good in everyone. There was no way I would take that away from you. So, purposefully, I stayed away. But I kept my eye on you as you grew up. I knew you played basketball and ran track in high school. I knew you were the valedictorian of your class. You excelled Tess, and you had normal high school years, just as I would have wanted for you," Chayse explains.

"How did you know all that about me? And who's after you?" I have so many questions and I'm starting to get apprehensive. What does he mean that there were people after him?

"I just looked you up frequently, and your accomplishments were all over the internet. I know I shouldn't have done that. I guess the word 'stalker' would have described me pretty accurately," Chayse laughs. "But, I couldn't help myself. I wanted to know what was going on with you. And I really was curious of where your life was going. And as strange as it may be, even though I didn't know you, a part of me was very protective of you. I don't know. I can't explain it, Tess," Chayse says, deep in thought.

I put my head on his chest. "My dad said to me that I had 'elite genetics'. Do you know what that means?"

Chayse starts playing with my hair. "I was told the same thing in the military. The theory is that some individuals may be born where their genetics match up just right. This may lead them to utilize their brain more efficiently, or they may be able to create neurological pathways faster than an average human. I was explained that these individuals may even possess 'sixth sense' or 'intuitions' or 'visions'. Also with these higher genes, they believe that these individuals are smarter, stronger, and faster. Guess their theories were correct. As far as I know, they only know of me. And I don't know of anybody else like me, besides you."

"You keep saying 'they'. Who are 'they' Chayse?" The more information he is providing me, the more confused I'm becoming.

"I know that when the special branch of the military recruited me, they already knew about me. They explained that if I joined them, they would protect me from the so-called wrong hands. There are people out there that would use me and you as guinea pigs, Tess. They could even use us as weapons. These are the people who I've been running from. So I joined this special military branch. They did many tests on me and I scored perfect in everything. They couldn't believe it. They've also done many blood tests and DNA tests to see what was different about me. They've explained that there's some variation in my chromosomes, specific genes. It sounds crazy, but they've been true to their word. They've trained me to fight, to use weapons, and to use my talents as an agent. I'm one of their best agents for obvious reasons, so they make sure to look after me. The only drawback is that I'm always watching my back. I have a lot of enemies, Tess, from my line of work. That's why I have to avoid bringing you into my world. I would never forgive myself if anybody figured out that you're similar to me. Trust me, this is not the type of world you want to be in. You deserve more, so much more." A look of panic suddenly flashes in his eyes.

"So there are people who you work for, that already know about you. These guys have trained you. And then there are others who are looking for you?" I draw him back to our discussion. It's important that I understand everything.

"Yes, Tess. My boss thinks they may want to study me. I don't know, maybe they feel they can create more people like us or something. I know if I end up in wrong hands, it could be detrimental," Chayse emphasizes.

"Ok, I'm trying to process all this, Chayse. How long have you been with the Special Forces in the military?"

"As soon as I finished college, this gentleman named Tom Sterns recruited me. He said he was the head of the Special Forces for the government and he thought he could help me. He told me he knew about me, and that they've been watching me for a while. So, I joined. Sterns is my boss. The pay is great, and it was a relief that maybe these guys would look out for me, you know?"

"Isn't it dangerous though, Chayse? I mean what type of assignments are they sending you on?" I ask, concerned for his safety.

"I'm not going to lie, Tess. Of course it's dangerous. But they've trained me well. Trust me, I have a knack for surviving through some tough situations. Must be my sixth sense or something," Chayse grins.

I frown. I don't like it. I've heard of Special Forces and the assignments they have to do. And I don't like the sound of people searching for him. "Now these other people who are searching for you, have you ever encountered them?"

"Not directly. I'm always on the go. Before I joined the Special Forces, I didn't stay in one place. Now, my team protects me. But yeah, indirectly, I've felt that somebody was watching me or following me. When I got those feelings, I just relocated quickly. Once, they actually broke into my apartment. I knew something was wrong before I even reached my apartment. I watched from a distance and I saw a bunch of men in suits leaving my place. I didn't even go back for my things. I just left. To protect myself, I continued to change my appearance and name often, as you know."

"I knew you as Joe, and then as Chris," I nod.

Chayse plays with my hair as he continues, "I found out that you were going to attend Stanford. It was perfect because we have a base near the university. I was also familiar with the area since I had spent four years of my college studies out there. I asked Sterns if I could be located out of that base for a while. I wanted to see you again. I *had* to see you again, Tessnia. You affected me so much during that first encounter. I had to know if it was still the same."

"I didn't even know you were Joe when I saw you," I say, deep in thought.

"No, you didn't. My hair and eyes were different," Chayse says.

"And you were bigger than I remembered you. And you were talking in that funny accent," I giggle.

Chayse smiles, deep in thought. "I remember watching you from the bleachers every day. I told myself that I was just curious, and that I would keep my distance. But each day that passed, I wanted to get closer. I hated myself because I was letting my emotions make decisions for me. I couldn't fight it anymore. I asked the coach if I could help train. He knew who I was, so he jumped on it."

I smile to myself. "I remember seeing you up there on the bleachers every day, and thought you were a stalker boyfriend of one of the girls."

Chayse laughs. "Oh I was stalking alright. You just didn't realize I was stalking you. That day when I came to the team and introduced myself to you, I feared that maybe you might recognize me. But you didn't, and I felt that same connection, if not stronger. You took my breath away, Tessnia, when I saw you. You were all grown up and beautiful as ever. God, I was so drawn to you. I convinced myself that maybe it was destiny. Maybe this was supposed to happen. I wanted to be close to you, but I fought my feelings. I knew once I let my feelings go, I was really in the danger zone."

"Destiny--my mom said something about destiny. Do you think us meeting and finding each other was destiny?" I ask.

"I'm not sure. I do believe that things happen for a reason, and that if it's meant to be, somehow it will be. But I also believe that we can set our own destiny. I believe that we can either make something happen, or avoid it from happening." Chayse pulls me closer into his arms.

"Yeah, I know what you mean." We lie in each other's arms without saying anything for a few minutes. Finally, I say, "I have another question. Why were you so distant when you were training me in track? And why wouldn't you just tell me who you were? You barely talked."

"Well, I was distant because I didn't want to get close to you. I was still going through my own inner struggles. It drove me crazy! And I was not going to tell you, because I didn't want you to know. You would be totally freaked out. I mean I had a fake accent and looked completely different, Tess," Chayse explains.

I giggle. "Yeah, I would have freaked out. I would have thought you were really crazy. But you *were* kind of a weirdo--not talking, always grouchy," I tease.

Chayse begins to laugh. "I was grouchy because I had no control of myself around you. And I hated that power you had over me. The more I got to know you, Tessnia, the harder it was for me to stay away. It got to the point when I just gave up trying to resist you. I'd find reasons to see you. I'd stalk you at your work for heaven's sake! I was pathetic!" Chayse says, shaking his head. I can't help but laugh with him, remembering our time together three years ago. "But you know what? This feels good to finally be able to tell you things now." Chayse scoops me up on top of him and then kisses me. I love his kisses. He thinks I have power over him? He has no idea how much power he has over me, over my body, over my heart.

I pull away and look at him. I can't help but think that we're destined to be together. Maybe my mom knew something that I didn't.

I take a deep breath and courageously say, "Chayse, I want you to make love to me."

Nineteen

Chayse doesn't respond, but I feel him catch his breath.

I quickly shield my eyes from him by looking away, and focus on a spot on his chest. I sneak a peek at him. He's staring at me, with a slight frown on his forehead. I try again, and say, "I know what I'm doing. This is what I want."

"Tess, last time, I took advantage of your vulnerability. I never forgave myself for that. I don't want to do that again," he says slowly.

"You didn't take advantage of me, Chayse. I wanted it then, just like I want it now. I have never been more certain of anything else in my life." He must understand that. How can he not see? He is the one, my only one. I lean into him and begin kissing him. I deepen our kiss, and he instantly responds. Our breathing changes, and our heartbeat quickens. The next thing I know, he flips me over and is on top of me.

"Are you sure, Tessnia? This is all I can offer right now. You know that right?" Chayse is still hesitant. He's making it very clear that he cannot make any promises for the future. I sigh.

"I understand, Chayse. Now just stop talking and make love to me!" I demand.

His lips come down hard. The kiss is full of desire and longing. I see that he's been holding back. Now, he lets it all go. Before I know it, my shirt is off. I have no idea how or when it happened. Damn, he's good. I fumble with his shirt, getting impatient. He helps me tug it off as he's breathing as hard as me. He looks down at me, watching me lie under him with my bra and jeans on. "You're beautiful, Tessnia. Do you have any idea how beautiful you are?"

I look up into his piercing gray eyes. They've turned a few shades darker with desire. I love this man. I love this beautiful man who was all alone in the world--a lost boy, not knowing who to trust. I love this intelligent man who somehow figured it all out, and discovered a way to survive. I love this man who eventually found his way to me. And I'm going to cherish every moment with him.

I grab him from the back of his hair and pull him toward me, to kiss him with all of the unguarded emotions I feel for him. I want him to feel how much I want him, how much I need him, how much he means to me. He kisses back with just as much need and passion.

He begins to kiss the nape of my neck and behind my ear. God, he's driving me crazy. I put my hand by his waist of his jeans and tug at them. I want them off, now! I unbutton the jeans, pulling his zipper down. I have never been this close to a man before. My heart is beating a million beats a minute as I start to tug his jeans down. Chayse pulls himself out of them, and I see that he's wearing fitted boxer briefs. I swear he has zero percent fat. I run my fingers on his defined abs and feel the tightness of his butt muscles.

I notice how turned on he is, feeling his hardness against my hips. For a brief second, I'm scared, fearful that this whole process is going to hurt. The thought leaves me as soon as he pulls my jeans and bra off. My anticipation increases, as we're both down to our underwear.

Chayse keeps kissing me and I arch my back to get closer to him. I am so ready for this moment. He has already seen me naked before, but I've never seen him. Well, I've never seen any man completely naked, outside of pictures and movies. It shouldn't be too shocking. I hope.

Chayse's hand is on my one breast, and his mouth is on my other breast. He starts with kissing and then sucking. He's driving me crazy. I moan. "I love hearing that sound, Tessnia," he whispers.

Chayse doesn't stop. He plays with my nipple with his tongue. How does he know exactly what to do? His mouth starts to play with the other breast. I grab the back of his head and hold him down closer to me. This feels so good. *He* feels so good.

While his mouth is working on my breast, his hand is exploring down my body. I feel him between my thighs. Suddenly, his hand is right on my panties. "Mm, you're good and ready for me, my Tessnia," he says slowly. I flush, knowing that he feels how wet I am for him.

"I want you, Chayse," I whisper shyly. It's the truth and that's all I can muster out. I can barely breathe. My body is completely under his spell, as I've lost all control.

"Last time, you said you hadn't been with anybody else. And I couldn't take your innocence away like that. I had so many secrets, and I felt like a total bastard, Tess. I'm so sorry," Chayse explains. Oh no, he doesn't realize that I still haven't been with any other man. Do I dare tell him? If I do, he will try to stop again. But if I don't, he will figure out sooner or later. I take a deep breath.

"Chayse, I have to be honest. I'm still a virgin. I haven't

been with any other man." I can't lie to him. He had poured his heart out to me, and had told me everything about him. I feel him stiffen up and he starts to pull away. I grab his face and force him to look at me. "Listen to me, Chayse. It never felt right with any other guy. If it didn't feel right, I was never the type to force it. But it feels right with you. Please don't pull away. I want this," I insist.

His eyes look sad and tortured. He shakes his head as if fighting his own inner battles. "Tess, I didn't know. You're so innocent. I don't even know what to say." Chayse is still shaking his head in disbelief.

"It never felt right, Chayse," I repeat, begging him to understand. "I know now. I was always waiting for you. I didn't even realize that, but it was always you."

Chayse buries his face into my neck. I feel him tremble with emotion. After a few moments, he finally lifts his head and looks down at me. "Is it selfish of me to want to jump for joy that no other man has seen you or touched you?" he asks, as a slow sexy grin begins to form on his lips.

I smile back. "No, Chayse, it's not selfish. I belong to you. I don't want anybody else."

"You're mine," he confirms. "Only mine."

"Only yours," I reassure him. I can never imagine being with anybody else. I know my destiny is with this man. He is my soul mate.

As soon as he hears me say I'm his, Chayse comes down on me hard. He finds my lips again, his breathing erratic. The thought of being his, and only his, is a turn on. Recognizing that he's my soul mate brings me to a whole new level. I want to give him my all, not holding anything back.

Before I know it, my panties are off and I feel his finger inside me. A moan escapes me. Damn him, he feels so good and he's driving me crazy. I start to take his boxers off and he helps me by slipping out of them. I stare at him. Everything about him is beautiful. He is perfection. I bravely put my hand on him to touch him. As soon as I touch him, he goes still. I start to kiss him again, and wrap my fingers around him and begin stroking him.

"Tess, you're driving me crazy," he groans. While I play with him, his finger plays inside me. We both are about to lose control. "It's now or never, Tessnia. Are you ready?"

"Yes," I whisper. He pulls out a condom from his wallet. "You have a condom with you?" I ask in disbelief.

"Remember what I told you? Always be prepared," he says, grinning.

"I guess so," I say. "I'm glad one of us is still able to think rationally."

He puts the condom on and takes his position back on top of me. "It might hurt at first. If it hurts too much, you have to let me know, ok?" Chayse looks at me for a confirmation. I nod.

With his legs, he spreads my legs. He lifts my legs up and I wrap them around him. He begins kissing me, and his hand automatically goes to my breast. I feel him, hard and smooth, pushing against me. I respond by arching into him. He begins slowly at first and it's driving me wild. I push against him hard. "Slow down, baby. I don't want you to get hurt," he whispers.

His pressure increases against me. I want him so badly. Suddenly, for a brief moment, it hurts. I feel myself tense up.

I almost push him off of me as I feel myself tightening against the pressure.

"Take a deep breath, baby. Let your body relax." Chayse stops pushing. He waits for a few seconds and then says, "Do you trust me, Tess?" I look up at him. He's staring down at me, his soul open for me to see. I trust him with my life. I nod yes, and find myself relaxing.

His lips touch mine. Gently, he opens my mouth with his lips. I instantly respond. His tongue penetrates inside my mouth as his kiss deepens and my body starts to move with the rhythm of his body. I hear him moan, which turns me on even more. God, he feels so good. He pushes harder into me, and as I relax, I know he's inside me. Chayse lies still for a minute, then whispers, "You ok?"

"Perfect," I reply. I stare into his eyes. "You feel really good, Chayse."

He smiles. "Do you have any idea how many times I've fantasized about this? About being inside you? I know it sound crazy, but I always tried to imagine how it would feel." Chayse takes a deep breath. His eyes darken, and he says, "It feels better than my fantasies, better than what I ever imagined."

Chayse buries his face into my hair. He begins to play with my neck with his tongue as he slowly starts to move. I find myself moving with his rhythm. He's gentle and tender. I want more. I move faster against him. I need more. It feels like I'm going to burst. He's driving me crazy. His hand finds my breast, and the other hand finds my buttock. He brings my hips up to meet him as he plays with my breast.

"Damn, Tessnia, you feel amazing." His voice is husky.

"Chayse, please," I say. The different sensations I'm feeling are too much.

"Please what, Tess. Say it." Chayse encourages.

"Please, I don't know what's happening." I'm too lost to even put into words what I want. My nails are digging into his back and I'm about to lose it. I kiss him frantically.

All of a sudden, as he holds us united, he rolls over so that he's under me, and I'm sitting on top of him. He has filled inside me even more now. He holds my hips and slowly starts to rock me. I moan. I open my eyes and look down at him. This perfect man is lying under me, watching me, eyes full of desire, with his hands on my breasts, playing with my nipples. The sight is a total turn on. I feel myself moving to the rhythm he has started, and I'm in heaven. He releases one of my breasts and brings his thumb where we're united. He touches me at my most sensitive spot, and I scream out his name. I close my eyes, as he starts to torture me with his thumb while moving his hips against mine. I can't stop my moans.

"Look at me, Tessnia. I need to see your eyes." I open my eyes and stare deep into his piercing gray eyes, full of yearning for me.

"Chayse," I moan.

"Let me have it, Tess. Come for me. I want to feel you." The combination of his voice, his thumb, him being inside me, his hand on my breast, his eyes seeking deep into my soul, is ecstasy. He is relentless as he keeps stroking and playing, and we start to move faster. Listening to both of our moans, with our powerful eye contact, is all too much, and I can't hold back any longer. I arch my back and I let it all go. Through it all, he continues playing with me. Through it all, he maintains his eye contact with me. I can't even focus anymore. Everything is so intense. *He* is so intense. I finally come back to Earth.

I look shyly at him, and he's smiling up at me. "I will never forget how gorgeous you looked just then. I have never seen a more beautiful sight than you losing control like that."

I want to hide my face, full of embarrassment. Chayse chuckles, finding it funny that I'm embarrassed. I slowly smile at him.

"You have nothing to be embarrassed about, Tessnia. Not with me. You are perfect. Your innocence is perfect. The way you lose control is perfect." I don't even know how to respond to that. To me, he's the perfect one--the flawless one!

Then, he starts to move again. He's moving faster and faster and he's deep inside me. I start rocking with him as I'm getting turned on all over again. This is crazy! We move and rock. I start playing with his chest and he goes faster. I open my eyes to look at him and he is staring at me. His soul is open to me. He lets me see it all. I see his eyes full of vulnerability, uncertainty, desire, conflict, and lastly, love. We hold our eyes as I hear him yell, "Tessnia!"

And he climaxes.

As he reaches his peak, I reach mine all over again. I collapse down onto him. The entire experience is so extreme, so powerful. When we both settle back down eventually, he turns me again and he's lying on top of me. He buries his face into my hair and I feel him shivering.

"Are you cold, Chayse?" I ask. The sun is shining down on us. Why is he shivering? Chayse doesn't answer. I lift his face to ask again. When I look into his eyes, I see they are full of tears. "What's wrong? Did I do something wrong?" My heart skips a beat. His eyes are full of unguarded emotions, and it's breaking my heart.

He shakes his head and attempts to bury his face into me again to hide his eyes from me. I hold him off of me, waiting for him to explain. Chayse sighs and after a few moments, says, "I'm caught up with emotions, Tessnia. I can't explain how much you mean to me, and to experience this with you... I just never even dreamed that I would ever get the chance." Chayse shakes his head, his feelings still exposed. He looks like a lost boy, full of confusion and sorrow. My heart feels heavy. I'm used to a strong, confident, and even cocky man, not this lost, sad boy full of uncertainty.

"That's my line, Chayse," I tease, smiling at him. "It was my first time, and it was amazing. You were amazing, so sweet and gentle." I reach for his face and kiss him. I kiss him gently, tenderly, and full of love. Even if I can't say the word "love" to him, I want him to feel it. Saying it out loud would be too much for him. In my heart, I know that he isn't ready for that yet.

He kisses back just as tenderly. When he stops the kiss, he looks down at me, and flashes me one of his rare, shy grins. "Are you ok? Did I hurt you?"

I shake my head. "To be honest, it hurt just for a bit, and then the pleasure overtook the pain. It was definitely one of my top memories. You are very good," I tease.

"Yeah, I've been told that before," he gives his sly grin and teases back.

"I'll bet you have!" I shove him off of me. Must he remind me that he's had other women before?

Chayse starts to laugh. He begins putting his clothes on

and hands me mine. "Tessnia, are you jealous by any chance?" Ok, so he's in his teasing mood. At least he has lightened up.

"Nope, definitely not!" I lie.

"Liar," Chayse says slowly. By now, we're almost fully dressed.

"Nope, I don't care about all your other women!" I insist. Truthfully, I hate them all.

He pulls me back into his embrace. He's still smiling. Then he says, "Would it make a difference if I told you that it never mattered how 'good' I was until right now? That the only person's opinion that I really care about is standing right in front of me?"

I smile and reply, "Yeah, I think it might make a difference. But let's not talk about all the women from your past. I want to scratch their eyes out, every single one of them!"

"Wow, violent! I didn't know you had that in you, Miss Tessnia. Ok, I will keep that in mind," Chayse laughs. Then he turns toward the fields and whistles for Gem. "Gem, let's go, girl!"

I can't even see or hear her. She has been gone for awhile and I haven't even checked on her. "Chayse, you think she's ok?" I ask, as I begin to worry.

"Of course. She heard me, trust me. She's probably heading back right now," he replies confidently. "Hurry, Gem!"

I'm about to suggest that maybe we should look for her, when suddenly, we hear her barking and running toward us. I stare at her running full speed toward us. She is so fast! I always knew she was fast, but I've never seen her run this fast before. It's not even a normal speed for a dog. Besides her speed, I'm amazed at her grace and beauty. She is leaping through the fields, demonstrating impressive agility, even for a dog. Before I can even acknowledge to Chayse about her speed, Gem is standing in front of us, wagging her tail and barking happily. She has gotten herself dirty out in the woods. She's going to need a good cleanup when we get back. Chayse and I kneel down and pet her.

"Good girl," I say.

"Told you she heard me," Chayse says proudly.

"You think she's like us, don't you?" I finally ask as we start to head back.

"Yeah, I do, Tess. Did you see how fast she was running?" Chayse asks.

"But how can this be? This is all so confusing, Chayse." Everything is so overwhelming. It just feels like the more I find out, the more questions I have.

"Your parents were in research weren't they, Tessnia? What was their specialty again?" Chayse inquires.

"My mom was doing genetic research, and my dad was into neuroscience. He specialized mostly on the brain," I reply.

"Well, don't you think that's too much of a coincidence? They gave Gem to you, Tess. They must have known about her," Chayse explains.

I remember my dad had told me that Gem was special. "But I don't understand." I am still confused.

"Look, Tess, I have no idea what type of research your parents were into, but I think Gem may have had something to do with that. Who knows? Maybe she's a product of one of their studies." Chayse is trying to make sense out of everything as well.

"Really? You think they made her?" I ask in disbelief.

"I think it's a strong possibility. I think they gave her to you knowing that Gem would have the assets to protect you if needed. Maybe it was the reassurance they needed."

I think about what he's saying. I guess if I open my mind to it, what he says makes sense.

God, I was so naïve growing up. I had no idea. I thought we were a normal family, with a normal life, and a normal dog. Boy, was that far from the truth!

Twenty

Chayse takes my hand and holds it while we walk back. It feels good. Gem trots alongside us, in her happy world. Yes, this is our happy world. It would be so nice if we could just live here, happily ever after, and forget about everything else. I sigh. I don't know how long our little escape is going to last, but I'm going to make every moment memorable.

When we get back to the house, I clean Gem up outside while Chayse prepares dinner. After Gem dries up, we go in the house.

Chayse is in the kitchen, cutting up some herbs.

He looks up and says, "You know, I'd like to have a romantic candlelight dinner with you tonight."

"Mm, sounds nice," I reply, smiling to myself.

"No, I mean I want us to dress up and have a candlelight dinner here. Since I can't take you out on a real date to wine and dine you, I'm going to try to make it as fancy as I can right here. I think I grabbed some dresses for you. Would you be my date tonight, Miss Sanoby?" Chayse asks, smirking.

"I'd love that, Mr. Pierce," I answer, giggling. "Do you want me to jump in the shower right now?" I'm getting excited about the romantic dinner.

"No, wait for me. I'm taking a shower with you," he says, as he flashes me a mischievous grin.

Suddenly, I'm shy again. What is the matter with me? I just made love with this man outdoors. I glance away quickly.

When dinner is in the oven, we both head upstairs.

In the bedroom, he showers me with tender kisses all over my body as he takes off each piece of clothing. All I can do is stand there and grab the back of his head, tangling my fingers into his hair, gasping with each kiss.

Before long, we both are naked. Chayse scoops me up in his arms and takes me to the bathroom. Once he puts me down in the shower, he takes the soap and begins to lather me. He even washes my hair for me, and I'm in heaven as he massages my scalp. While we shower, Chayse is loving and tender. He claims my lips and I want nothing more than to make love to him, right here, right now.

I pry myself away from him, take the soap, and say, "My turn." Two can play this game.

I follow his movements and lather him up. Chayse is hard as a rock all over. This man is all muscle. Lathering him and feeling him respond to my touch, is arousing me even more. I shift my gaze up at him, and start to kiss him. As I deepen our kiss, I rub my body against him so he knows what I want.

As we're both gasping, trying to catch our breath, I feel him pulling me off of him. I hold tighter in protest. "Tessnia, we're going to wait. It's all about the anticipation. Trust me, the evening will be that much more interesting," he whispers in my ear.

I am intrigued.

When we step out of the shower, he dries me with the towel. He kisses me deeply and shows me exactly what's going to be on his mind all evening. I kiss back just as deeply, to keep him wanting more. By the time he stops, Chayse is breathing hard.

His voice is husky when he says, "I'm going to go change. I'll see you downstairs when you're ready." He turns and walks to the other bedroom.

I put on my matching black lace panties and bra. I want to feel sexy tonight. I look in the closet, contemplating what I want to wear. I guess my mom was right when she had once told me that I'll worry about what I wear once I fall in love. I sigh, missing her. "I wish I could talk to you about this man I love, ma," I whisper. As my eyes become misty, I quickly start focusing on my clothes again, not wanting to cry.

I eventually choose my black fitted, sleeveless mini-dress. It's the same one I had worn during my Vegas trip. I don't have any jewelry here, but I do have some makeup. I haven't used much makeup lately, so I'm looking forward to the transformation. I even apply some eye shadow to give me a smoky, mysterious look, making my brown eyes look even bigger. My mascara adds length to my already long eyelashes. I use my dark red lip-gloss to emphasize my full lips. I search in the closet to see what shoes he grabbed for me. I can't believe it! He brought my black heels. Maybe he planned to have a dress-up dinner all along. I don't think I will ever fully understand this man.

I slip the heels on and examine my final appearance. I smile at my reflection. I feel sexy. The dress emphasizes every curve. My lips look full and pouty and my eyes are exotic, emphasizing my natural, mysterious look. My hair is pulled up in a bun with loose curly strands shaping my face. I see a beautiful, elegant, carefree young woman, full of life. I take a deep breath and head downstairs.

As I'm walking down the hall, I notice everything is dim,

and I hear soft music playing. My heart beats faster from nervousness, anticipation, and excitement. I can smell the delicious lasagna that's baking in the oven. When I enter the kitchen, I notice there are candles on the kitchen table, and throughout the room. I smile and I feel him approach me. I look up and there he is in a black suit. I stop breathing. Wow! He has finally shaved his face, and his hair is neat and tamed. The suit fits him beautifully. I've never seen him dressed up like this, as he usually wears t-shirts and jeans. Not only does Chayse look dashing, but he looks sexy as hell.

He takes my hand, kissing it, as he bows. "You look beautiful, my lady," he says.

I laugh. "You look beautiful, too." I reach for his cheek and kiss it. "Thank you. This is amazing."

He guides me to the table and pulls the chair out for me. The silverware, the plates, and the wine are already set on the table. The dinner consists of salad, garlic bread, lasagna, and ice cream. By the time we're done, I'm stuffed.

"You know you're killing me with all this food," I complain to him. "Where did you get the wine?"

"You need to eat. I know you've only been here for a few days, but you're getting some healthy color to you again," Chayse smiles. "And what's a candlelight dinner without wine? I've got an emergency stash hidden away."

"Hey, I'm not complaining. This wine is just what I needed," I laugh. "Oh, and I think the healthy color may be because you always make me blush." Chayse just has to glance my way, and my cheeks go on fire. It's unbelievable how much control he has over my emotions.

"Do I now?" he teases. He stands up and soaks our dishes

and utensils in the sink. "Come, let's dance." Chayse leads me to the living room. The music is slow and hypnotizing. He holds me against him and starts to lead me. I'm not surprised at his graceful dancing skills. He is light on his feet, moving just right with the beat of the music, his hips moving against mine. I let myself go, relaxing my body against his, and allow him to take control of the rhythm and the beat. The wine is doing its wonderful magic to my senses. Chayse leads and I follow. It's exhilarating.

"I have to admit, Tessnia. This little dress of yours is really turning me on," Chayse whispers in my ear. My heart stops and my body automatically responds. He just has to use his soft whispers to have this type of effect on me! I feel my body sinking into him more. "That weekend when you visited your friend, Jack, in college, I nearly lost my mind. I know I had no right to you, but do you know I literally went insane? I couldn't bear the thought of any man kissing you, or touching you. I kept trying to calm myself down, told myself to think rationally. I couldn't. I wanted to track you down and drag you back. It took everything out of me to wait until you got back to your apartment. And even then, I acted like a fool."

"I told you, Jack and I are just friends. That's all it has ever been," I explain. I remember how Chayse had reacted when I had returned.

"But he has strong feelings for you, Tessnia. It's so obvious," Chayse says, shaking his head.

"How would you know that?" I ask.

"I make it my business to know who goes in and out of your life. I've been keeping an eye on you for years now, you know that."

"Is that how you knew my parents died?" I ask. I don't want to talk about this, but I have to know.

"I was notified of your parents' death. My team kept an eye out for me, to make sure you were ok. I was hoping you would eventually get out of the depression. But the reports I was getting said you were getting worse."

"Wait, what? There were people spying on me?" I ask in disbelief. I stop dancing, and wait for his response.

"Tess, yes, I do have my team watch over you when I can't. Maybe it's not right. But that's the only way I could get myself to go on assignments. I needed regular reports on you. When they told me you didn't look so well, and that you were not bouncing back, I had to check it out myself. So I asked my boss to pull me out of my last assignment. I had to see you myself. One day, I waited until you finally took Gem for a walk. I couldn't believe how different you looked. Besides the weight loss, I could tell you had just given up. The light in your eyes had disappeared. I almost ran to you right there to yell at you and shake some sense into you. But I had to think it through. So I came up with this elaborate plan. I knew I couldn't just show up at your door. You were probably still angry with me from our past. Besides that, I wanted to get you away from there. I prayed that if I got you away and alone with me, maybe I could help you. I wanted the opportunity to talk some sense into you. I was not going to let you go until you got better. So I came up with these drastic measures. Before getting you, I stored this place up with groceries, dog food, and some essentials that would last us for a while, since we're in the middle of nowhere. I know that drugging you and then kidnapping you seem extreme. But I was ready to do whatever it took to help you," Chayse explains.

"I think you did more than talking, Chayse," I tease, as I begin dancing with him again.

"I guess I did. Are you complaining?" he asks, grinning and lifting his eyebrow at me.

I look at his beautiful lips and I reach up to give him a kiss. "No, I'm not complaining. You gave me strength again. I haven't felt like myself in a long time. I think I did give up. There were so many times I had wished that I was in the car with my parents."

"Tessnia, your parents would not want that. You must know that," Chayse says, exasperated.

"I do, Chayse. But, I felt so alone. Even though my aunt, and my friends did everything they could to help me, I wasn't ready to accept their help. You honestly did save me," I confess.

Chayse stops dancing and holds me close. "I want you to promise me something. I want you to promise me that no matter what life brings you, you will find a way to live. I couldn't bear it if anything happened to you. Promise me you will find the strength and the will," Chayse insists.

I thought about Chayse being alone in this world his whole life. He always found a way to survive, even though he had nobody. He's right. I have to be stronger.

"I promise, Chayse," I assure him.

Chayse leans forward and kisses me. And I melt.

"You look so beautiful, Tessnia. It's driving me wild," he whispers, as he starts moving me to the music again. He wasn't kidding about the anticipation thing. I want him, and the waiting is making me want him even more. Chayse buries his face into my hair as we dance. “You look very elegant tonight. I can’t wait to undo this beautiful bun of yours. And you smell delicious,” he softly whispers, seducing me.

I smile to myself, because I was just thinking that he smells heavenly. I put my head against his chest and I feel his strength and power flowing through me. I can’t even imagine my life without him. It feels like ever since that first day I met him, he’s always been with me. He found a place in my heart from the very beginning. I just hadn’t realized it.

I sigh. I can’t allow myself to think about how much time I have left with him. If I dare, I won’t be able to live for the moment as I am right now. I cling to him. If time stops right now, I would die a happy woman.

Chayse holds me tighter. He brings my hips against his, and I can feel his arousal. I reach up and kiss him, to show him that I want him just as badly.

Suddenly, Chayse picks me up, cradling me in his arms like a baby. I hold on to his neck and start giggling. “What are you doing?” I ask.

“Can’t wait anymore. I’m carrying you up to the bedroom and making love to you--on the bed this time, Tessnia. I want you,” Chayse says, as he carries me up the stairs. We kiss passionately all the way to the bedroom. He kicks the bedroom door open. Somehow, he makes it to the bed and throws me down. He steps away, watching me, his gray eyes full of desire.

I watch him in fascination as he takes his black jacket off, and then his tie. He unbuttons his white shirt, slowly, seductively, throwing it off of him. My breathing quickens as he unbuttons and unzips his dress pants. I am paralyzed as I watch his pants fall to his ankles and he steps out of them.

This heavenly man, with a body of a Greek God, slowly strolls toward me, as he pulls his undershirt over his head.

Chayse looks sexy as hell as he grabs me by my ankles, lifts my feet up, and throws my shoes off. He then kisses my toes, one at a time, and begins to trail up my leg with soft kisses. I moan. He pulls me to a sitting position and begins kissing me. As his kiss deepens, I feel his hand unzipping my dress, sliding it off of me.

Then, his hand reaches the back of my hair, pulling the pin out of my bun. My dark curls flow down, thick, curly, and wild. Chayse plays with my hair with his fingers, and whispers, "Mm, perfect. I love your hair, Miss Tessnia." He buries his face into my hair and holds me tight. Chayse then proceeds to lie me back down while he kneels over me.

"Chayse, I want you," I moan.

He looks down at me, his gray eyes a few shades darker. "You are so fucking beautiful, Tess. You have no idea of the power you hold over me!" he says hoarsely. He runs his finger down from my neck to bellybutton. The movement is slow and deliberate.

I close my eyes and arch my back. I want him to do whatever he wants with me. I've surrendered myself to him.

I gasp as I feel his mouth on my navel. He begins playing with my navel with his tongue. Can he drive me any crazier! He travels upward and buries his face between my breasts. He reaches behind me and unclasps my bra strap. Once the bra is pulled off, his face is buried against my bare breasts.

"These are gorgeous. So round and perfect," Chayse moans. I grab the back of his head and intertwine my fingers into his thick lock of hair. He moves from one breast to another with his hands and with his mouth, torturing me. Damn it!

"Chayse, I'm about to lose it!" I gasp.

"No, not yet Tessnia. Let me taste every inch of you," he says, his voice husky. When he's satisfied with my breasts, he starts to travel downward. Oh my god! I vividly remember this from years ago. The anticipation alone is making me want to burst.

"Chayse," I say. I can't recognize my own voice.

"Open your eyes, Tessnia. I want you to look at me. I want you to look into my eyes," Chayse demands. My eyes spring open. The sight of him down there like that is too much.

I notice that his boxer briefs are already off. As I stare down at him in awe, he flashes his famous lopsided grin right before burying his face on top of my panties. I can't hold back a moan. I continue watching him as he slowly removes my panties.

"I've been dreaming of tasting you again since that first time." And Chayse goes to work with his tongue. My moaning gets louder, and my body is on fire. I grab him by his hair again as I start to move against his tongue. This feels too good. Just watching him with his head buried inside me, is about to make me explode. I can't hold back anymore. I finally let go as I scream his name. This is heaven! Chayse doesn't stop until I eventually settle down.

I'm still breathing really hard when he moves himself up toward my face. He stares down at me as he caresses my face. He then leans over and kisses me passionately. I'm already aroused, wanting more from him. How does he do this? I have no control left of my body or heart anymore. And I don't even care. This just feels too damn good. His kiss deepens, and his tongue plays in my mouth. He starts to spread my legs.

"Not so fast," I say. "My turn."

Before he can respond, I roll on top of him. I start to travel south. "Tess, you don't have to, you know. Maybe this is too soon for you," he says hesitantly.

"Are you kidding me? I've been fantasizing about this all day," I confess.

Chayse smiles and says, "Is that so? Well, I'm glad I can fulfill your fantasies, my lady."

"It's revenge time," I threaten. But I'm nervous. I'm not sure if I know what to do. Kylie had told me about this but to actually do the act? And to do it right? I take a deep breath, and slowly and timidly, I lick him. Hearing him gasp, makes me smile, and gives me the confidence. Yes! I'm in control this time! And I go for it. I suck, lick, and do my tricks with my tongue. And the more he's getting aroused, the more I'm getting aroused. My body automatically reacts with him. I hear him moaning and calling out my name. Damn! That sounds so sexy.

"Tess, stop. That's it. I won't be able to control myself," Chayse begs. But I don't stop, rising to the challenge. I take him deeper and moan. I take him in and out, sucking at the same time. He's doing everything in his power to control himself. I hear him moan again, deep from his throat.

"Damn it, Tess!" he yells. Suddenly, he pulls me up and rolls so that he's now on top of me. He reaches for the condom on the bedside table and hastily puts it on while he starts to kiss me. "I can't hold back, Tess. This may be a little rough," he warns.

Chayse spreads my legs and in one swift thrust, pushes himself into me. I gasp, not expecting that. And wow! How he fills me! He begins to move, in and out, and I move with him. He's much rougher than earlier. But I like it. He's deep inside me, and he's hitting my tender spot just right. I'm rising fast with him.

"Chayse," I moan breathlessly.

He kisses me again. We're gasping and kissing, moving and licking. He's thrusting into me hard, over and over. And I can't hold back anymore. It's magical. I scream his name again. As I climax, I hear him scream my name as he joins me. As we reach our peak together, and eventually begin descending again, I hold on tight, not wanting to let him go yet. Once our breathing becomes somewhat normal, Chayse lifts his head and looks at me.

"Sorry, I was a little rough there. You ok?" he asks sheepishly.

I smile shyly at him and say, "I liked it."

He lifts my chin up as he smiles, and says, "Hmm, I'll remember that next time, Tessnia." Chayse kisses me again. "You drove me insane earlier. How the hell did you know how to do that?" Chayse narrows his eyes at me suspiciously.

"Wouldn't you like to know?" I tease.

Chayse goes still. He looks at me again, with a slight frown. "Seriously, Tess. Don't tease like that."

"About what?" I continue teasing. I can't resist.

"Ok, you said you had never been with another man. I guess I assumed you meant in every way. Maybe it was a false assumption? I didn't realize you meant just sex." Chayse is getting more serious.

"Maybe it *was* a false assumption," I respond. I like to see him flinch like this.

Chayse stares down hard at me. His eyes change. They're no longer teasing. "Who, Tess? I want to know who the hell you did that with?"

"Why? What difference does it make?" I ask. In reality, there was nobody else. But I'm having too much fun making him squirm.

"I don't like this feeling, Tess. You fucking did that with another guy? What the hell! Damn it!" Chayse is getting upset. "What else have you done?"

"You're acting totally unreasonable right now, Chayse. I never asked what you've done with different women. I mean the past is the past," I say, shrugging my shoulders.

Chayse comes down on me hard. He starts to kiss me, but this time it's much rougher and almost punishing. I can feel his anger and frustration. I don't like it. I try to tell him that I was just joking but I can't even get a word out. As he continues his rough kisses, I finally muster enough strength to push him off of me.

"Damn it, Chayse! I was kidding! You're acting crazy. Look at you!" I yell at him.

Chayse goes very still. He buries his face into my neck and settles his hard breathing down. When he's calm, he says, "I'm sorry, Tess. That was totally inexcusable and unacceptable. God, I am so sorry. The thought of you doing that to somebody else, I can't bear it! Call me a hypocrite! But I can't bear it. I know it's selfish. How am I ever going to let you go, Tessnia?" he mumbles into my hair. It's as if he's just talking to himself. "I can't let you go. What am I going to do? I'm nothing without you."

I lift his face to look at me. "Chayse, I am yours. I don't know what's going to happen in the future with us, but trust me, I will always be yours."

Chayse holds my face with both his hands and stares into me, as if he is unveiling my soul to him. "I am a selfish man, Tessnia, to even expect that from you."

I bring his face down again into my neck and hug him tight. Sometimes I think that if I hold him tight enough, nobody can take him away from me. Chayse is holding me just as tight. Eventually, we fall asleep, clinging to each other.

Twenty-one

"Mm," I purr, as I open my eyes the next morning. Chayse is awake, propped up on his elbow, and is watching me. His eyes are distant, deep in thought.

"I love watching you sleep, Tessnia. You look so innocent and pure. Just watching you sleep brings peace to me," he whispers.

I shift my weight and try to move. I am exhausted! "Mm, sore body," I mumble, as I stretch.

Chayse laughs. "I'll bet! You were very active yesterday, Miss Sanoby. You apparently used muscles you never used before."

"So true, Mr. Pierce," I smile. "But right now, I have to get up and get myself cleaned up." I jump out of the bed, wrap the blanket around me, and dash toward the bathroom.

"Why are you covering yourself? I'm pretty sure I've seen every inch of your body by now!" Chayse teases.

As I get even more embarrassed, I run into the bathroom, holding tight to my blanket. I quickly lock the door, wanting some privacy to clean up. I don't trust him not to follow me in here.

"I'm shy, ok?" I yell from the bathroom.

"I guess so," he yells back. "But not for long, Tessnia--at least not with me!" He is so demanding!

Without replying back, I leap into the shower, and let the hot stream hit my aching muscles. When I come out, he's already left the bedroom. I put on my workout clothes and head downstairs. He's nowhere to be seen so I step outside.

Chayse is sitting on the swing on the porch, wearing his workout clothes. "Do I get my morning kiss now, Tessnia? I've been waiting patiently," Chayse says, with his famous smirk, and his eyes teasing. I walk up to him on the swing, and he pulls me onto his lap. "Come here, woman," he says in his seductive voice.

I lean forward and kiss him. It's a gentle kiss at first, but turns passionate as we continue kissing. I want him, right here, on the porch. "Chayse," I whisper, as I'm trying to catch my breath.

To my disappointment, Chayse pulls away, but continues to hold me on his lap, and my arms stay wrapped around him. He has his face buried into my hair. "You smell delicious, Tessnia. Thank you for that good morning kiss." Chayse looks at me, smiling. "But if we continue kissing like that, we'll never get anything done today," he laughs.

I laugh with him and say, "I want to work out again this morning."

"Ok, I told Gem to go for a run already. Do you want to do that same workout as yesterday?" he asks, twirling his fingers through my hair.

"Yeah, I would. I also want to learn some new moves," I answer. It now makes sense to me why Chayse and I are able to perform such a difficult routine.

Also, I see now that the card tricks were no tricks. We were able to guess the actual number because of our intuition or "sixth sense", as he calls it. Now that I understand our "talents" more, I want to learn as much as I can about how to use them.

"Let's go then," Chayse says, pulling me off as he stands up. We head back to our spot and workout for an hour. He teaches me to be on offense while he stays on defense, showing me some attack moves. I try them all on him, not holding back. He is easily able to block all of them.

Chayse is training me, wanting me to be ready in case I ever need to use the moves. I feel more confident in myself, pushing myself to be better, faster, smarter, and stronger. I start using the combination moves, consisting of kicks in the air, fast punches, spins, and flips, determine to land something. But he deflects them all, and before I realize what's happening, he grabs me, and has my back pinned against him. He's holding both my hands and is right behind me, restricting my movements. Damn him!

"Impressive," he whispers in my ear.

"Not good enough," I say, mad that he's able to get me into the compromising position so easily. I'm out of breath, but his breathing is calm as if he hadn't moved at all. One of these days, I'm going to get him!

Chayse releases me, and says, "You'll get there. Let's go for a run now. We haven't run together in a while. And I miss it."

"Ok, let's get some water first," I agree. After drinking some water, Chayse calls for Gem. She comes running and all three of us set off for our run. I keep up with his pace, giving my all because I know he's pushing me to be faster. I'm surprised how fast my legs are moving. It's just like he always tried to teach me in track. He said to stop analyzing about the run, and just do it. He said to visualize, and shut everything else out except running. He was right. I am in my zone.

When we head back, I start running past him, laughing. I take off, through the meadow, and through the wild flowers. I feel him behind me. I know he's closing in. I can't help but laugh as I run even faster. Suddenly, I feel a hard body slamming into me. I'm on the ground with him on top. We're both laughing uncontrollably.

"Nice try, but I will always be able to find you and catch you, Tessnia," Chayse says and he kisses me. I wrap my hands around his neck to kiss him back. This feels good. I'm in my happy place, right here in this beautiful meadow, with the man I love on top of me, kissing me so lovingly. Maybe it's not good for me to be this happy. But I push that thought away as soon as it enters my mind. Chayse helps me up and we finish our run back to the house.

As we approach the house, we stop running, and I ask, "So whose house is this anyway?"

"It's just one of the places that my bosses own--you know, for the team to use. They own places like this all over the world. They're usually in remote areas. They're not even on the map. These places can be used for hideouts, an escape, or even vacations. I just have to let my team know I'm here, just in case I need them or they need me."

That explains why we're in the middle of nowhere. I wonder about his team. It's apparent that he takes a lot of pride in them. I'm happy that Chayse found a purpose in his life. I reach for his hand and squeeze it. He looks down at me questioningly, and I smile back, so proud that he made it.

After breakfast, Chayse asks what I want to do for the rest of the day. I love our hilltop by the lake, so I suggest that we go back and have a late lunch there.

"Alright let's leave after we shower. I'm going to bring my guitar too. I haven't used it in a while, and it would be nice to pull it out again," Chayse says.

"You have your guitar here? I'd love to hear you sing again!" I exclaim. I give him a hug and a kiss. "I'm jumping in the shower. I stink!" And with that, I sprint up the stairs.

After the shower, I dress in my cutoff jean shorts and my light blue tank top. When I get downstairs, Chayse is waiting for me, with the backpack ready and his guitar case hanging off of his shoulders. He's wearing beige khaki shorts and a fitted white t-shirt, looking sexy as hell.

"Ready?" he asks, smiling at me. "And your legs look hot in those little shorts of yours by the way."

"Thank you! You look pretty hot yourself." I return the compliment as I approach him. Chayse kisses me on my forehead and embraces me.

"I'm very lucky, Tessnia," he whispers.

Chayse, Gem, and I hike to "our spot." When we arrive there, he spreads the blanket down, and tells Gem she can go exploring. With his arm around my shoulders while I rest my head on him, we both sit and stare down the hill at the water. I feel the peace spread through me, as I savor this moment.

Chayse pulls out his guitar and starts stroking the strings.

He tunes it until he's satisfied and plays with it. He then sings some tunes from John Mayer, Michael Buble, and even Bruno Mars. He sings the songs in his own version, always mellow. I'm mesmerized by his unique voice and his singing style. Time stands still; the only thing that matters is Chayse and his singing.

When I first saw him, it was his music and singing that drew me to him. Later, it was his singing that helped me see the truth that Chris was really Joe. Nobody can sing like him. It's magical, and I lose track of any rational thoughts.

Chayse starts another song and I recognize it as "A Drop In The Ocean" by Ron Pope. I stop breathing as soon as Chayse's version of the song starts. He never looks up while he's singing. His thick beautiful lock of hair falls in front of his forehead.

I travel back in time as the vision of Joe singing six years ago at *The Angels* flashes before my eyes.I can't move. I can't even breathe. He sings his heart out with every verse, every line, every word. I have goose bumps and my heart feels unbearably heavy.

Chayse slows his singing down, and sings the last verse a few more times. He sings, with no barriers, no walls, all of his emotions exposed for me to see. When he finishes humming and stroking the verse with his guitar, he looks up, directly into my eyes. He wants me to see what's in his heart.

I scoot closer to him. Chayse puts his guitar to the side. I slide into his lap and I bury my face into his neck. I wrap my arms around his neck while he holds me tight, cradling me on his lap. We sit like this for a long time. I will forever cherish this moment. I will remember his scent, the breeze blowing, the sun shining on us, the sound of the waterfall, our hilltop, how he held me, and how he sang to me. I never want to let him go.

But both of us know that this is temporary. Both of our intuitions tell us that this will be over soon. It makes me hold him tighter. I want to be with him, always. Chayse holds me just as tight.

Chayse turns my face to him and his eyes, full of emotion, penetrate into me. “I want to make love to you, Tessnia. Right now.”

Chayse and I make love on our hilltop. Our lovemaking is gentle, sweet, tender and loving. Chayse takes his time, both of us wanting to make it last, cherishing this moment.

After making love, we lie there, lost in our own thoughts. He finally turns to me and says, “You know, ever since I remember, I’ve always had the same dream, too. Except my dreams were not like yours.”

“What?” I asked, confused.

“Yeah, it was always of a girl. She had long, dark, curly hair. But I could never see what she looked like. I never understood the dream, and finally I just gave up trying, accepting that these dreams will always haunt me. Then, when I saw you at *The Angels* six years ago, I knew you were the girl from my dreams. I just knew. I had no idea what it all meant, but there you were, standing before me,” Chayse whispers.

“What happens in your dream?” I ask, curious.

“The girl is walking away from me. I never see her face. In every dream, I try to reach her, desperate to stop her. But she continues to walk away, with her back toward me. No matter how much I try to catch her, she walks further and further from me, until she eventually disappears in the distant.”

Chayse turns to look at me, and I notice his eyes glisten with unshed tears.

Sadness overcomes me. "Chayse, why didn't you tell me before?" My voice quivers as the tears start rolling down my face.

"It's not something I want to think about, Tessnia. I don't know what it all even means. Even all this, you and me together like this, seems unreal to me. I just never even imagined that I'd ever get this opportunity with you. But I know that I have you now. And I have to just hold on to that." He pulls me closer to him, and kisses my tears away.

I sigh and hold him tight. I don't understand his dreams at all. "I would never leave you, Chayse," I whisper. "When was the last time you had the dream?" I have to know.

Chris shudders and slowly answers, "Last night, Tessnia."

My body tenses. "Chayse, I don't understand."

He caresses my back and holds me just as tight. "Let's drop this, Tessnia. Let's just enjoy each other for now."

He's right, of course. We can't waste our time together. The rest of the afternoon, we eat, explore some more, and talk about nothing and everything. We hold hands, laugh a lot, and even chase each other. Neither of us bring up his dream again.

When we finally arrive back to the house, it's late. We sit on the outdoor swing on the porch, while Gem stretches out on the steps of the porch.

I receive a text from my aunt. As I'm replying back, Chayse asks, "How is she doing, Tess?"

"She's ok. I think she's still worried about me. I did talk to her yesterday and tried to assure her I was fine," I reply. I answer back to her text. I have to text her every day to let her know that everything is ok.

"How are *you* doing, Tessnia? I know it was rough for a while. And I want you to be honest with me. How are you really?" Chayse asks, full of concern.

"You know, my parents always taught me that everything happens for a reason. I just couldn't understand what the reason was for their death. And I still don't. But my mom also was big on destiny. As bittersweet as it may sound, I think their death brought you back to me. Truthfully, I had given up on life. But being here with you, I feel more alive than I ever had. I owe you my life, Chayse," I say sincerely. Truth be told, Chayse had saved my life.

"You're stronger than you realize, Tessnia. I know you are. You have to believe that. You have to give yourself more credit." Chayse reaches for my hand and squeezes it.

"Everything is making more sense now, Chayse. I understand my strength now. I won't give up like that anymore. That was a horrible place to be. I never want to go back there again." I shudder, just thinking about that miserable point in my life. I vow to myself that no matter what, I would somehow always find the strength to keep going, to not quit.

Chayse reaches for me and pulls me into his arms as we keep swinging. I sigh and rest my head onto his chest as all three of us watch the sunset. There's an orange haze above the horizon, lighting up the sky. The sun over the open fields is accompanied by hanging clouds, which are splashed with beautiful colors of pink, purple, orange, and blue. It's a breathtaking sight. The sun slowly starts dipping lower and lower, until it disappears completely on the other side of the horizon. Neither of us say a word, both of us holding on to the moment.

As the sky finally becomes dark, covered with shiny bright stars, I hear Chayse sigh and say, "Come on, we better go inside and eat."

"I'm still full though," I complain.

"Too bad, you're going to eat. I told you, I'm going to make sure you get your three meals and you *will* gain your weight back. I'm not going to change my mind, no matter how much you whine. Now stop rolling your eyes and let's go inside," Chayse chuckles.

How does he know I rolled my eyes? It's no use arguing with him. He would make sure I ate. "Let's just have salad or something light then."

"Fair enough. Come on, Gem, let's go in." Gem trots toward him, while wagging her tail. Chayse kneels down and rubs behind her ears as she licks his face.

I start laughing. "I think she may love you more than she loves me."

"Nah, she's your baby, and she'll always be loyal to you, right girl?" Chayse says. Gem barks in response. "But I love her, too. She is definitely on my top female list!"

"You have a top female list? Do tell," I tease.

"Of course, doesn't every guy?" he teases back, raising his eyebrow.

"I wouldn't know. Tell me who's on this top female list of yours," I say. Ok, so maybe I'm getting a little jealous.

"Wouldn't you like to know?" he smirks.

I put my hands on my hips. He better tell me. I'm ready to force it out of him if I have to. "Well?"

Chayse starts laughing. He grabs me and pulls me out of my "ready to win this battle" stance, and hugs me.

"I love when you get feisty like that." He kisses me, and says, "I only have two names on this list. That's Tessnia and Gem. Happy?"

I kiss him back. Only Chayse possesses the power to make me feel this elated.

"Yes, very happy," I whisper.

After taking a shower together, we make a salad for dinner. While we're eating, I ask, "So these people who are after you--how do they know about you? I mean you tried really hard not to stand out, purposefully not performing to your full potential. How did they even find out that you existed?" This has been puzzling me.

"I've wondered that myself. My team has tried to find some answers as well. The only theory is that somehow my parents are the link. My team thinks that maybe these people found out something from my parents when they were alive. Maybe my parents may have mentioned something unique about me to even one individual. Or maybe there's some type of documentation about me that was discovered. There have been no concrete connections though," Chayse says, with a faraway look in his eyes.

"And your team was not able to find out anything about your parents? Maybe they were scientists like my parents," I wonder.

"No information. Not one thing. That's why I wonder if we even know their real names." Chayse runs his hand through his hair in frustration. This is a tough subject for him to discuss.

I decide to change the topic. "Why did you have to leave so abruptly three years ago? You said in your letter that you had no choice." I remember my pain, as if I was stabbed through my heart. He hadn't even said goodbye in person, leaving me no explanations.

"After I left you that next morning, my boss contacted me before I even got back to my apartment. He said somebody had broken into my apartment. Nothing was robbed, but they were going through my things, as if searching for something. I couldn't believe that I was found as Chris. My boss instructed me to not return to the apartment, and that I had to get out of there immediately. He said he would get me out of the country on a long assignment. I told him I wanted a few more hours before I left. He forbade me to make contact with you, saying that if these people were tracking me, I would be putting your life at risk. But I couldn't leave without seeing you one more time. I went to that bar by your apartment, just to be closer to you. I wanted to stop by your place, but I couldn't chance that," Chayse says, desperate for me to understand. I nod, encouraging him to continue. "At the bar, I kept racking my brain on how I can see you one more time without making it obvious. When I saw your roommate come into the bar, I knew she would contact you. So I came up with a plan. I wanted you to know the truth about who I was. And in my heart, I knew that if you heard me sing, you would know. That was my only chance, without risking your life," Chayse sighs, shaking his head. "And when you ran out of there, I knew that you knew. I snuck back to your apartment, making sure nobody saw me, and left you that letter. I left immediately afterwards. You have no idea how difficult it was for me to walk away from you. But I knew I couldn't put your life in danger. I would never have forgiven myself, Tess. You do realize that, right?"

I reach over and squeeze his hand. I feel his frustration, my heart bleeding at the thought of his life always on the run. Poor Chayse--always hiding! I can't imagine a life like that. As I continue to hold his hand, Chayse looks at me with his piercing eyes.

"I liked the roses I received for my twenty-first birthday," I slowly say, with a shy smile.

"You knew?" Chayse raises his eyebrow at me.

"How could I not? All of the memories of "us" came flooding back again. God, so much time wasted," I say, shaking my head.

"Let's not brood on this. It's quite depressing. And this is our time--our happy time," he says, smiling at me.

I smile back, wondering how long our happy time was going to last. We have not brought up our future. Neither of us wants to discuss that yet. I noticed that he had stocked up enough food here to last us for at least a couple of more weeks. I sigh. Why bother worrying about this right now? He's right. This is our time and I'm not going to ruin it by thinking about when it's going to end.

That night, we make love again. It is sweet and beautiful. We wake up in the middle of the night, and make love again.

During the weeks that follow, we work out every morning,

consisting of running and the battle moves. We also hike to our hilltop by the lake every day. Chayse makes sure we eat three full meals. And we make love--lots of love. We make love in our bed, in the bathtub, in the shower, on the kitchen floor, on the floor by the fireplace, and on our hilltop. I become familiar with his body, and I learn what makes him feel good. Slowly, I lose my shyness as he shows me different ways to fulfill our needs.

If there is heaven, this place is it. Even Gem agrees with me. She's constantly happy and loving the routine that we have set for ourselves. As each day passes, I become stronger and faster. I've even gained most of my weight back. I'm able to keep up with Chayse with not only the running, but also his workout routine. He has taught me defense moves, specifically how to block his punches and kicks. On some days, I'm able to give him a run for his money. But then again, he may be holding back and going easier on me to help build my confidence. It doesn't matter though, because it's working.

One night, when I come out of the bathroom, I have my black nightie on. It's revealing in all the right places. I have all my hair up in a bun. Tonight, I'm going to take control and throw all my inhibitions out the window. I'm going to be wild and spontaneous.

He smiles when he notices what I have on. I turn on soft jazz music from my iPhone. As the music plays, I pull my bun off so that my hair falls loose and wild past my shoulders and mid back. I feel sexy. I start to slowly take my nightie off. I'm nervous at first, but damn I just want to have my fun with him. I think he's just as surprised as me when he realizes that I'm about to perform a strip show for him.

I begin seductively moving my hips to the music, and slide the nightie slowly off of my shoulders and step out of it. I'm down to my black, lacy bra and matching thongs. I dance sensually, biting my lower lip and closing my eyes. I hear him moan so I know he's enjoying the show. I tease him more by taking off my bra. As my bra comes off, he watches me touch my breasts. His mouth opens in surprise. I love his reactions! As my hips move side to side with the music, I start working on my panties. When I pretend to take them off, I hear Chayse catch his breath. I hold back, teasing him some more. I dance with my back to him so that he can see my back view. As I sway my hips to the music, Chayse groans. I smile, knowing how many times Chayse has complimented me on my round butt. I take advantage of this. I slip my panties off on one side first, and then the other. I tease Chayse some more, and then I slowly and deliberately slip them off of me.

"Tessnia," Chayse says, his voice husky.

I dance with my back to him, seducing him with my sensual dancing. I slowly turn to face him, standing before him completely naked, still dancing and playing with my breasts.

"Damn, you're driving me crazy, Tessnia," Chayse says hoarsely.

This erotic dance and his reactions have turned me on. I seductively stroll toward him as my hand slowly moves from my breast, down past my belly, and I touch myself. I keep watching him as he watches my hand, his gray eyes full of desire. His reactions give me the confidence to push the limits. As I watch Chayse fall apart in front of me, I'm loving this control I have over him. As I stroke myself with my finger, I moan.

"Come here!" he commands.

I climb on top of him, and he grabs me. Chayse holds my hand by my wrist, and puts the finger that I had just used to touch myself, in his mouth. His eyes penetrate mine as he sucks my finger. My heart is beating out of control. Chayse takes the finger out, and kisses me hard. I want him! God, I can't get enough of him.

I want to taste every inch of him as I trail kisses down his body. I go lower until I find my target. This time, I want to taste him. He has never lost control with me, but tonight, I'm going to take charge. I stroke, lick, and suck. I stroke some more, lick, and suck some more. When I hear him moan hard, I go faster.

"Tessnia, I'm going to lose it!" Chayse chokes out the words.

"I want to taste you, Chayse. Stop holding back!" I demand.

"Tess, stop. You're killing me," he begs. I'm not stopping this time. No, this is my show, and I'm in control. He tries to pull me back up but I resist, relentlessly using my mouth and tongue to drive him wild. I torture him with the stroking, sucking, and playing with my tongue. Chayse releases a sigh of defeat as he finally stops resisting me. I feel his hips move up and down with my rhythm. I hear him moan with every suck and I take him deeper.

"Tess!" Chayse yells. And he starts to move faster. I suck harder. Faster, harder, deeper. Suck, lick, stroke. All of the sensations, and listening to him moaning, is about to put me over the edge. He has his hand tangled into my hair and damn that feels good. His moaning and thrusting of his hips becomes more intense.

And then, with a final strong thrust as I suck him hard, he moans, "Tessnia, yes!"

And he loses all control, reaching ecstasy.

I keep sucking and swallowing until his tremors subside. The experience is so erotic, that I'm about to burst. I want him!

Chayse pulls me back up to him. He kisses me. He kisses me hard.

"You're crazy, my little vixen," he whispers. "And amazing! And I'm not done with you. We're just getting started. It's time for revenge," he threatens. I have no idea how he's already geared up for round two, but I'm ready for whatever he has in mind!

Chayse rolls me onto my belly and begins kissing my hair in the back. I feel his tongue licking my back, slowly, deliberately, and sensually. My body trembles under his touch as the goose bumps begin forming. I want him to take me right now! I need him to take me! I've never been this turned on before.

His hands slip under me and find my breasts. He plays while licking my back and I feel his hardness against my thighs. Slowly, Chayse's mouth travels lower, savoring every inch of me. He kisses my one buttock and then the other.

"I love this right here, Tessnia!" he says hoarsely, as he purposefully bites one of my butt cheeks. It's not a hard bite, but just enough pressure to catch me by surprise and turn me on even more. His hands travel to my front. As he kisses and licks my buttocks, his finger goes inside me, exploring. Damn it! This is too good. *He* is too good. He pulls my hips up so that they are elevated and I am propped up on my knees. Chayse spreads my legs and strokes me as his mouth focuses on my buttocks.

I moan, begging for a release. “Chayse, I need you now!” I yell.

I feel his hardness against me and with one quick thrust he is inside me. He’s going in and out, deep and hard. And I love it. I moan at every thrust. As he goes faster, I scream louder. He thrusts harder, as his finger continues to stroke me. My hands find my breasts as I stimulate my nipples. My body is on fire.

“Tess, now, baby!” Chayse yells.

I can’t hold back anymore and I explode! “Chayse!” I yell.

Chayse joins me and we both climax together. I collapse onto the bed, exhausted. Chayse collapses on top of me, just as exhausted. As we both settle back down, he takes the condom off of him. I don’t even remember when he had managed to put that on.

“That was amazing. *You* are amazing,” Chayse whispers into my neck. He turns me around so that I’m lying on my side facing me. “And you’re beautiful. And you’re mine.”

“Mm, yes, always yours,” I whisper back, snuggling into him. Content and happy, we fall asleep, with our arms and legs tangled into each other.

Twenty-two

In the middle of the night, I wake up to Gem growling. Chayse jumps out of bed. He stares at Gem for a few seconds, and she continues to focus toward the window, still growling.

"Something's wrong," Chayse says, as he slips into his black sweatpants. "Get up. I want you to put some black clothes on. We have to go!"

"What? What's going on?" His voice is starting to scare me.

"Please, just get up, Tess! Now, and move!" Chayse pulls a black t-shirt on, and slips into his gym shoes.

I run to the drawer and put on my black sweats and black t-shirt. I grab my gym shoes and he pulls his phone out, calling somebody.

"I need back up. Now! I think they've found us. We're going to try to leave the house if we can. We're not going to take the car--too risky. We will be on foot, and we'll head for the woods. Tess and her dog are with me. Priority is to save them. Understand?" Chaye talks abruptly as he gives orders. He ends the call.

"Who were you talking to? What's going on? You're scaring me," I whisper. I'm not sure why I'm whispering, but I know something is not right.

Chayse walks up to me and grabs my shoulders. "Look, Tess, the only thing that has saved me all this time, is my instincts. Can't you feel it? We have to get out of here. I think they're on their way. But I don't think they're here yet."

"Who?" I am so scared. My heart is beating uncontrollably. I can't believe this is happening.

"The people who've been after me! Look we can't talk now. Let's go! I asked for back up, so hopefully my team will get to us in time. But they are far. We are in the middle of nowhere. And you have to understand something, Tess," Chayse says while he lifts my chin up to look at him. His eyes have hardened. "They already know about me, but no matter what, they can NOT know about you. Do you understand? You stay hidden. And if we get caught, you tell them a different name. They can't know that you're like me. Promise me!" Chayse is shaking me.

I nod, terrified.

"No, say it, Tess. Promise me!" Chayse insists.

"I promise!" I whisper. I run for my shoes, and grab my cell phone. I quickly put the phone in my pocket of the sweatpants, and zip it up.

"And you too, Gem. They can't see what you can do. Do you understand?" Gem barks as if she understands. "Your responsibility is to protect Tess. No matter what happens. Do you understand?" Gem barks again.

Chayse runs to the garbage can, pulls the used condom out and flushes it down the toilet.

"What are you doing?" I'm still having a hard time comprehending everything.

"Trying to avoid having easy access to my DNA. Let's go."

Without turning on any lights, we slip out of the back window. I don't see anything out of the ordinary but I have the same feeling as Chayse; something is closing in on us.

I take a deep breath. I have to stay calm. Chayse will make sure we'll be ok. Besides, he said his team is on the way.

All three of us start running through the grass and the open field. We try to stay light on our feet to avoid leaving any tracks. I have no idea where we're going. All I know is that I have to keep running and not slow him down.

The loving, gentle Chayse is gone. Chayse is in his survival mode. He has a cold, calculated look in his eyes now.

We're running, without looking back. We have to get away. We're running for our lives--just like my dreams.

And then I hear them. I hear the cars, the slamming of doors, and the voices. It sounds like they've found the house. My heart starts beating faster. We quicken our speed, desperate to gain some distance.

After a few moments, I hear the cars driving again. They must have realized we're not at the house. Oh no! They're looking for us in their cars. How are we supposed to out run the cars? But we keep running, not losing focus.

I'm living my worst nightmare. The girl in my dreams was always running to escape from the unknown. But this time, it's not a dream. This time, it's reality.

The sound of the cars disperses in different directions. "I think they're splitting up," Chayse says, as we keep running. We run deeper into the woods, hoping the trees and bushes will protect us. They can't drive in the woods so there's a good possibility of us escaping.

"Maybe you should call your team again to see if they'll get here in time to help us," I suggest. I wonder how far his "team" is from this place.

"No, I destroyed my phone back at the house. Even though my phone is not traceable, they have the latest technology, Tess. I'm not willing to take that chance." Chayse lowers his voice.

"Should I throw my phone away?" I whisper.

Chayse stops in his tracks. He turns around to look at me. "You have your phone with you?" he asks incredulously.

Oh no. My eyes widen with fear, as I pull my phone out. He reaches his hand out and snatches the phone. Without saying a word, he throws it on the ground and smashes it with his foot.

"They can't pick up the signal if we haven't used it, right?" I ask, panicking.

"Tess, I'm telling you, they have the means. I've seen tracking devices that can track cell phones without the phone being in use. The mere fact of the phone being on, can trigger a signal into their system," Chayse explains, shaking his head in frustration.

"I'm sorry, Chayse. I had no idea," I say, keeping my head down. Damn it! Why didn't I just ask him at the time?

Chayse pulls my chin up. "Look, don't worry, ok? They probably don't even know you're with me. Hopefully, they think I'm alone. And if that's the case, maybe they weren't even tracking the signal for your phone. Besides, the tall trees probably disrupt the signals anyway," Chayse assures me, pulling me into his embrace. I know Chayse is just trying to make me feel better so I don't worry.

Suddenly, we hear a different engine sound, and it doesn't sound like a car. There are several of these sounds. Oh my god. What is that?

"We have to go, Tess. Sounds like they came with motorbikes."

I hear apprehension in Chayse's voice. They can drive their motorbikes into the woods. We're in trouble.

Gem snarls. "It's ok, girl. You have to stay quiet. We'll make it," I whisper to her.

All three of us start running again. We weave through the trees, our legs moving us faster and faster. I can feel the pine needles cracking under our feet as we dart around the low branches. Once, I trip over a log and begin to fall forward. I'm falling face first. But before I can hit the ground, Chayse wraps his strong arms around my waist and catches me. He grabs my hand and we sprint again, desperately trying to find our escape. We're descending deeper and deeper into the woods. We run like this for another hour, stopping only to catch our breath. Thankfully, I don't hear those motorbikes anymore. But I'm exhausted, physically and mentally.

"We have to find a hiding spot," Chayse says, as he comes to a stop. "We have to try to hide out. The sun will be rising soon." As he explores our surroundings, his keen eyes spot an opening which is covered by bushes and shrubs. He leads us to it after investigating it.

Gem and I squeeze into the opening after him. Once we're situated, he pulls me into his arms. I'm trying to be brave, but I'm scared out of my mind. I start trembling. Chayse holds me tighter.

"I'm scared," I whisper.

"I know, Tessnia, I know. I'm scared, too. But I promise you, I will not let anything happen to you," Chayse says with conviction.

"Do you have a gun?" I ask. I have to know.

"I left it at the house on purpose," Chayse answers, shaking his head. "If I use a weapon on them, that would give them a reason to use their weapons. And there are too many of them. I can't take that chance--not with you and Gem with me."

"But I don't want anything to happen to you, Chayse," I say, my voice quivering.

"They won't do anything to me. They want me alive. You know, probably to use me as their precious lab rat," Chayse says dryly.

I shudder at the thought. My beautiful Chayse at the mercy of somebody, helpless, while they do as they please with him.

Chayse pulls a bag out that was hanging on his back. I don't even remember him grabbing a bag. He takes out some water bottles and some energy bars. He pours some water into Gem's mouth as he hands me one. I look at him questioningly.

"It's my survival bag. I always have one ready. You know, the basics: water, some energy bars, something to light a fire, a pocket knife, and this watch. The watch activates as soon as I turn it on. It's got a tracking device that's connected to my team's device. No other device can pick up the signal, except the device this watch is connected to. We are in the middle of nowhere, so it will take my team a while to get to us. But I'm hoping this will help them find our location." Chayse activates the watch and puts it on. He slowly smiles at me, almost an apologetic smile. "I can't believe I got you into this mess, Tessnia."

"Chayse, I'd rather be in any type of mess with you, then you having to face it alone. You do know that, right?" I look into his eyes to make him understand. His beautiful gray eyes are full of sorrow and regret now.

"No, don't say that. You don't deserve any of this. Damn it! It's my fault. I dragged you into this. If you weren't here, you would have been fine," Chayse whispers fiercely.

"I was not fine at all. I wouldn't trade any of this, Chayse. None of it!" I whisper back just as fiercely, holding his face with both my hands. Chayse sighs, shaking his head.

I rest my head into his chest, hoping to relax in his arms. As Chayse holds me tight, transferring some of his strength into me, we both seem to settle down. He makes sure I eat the energy bars and drink some water.

It must have been an hour later, when Gem's ears perk up and she begins a low growl. Chayse and I are on high alert, and we hear the motorbikes. This time, they're getting louder. Oh no! I'm tense, and I can feel that Chayse is even tenser next to me. Gem's growl gets louder. "You have to stay quiet, Gem, ok? No noise," I whisper to her. She makes no noise but her teeth remain exposed. She is furious.

Suddenly, we hear voices. The motorbikes drown out the voices, but the bikes have slowed down. I know they're in close proximity to us. I look at Chayse, and he puts his finger on his mouth, signaling me to not make any noise. The noise of the motorbikes subsides, as the engines are turned off. I'm gripping Chayse's hand for dear life.

They are so close, we can hear them talking. "He has to be in the woods somewhere," one man says.

"Yeah, how far can he go?" I hear a second man.

"We've been looking all night for him. I'm tired. Just wanna finish him off and get on with it," the third angry voice says.

"No, he cannot be hurt. Those were the orders. They want him alive and healthy. Understand?" This first voice commands.

One of the other men grunts. I wonder why they decided to stop here. Then, I hear them taking a leak. I pray they go on their merry way once they're done with their business.

Chayse looks at me and holds three fingers up indicating that there are three of them. I nod.

"I say we hang out here for a bit. I'm exhausted," the second man says.

"What about the others?" the third man asks.

"Who gives a fuck about the others? What's wrong with us taking a little break?" the second man says angrily.

Please don't stay, please don't stay.

But unfortunately, we hear the first man say, "Yeah, I guess we can stay here for a bit. At least until light comes up."

I look at Chayse. He gestures for me to stay at my spot. He then points to himself and points out toward the men. I shake my head no vigorously. Why would he want to leave our hiding spot? He sighs, and nods his head. He then mouths, "Trust me." I shake my head no again. "Stay here no matter what!" Chayse mouths. He gestures to Gem to stay. I try to grab him as I panic, but he pulls my hands off of him. He plants a quick kiss on my lips and silently sneaks out.

As Chayse crawls out, I can see the men. Their backs are to us as they're still chatting and arguing amongst themselves. They're wearing military fatigues, their clothes camouflaging them.

I try to find Chayse but before I can even register what's happening, he leaps from nowhere and springs forward. By the time any of the men can turn toward the sound, Chayse is already on them. He knocks one of them out with his kick. He grabs the second one and flips him over. The third one charges at him with his knife out, but Chayse is ready. He blocks him, knocks the knife out, and tackles him down. He then springs to his feet and does his flip in air and knocks the second guy out as he's trying to get up. As the third guy attempts to get back up after being tackled, Chayse is already on top of him. He grabs him by the neck and performs a maneuver, and the guy goes limp. Chayse has dominated over all three guys, knocking them out, in less than two minutes.

I release a long sigh of relief. I must have been holding my breath the entire time. Those guys didn't stand a chance. My gaze turns from the men on the ground, to Chayse as he towers over them. I shudder. He looks deadly and dangerous. He comes back to us and pulls us out. He approaches the men again and checks their pockets for any clues. There's no identity, but he finds some knives on them. I shudder at the site of the sharp knives.

I wonder why these guys don't have any guns on them. I then remember that they were given strict orders not to kill. They probably are not allowed to carry the guns. That knowledge makes me feel a little better. When Chayse finds their cell phones on them, he steps on all three phones and destroys them.

I look down at the men. "Are they dead?" I hesitantly ask.

"No, I just put them to sleep for a bit. Come on, we have to get out of here. I don't want to use their motorbikes to escape because the noise will draw too much attention on us," Chayse says, as he if thinking to himself. "Besides, we can hide ourselves better if we have less things to hide."

Chayse hangs his bag on his back, grabs my hand, and all three of us start running. I know he wants to get some distance between us and those three goons.

We run for a couple of more hours. It has started to rain, so we're now wet and cold, and trying to run through the slippery ground. Daylight is upon us. We need another hideout.

Chayse finds a small cave. We all squeeze in there, and he tries to close up the opening with bushes and shrubs. He gets more water out for us. Gem is probably hungry too but she's being a good sport about it. We're all soaking wet.

I start shivering. I'm not sure if it's from being cold or my body going into shock. Maybe it's a combination of both. We try to warm ourselves up with our body heat. Chayse pulls me tight into his arms. I'm exhausted. Why hasn't his team found us yet? I sneak a peek at him. He appears tense, stressed, and worried. I want to wipe the worry lines off of his forehead. My beautiful Chayse. This isn't fair. I finally doze off--cold, hungry, and exhausted.

When I wake up, I'm alone, with no sign of Chayse or Gem. I jump up. Damn it! Where are they? Nothing seems out of place. I peek out. Right then, I see them walking back toward the cave. It's still light out, probably around mid-day. Chayse crawls back in the cave and Gem follows.

"Where did you guys go?" I ask.

"I let Gem hunt for a bit. She needed to eat some food. I also found us some berries to munch on. They should give us some energy. And don't forget, I still have those bars from earlier."

"Did Gem find anything to eat?" I ask, curious.

"Yeah, she caught a rabbit. I'm sure she's full now," he says, as he smirks. Oh how I miss those smirks! I lean forward and kiss him. He smiles at me, but his eyes are not smiling. They're full of sadness, regret, and remorse.

I want him to know we're going to get through this together. I rub his cheek with my hand, looking deep into him, to let him see that I have hope; I believe in him, in us. Chayse holds my hand against his cheek and sighs.

I take some berries from him and force myself to eat them. I have no desire to eat anything. I feel nauseated with worry. But I know I have to eat to keep up my strength and my energy.

After a few moments, I hear Chayse ask me, "What are you thinking, Tess?"

I turn toward him and say, "I guess that girl from my dreams *was* me. All these years the girl was running through the woods, trying to escape. And here I am, running through the woods, trying to escape. Maybe a part of me always knew, but just wasn't ready to accept it."

"Does she ever get caught in any of your dreams?" Chayse questions, raising his eyebrow.

"I always woke up right before she was caught. I have no idea, Chayse," I say, shaking my head.

"I'm going to fix this, Tessnia. You are in this predicament because of me. I'm going to make it right. I promise you, Tess, I will protect you 'till my last breath." Chayse is staring deep into my soul, making a silent promise to himself.

"Stop talking like that! Chayse, we're going to get through this together. I don't know how, but we will," I promise him, uncertain about that promise.

"It doesn't matter. I'm going to make sure you're ok. No matter what happens, I will not let them harm you," Chayse insists. "Listen, if for some reason, we end up in a situation where they're trying to find your identity, you don't give it away, ok? You make up a name, and give away nothing. Just like I explained to you last night. They can NOT know about you. Do you understand? Otherwise, your life as you know it will be gone. And God only knows what they would do to you if they found out about you."

I stare at Chayse, starting to panic. "Chayse, we're not going to get caught." I can't even think of that possibility. This is way too much for me to process right now.

"Do you understand, Tess?" Chayse asks again, this time squeezing my shoulders to make sure I'm comprehending his instructions.

"Yes, Chayse, I understand," I reply. "But nothing can happen to you. I can't live without you Chayse. Please promise me."

"I told you, Tess, they won't hurt me. They want me alive. But don't say things like that. You have to live. No matter what. You have to live. You have your whole life ahead of you. You're going to be an amazing physician, and you're going to fall in love and have lots of kids. I want you to have a normal life." Chayse's voice is persistent, but he's sounding crazy to me.

"What are you saying?" I start shaking my head, wanting to shut him out. "Chayse, I don't want to be with anybody else but you. Why are you saying that?" The unshed tears sting my eyes. It feels as if he's saying goodbye. How can he not see that I've already fallen in love?

"Listen, Tess. That's my wish. If something should happen that I can't control, you have to go on. I want you to have a normal life." Chayse's grip on my shoulder gets tighter. He looks desperate, trying to make me understand.

As tears threaten to fall, I start to shake my head. This is a nightmare. I'm losing all control of my life again.

"What have I always taught you, Tessnia? You have to be strong. No matter what life brings you. Your parents always taught you that. Remember your parents, Tess!" Chayse insists.

"It sounds like you're saying goodbye," I whisper. Now the tears are freely falling down my cheeks.

Chayse pulls me into his chest. "Don't, Tessnia. I can't bear it," he whispers. I take a deep breath, gathering all of my courage. I have to be strong for him. If I fall apart now, it's going to take the fight out of him.

"Just promise me that you'll do everything possible to save yourself, too. Can you at least promise me that?" I need that reassurance.

"I promise that I'll do everything in my power to get all three of us out of this, ok?" Chayse lifts my chin up to look at him. "But right now, we need to rest. We'll travel again at nightfall." Chayse moves my hair out of my face and tucks it behind my ear. He gently kisses my tears away from my cheek.

I close my eyes to cherish this moment with him. I force my body to relax and eventually fall asleep in his arms. I dream that he's chasing me through the flowers. As I laugh and run, he catches me, and kisses me all over. It is such a wonderful dream; I don't want to wake up.

Twenty-three

"Tess, wake up," I hear Chayse whispering to me. My eyes fly open. "It's going to be dusk soon. I already took Gem to hunt and fetch her some water. I want you to eat and drink some water because we're going to be leaving this spot. I feel like we're sitting ducks here. We're going to head back to the house even if they're still monitoring the house. The chances of my team finding us there are better than this tracking device on this watch, in the middle of the woods. Besides, I know they'll go there first."

I nod. I drink more water, and eat another energy bar. He hands me more berries, so I eat some of those as well. I'm muddy and dirty. I've never missed a shower as much as I do right now.

I glance up at Chayse. He's just as muddy as me and has stubble on his face from not shaving. His hair is a curly mess from the rain. His gray eyes are piercing, strong, like those of a warrior. He looks rugged and dangerous.

Suddenly, Gem's ears perk up and she leaps up. Her snarl returns and Chayse springs into action. With my heart beating fast, I jump up with him. He motions Gem to stay quiet. She stops growling, but her fangs are ready to attack. My heart is about to explode. Something is terribly wrong.

And then I hear those dreaded motorbikes. They are still distant, but they're getting closer. I look at Chayse. He's peeking out of our hideout. It's starting to get dark, but not dark enough. Our little cave is not a good hideout. If they head this way, the likelihood of them finding us is good. From the sound of the motors, it seems like they're heading straight this way. And there's no way we can make a run for it. If we leave our cave, the chances of them spotting us are high. We're in a bad predicament, whether we stay hidden or make a run for it.

Chayse turns to me, and then quietly, but sternly says, "Listen, I'm going to try to lead them out of here. You and Gem have to stay hidden. When everything is clear, you have to start heading toward the house. Gem can get you back there. My team will find you there. Just stay in the outskirts, because it may still be monitored."

"What are you saying? No, NO! We are staying together, Chayse," I say, my voice half full of panic and half full of anger.

"No choice. Don't argue. I will meet you back there. We can't run now, it's too late. They'll see us. I can't have them come through here, they'll catch us. I will lead them out of here so that you guys can get away. They don't know you guys are with me, Tess. Come on, think."

"We can all fight, Chayse. You've taught me. We have a better chance if we fight together," I insist. I'm furious at what he's suggesting.

"NO, TESS!" he exclaims. "They can NOT see you in action. They'll know. You promised." Chayse looks back out again. The sound of the motorbikes is getting louder. He turns to Gem. "Stay with Tess, Gem. Your job is to protect her at all cost. When everything is clear, you find your way back toward the house again, ok?" Gem looks up at him and bows her head to him. He gives her a hug.

My eyes are tearing up again. I don't want to cry. Not

now. I blink them away. He turns to me and grabs my hand and gives me a quick kiss on the inside of my palm. After the kiss, he holds my palm to his cheek for a brief minute, closing his eyes. When his eyes open, they are dark, determined, and fierce. Then, just as quickly, Chayse releases my hand. He doesn't say anything more. He is all business now, not giving me a second glance.

Chayse crawls out of the cave and creeps toward the direction of the motorbikes. I can see him from where we're hidden. He's stooped low and is creeping through the bushes. Chayse stalks as a predator, about to attack his prey.

But then I see the bikes. There aren't only three this time, there are probably thirty! No, this is a mistake! We should have made a run for it.

Chayse jumps out in their path so that they have a visual of him. They begin shouting and start veering toward his direction. He starts to lead them away from the cave. Oh my god. He can't fight them all. There are too many of them!

"Don't shoot him!" I hear somebody yelling. "We have to take him in alive and well!" So they *do* have guns?

At least I feel somewhat better that the instructions are to not shoot him, but not much better. I can still see him, but he's going further and further away, with all those horrible men following him. Although Chayse is fast, I can already tell that the motorbikes were closing in on him. There's no way he would be able to outrun those bikes!

I look at Gem and she looks just as worried as me. She's staring out and her ears are perked up. Her senses are on high alert just as mine. As they gain more distance from us, I lose all visual on Chayse and the motorbikes.

Suddenly, I notice that we can't hear the engines of the bikes. It's as if they stopped. I hear yelling, but I can't make out what they're saying. Even though Chayse's strict instructions were for us to run toward the house, my mind is racing with anxiety. Did they catch up to him?

"I can't take this, Gem," I whisper to her. "We have to check and make sure he's ok. I need to know if he got away. We can't just sit here."

Gem wags her tail in agreement. We both slowly sneak out of our hidden cave, and start to head toward the sounds. My heart is beating out of my chest wall, but I keep edging forward. We're careful to not make a sound. Some small part reminds me that Chayse will kill us if he finds out what we're doing. But there's no way I can leave without making sure that he has gotten away.

Finally I get a visual. I catch my breath as I see him standing in the middle of them all. He is surrounded! I gasp, and put my hand on my mouth, as my heart is about to burst.

Chayse is assessing his threat, not moving a muscle. The men are slowly circling him. Nobody is making a move. Chayse looks tall, strong, confident, and fierce. He's watching them closely, waiting for them to make a move. There are roughly thirty men circling around him. Nobody is making a sound. I hold my breath. There's no way he can fight all these men off.

Suddenly, there's a quick motion from a corner. Somebody throws something toward him. Chayse quickly dodges out of the way. Oh my god, what the hell was that?

Another man yells, "No killing! We bring him back alive!"

I focus on the object that was thrown, now lying on the ground. It's a knife! A fucking knife! Damn it! Before I can process this, a few of them move toward Chayse. One takes a swing, but Chayse is ready. He ducks out of the way of the strike. He attacks back and the guy is thrown across to the other side of the circle. I know Chayse has his pocket knife with him, but I'm not sure if he's going to use it. If he uses it, then these men may think it's a fair game to use weapons. And to my dismay, it sounds like they probably have guns as well.

I hold my breath as I watch three men jump on him at once. Chayse strikes back, his movements quick as a lightning. He's able to dodge most of the blows. He's kicking and punching, flipping out of the way. Chayse is moving so quickly and ferociously during this battle, that my eyes can barely keep up. I've never seen him move like this. I guess he *had* been holding back with me during our morning routines.

Chayse is fierce and he's a warrior.

To my horror, I notice most of them are trying to attack him at once. Chayse can't make a run for it, because he's surrounded. Plus, they would catch him on their motorbikes. But he fights like a caged animal. He's agile, and his strikes are fluent and precise. Even these men are taken aback when they aren't able to bring him down.

But as I watch helplessly, I see that some of their blows are meeting their mark. Each time Chayse gets struck, I feel the pain. But he doesn't budge. He doesn't even flinch. He keeps fighting--striking, kicking, dodging, blocking.

The battle goes on for another thirty minutes. I don't know how much longer Chayse can hold them off. I can tell that he's starting to become fatigued. I can't bear this. I look down at Gem and her fangs are flashing as she's snarling. She looks just as upset as me. We both know that Chayse is not going to be able to get out of this one. There's too many of them.

I gasp as some of the men catch him by surprise and tackle him. Chayse is trapped under them. Oh no, no, no! But somehow, Chayse throws one man at a time off of him. He springs back up on his feet. But he's weak and shaken up. I can't watch any more. It's killing me!

Gem and I look at each other and we both know what we have to do. I nod to her, and we both sprint toward the battle scene. Gem has the lead instantly since she's so much faster than me.

As we're running toward him, I see one of the men charging at him with a knife again! Chayse doesn't notice because the man is charging from behind him, and Chayse is too preoccupied fighting the men in front of him. Oh no! I have to run faster! I can't watch him get stabbed right in front of me! But there's no way I can reach there on time. Dear God, no! My heart stops beating, and time stands still.

Just as the knife is about to strike down, stabbing Chayse in the back, Gem leaps up in the air. The guy with the knife is tackled, with Gem on top of him. Just as quickly, she snaps his neck with her fangs, as if he's just one of the rabbits she had killed earlier. He is dead.

I fly there and I'm about to attack the guy who was going to swing at Chayse, but something catches me. I can't move. It's Chayse. He has grabbed me by my waist and is holding me back. I'm uncontrollably furious, wanting to get my revenge for hurting Chayse like this. I want to kill them.

"No, no," Chayse is whispering in my ears. "They can't know. You promised." I'm still trying to get free of him, screaming at him to let me go. The men stop advancing, trying to process what's happening.

One of them yells, "That bitch killed Ken!" He has his gun pointed toward Gem. Gem is growling at him, fangs exposed, ready to strike. She looks like a wild animal, about to attack for her next kill.

"Stop!" yells Chayse. "I'm surrendering. I'm giving up. Just don't shoot!"

"That bitch killed Ken!" the man repeats. The man's hand shakes as he's holding his gun. He's terrified of Gem.

"Please!" Chayse says. "She was just protecting me. Nobody else will get hurt. I told you, I'll go with you willingly."

Chayse still has a hold of me. He sounds defeated. I quickly glance up at him. His bottom lip is bleeding, and his cheek is bruised.

"Who the hell is this girl?" another man asks.

"She's a friend, that's all. She's harmless. You have no need for her," Chayse replies.

"A friend, huh? So all the female clothes we saw in the house must have been hers! Seems like she's more than a friend. And you won't be telling us who we'll be needing!" the man yells angrily. It appears as though he may be the leader. He walks up to me. He has dark hair, a beard that's a tangled mess, and beady brown eyes. He has a scar about two inches long by his right eye. He smells like filth.

He slowly inspects me from top to bottom, and a nasty grin forms on his face. "I like what I see." He starts to reach his nasty hand toward me to touch my hair.

Chayse grabs his arm midway. "If you even think about touching her, I promise you, I will rip your heart out!" His tone is deadly enough to stop the leader in his tracks.

Deciding not to challenge Chayse, he drops his arm and says, "She comes with us. We will let the big boss decide what he wants to do with her. And the dog dies."

"No, no deal. Your big boss wants me to cooperate. You leave her alone. You don't kill the dog. Just let them go," Chayse insists.

"You know, I change my mind. All *three* of you come with us. The big boss will decide on *all* your fates. Let's go," he commands.

I look at Chayse, waiting for some type of signal. But there is no signal. There is no way out of this without one of us getting killed.

"Just do as they say and don't fight back," he instructs Gem and I. There's no arguing the matter. Chayse has taken charge and there's nothing else we can do.

I drop my head down in defeat. We're all caught. It's over. The leader tells Chayse to tie up Gem's mouth so that she wouldn't be able to bite. They must be scared to go near her.

Chayse grabs the rope from him and starts heading toward her. He kneels down to her and kisses her forehead and hugs her. Because I know their relationship so well, and have watched their encounters a thousand times, I know during the hug, he whispers something to her. I also know that there's no way the men would have any idea of that exchange. Right when Chayse pulls the rope out to tie her mouth, Gem nips his hand. Chayse jumps back, shaking his hand and yelling, "Ouch!"

And Gem takes off. The men pull out their guns to shoot her, but Chayse remains in the way. He knows they aren't going to shoot at him.

"Move, she's getting away!" yells the leader.

"Damn, she bit me. Sorry," replies Chayse, shrugging his shoulders innocently.

By the time they try to shoot into the woods, Gem is nowhere to be seen. She's gone, disappearing into the deep wilderness. Both of my hands are clasped on my mouth, eyes wide, holding my breath during the entire exchange. My Gem. I say a silent prayer for her. Please let her make it. God, please take care of her.

"You did that on purpose!" The leader is upset.

"What are you talking about? Didn't you see her bite me?" Chayse sticks to his story.

"Take her!" the leader instructs to one of his men. The man comes up to me and grabs me from my arms. Before I can react, he pulls a knife out and holds it to my throat.

"What are you doing?" Chayse yells, as he starts advancing forward.

"One move and she dies. I suggest you stand very still!" yells the evil leader.

"Just let her go, ok? I won't move." Chayse lowers his voice, hoping to calm everybody down.

The cruel leader walks up to Chayse and punches him twice in the stomach and his jaw. Chayse doubles over in pain but does not fight back.

"Stop! What are you doing? Leave him alone, so help me God, I'll kill you!" I scream, trying to get at him. But the man with the knife restricts me.

I hear a horrible cackling laugh from the leader whom I now despise more than ever. "She's going to kill me? Pathetic!

You must really care about this guy! This is getting better and better! We're going to have fun with this! No matter. Tie them both up!" the leader commands. The man with the knife lowers his knife but ties my hands behind my back. After Chayse's hands are tied, they lead us toward their motorbikes.

I look at Chayse to see how he's doing. His other cheek now has a bluish bruise already forming. I'm beyond angry! They are not supposed to hurt him!

They make Chayse sit in the back of one motorbike, and me in the back of another. They put blindfolds on both of us.

"Is this really necessary?" Chayse asks.

"Yes, I don't trust your ass! And there's no need for you to know where we're going," the leader replies.

I feel even more helpless with the blindfold on me. I hate the feeling. I hold on to the back of the motorbike as they're driving. We must have driven like this for at least a couple of hours. When the bikes stop, we're pulled off of them and shoved into a car.

"Chayse?" I call for him.

"I'm here," I hear him right next to me. I snuggle closer to him. I need to feel his strength next to me. I wonder what they're going to do with us. From my estimation, it's probably nightfall by now. The blindfolds stay on us. I don't know how many other men are in the car with us.

I wonder where they stored the motorbikes. I hear cars, but then I also hear stronger engine sounds. Perhaps they have bigger vehicles where they might be storing the bikes.

Chayse leans into me. I feel his lips on top of my head and he finds my cheek and gives me a kiss. It's a kiss of reassurance. I'm numb by now and beyond exhausted.

All I can think about is that Chayse is hurt and I want to tend to his wounds. We both lean onto each other during the entire car ride. His touch gives me hope.

We're driving for hours. I even fall asleep frequently. We probably drove throughout the night. I'm glad that I took care of using the bathroom right before we heard them earlier.

My thoughts drift to Gem. I say another prayer for her. Please let his team find her. Please let her be ok. My Gem, my girl, who has been through hell and back with me.

How did we get ourselves in this mess? Maybe I can offer them money for our freedom. Maybe that's all they want. I whisper my idea into Chayse's ear.

He shakes his head no. "That's not what they want. Please trust me," he whispers back in my ear.

"Hey you two, stop talking back there!" I hear the leader's voice. God, I want to kill that son of a bitch!

Twenty-four

Chayse and I stay quiet the rest of the trip. We travel through the night. Finally, the car stops and we're dragged out. I feel the heat from the sun on me, so I know at least it's daytime. I have to pay attention to any clues of our whereabouts. It may come in use if we find a way to escape.

With our blindfolds still on, we're taken through a doorway. As we all stand there, my stomach drops. We must be in an elevator, but it feels like I'm falling into an abyss.

When the elevator stops, we're guided through another doorway. After walking straight for fifteen steps, we're escorted down the stairs. It's a long descent because I count forty-seven steps. One of the men is holding my arm to prevent me from tripping. Where the hell are we? When we're shoved through the last doorway, I hear the door close behind us.

"I'm here, ok?" Chayse whispers to me. I have no idea where the hell we are. I'm petrified.

Chayse and I walk toward each other's voice. He gets behind me, and unties my blindfold with his teeth. As soon as I open my eyes, I have to close them immediately. The room is so bright, it's hurting my eyes. Slowly, I open them again. I note a big, empty white room, with florescent lights.

I quickly run behind Chayse. He kneels down so that I'm able to reach him. I untied his blindfold with my teeth as well. As soon he's able to see, he goes to work on my hands that are tied together behind my back. He frees my hands shortly with his teeth. Once my hands are free, I untie him. He pulls me into his embrace for a brief moment.

"You ok?" he asks softly.

I nod. "Are you?" My eyes tear up as I remember how he had fought so fiercely.

"Yes. Don't worry." Chayse releases me and we glance around the room. It's completely bare, with white walls and white tiles. In a corner there's a toilet and a curtain that can be pulled around it. One of the walls has a large mirror.

"They're watching us from there," Chayse whispers to me.

I turn away from the mirror and focus my attention on him. Chayse is badly bruised up and has cuts on his face. I reach to touch his bruises. "You're hurt," I whisper.

"It's ok. I'm ok," he says. He then walks away from me and heads straight to the mirror. "What's next?" he yells. "You've got me. Let her go." There's no response.

I'm physically and mentally exhausted. I want this nightmare over. Chayse approaches the door, and tries his luck to break it open. It's no use.

I walk up to him and pull him to me. I know he's stressed out. And I want him to rest a bit so he can gain his strength again. He's resistive at first. But I persist and pull him into my arms. As he sighs in defeat, I feel his body relaxing. We both sit down against the wall in each other's arms. We fall asleep from exhaustion.

We're awakened when we hear noise outside the door. We both spring up and Chayse pushes me behind him. Two plates of food are slipped into a slot that's next to the door. What the hell! For all we know, they may have poisoned the food!

I glance toward Chayse, and he's also looking at the plates with suspicion. We haven't had a real meal in over forty-eight hours, but neither of us want to take a chance and eat this food.

Chayse picks up the food and throws the plates to the mirror. "I want your boss to come talk to me!" he yells. There's no response. "I know he wants me alive and well. But know that I'm not going to eat until we talk. I have a proposal for you." No response. I look at him questioningly, but he doesn't make eye contact with me. I suppose we can't really talk anyway since they're watching our every move and probably can hear everything we're saying.

I sit back down at our spot and think about Gem. I'm relieved that she has gotten away. I wonder if she made it to the house. If she did, his team certainly would have found her. They know that Gem and I were both with Chayse. He had mentioned that his team would head to the house first.

I wonder if they're still able to track us from his watch. I don't seem to have as much faith in his team as apparently he does. I don't understand why we're still with these horrible people. His team should have located us by now.

Chayse sits next to me, and pulls me in his arms. "I'm going to make this right. I promise, ok, Lori?" I look up at him. Why is he calling me Lori? He's staring back at me, willing me to understand. I see. He's giving me a fake name because he doesn't want them to know my true identity. Ok, I guess I'm Lori. I nod and snuggle closer to him. I want to feel his body against me, hoping it would somehow make me feel better.

A few hours later, they slip more food into our room. Chayse throws it to the mirror. As time passes, I'm feeling more and more hungry. I wonder if they really would drug the food. I guess it doesn't matter. I have to follow Chayse's lead.

I need to use the bathroom as well. No use being modest now. It's all about practicality. I get up, close the curtain and use the toilet. To my relief, it's spotless clean and it flushes. Chayse uses it after me.

That being done, next is to formulate a plan to get the hell out of here. Even though Chayse has already shot the idea down, I still think about offering them money. But a part of me knows Chayse is right. It's not money they're after. Unfortunately, Chayse and I can't even discuss any plans because they can hear us.

Chayse walks to the one-way mirror. He says, "It's useless. We will not be eating or cooperating until the person in charge talks to me."

Finally, there's a response. "Hello, Mr. Chayse Pierce. I understand you've been requesting to speak to me," a male voice says. I guess they know Chayse's true identity. The unfamiliar voice is deep and has an accent, although I can't place it. But then again, he can be disguising his voice for all I know.

"Yes, I'd like to speak to you. You have me. I know you've been after me. I will cooperate with whatever you want of me, but let her go," Chayse says to him, gesturing toward me.

"Now, Mr. Pierce, why would I let her go? I can tell that she is your weakness. She means a great deal to you, and therefore, she's a great asset to me," the voice replies, giving me the chills.

"Sorry to disappoint you, but she means nothing to me.

She's one of hundreds," Chayse replies with a hard tone. My heart stops when I hear those words. No, he doesn't mean that. He's lying to them to protect both of us. But his tone is mean and cruel. I don't dare move, afraid that I may ruin whatever Chayse is trying to accomplish.

"Nice try, Mr. Pierce, but I've seen the way you look at her. You love her," the voice laughs. Chayse laughs too, a cruel, hard laugh. It's as if he's laughing at this man for actually believing that.

"Trust me, I love nobody." I want to vomit. His words cut like a knife. He sounds so convincing. "But that doesn't negate the fact that she's innocent. And I protect the innocent. I don't want any harm to her. I want her to go back to her life as if nothing happened. And like I said earlier, in exchange, you will have my full cooperation."

The silence, as we wait for a response, is unbearable. Finally, the voice says, "She knows too much. I can't let her go."

"Yes, you can. I know you have the means to erase her memory for the last few weeks. She will not remember anything. You will be safe. She will go on with her life, and you will have me. But, if you don't agree, I will fight you every step of the way. You know I'm strong enough to do that, both physically and mentally. It wouldn't matter how much you try to get into my mind--all of your tactics will fail. We both know that I can resist them."

I'm staring at Chayse in utter shock. What is he talking about? Erase my memory? Why would he want to do that? Maybe he's working on some strategy. I step toward him and place my hand on his arm. I need some type of reassurance that he knows what he's doing. He flinches his arm away as if my touch burns him. He also throws a look of disgust in my direction. I have never seen him look at me like that. It's as if I'm a nuisance and he hates me. I must have looked shocked at his response, because I hear a cruel laugh from the horrible man on the other side of the mirror.

"That was cold, Mr. Pierce. But then again, I have heard about your reputation," says the harsh voice. He laughs again.

"I told you, when I'm done, I'm done. I want her out of here. Do we have a deal?" I want to scream at him. But I hold my tongue. He probably has some plan. He must! But does the plan have to include being so ruthless? I'll have to wait to ask him what he's up to.

"Who is she anyway? What were you doing with her?" the voice inquires.

"She's a nobody! I told you that. Her name is Lori. She was able to meet certain needs of mine. But frankly, I was getting tired of her. Like I said, she's one of hundreds. I just feel sorry for her. She needs to go on with her business, her life. So I ask you again, do we have a deal?" Chayse is horrible. The pain in my gut feels like he's stabbing me with a knife into an already open wound.

"I need to think about your proposal, Mr. Pierce. I will get back to you on this." And the voice is gone.

I wait for Chayse to look at me and give me some type of a secret signal. But he doesn't. He completely ignores me. He doesn't even look my way.

Finally, I whisper, "Chayse, we need to talk."

"Stop, just stop," Chayse interrupts abruptly.

"Are you kidding me? No, I'm not going to stop. What the

hell is going on?" I ask, becoming more annoyed. The least he can do is let me in on this crazy plan of his. He can't talk about it, but at least he can give me some type of a gesture or a signal.

"Look, like I said, I'm sorry I got you in this mess. But I want you to just go about your life like nothing ever happened, ok?" Chayse is just as annoyed as me.

"Are you fucking joking?" I ask incredulously.

Chayse finally turns to look at me. His eyes are uncaring and full of anger. Gone are the tender, loving eyes. "Would you just shut up? What we had, was fine while it lasted. But it's over now. You need to move on with your life and I need to move on with mine. Just accept it!" Chayse exclaims, his voice cold as ice.

"First of all, you're insane! And furthermore, what the hell are you talking about erasing my memory? I will not allow that! And I won't leave you here with these crazy people!" I want to jump on him and hit him. I want to shake some sense into him. What the hell is wrong with him? This is not the same Chayse I fell in love with. This Chayse is cruel, cold, and hard. This Chayse cares about nobody.

"I don't want you with me anymore! We are done. Get that through your head!" Now, Chayse is yelling at me.

It's useless talking to him. I turn toward the one-way mirror and yell, "I have money. I can pay for both of our freedom." I have to try. Chayse throws his arms in the air and walks away, exasperated.

The voice on the other side laughs--another harsh, cruel laugh. "This is quite entertaining. And no, we have no use for your money. We have plenty of that. But hey, can't blame a girl for trying. Mr. Pierce, somebody will be in to get you shortly. I'd like to talk to you about the details of the proposal." I'm left staring at the mirror, dumbfounded.

I turn to look at Chayse. He abruptly turns away. That's it! I'm going to force him to look at me. Just as I begin to charge toward him, the door opens. We both turn toward the door. Four men with guns are standing there, dressed in military attire. They signal Chayse to follow them and me to stay. I have no other option but to stay.

Once Chayse is gone, I try to open the door. Not surprisingly, it's locked. I begin pacing. This is getting more and more out of hand. Chayse is not Chayse. He's beyond cruel. Besides his cruelty, I'm becoming apprehensive about this memory erasing plan. I refuse to believe that Chayse would let them harm me in any way. No, he wouldn't. Even if we are "done", as he put it, he would still protect me. I'm sure of that. But I'm weary about what their plans are for me. I need to formulate an escape plan.

Chayse said they wouldn't hurt him. But there's nothing stopping them from hurting me. They want nothing from me. I'm useless to them. At that moment, I decide that if they come for me, I'm going to put up a hell of a fight. I'm going to use everything I learned, all my speed, all my strength, and fight until I have nothing left. I don't care if they figure out what I'm capable of doing. What does it matter now anyway? It already seems like Chayse has turned his back on me.

About half an hour later, the door opens again. I'm ready to attack. I spring toward the person, but I don't get far. Chayse has walked in, and he blocks my strike. He instantly has me under his hold, leaving me no hope of getting out. I struggle and struggle, but I'm no match for him.

"Calm down. What the hell are you doing?" he asks.

"Let me go! I don't want you to touch me!" I yell back at him.

Chayse doesn't say anything but he does not release me. He holds me until I eventually stop struggling. When I stop moving, I notice he has come alone. The door is already closed.

"Are you calm enough to listen to me now?" he asks. His tone is impersonal and unemotional.

I don't reply. He proceeds to release his hold. I jump away from him. I can't bear him touching me. His touch is not comforting to me anymore. I don't trust him. And he said some awful things earlier.

Chayse stares at me for a couple of minutes before saying, "Look, I'm going to get you home, ok? But you have to listen to me."

"Why would I? I don't trust you!" I snap at him.

"You shouldn't trust me. You shouldn't trust anybody. But you still need to listen to me. You have no choice," Chayse replies calmly, folding his arms in front of him.

"You want those horrible people to mess with my brain!" I yell. I don't give a damn who hears me anymore.

"It's not what you think! Please, calm down and I'll explain, ok? It's nothing invasive. I told you, they are very advanced. They have the technology to block memories. They will block the last three weeks and any other interactions you've had with me. I will be supervising the whole thing. You will be asleep the entire time. You will be taken back to the house and my team will get you from there. Then, my team will bring you to your own house. When you wake up, you will be back in your home, safe and sound." Chayse explains the plan with no emotion. I can't even follow his explanations.

"What do you mean any interactions with you?" I catch on to what he said to me. First he was talking about the last three weeks, and now every moment with him?

Chayse looks straight into my eyes. His eyes are intense. After a moment, he finally answers, "Yes, everything. It will be as if we never met." He says these words slowly and deliberately as if allowing me time to process it.

"Why?" I don't understand any of this.

"They want no loose ends. This was their part of the deal to let you out of here safely. They will never bother you again--that was my part of the deal."

"Why would I want them to erase my memory of you?" I ask. "Why would *you* want that?" I whisper. I can't help but feel hurt. My every interaction with him has made me who I am today. He's been a significant part of my life, directly and indirectly. Every moment with him is memorable, from the time I was sixteen until now. He has influenced me as Joe, Chris, and finally as Chayse. All three of them have helped me in their own way. I have some of my best memories with him. And my memories are all I have.

I've always known that I wouldn't be able to keep him, that it was always temporary. He had made that very clear. But I cherish our time together. They are *my* memories to keep. He has no right to them!

"We have no choice," he whispers back. For a brief second, I feel his emotions. I see the old Chayse I remember so well. But it's just for a brief second. Just as quickly, he becomes his cold, calculated self again. "That's how it's going to work.

You had nothing to do with any of this. I got you into this mess. And the only way to safely get you out is to block your memory. They don't want you to remember anything. Again, let me emphasize that they want no loose ends. Trust me, this is better than the alternative."

The alternative? What could be worse than somebody messing with your mind? Suddenly, I understand what he means. No loose ends. I'm a liability. The alternative would be to kill me. I swallow hard.

"My memories are all I have," I whisper, looking down. I don't want him to see the tears filling my eyes. I have to toughen up. I take a deep breath and with a stronger voice, I say, "What could I possibly do anyway? Why do they care? I'm a nobody."

"They don't want you to remember this place, and they don't want you to remember me. It's very simple. The only way they agreed to my deal is if they can be guaranteed that you would not remember me. Like I said, they want no loose ends. Look, I'm trying to explain this to you, but you're not even being reasonable. It's time to grow up. This is your way out and there are no other options." Chayse is frustrated and not holding back his annoyance toward me.

I change the subject. "Why do you think your team would get me from the house?"

"Because that was also part of the deal. I was allowed to put a word out to my team to get you from the house and back to your home safely. I also told them that your dog should be near the house and to bring her back to your home with you. They will be expecting you there in the next twelve hours. Within twenty four hours, you will be back in your own home," Chayse explains. I keep searching for some tenderness or understanding from his eyes. I get nothing.

But then, my mind starts racing. If he was able to put a message out to his team, surely there's a way they can trace that. And maybe there's hope of them still getting here on time. "And the message was non-traceable," Chayse explains, as if he can read my mind. My thoughts shift to the watch. Why haven't they traced the watch yet? "This is a trace-proof building. We are underground. The entire area for miles is trace-proof. There's no reception for anything, unless their own technology is utilized. That's why they brought us here. You see, they planned this well." I swallow hard, forcing myself to recognize that there's going to be no rescue. I've been waiting for his team to rescue us, and Chayse's desperate actions prove that we are on our own.

I sigh deeply. There has to be another way out of this besides his plan. Why would he think that I would leave him with these crazy people? If I leave him, how would anybody even rescue him? How can they possibly find him? Lifting my chin up, I look dead at him, and say, "I'm not leaving you, Chayse. I *will* put up a fight."

"They won't harm me. I already told you that," Chayse insists.

"They already hurt you!" I yell.

"I mean they won't do any serious harm to me. There's no more time to go back and forth on this." Chayse towers over me, his voice cold and hard. His intimidation tactics are not going to work!

"I don't care! I'm not going to let anybody mess with my

mind, let alone even consider leaving you. I will face whatever they want to do with me. I would rather die than hide like a coward!" I'm furious! He's not allowed to make decisions for me!

Chayse smirks, but it's not a happy smirk. His smirk is sarcastic and bitter. "Brave words, but not going to happen." Chayse moves quickly and before I even process what he's about to do, he has me in his hold. This time, he's holding my mouth as well, and I'm unable to say anything. I try to bite him and hit him to get out of his hold. I even try to kick him. It's useless. He's way too powerful compared to me. "Ok, we're ready," Chayse yells toward the one-way mirror. "Open the door, and I will bring her where you need her."

I panic. Oh my god! This is really happening. I try to scream and shake him off of me, giving my all. The door opens, and I try to kick the men who come through the door. But Chayse swings me away so my kicks don't land. I hate him!

As soon as I get the opportunity, I'm going to tell them everything. That is the only way. I don't care about Chayse's instructions. I'm going to confess to them that I'm just like him. I have those same super genes. At least if they know that, they won't mess with erasing my memories. They will probably keep me here with Chayse to study both of us. Maybe if I stay with him, there might be a better chance of Chayse escaping. I can't leave him alone. There's no way.

Chayse drags me out of the room. He never releases his hold or his hand over my mouth. I struggle the entire way. I'm not going to make this easy for him.

I try to look for a way out. We're underground he said. But there has to be a way out. Where are the stairs we used?

But I see no stairs. All I see are white walls. He drags me down a long narrow hall and I'm forced into another room. There are six men standing there with white lab coats.

"Throw me that handkerchief. I'm afraid if I let her go, she'll scream the entire time, and I don't want to deal with that," Chayse instructs one of the men with the white coat. I'm desperate, trying to use all my strength to get out of his hold. It's now or never.

But before he releases his hand from my mouth, somehow he has the handkerchief wrapped around my mouth. He ties it up quickly, as I relentlessly shake my head to try to wiggle out of it.

Chayse releases his hold on me to use both hands to tie the handkerchief. This is my chance and I take it. I kick him hard right in the shin. I must have caught him off guard for that brief moment, because he reflexively draws away. My hands quickly work on untying the knot on the handkerchief so I can tell them the truth about me.

To my dismay, I'm only able to soften the knot before Chayse is already on me. He tackles me to the floor, with my face to the ground. Just before I'm about to hit the floor, Chayse controls my fall to avoid a hard landing. I'm now lying on my stomach, with him on top of me. He holds me down with his body and ties the knot tighter on the handkerchief. Now, I'm completely unable to move at all. Damn him!

"She's a feisty one, huh?" The cruel boss laughs ruthlessly.

I try to see where the voice is coming from. All I see are those men in white lab coats. Then, I notice a similar mirror like in the other room. He must be hidden on the other side, not showing his face. Coward!

Chayse pulls me up to standing. He drags me to a table with straps. He picks me up and places me on it. I try to roll off, but he quickly fastens the straps around one of my wrists. I try to hit him with my free hand but he blocks it and then reaches over, fastening the strap on that arm as well. He quickly straps both of my legs even though I'm kicking ferociously to avoid it.

I'm pulling on the straps with all my might to free myself. Please, let me be strong enough to break out of these. But they're leather straps and it's useless.

Two men with lab coats approach me and place electrodes in various places around my head and forehead. I'm vigorously shaking my head but Chayse holds my head steady for them.

"Ok, we are ready," I hear a different voice. No, no, this can't be happening. Please stop! I'm screaming but it's muffled. I'm giving my last fight, with everything I possess inside me. I wiggle, pull, kick, scream, and try to throw my body around. I need something, anything, to get me out of this mess. I fail. There is nothing left of me. I'm defeated.

Chayse holds my arm steady, and they insert the needle into my vein. The IV is attached with a clear liquid. Saline? But within seconds, I'm having difficulty staying focused. Damn it! It's not just saline.

I focus on Chayse, trying to look into his gray eyes, into his soul. I want to remember him. Please God, let me remember him. Let me remember all of the clues of this place. I have to come back for him, to save him. I can't leave him like this with these horrendous people. He's looking down at me with no emotions, as if I'm a complete stranger. He has completely disassociated himself from me.

I feel the tears rolling down my cheeks. Everything is becoming blurry now. No, no. Not yet. I want to remember. I have to remember.

Then, I feel Chayse kneeling by me. He gently wipes my tears with his hand, and whispers in my ears, "I'm so sorry. I may be in hell, but I will never be too far from you. You are my heart. Remember that." His words are so soft that only I can hear.

Even though I'm having difficulty focusing, I give it my all to catch every word. I have to remember, he said. I feel him squeeze my hand. I try to squeeze back. I want him to know that I heard him.

I'll never know whether I was able to squeeze his hand, because suddenly, everything goes black.

Twenty-five

She is running again. But this time she's laughing. She's not scared. She's happy. She's running through a field. The sun is shining, the birds are singing, and there are flowers everywhere. She is laughing and running. Something is chasing her. But she's not scared. It's a game. She's playing a chasing game. She's tackled. Something is lying on top of her. She starts laughing even harder. She is being tickled. She opens her eyes to see. She can't see what is on top of her. She tries to focus harder. She sees gray laughing eyes. The eyes are smiling at her and they are full of happiness and something else. What else? Love, yes it is love. The eyes are full of love. "You are my heart," the eyes whisper to her. She reaches up. But the weight of the body is being pulled off of her. She sees the figure with the gray eyes fading off of her. "No, don't go," she says to the gray eyes. She starts to panic. If the gray eyes leave her, they will be gone forever. She has to hold on. But the gray eyes look sadly down at her. They are leaving. She tries to reach up, but it's too late. She can't touch anything. It's just empty space. The gray eyes are far off in the distance and soon they disappear.

"No!" I yell. I sit up. I'm breathing heavily. I force myself to settle down. I look around me. I'm in my room. Gem is on top of me, kissing my face. She's whimpering. I pet her. "It's ok, girl. It was just another strange dream." Gem keeps whimpering. "I'm ok, girl," I repeat.

That was an unusual dream. My dreams have never been like that in the past. Before, the dreams were always about the girl running for her life, terrified of whatever was chasing her.

She was never laughing in my dreams. This time the girl was happy. But who was chasing her? The gray eyes, they were so intense, and so full of love. But then they disappeared!

My dreams are getting stranger and stranger. I sigh. Shaking my head, I look around my bedroom. The sun is shining through the window. I guess I better get up. I'm so tired though. And boy, do I need to use the bathroom! I swing my legs off and force myself to crawl out of bed. Even my muscles feel sore and fatigued.

I waddle into the bathroom. I quickly use the toilet and jump straight into the shower. Ahh, the shower feels fabulous on my achy muscles. After the shower, I glance into the mirror. I cringe at the sight. My eyes are staring back at me, looking wide and haunted. Not wanting to look at myself any longer, I shift my attention to putting on my sweat shorts and t-shirt.

Gem is still whimpering. Maybe she needs to go outside to relieve herself. I come out of the bathroom and head downstairs. I open the back door for her to run in the yard. Apparently, she has no desire to go outside because she sits by the door whimpering to me again.

"What's wrong, girl?" I ask her. She whimpers even louder. I check her food and water bowls, but they're both full. "You're not getting sick on me, are you?" I tease. Gem keeps crying. She puts her head down on the floor and lies down, burying her face under her paws.

I sit on the floor with her and pull her into my lap. She looks so sad, it's breaking my heart. I hug her tight.

"You look like you lost your best friend, girl." I slowly say to her, scratching behind her ears and holding her tight. Gem howls sadly. She looks into my eyes, penetrating deep, as if looking into my soul. It's the same look Thunder, the black stallion, had given me in Jamaica. The look that makes me feel like she knows something that I don't. I bring her face up to mine and search her eyes, hoping I can understand. "I'm sorry, Gem. I don't know what you want," I say softly to her. She puts her head down in my lap in defeat.

As I hug her, I begin thinking about my dream. What a bizarre dream! They looked like the same gray eyes as my previous dreams. But this time, the dream wasn't scary. At the end though, the gray eyes just disappeared. I shudder. What does it mean? I shake my head. I have to stop thinking about this. Besides, I'm starving.

I get up and look at the time. It's almost noon! I better check my cell phone to see if anybody called to check on me. I run up to my room to search for my phone. I don't see it plugged in at the normal place. That's strange. I search in the kitchen and the family room. No phone. I grab the house phone and call my cell phone to see if I can hear the ring. I don't hear anything. What the heck! I dial Kylie's number.

Kylie picks it up before the first ring even ends. "Tess?" She sounds frantic. What's wrong with her now?

"Yeah?" I ask.

"Where the hell have you been? I've been trying to reach you! I almost called the police! Why didn't you text or call? Never mind, looks like you're finally home. I'm on my way." I hear a click as she hangs up.

I'm left staring at the phone, shaking my head. I have no idea what she's talking about. Kylie is being her usual dramatic self! I shift my attention to the fridge in search of food.

Nothing! I open the pantry and find some chips. As I start munching on the chips, I notice a can of chicken noodle soup. Good enough for now!

I begin warming up the soup as I continue devouring the chips. By the time the soup is warm, the doorbell rings. It must be Kylie. Before I reach the front door, she has already unlocked it with her spare key. She comes running down the hall and hugs me, holding me tight. I start laughing. I don't know what has gotten into her. When she releases me, I'm attacked with another hug. It's Jack!

"So good to see you, Tess," Jack says, as he twirls me around. "Where have you been?"

"What do you mean?" I ask. "And, I didn't even realize you were coming with Kylie."

"I was with Kylie when you called. So I jumped in the car with her to see you," Jack explains.

Kylie starts crying.

"Why are you crying?" I ask. Their behavior is so odd.

Gem comes running, wagging her tail. At least she's happy about something. Maybe she'll stop moping around! Jack and Kylie both get down and hug her.

"I missed you, girl!" Jack exclaims. Then he turns to Kylie and me and says, "Let's all just sit down. We all have a lot to catch up on."

We sit at the table so I can finish my soup. They both watch me cautiously.

Finally, Kylie says, "You look good, Tess. You've gained most of your weight back, and your color looks much better."

I don't even know how to respond. I thought I looked like

crap when I saw myself in the mirror earlier.

"What's going on here? Why are you guys acting so weird?" I ask.

"You're kidding, right? You've been gone for over three weeks! Not telling anybody where you were. Last couple of days, we couldn't even reach you. Every time we called, it wouldn't connect. What's wrong with your phone? And when did you get back?" Kylie starts firing off her questions.

"First of all, I didn't go anywhere. And I can't find my phone. I've been looking all over this morning." I shake my head. I'm confused at why they would think that I was gone.

"Why are you changing your story now? You've already texted us and told us numerously that you needed some space and that you're fine. Here, let me show you the texts." Kylie pulls out her phone and pulls up my texts to her. I skim through them. Every one of them says, "*I'm fine.*" "*I'll be back soon.*" "*Don't worry.*" "*I'm doing much better.*" I can't believe it! I never sent these texts to her.

"I didn't send these to you, Kylie." I whisper. This is all so confusing. "I've always been here, Kylie. Remember? You guys would make me food and make me eat. You would come and take Gem for walks."

"Tess, what are you saying? We've been here almost every day since you've been gone. You haven't been here. You and Gem were gone! You kept in touch with us but you never told us where you were, or who you were with. Don't you remember?" Kylie is getting frustrated.

And I'm getting just as frustrated. I don't remember any of this. My head starts to hurt. I put my hand on my temple, closing my eyes because the room is now spinning. I have to settle myself down.

"Kylie, back off!" Jack commands. "Remember what the doctors said about post traumatic syndrome?"

There's a silence. Nobody says a word.

I take a deep breath and ask, "What's the date today?"

Jack replies, "It's August 20th, Tess."

August 20th? How can that be?

"But didn't you just take me to the park yesterday to lecture me on my life? Remember? We talked about my dreams of becoming a physician? Your lecture must have helped, because I do feel stronger." That's what I remember. That was yesterday.

"Tess, that was at the end of July. That was easily three weeks ago. And the next day you were gone. I blamed myself. I thought it was something I had said. But you truly sounded happy on the phone whenever we talked. So I figured you were getting the extra help that you needed--whatever that may be. And that's all that mattered to me," Jack explains.

That was the end of July and now it is August 20th! I have no recollection of anything since that day. I look at Gem. She's looking right at me, with that same penetrating gaze. She knows. She knows where we've been and what happened. She was with me the entire time. Oh my god, why can't I remember? It's all a blank slate.

I must have really looked in distress because Kylie gets up, takes my soup bowl and says, "Look, let's not analyze this too much. Maybe your mind is just not ready to remember everything. The real point is that you're back now, and you really do look stronger, Tess. You were so helpless when you left, having no will or motivation to do anything. You're totally different now. Even your eyes, I don't know, it's as if you found your will again. Eventually, when you're ready to remember, you will remember. You'll see. I don't want you to stress about this anymore. You need to continue getting stronger, Tess."

But why am I not remembering? This is crazy. I was gone, but nobody knew where I was. Gem was with me. I kept in touch with them. According to Kylie and Jack, I just returned. Last night? This morning? But I don't remember leaving or coming or anything in between. I have never experienced anything like this. It's as if three weeks of my life are gone--vanished. Damn it! I have to remember!

Jack reaches for my hand, and says calmly, "Kylie is right, Tess. Please don't push it right now. It will all come back. You will see--when you're ready. Things happen for a reason. There's a reason for this. You've gone through so much stress lately. You've been through hell and back. And this may be your body's way of protecting itself. Who knows how all this works? Just please don't stress about it right now." I look up at him. Ok, maybe he's right. Maybe it will all come to me within a couple of days.

That's when the doorbell rings. I wonder who that can be. Maybe it's Aunt Jenna. Great, more questions!

When I open the door, I notice a man standing on the front porch in a suit. He seems like he's in his forties, and he looks vaguely familiar.

"Hello, Miss Sanoby. My name is Tom Sterns. I met you at your parents' memorial. I'm not sure if you remember me?" Mr. Sterns has a strong, authoritative voice.

Ok, that's why he looks familiar. "Yes, I remember you. You worked with my mom with her research, right?"

"Yes, I did. I'd like to talk to you about something. May I come in please?" he asks.

"Well, I have company right now," I reply hesitantly.

"This is rather important, Miss Sanoby. And I think you'll want to hear it," Mr. Stearns insists. I guess I might as well see what he wants.

"Ok, come in then." I step out of the way and Mr. Sterns enters. We walk into the kitchen where Jack and Kylie are still at the table, whispering to each other. When we walk in, they stop abruptly and look up.

"Jack, Kylie, this is Mr. Sterns. He knew my parents through work." They both greet him. I lead Mr. Sterns into the study so we can talk in private.

Once we enter, he sits on the chair and I sit behind the desk. "I'm going to make this quick, Miss Sanoby. I have a proposal for you. I knew your parents well. And I was very involved with their line of work. I'd like you to take over the research that your mother was involved with. I know you just graduated from college. And I also know that your goal is to become a physician. I can help you with that."

"I'm not sure if I'm following you, Mr. Sterns," I reply suspiciously.

"Let me start from the beginning. You see, I work for the government, in a special military branch. I'd like you to come and work for me. I will train you and we will also put you through our accelerated medical program. I know you have the brains," Mr. Sterns says confidently.

"What sort of branch of government? And what type of

training?" I still don't comprehend what he's saying.

"It's special services. And it's top secret. We would only fill you in on the details if you decide to join us. Your mom wasn't directly *in* special services, but she did work for us indirectly. And your training would consist of everything. Outside of your medical education, we would train you on weaponry and combat. Your training would challenge you physically, psychologically, and cognitively. We would excel your current skills. We would train you to be not just a secret agent, but one of the top agents. I strongly believe that under my program you would excel, Miss Sanoby. The pay is very good as well. I want you to consider my offer. If you're interested, I can fill you in on the details. But you're the only one who can finish what your mother started."

"This is a lot to take in. Can I contact you tomorrow?" I ask. I'm not sure what made me say that. My instincts already tell me that this is my calling.

"Absolutely, Miss Sanoby. Here's my card. I look forward to hearing from you. But I'd appreciate it if you don't repeat the information about special services to your friends or anybody else. Like I said, this is confidential information. We can't have general public find out about us," Mr. Sterns explains.

"I completely understand, Mr. Sterns." I stand up and take the card. I shake his hand and we both walk out of the study. Kylie and Jack are still engrossed in their conversation, with worried looks on their faces. Mr. Sterns nods his head at them and walks out the front door.

"What was all that about, Tess?" Kylie asks.

"Oh, he worked with my mom. It was a job offer, and he

said he'd help me get my medical degree as well, through his accelerated program." I try to sound casual about it.

"Wow, that sounds interesting. What do you think? What about all of the other medical schools that offered you a spot? Have you decided anything?" Jack inquires.

"Not sure if I want to go the traditional route any more. This sounds more interesting. But I'll have to think things over, I guess," I reply. I take a deep breath. I know they're worried about me. Hell, I'm worried about me, too. But I know that I'm much stronger now. And I have to hold on to that. "Listen, I can't explain what happened to me in the last three weeks. Maybe it'll all come together for me, I don't know. But I *do* know that I'm not the same as I was three weeks ago. I'm stronger now, and more focused. I admit that after my parents' death, I had given up living. But I don't feel that way anymore. I feel like there's a purpose for me here, a reason why I'm alive. I have no idea what that purpose is, but I know I'm supposed to live! And that counts for something, right? I'm going to focus on that for now! I don't want you guys worrying about me. I'm much better, trust me. And thanks so much for always sticking by me--through all of my ups and downs. I honestly am so lucky to have you guys." I mean every word. For the millionth time, I'm thankful for Jack and Kylie being in my life.

Kylie has tears flowing down her face. They both come up to me and all three of us hug each other--our friendship hug. We must have stood like that for a few minutes, because then Gem comes and tries to jump on us. We all laugh and hug Gem as well.

Later, Jack takes Gem for a run, while Kylie and I cook dinner. I talk with Aunt Jenna and explain to her that I lost my cell phone. I tell her that I'm home now and assure her that I'm absolutely fine. I definitely don't need her to worry about me and my memory loss.

We decide to eat an early dinner since I only had soup all day and I'm still starving. I ask Jack and Kylie about their jobs. I know they were applying for places but I haven't even inquired what they decided. I've been so wrapped up in my own life the entire summer.

Jack tells me he's joining the FBI, and Kylie tells me she got a job at the local newspaper firm. They're both excited to start the new phase in their life. I can't believe Jack is going to be an FBI agent! And Kylie got the perfect job!

After we eat dinner, Jack and Kylie give me another hug before they leave. Jack kisses me on my forehead, and softly says, "I'm proud of you, Tess."

Once they leave, I climb back up to my room. I search around for clues. Maybe I brought a souvenir back from where I was for the last three weeks. But I find nothing.

I open my drawers and notice that my clothes are all in my drawers. How strange! They're not organized like how I normally organize them. The clothes are all folded in different drawers. I certainly don't remember putting these away. I shake my head in frustration. This is all too much.

I walk to the jewelry box. I like to look at the locket because it always gives me strength. I see my parents' rings. I pick them up and hold them to my heart, closing my eyes. I then take out the locket. I notice two folded pieces of paper under the locket. I pull the first paper out and unfold it. What is this? Huh, it's a letter. I start reading it.

Dear Tessnia,

I never meant to hurt you. Ever. I can't even express how sorry I am for dragging you into my mess. I have to leave. I don't have a choice. But before I leave, I want you to remember when we first met on your 16th birthday. I want you to know at least that much about me, with the hope that it helps you hold on to some good memories between us. I know you are probably wondering why I never told you the truth. Again, there's probably another time and place for that.

Please remember what I said. Don't trust anybody. But always trust your instincts. Embrace your gifts!

Tessnia, please know that if there is any way that I could spend even one more minute with you, I would in a heartbeat. I never got the chance to even begin to explain what you mean to me. I guess some things are better left unsaid.

Please don't look for me. You won't find me.

Yours always...

I begin shaking. Who is this? Who wrote this letter to me? I have to sit down on my bed because my legs are struggling to hold me up. If I saved the letter, that means this person had meant a lot to me. But why can't I remember him? And he said we had met on my 16th birthday. That was so long ago. But I can't remember meeting anybody out of the normal! Oh my god, I'm completely losing my mind.

As I unfold the second paper with my hands shaking, I catch my breath. It's a beautiful sketch of me. I'm studying with my pen in my mouth. So typical! Somebody drew this of me--somebody who knew me well. On the corner, it simply states:

"Happy Birthday, Tessnia."

It's the same writing as the letter. The person who had written this letter also had given me this sketch. My heart is racing so fast. I start having a panic attack, and I'm not sure why. This isn't right. Why can't I remember? This person was important. I must remember! Beads of sweat form on my forehead from the anxiety. The room starts spinning and I find myself gasping for air. I feel it in my bones that something is terribly wrong. I force myself to take some slow deep breaths to calm my racing heart.

"Think, Tess!" I yell to myself. I stay on my bed, with my head buried into my hands for half an hour. With my heart beating fast and my head spinning, I desperately search in my brain for something, *anything*, regarding this letter and the sketch! Nothing.

I have to get a grip. I have to get control of my life. And I have to find some answers. But sitting here and racking my brain is getting me nowhere.

After I miraculously calm myself down, I grab the locket, the letter, the sketch, and Mr. Sterns' business card. Holding all of the items in my hands, I go back downstairs.

I take Gem out in the back yard and sit on the porch. I need fresh air to clear my mind. I notice the sun is about to set. It's beautiful. Gem and I watch the sunset together. It feels like déjà vu. At that moment, I feel content, but at the same time, I feel empty. Something is missing. I sigh. Gem puts her head onto my lap and whimpers.

As I pet her, I look down at the locket. Again, I read the message:

Strength
Peace
Happiness
Always

Strength. I breathe in deeply. My parents always wanted me to be strong. I feel much stronger now than I did three weeks ago. I was in a horrible place then and I never want to go back there again. I finally understand the people who give up their will to live. I promise myself that I will always find the strength to keep going, no matter what challenges life may bring my way.

Peace. Am I at peace? I have so many unanswered questions. I don't understand why I can't remember the last three weeks of my life. To make matters worse, I don't understand how I can't remember who wrote me this letter and drew this beautiful sketch. It's all just a big blank. I'm so frustrated! But

I'm not going to give up. One way or another, I'm going to remember.

Happy. I sigh. This one is tough. I'm not sure where my happiness lies. It feels as if I have some type of destiny to fulfill. Maybe it has something to do with the research my mother had started. I glance down at the card that Mr. Sterns gave me. Maybe the answer lies with him. Maybe he's going to be able to help me put the gaps together in my life.

I look at my sketch again. The drawing is so detailed and heartfelt. This person has portrayed me as not only beautiful, but also as a deep, determined girl, ready to conquer the world. Who is this mystery man?

I think about my dreams. So many times, I've had dreams where the girl was running from something, or somebody. It was always the same theme. Maybe the dreams symbolize me running from my problems. Maybe my whole life, I've avoided conflicts. Well, no more. I'm done with running or hiding. Whatever life throws at me, I'm not going to run. I'm going to face it head on!

I rub Gem's fur as the sun slowly disappears. The sun whispers, "Farewell" as it vanishes into the horizon. The disappearing of the sun is bittersweet. It feels as if a significant chapter of my life is coming to an end. I sigh, trying to let my old life go, saying goodbye to my parents.

I lift my chin up with courage because I know that tomorrow the sun will rise again, shining bright. And as the sun brings another day, I brace myself for the new chapter of my life that's about to begin.

About the Author

Jalpa Williby was born in India and immigrated to the United States at the tender age of eight. A voracious reader, Williby's adolescence was marked by a promising academic career. After graduating with a Bachelors of Science from the University of Illinois, Williby went on to earn Masters in Physical Therapy from Northwestern University. Her passion for helping her patients led her to a specialty in neuroscience, focusing on children and adults with neurological impairments. Juggling her time as a wife, a mother, and working full-time, her love for books never subsided. Williby introduces her debut novel, Chaysing Dreams, as she writes with her heart and soul, her passion flowing through every page.

CPSIA information can be obtained at www.ICGtesting.com
Printed in the USA
LVOW13s1546130913

352331LV00003BA/219/P